PRAISE FOR
JON COON'S FIRST N

THIEF OF THE DEEP

"With *Thief of the Deep,* Jon Coon has established himself as one of America's top writers of modern sea adventure. A great tale with suspense and romance at every turn."

—Clive Cussler

"The best diving fiction I've read in years....Hopefully there's more to come...I'm waiting."

—Walter Comper, *AquaCORPS Journal*

"...a complex plot involving underwater raiders...an undetectable state-of-the-art submarine à la Tom Clancy... the drama is tense."

—*Publishers Weekly*

"Jon Coon has provided us with an archaeological subterfuge having all the elements of an exciting underwater thriller. The plot twists and turns through a series of adventures that both divers and non-divers will thoroughly enjoy."

—R. Duncan Mathewson III, Ph.D., archaeology director for Mel Fisher's hunt for the treasure galleon *Atocha.*

"Action is where *Thief of the Deep* excels, and Coon plunges you into it from the first word. His action scenes...(are) tightly written and more believable..."

—Karl Shreeves, *Scuba Times*

"...captivating....Do yourself a favor and read this book. You'll enjoy it...."

—*The Rappahannock Regulator*

"Jon Coon has hatched a tense plot involving drug smuggling, murder, and wreck piracy in Bermuda waters. He weaves into the story much fascinating Bermuda maritime history and...portrays the controversy between wreck hunting and archaeological digs. The resulting story is both tense and informative."
—Stan Waterman, Emmy Award-winning underwater filmmaker

"Jon Coon knows his diving. He also tells a rattling good yarn of drug smuggling, murder, CIA skulduggery and buried treasure....a thoroughly good read."

—*Sport Diver,* England

"Jon Coon very skillfully tells the tale, drawing on his own experiences...provides the reader with interesting and educational insights into various aspects of diving.... Romance is tastefully intermingled with the high adventure and technical wizardry, rounding the book off very nicely....provides exciting and interesting reading... deserves a place on all of our bookshelves."
—John Lippman, author of several technical diving books

"...space-age technology, top-secret CIA operatives, drug smuggling, murder, intrigue...highly successful modern adventure novel."

—*Scuba Diver,* Australia

"...blends plenty of action with credible undersea scenes with a cast of somewhat larger than life characters to provide good entertainment with a different twist."

—Paul Sullivan, *The Free Lance-Star*

BLACKWOLF

A NOVEL BY

JON COON

AQUA QUEST PUBLICATIONS, INC. ■ NEW YORK

This is a work of fiction. Characters, institutions and organizations in this work are either the product of the author's imagination or, if real, used ficticiously without any intent to describe their actual conduct.

 For further information about this book contact: Aqua Quest Publications, Inc., P.O. Box 700, Locust Valley, NY 11560-0700. Telephone: 516-759-0476. E-mail: aquaquest@aol.com

Library of Congress Cataloging-in-Publication Data

Coon, Jon, 1944-
Blackwolf : a novel / by Jon Coon
p. cm.
Sequel to: Thief of the deep.
ISBN 1-881652-15-7 (alk. paper)
I. Title
PS3553.0577B58 1999
813'.54—dc21 98-31483
CIP

Printed in the United States of America
10 9 8 7 6 5 4 3 2 1

For Rachel,
my partner in the great dive into life.
And for the many divers and friends with
whom it's my privilege to share a life of diving.
Thanks to you all. Life is good.

ACKNOWLEDGEMENTS

Thanks to dear friends and consorts Marsha and Keith O'Daniel, whose enthusiastic guidance is always appreciated. My sincere thanks to Gordon Watts, Ph.D. who has been kind enough to let me share several summer adventures in Bermuda, learning about archaeology and the virtues of rum and ginger beer. Thanks to Teddy Tucker, an authentic Bermuda treasure, who has ignited my passion for wreck diving and enthralled me with his great stories. To Towny, Alison, Mickey and the crew from the Maryland Archaeological and Historical Society who graciously allowed me to participate in some of their projects, thanks for some great experiences. There is so much ocean and so little time.... Finally to Tony and Josie Bliss of Aqua Quest Publications, whose cherished friendship has been the highlight of this whole adventure.

BLACKWOLF

CHAPTER 1

John "Doc" Holiday, 48-year old doctor of American Literature and ex-Navy SEAL, woke as the eastern sky began to lighten. His neck and chest dripped with sweat. The instant his eyes opened, he was fully awake and tensed for action as if he were back in the jungle on Vietnam's Rung Sat River.

It had not been a good night. Flashbacks of his daughter, Debbie, trapped in a dead sub four hundred feet down, gasping for breath while he hovered helplessly outside the glass dome port, had robbed him of any restful sleep. The dreams were all too real. The nightmares had been a reality—video clips replayed by a malicious subconscious with Doc as a captive audience. Unfinished business. Enough. Today he would fight back.

He lay back on the pillows trying to refocus as soft morning light filled the cabin. He breathed deeply and slowly, regaining his composure, letting the gentleness of the morning calm him for a moment before getting up and letting the monsters of the night go back to their dark closets.

Doc began by going over each step of the upcoming dive while staring at the ceiling mirrors of the yacht's hand-rubbed teak paneled master cabin. Sleeping nude as usual, Sheri Benson, 18 years younger, much softer and certainly prettier, nestled close beside him. At five-foot-eight she looked small in the bed compared to his bulk. Doc smiled at her tousle of sun-streaked blonde hair and the upturned Swedish nose. Her shoulders and arms were strong from lifting tanks as part of her work in the Bermuda Maritime Museum diving locker. And even though it was only late March, she was deeply tanned. Covered beneath the sheet, he could see the curve of her thighs, developed by her passion for running. The sheet was pulled up only to her waist and there were no tan lines on her upper body. Frequent sunbathing when they took the boat far enough out to be alone had solved that problem. And the services of a friendly plastic surgeon at Atlanta's Northside Hospital had generously enhanced her natural endowments. Not wanting to lose focus completely, he gently kissed her and slipped from the bed.

His shorts and tee shirt were across the stateroom, behind the chair where she had thrown them last night, along with her own. The welcome home party, at which he had been the only guest, had left them both satisfied and exhausted. He smiled at her. At times she was amazing and he wondered how he'd ever been fortunate enough to share her life.

He stepped into his shorts and pulled on the shirt. The length of the sleeve was just long enough to cover the smiling red seal on his right arm and the neck just high enough to hide the worst of the scars on the left side of his neck and chest.

He stretched, ran his large hands through thick salt-and-pepper hair and then across the gray stubble on his chin. He would shave later.

The Navy Mk-17, closed-circuit mixed gas recirculator was where he'd left it on the salon floor last night. He'd begun setting it up for today's dive when Sheri got spontaneous. Sometimes she reminded him of an irrepressible puppy demanding his full attention and willing to go to comical extremes to get it.

Those were the best of times. Until meeting her he had become so self absorbed in the sobriety of his work and grief over the death of his wife, Nancy, that he had forgotten how to play. Sheri demanded that he play. For that and for her loyalty, he had come to love her. Even when her unrelenting playfulness kept him from his work and drove him nuts.

He opened the salon door and stepped out onto the stern

deck. The Bermuda Royal Navy Dockyard marina was pink in the early sunlight and quiet. The large stone buildings looked much as they had a hundred and fifty years ago. The Dockyard's high stone walls had withstood a hundred hurricanes and provided a safe haven against intruders.

On the hill above the Maritime Museum, the commissioner's house looked as spooky as ever, and across the water the old warehouse with its majestic twin towers stood as it had when proud sailing ships of her majesty's Royal Navy still called the Dockyard their home port.

To the west lights still flickered on the hills above Hamilton, and north at the rim of the Great Sound, buoy and tower lights flashed, marking a narrow channel through dangerous reefs which have claimed hundreds of unwary vessels making Bermuda a repository of wrecks unequaled in the Western Hemisphere. The wind was flat, the sky clear and air crisp. It would be a good diving day.

As was his habit upon rising, he quickly checked the mooring lines and looked over the sixty-five-foot sport fisherman from stem to stern. He and Sheri had renamed her *Kratos,* in Greek meaning to care for and to be held accountable for the outcome. It was the same word used in the Old Testament to describe God's intended relationship between man and the earth. Having a boat with that unusual name gave Doc the opportunity to share a little of his own creation theology from time to time. He left the preaching to Chaplain Bill Stone at the Naval Station, but still it was a good conversation opener, that name, *Kratos.*

Satisfied that everything was secure, he returned to the salon and after turning on the coffee pot and one light, he dropped to the deck to finish shaking the fine pink dust out of the recirculator's CO_2 absorbent canister. As he locked the canister down in the unit, he heard Sheri call from their stateroom. He left the recirculator, filled two coffee mugs and took them down the short stairs to his drowsy princess.

"'Morning," she said from the bed. "Thanks. Smells wonderful." She sat up amidst a pile of sheets and pillows. He handed her a cup, kissed her and then sat down beside her, admiring the view.

"You're dressed. It's Saturday and it's still early. What's up?"

she asked.

"I'm diving, remember? When we're done we'll cruise to Hamilton and have lunch."

"Not so fast. Why don't I get to dive?"

"Just humor me on this one, okay? The dive may be longer than you could do on a tank, that's all."

"Oh no, that's not all. You're talking about the tunnel. No way."

"Pizza for lunch, and I'll be careful. Listen, the only way I'm ever going to prove the capacitor fragment I found was from one of Behrmann's torpedoes is to find one of Behrmann's torpedoes. His old base is our best shot."

"But why the recirculator?"

"Just in case I get lucky."

"You're the stubbornest man on the planet, Doc. You've been gone nearly a month and it's our first day to play and now you're sticking your nose in the Navy's business again. You're never going to let this go, are you?"

"Nope. Good men died on that ship along with the Secretary of State. I won't give up until we can prove what really happened, but I will buy you a pizza."

"Anchovies?"

"All you can stand."

"Alright," she said, shaking her head with disgusted resignation, "but this is our only morning to sleep in...are you sure there's nothing I can do to change your mind?"

He ignored her come-on smile and the way she arched her back and shook her shoulders...well, at least he tried to ignore it.

"Just smell that pizza." He held the imaginary pan in front of her nose, wondering if her passion for pizza was greater than her passion for other things which he had enjoyed.

Twice the Secretary of the Navy, Andy Anderson, had asked for his help. And twice Doc's arguments to prove Captain Hans Behrmann responsible for terrorist acts had been ignored. First was the sinking of an inconsequential freighter hauling grain to Costa Rica. Target practice for the sub. The ship was lost with all hands, but the blast was witnessed by a passing sailboat. The description of the explosion and the dive convinced Doc that *Blackwolf* was still operational. The second call came just after explosions which sank a private yacht on which the Secretary of State was meeting with a treaty delegation from five Middle East nations. More than target practice, but the political overtones of this incident were staggering. Rumors were rampant that Iraq, not invited to participate, was somehow responsible. Doc was very skeptical. Then, on the underwater inspection of the wreck he found a scrap of aluminum, which he was certain matched the capacitors he'd seen eight months ago aboard *Blackwolf* as part of the firing system of the sub's deadly little torpedoes.

Sheri inhaled the imaginary pizza, laughed then put her arms around him and pulled him down on top of her. *The lady wants my undivided attention right now,* he thought. *Resolving the quandaries of international terrorism will have to wait.*

An hour later, they were anchored a mile off the west side of the Dockyard where a deep unmarked channel abruptly ended in a tunnel entrance hidden by coral-encrusted ledges.

The ocean was green and clear. Morning breezes created only delicate whispered facets across the glossed surface. Doc sat on the starboard rail wearing the recirculator and ran a final systems check.

"I should be going with you," Sheri said, her stubborn streak showing.

"We have only one recirculator." He was impatiently patient.

"Mike and Ian won't like your doing this without them." Using the U.S. Naval Station's security chief, Lieutenant Mike Berry, and the chief of Bermuda's Marine Police, Inspector Ian Cord, to strengthen her argument was a last ditch effort. But as soon as the words were out of her mouth, she knew her effort was futile. His mind was made up and anything more she had to add was only going to make matters worse.

"This is my job." He glared at her for not trusting his competence and his decision. "It's what I was trained for. Don't worry, I won't be long."

He checked both the recirculator's pressure gauges again, then looked around the boat. Even though they were an hour later than he'd planned, there were no other boats out this early. He fitted his mask in place, zipped the wet suit all the way up, opened the mouthpiece valve, and rolled backward into the water. As he swam to the bottom eighty feet below, he focused again on the problem which had kept him awake for the last six months. *The Navy had answers, but not the right ones. Doctor Hans Behrmann's sub, Blackwolf, had vanished and the tunnel to his secret base was sealed by an earth-shaking explosion set off by Behrmann himself. Now it was as if the Navy had reformatted the computer hard disk to erase all memory of the sub or the events surrounding its second disappearance. As far as they and the rest of the world were concerned, Blackwolf had never existed.* But Doc knew better, and he had a score to settle. *So the question wasn't what Behrmann or the Navy had done; it was what else they might be doing and why.*

He leveled at fifty feet, took a compass bearing and swam forward. He shivered as water ran down the back of his neck. The cool water was normal for late March, but with it came visibility of over a hundred feet. His body quickly warmed the water in the wet suit, the chill passed and he found the rock pile created by Behrmann's blast. A second blast had supposedly destroyed the sub and its crew, including the brilliant old scientist turned pirate or worse, Behrmann himself. At least that's the way the Navy reported it, in spite of the fact that not one piece of the sub, not one life jacket, dismembered corpse or fragment thereof had been found. Doc didn't buy any of it.

But then no one had cared much what Doc bought or thought. That was the heart of it. The bottom line. Hell hath no fury like a woman scorned or a hard-headed Navy SEAL pumped on righteous indignation with a story to tell and no audience.

"I've always been an optimist and a trusting soul," Doc noted one dark and stormy evening, as he savored Dark and Stormy, the dark rum and ginger beer medication reserved for chronic gout, severe depression, or mild thirst and the company of friends. "But this business with the Navy, it's enough to make a man start thinking about pulling up anchor, if that's the way things are going to be."

He swam a large set of circles out from the entrance looking for another opening. Nothing. *Go back...start again.* He hovered glaring at the rock pile and wondered if he could get away with using explosives to clear it.

As he glared at the rocks, a blue and green wrasse about a

foot long emerged from the rock pile. Doc dropped to see where the fish had come from. He couldn't see much, certainly not an opening he could get through, but if the fish got through...he began tossing rocks from the pile. Soon he was breathing hard as he strained to dislodge the larger boulders. Thirty minutes later he had opened a hole large enough to crawl through...if he took off the recirculator and pushed it in ahead of him.

He pushed, scraped and crawled through the tight opening before putting the recirculator back on and checking the pressure gauges again—plenty of gas. Then he checked his three dive lights. Satisfied that everything was working, he turned off the larger light and rose to the tunnel roof. He was looking for the guide wire used by Behrmann's sub to navigate the twists and turns of the mile-long passageway.

The tunnel looked clear. Doc wished he could clear his mind as well. Memories of his last swim through this tunnel to rescue his daughter from Jason Richardson, Behrmann's grandson and the former director of the Maritime Museum, rushed at him like hungry barracuda. He remembered finding the booby trap Richardson had set to keep Behrmann from escaping with *Blackwolf*. Had the timer run a minute longer, there would have been a new entrance to the tunnel.

But even after disarming the bomb, Doc had arrived in the tunnel too late. Debbie, his daughter, was gone. She was taken by Richardson in a stolen tourist sub, which then lost a hard-fought sea battle when Jason tried to outsmart a treacherous drug runner. Richardson's sub went crashing to the bottom four hundred and eleven feet below, trapping everyone who survived.

In the darkness Doc could still see his daughter looking out at him through the downed sub's bow hemisphere. Near death, his only chance to save her had odds worse than winning the lottery. He had to flood the sub and then force his way in before she died from lack of air.

He shook it off. It was history. His million to one shot had paid off. Debbie and Tom, newly married, were safe and living on the island. Still, there was a score to settle.

He focused on the small black wire above him, determined not to let the memories bother him. *Before the blast the tunnel had been open. But would it have normally been unprotected, unguarded? Why had it been so easy to get in the first time?* The question kept coming back like an old song.

He was now a thousand yards into the darkness. The silence of the recirculator was comforting. No bubbles from a scuba regulator hammering against his ears, only the plop, plop of the big diaphragm and the occasional click of a solenoid as the unit automatically added oxygen to the scrubber's canister. Soft green lights on the wrist display told him everything was fine. *Total darkness...total silence: total darkness...photo cells would pick up a firefly at a thousand yards...acoustical monitors could hear a ship at a hundred miles. Photo cells.... Perhaps that's how Behrmann had known he was coming. Could they still be operational?* He turned off the dive light and kept swimming.

It was so dark without the light he couldn't tell if his eyes were open or closed. He kept his breathing slow and deep, and gently ran his fingers along the wire. As he became more comfortable, he increased his speed. This was simply another of hundreds of blackwater dives. Then as if he had fallen out of bed, he lost the wire and in the total darkness was suddenly completely disoriented.

He stopped short, cracked his mask seal and partially flooded his mask. Now as long as he could feel water in his nose he was headed up. He put one hand above his head and began kicking until he hit a steel beam. He stopped, grabbed the beam and began feeling his way through a maze of big beams, pipes and large steel gears. His hands did the looking and his brain raced to translate. Above him he felt the roughness of thick steel cables woven into a heavy net. He moved along the net's length, trying to visualize its size and the machinery which operated it. Experienced in blackwater work, he quickly put together the images his fingers were "seeing." It was a submarine net on a huge drum. He could feel heavy chains and the teeth of a large gear. What could the trigger be? Where were the controls? He wanted desperately to use the dive light, but if the triggers were photo sensors.... He imagined how the circuits would be laid out: electromagnetic servos to operate a trip lock, a counter weight to turn the drum. Simple, ingenious, terminal.

He began preparing a check list of what he would need

for the next dive. *Heavy chain to bind the gears and explosive cable cutters to disable the machinery. A cutting torch with Mapp or Apache gas wouldn't be a bad idea either.* He worked his way back toward the steel beams. Experience gained by surprises frequently resulting in scars had taught him to be patient. *No surprises...a good motto for divers who want to stay alive.* Another day, another dive might give him the edge he needed to survive Captain Behrmann's deadly snare. He didn't have all the answers he'd come for, but experience, that most difficult of masters, demanded that he be patient. *Slow down and do it right. Impatient pioneers are the ones found face down in the dust with arrows in their backs.*

He searched carefully until he found the ceiling wire again and began slowly backtracking to the tunnel entrance. He would not risk penetrating the tunnel further or using lights until he was certain the net was out of commission. He breathed easier now. He was doing it the right way and perhaps, just perhaps, this time he would find the proof he was after.

He had gone only a few yards when he was stopped short by the deafening screech of rusted gears and the rumbling of heavy chain. The huge net was dropping behind him.

He turned and beneath him, fifty feet back in the tunnel, he saw the flicker of a dive light. *Sheri must have gotten worried and followed me in. She won't have enough air to make it to the cave. Damn that hard headed woman!*

He snapped on his dive light, pushed off the ceiling and with powerful kicks swam as hard as he could to the falling net. It was close. He grabbed the "I" beam at the net's bottom and rolled under just as it crashed onto the hard stone floor. Now they were both trapped. And, appropriately, the tunnel again became silent as a tomb.

He caught his breath and looked for Sheri. She was on the bottom, stunned and motionless. He swam to her and when he could look into her mask, he saw her eyes wide with fright and an "I'm-sorry" look. He held back his anger at her, gave himself another moment to regroup and then gave her hand a gentle squeeze. He checked her pressure gauge. Her tank was two thirds full. Good, but not enough to make the mile long swim to the cave, especially not at the rate she was breathing now. He took her hand and motioned to her to relax and slow her breathing. She nodded, exhaled deeply and then began slow, deep controlled breaths. She gave him an okay signal and he pointed toward the ceiling. They rose thirty feet and began swimming. Two hundred fifty yards from the net, just past an abrupt right turn, they came to a dead end.

This dead end was not a cave-in. The tunnel simply stopped as if the miners had gotten tired and gone home. The walls were covered with dark algae and loose stone was piled on the floor. He picked up a piece of stone and studied it. When Bermuda stone is first cut it's almost white. All the sides of this stone were dark, like the walls. Now what?

They must have missed something, he thought, trying to be optimistic. He panned the walls and ceiling with the dive light. Nothing but the algae-stained stone. Nothing, and then it hit him: where was the wire? He had not been following it after the net came crashing down, but the sub would have. So where had the wire gone? He took Sheri's hand. She was trembling. He gave her an okay signal and she shook her head doubtfully. Still she followed him back up to the ceiling and wondered what the devil he was looking for.

Doc found it just before the curve. The tunnel went hard right. The wire went straight ahead—straight into another stone wall.

But the wire suggested something else entirely. Doc pulled out his stout-bladed Randall knife and went to work on the mystery wall. The texture was different, not stone at all but more like very old latex rubber. Beneath it were woven steel cables. This wall was really another net, cleverly disguised so that anyone who wandered in would believe he'd come to a dead end and that would be the end of the story. *Congratulations. So that's how they kept it a secret for all those years. Sure there's an old tunnel, and it's long and dark and spooky, but it doesn't go anywhere....* He checked the recirculator. Its six-hour gas supply was down to four and a half hours. *Must have been doing a little heavy breathing—Sheri must be close to half a tank. Good guess—1,500 psi.* Her breathing was still nearly double her normal slow controlled rate. *Impossible not to hog your air when you're scared to death. Still, we might last two hours buddy breathing. Plenty of time...that is if we can kick one of the ends out of this coffin and turn it back into a tunnel. Two hours. Good news, bad news. That's a long time to wait if we don't find a way out.*

The tunnel and its steel net doors was impressive, but how the hell did it work? *It has to be the ceiling wires. The sub somehow made contact with the wires which triggered relays that open and close the doors just like a street car or a train on a switch track. It's probably a low voltage system. The wires are small and the contacts might even be...the sub didn't make direct contact to trigger the relays. What if...?*

He started swimming faster, dragging Sheri behind him and looking more closely at the wires. Half way back to the net he found what he was looking for, and excitedly pointed to the tiny relay box. Sheri didn't get it so he closed the mouthpiece valve, took it out of his mouth and grinned at her. It didn't help much; her eyes were still big as saucers. He replaced the mouthpiece, reopened the valve, exhaled and then took a breath.

At the junction box was a new circuit leading to twin photo sensors. They were the eyes in the darkness, the watchful tiger who had triggered the net.

He needed two short pieces of wire and used the Randall to cut them from the photo cell circuit. Once the wires were stripped he took the back up dive light and removed the lens cap. Water pressure held the sealed head lamp bulb in place, but the butt of the Randall solved that. He smashed the lens and quickly connected the wires to the lantern battery and handed the other light to Sheri, pointing it at the relay box. She nodded and he set to work to find the right contact points to trip the relay. He glanced at her pressure gauge. She was in the red: less than 500 psi remaining. *Time to start thinking about buddy breathing.* It was more complicated with the recirculator's double hoses and valved mouthpiece. *Have to be careful not to let water get into the scrubber's canister.*

He tried the second combination of contacts. Still nothing. He reversed the wires and tried again....

Contact! From the inner end of the tunnel they heard the screech of rusted gears. The wall which was really a door was opening, but the net which kept them from going back to the boat remained closed.

By the time they reached the opened door Sheri was nearly

out of air. Doc showed her the valve lever on the recirculator's mouthpiece and motioned for her to get behind him and hold onto the recirculator. She did and then he passed the mouthpiece over his head and back to her. She took it, opened the valve, took two breaths, closed the valve and passed it back. She gave him an okay and they started forward again. Doc was a strong swimmer and enjoyed long distance workouts. During the past winter months he had swam in the ocean nearly every day. The cooler water didn't seem to bother him, which added to his reputation as the marina's resident crazy person.

But that's alright. Most smart folks give crazy people a wide berth. A mild mannered professor wouldn't want to cultivate that image. But then he'd ceased being mild mannered the night his daughter was kidnaped. Having crossed the line then, he saw no reason for turning back now.

He swam quickly, pulling Sheri who was exhausted. And they worked into a buddy breathing rhythm so well that it hardly slowed him down. Twenty five minutes and seven hundred yards later, they surfaced in the cave—the secret base of Doctor Hans Behrmann and the crown jewel of Behrmann's engineering career: the antidote for nuclear power, *Blackwolf.*

CHAPTER 2

A faint light filtered down through the single ceiling vent sixty feet above, illuminating only the top tier of the catacomb-like rooms. Doc swept the walls and catwalks of the other three tiers with his dive light causing rats to scurry across the stone terrace. Doc and Sheri swam to the stone pier where *Blackwolf* had been moored and rested for a moment before pulling off their fins and climbing the roughly hewn, slime covered stone stairs.

"Mike and Ian will find us," she began as she shivered in her wet suit. "But I hope I don't freeze to death first."

"We'll get a fire going. They had a generator. We'll find it and turn on the lights. Maybe they even left us something to eat."

"You promised pizza."

"And you were supposed to stay in the boat."

He was right and she knew this was not the time to be complaining about starvation, cold or even a broken nail. She could have very easily been dead an hour ago and it would have been her own fault. Better to suffer in silence.

They left the equipment by the water and began exploring. From his last visit Doc remembered hearing the generator noise from the far left corner of the cavern and they set out in that direction.

"What about snakes?"

"Taste just like chicken. Unfortunately, there aren't any in Bermuda."

"Oh, that helped. My stomach stopped growling at the mere idea. I just imagined a plate of spaghetti that moves."

The generator shack door was bolted. He pried back the rusted bolt and the heavy door creaked as it opened. The shed held two large yellow marine generators with racks of batteries. He checked the fuel and oil of the first, then hit the starter. The engine turned over twice and then fired. He let it warm up for a minute and then closed the knife switches to turn on the lights. He stepped from the shed and closed the door just in time to see startled bats fly for darkness from the dim orange lights, and a large rat run in a confused circle before scurrying to a trash pile of crates and fuel drums.

"You going to put him on your menu too?"

"Rataroni? Rat parmesan? Rat alfredo?"

"You're impossible."

"Nearly, but as you have proven, with patience and determination, even I, a pillar of strength and moral rectitude, can be diminished to ash at your altar."

"Oh, 'ash at my altar,' I like that. Your lines are improving." She laughed, took his hand and they began their search.

The pueblo-like structure was four stories high, built of the blocks cut from the tunnel and beams from timbers of old ships. The timbers, now sagging and rotten, were braced and spliced with odd pieces of iron and piling, none of which looked too sturdy. With the wooden stairs and balconies gone, the rooms were connected by rusting steel scaffolds and planks, and strung with reels of electrical cord and dimly glowing bare bulbs. Black and green mold covered much of the stone, and moisture dripped from the iron.

They found the mess hall and C rations from the Second World War. Sheri gracefully declined. Two stainless steel refrigerators contained moldy bread and other unidentifiable remains. Everything was damp and moldy, like the matches Doc found which crumbled when he struck them. Sheri shivered again as her visions of a warm fire crumbled with the wet match heads. Doc put his arm around her and smiled. *Things will get better. They always do if you keep your attitude right.*

They moved on to Bill Roberts's computer room. The

equipment racks were empty; the equipment was now aboard *Blackwolf*. There were two telephones. He picked them up. Both were dead.

"Did you really think it would be that easy?" she laughed.

"A pessimist...I knew you were a pessimist. Just for that, no pizza."

They found blankets in plastic storage bags. Doc used the Randall to convert them to ponchos. Sheri was still shivering even though she was still in her wet suit. Doc hadn't forgotten about the fire; it was just that the key element, ignition materials, had not yet presented themselves. They moved on to a gloomy, smelly, crowded laboratory. There were piles of encrusted metal, tanks soaking artifacts and Nalgene chemical bottles. They also found coin beds for reverse electrolysis and an old X-ray machine. A lead apron hung over its barrel. One tank contained several old guns in various states of restoration.

"Flintlocks from the 1814 wreck," Sheri said. "So Lisa was right. Jason Richardson had been raiding those sites. He had some nerve to blame it on sport divers. He belonged down here, with the rest of the rodents."

"Not that we ever doubted his integrity," Doc added sarcastically.

Doc found tongs and lifted one of the guns from the tub. He pried the flint from the firing lock, dried it on the blanket, and struck it against the notched back of the Randall. Sparks flew and visions of a fire came back. He returned the gun to the tank and looked over the selection of chemicals. He smiled when he spotted a bottle of naphthalene. *Why settle for a camp fire when you can have an inferno?* However, his better judgment took over when he spotted a gallon of less volatile alcohol. Now they would be warm. On the way to Firebuilding 101 Doc noticed a notebook sticking out of a half open desk drawer. Thinking the paper might be of use, he pulled it out and flipped it open.

"What?" she asked.

"Have a look," he said and handed her the pad. The first pages were nudes of Karen, Sheri's diving student who had fallen under Jason's spell, and after being shot was taken hostage aboard *Blackwolf* by Captain Hans Behrmann.

"Jason was a good artist, wasn't he?" she said. "I wonder if he survived the head wound he got when the sub crashed."

"He didn't look so good when we put him aboard *Blackwolf.*" Doc turned through the next few pages, more torsos at various angles, and then added, "The first time we met he told me he was on a quest to find the perfect pair of boobs—a more honorable endeavor than many academic quests. One must admire that level of scientific dedication. Karen was certainly a contender."

"So what made him different from any other male? That's neither politically correct or even funny, considering all the pain he caused. Have you forgotten how close you came to losing Debbie because of him?"

"I'm probably too old for political correctness," he laughed and flipped past the rest of the nude sketches until he came to detailed drawings of an elaborate wine goblet.

"Isn't that...?" Sheri asked.

"Yes, the goblet old Ben Travis claimed was Socrates's poison cup."

"So Jason had that too."

"Yes, and another question I've not been able to answer is, why did he send it back to old professor Travis?" Doc said.

"Didn't Travis tell you it was to taunt him, that Jason did it to prove he had won the final round and found the hiding place for all the loot Travis and his students had stashed?"

"Loot? Is that a politically correct archaeological term?"

"You know what I mean. Artifacts. Priceless relics of antiquity."

"Much better," he laughed. "Yes, that's what the old man said. But I can't help thinking the chalice was worth a fortune and that if Travis was telling the truth, it held the key to the locations of more very rich wreck sites. There must have been other things Jason could have sent that would have conveyed the same message. Why send the chalice, particularly if everything Travis said about it was true?"

"So you think Travis might have been wrong? Jason might have sent it as a kind of peace offering or something? That's an interesting twist."

"Just another possibility, that's all. Perhaps someday we'll get the chance to ask Jason in person—just before I wring his neck for what he did to Debbie."

Doc turned the remaining pages of the sketchbook slowly, examining the remaining drawings. There were rifle firing mechanisms, shards of pottery and military uniform buttons. On the last page was the torso of another well-graced female. He held it up to the light and looked back at Sheri.

"Turn to your left a bit and take off that blanket," he said looking at her and then back at the sketch.

"No way, Doc. That's not me! I never took off anything for Jason." She grabbed for the pad. He held it above her reach and kissed her when she jumped for it.

He laughed again and then glanced back at the sketch as if trying to make a definitive comparison. But in better light, closer to the orange bulb, he could see the indentations of another drawing on the page. Fragments of torn paper in the wire spiral confirmed that the preceding page had been torn out. Sheri jumped again and this time grabbed the pad. She was still laughing and hadn't yet caught his sudden change of mood.

"Wait. Stop it! Look at this. Find me a pencil. This looks like a map."

She found a pencil and he began shading over the indentations on the back of the page.

"What is it?" she asked.

"Have a look. What do you think?"

"It's like Bermuda, here's Hamilton, the Dockyard would be here.... No, it doesn't work. There's nothing out here where St. George's should be."

"Good. I don't think it's Bermuda either."

"Then what?"

"I'm not sure yet, but it was important enough that he didn't want anyone else to see it. We'll hang on to this until I can check it out. Now let's find something to build that fire."

The only room remaining was a workshop, but it had been picked clean of everything except a half dozen plywood packing crates. Doc opened one and discovered the foam liner cut to hold the cylindrical sections of *Blackwolf*'s torpedoes.

There were workbenches where the torpedo sections would have been assembled, a traveling chain hoist for lifting them, and wheeled dollies for moving them to the sub. Frustrated that he'd not found anything to prove the aluminum shards he'd found had come from one of these torpedoes, he went to the trash pile with visions of a roaring fire.

"How did these get down here?" she asked pointing to the oak palettes in the trash pile. "And how did they get those generators down here? They're too big to come down the stairs and certainly too big for the hatch of any sub. So, how did they get here?"

"Good question."

"Well, come up with something. You're supposed to be the brains here. I'm along only for sex appeal, remember?"

"Now, who's being politically correct?" He gave her a dirty look and swatted her bottom.

Getting the fire going didn't take long and as the fire grew, he dragged mattresses next to the blaze. Sheri peeled out of her wet suit, then lay wrapped in the blanket on her side with her back to the fire, enjoying the heat like a Minnesota cat in front of a December wood stove.

"I'm still waiting for you to tell me how they moved heavy stuff, like those torpedoes or fuel drums for the generators, without an elevator," she said.

He lay back with his head on her stomach and looked at the ceiling.

"There has to be something," she continued. "Look, how come that trash pile is so small? Where are the empty tin cans, beer bottles, dirty dishes and grocery bags? If they had been burning stuff like we are, someone would have seen the smoke or smelled it. If they were dumping trash in the water, some of it would have been in the tunnel and there wasn't a piece, not one. No anthropologist or archaeologist would buy this: no chicken bones or McDonald's bags. No primary cultural deposit. They had a disposal system we haven't found yet."

Doc got up, tossed another oak palette on the fire and then lay back down beside her. Together they watched the flames rise toward the roof. As the light grew brighter, he could see the answer to her question in the ceiling above them.

"Up there, look, it's a lift. It must go into one of the warehouses by the boat pond. You were right, they had an elevator." He got up and grabbed the Randall.

"Where are you going?"

"To find the controls for that lift. The main staircase is blocked so that lift might be our way out."

"Great idea, but not now," she smiled. "Why don't you just stay here and keep me warm? I haven't thanked you yet for saving me." She tossed her swimsuit out from beneath the blanket and gave him an inviting, teasing smile.

Suddenly the lights went out and the generator was silent.

"Now you have to stay. You wouldn't leave me alone in the dark would you?"

"I should see what happened to the generator."

"It quit. Stay with me. I won't quit."

"Now there's an amazing revelation. Almost as amazing as last night...and this morning. But, I thought you were starving?"

"I am, so see if you can get my mind off food for a while. Besides, Mark or Lisa will see the smoke. I feel kinda sexy here by the fire."

"What a salesman."

"Salesperson, if you please."

"Sorry, I should have known our new found political sensitivity includes the area of gender exclusivity."

He lay back on the mattress and they watched the fire's shadow dance on the pueblo walls. He reached beneath her blanket and stroked her bare back. But when he reached for her with serious intent, she jumped to her feet and with a war hoop danced around the fire, twirling, bobbing and weaving like a primal creature, writhing to ancient rhythms. Her shadow grew as the flame flickered higher and then with fire in her eyes, she slipped out of the blanket and danced with it as a twirling cape.

She circled him once, twice and on the third time attacked. He put up a mock defense, but was quickly overcome. *Only an idiot would fight off this attack.*

She moved with that same primal energy atop him, arched her back and screamed when she came. A bit melodramatic perhaps, but highly satisfying. Her cry echoed off the walls, sending bats in flight. Doc lay back laughing until she collapsed on his chest.

"I should have guessed you were an Indian," he said while gently stroking her back with the tips of his fingers.

"That's Native American if you please and yes, I'm part of a very old tribe, the Fugawee...perhaps you've heard of us?"

"Weren't they known as great sailors?"

"Discoverers, actually. But they never got credit for their discoveries because of a failure to communicate...."

"Really, like with Paul Newman in *Cool Hand Luke*?"

"Precisely, and it must have been terribly frustrating for them."

"Well, don't keep me in suspense," he said grinning, fully aware that he was being had and loving every minute of it. "What was their problem?"

"Well, whenever they'd get to a new place, they'd say something like, 'Yo, we're the Fugawee,' and the other Indians would always think they were from New York and lost. Isn't that just terrible?" she laughed.

"Simply heartbreaking." He laughed again then ran his fingers through her mop of blonde hair, pulled her closer and kissed her again. Later, when she came up for air she asked, "How the hell are we going to get out of here?"

"We could try putting a note in a bottle," he answered.

"Brilliant. What would you write?"

"Having a wonderful time. Send vitamin E."

She kissed him again and when he started to get up to check the generator, she pulled him back down and whispered, "Not yet." She pulled the blanket over them and began kissing his neck. Later they slept and when she awoke, the fire was only glowing coals and the air tasted damp and cold. Light no longer filtered down through the ceiling crevice and she wondered how long they had slept. He was on his side with his arm protectively holding her. The radiant hands of his Rolex said it was nine-thirty. She had slept for two hours and her stomach was screaming.

A rock fell from the ceiling and bounced from the pueblo walls to the cavern floor. Then lights flashed above them.

"Doc, we've got company. You awake?"

"No," he whispered back.

"That's what I thought. Do you remember where I left my suit?"

"On the deck behind the chair? No, that was last night. Stay put. I'll find it."

He pulled on his blanket poncho, found the dive light, handed over her swimsuit and pulled his on as well. He stuck the Randall's sheath in the back of his suit then tossed the last of the wood on the fire. The dive light's beam was not bright enough to reach the ceiling sixty feet above, but Doc recognized Lieutenant Mike Berry's voice when the lieutenant shouted, "Anybody home?"

"You the pizza delivery guys?" Sheri shouted back.

"I'll check the generator," Doc said and left her by the fire. He took the light, walked to the shed and pulled open the heavy door. He was greeted by the strong smell of diesel fuel. In the dive light's beam he could see a pool of fuel on the stone floor. He knelt to look for the source and saw cut fuel lines spewing fuel. He jumped back, but not quickly enough. The door slammed behind him and he heard the bolt being hammered into place. He turned with the light looking for something he could use to beat down the door. Hanging just above the diesel fuel was a broken light bulb on an extension cord. He dove for it, grabbed the cord and jerked as hard as he could. He heard a groan from outside the shed followed by a short burst of profanity. He pulled the cord until he had the other end in his hands. The wires were stripped ready to make contact. Whoever had slammed the door evidently had a taste for barbecued English professors.

He found the fuel valve and turned it off. The generators were fresh water cooled with heat exchangers. He opened the spitcock at the bottom of the heat exchanger and saltwater flooded the floor, diluting the fuel. The fumes were still overwhelming, but it's better than being roasted. He went back to the door and yelled to Sheri. No answer. The shed had been built to be soundproof—apparently she couldn't hear him. *What now? Turn the lights on so Mike can see what's going on, that's what.* Doc cut the leather lanyard from the Randall's hilt and tied the broken lines with a patch he cut from the spare generator's water hose. After closing the spitcock and turning the fuel valve back on, he hit the starter and when the generator came to life with a deafening roar, he slammed home the knife switches and waited.

The lights came on. Lieutenant Mike Berry had just landed on the pueblo roof and was removing his rappelling gear when the Marine above him shouted and pointed toward Sheri. A man was approaching her with a knife. Mike shouted to warn her and then opened fire. Sheri screamed and stumbled to her feet. The man, his face covered by a black cloth mask, lunged at her. She jumped backward and then he grabbed the notebooks and sketch pad and ran to the far end of the cavern with a trail of gunfire following him. He crossed a flimsy timber bridge and vanished. Sheri screamed at the shooting and when it stopped, she ran to the generator shed.

The hasp was bolted. She struggled until she got it open. Doc emerged drenched in diesel and holding his ears. Mike and two of his men came running down the scaffolding. Doc pulled off the diesel soaked blanket and tossed it aside.

"Come on," Mike shouted. "Let's get him."

He handed Doc a nine millimeter Glock and led the way toward the plank bridge. As they ran Mike started, "What the hell are you doing down here? Why didn't you wait for me? Now you've got the whole damn Navy involved again."

They crossed the bridge, entered a crumbling stone-walled room and in back of a wooden storage cabinet, found a path which led to a long stone stairway. "This must be how Jason and Karen got away from us at his party," Doc said. "I'll lead."

Mike didn't argue and they began the climb. The stair wound around an open shaft and then ended in a short tunnel.

"Doc was afraid of the booby traps," Sheri said when they came to a landing. "He didn't want you getting hurt and none of this would have happened if I'd waited in the boat like I was supposed to. But I got worried and followed him into the tunnel."

"Sub nets controlled by photo cells," Doc added. He was breathing hard. "Her light triggered them and we were trapped."

They came to the top of the corkscrew and the tunnel took a hard left. Doc kept to the inside and rolled cautiously around it. Then above them they heard shouting and saw a light.

"Come on," Doc said and they began running.

The shaft ended abruptly in a massive cedar door. It was open and beyond it they found themselves in the Commissioner's house in what had been Jason Richardson's elaborately decorated bedroom. Lisa, the museum conservationist, was standing on the bed wrapped loosely in a sheet, screaming as if she'd been attacked by a regiment of cave rats. Mark, her invited guest and lab assistant, had chased the uninvited guest out of the room and down the hall. Lisa pointed. Doc and Mike followed. Sheri stayed with Lisa. When they came to the bottom of the stairs in the conservation lab's courtyard they found the gate open and Mark sitting, stunned and bleeding on the edge of an artifact holding tank.

"I almost had him, Doc," Mark said. He was not a pretty sight catching the free flowing blood from his broken nose with his hands, and in turn covering his arms and chest with it. "Son of a bitch slammed the gate in my face. Damn, this hurts. I saw the smoke and called Mike. Knew it had to be a signal from you—especially with *Kratos* anchored out there. We took the inflatable out and brought her in. She's safe in your slip. I'd have come after you myself, but there was no climbing gear. Couldn't even find a decent rope.

Then Lisa called: "What'd you find down there?"

"Trouble," Doc said. "Come on, let's get the first aid kit and some ice. We'll pack your nose and get that bleeding stopped."

"Any idea what that was about?" Mike asked later as they searched the warehouses around the small boat pond called the Keep for the elevator Doc had seen in the cavern.

"Someone came to see what we were up to, I guess. I'm not surprised they were watching. I should have been more careful."

"You'd think after seven months and nothing..."

"That it's over? *Blackwolf*'s still out there, Mike. I know it, you know it and somebody's still worried that we might be able to prove it. Now I'm sorry I waited so long to make that dive. And here's one you can put in the bank. Any doubts I had that I'm right about *Blackwolf*...well, this little stunt tonight removed them all. I swear I'm going to find out what's going on here. And when I do, there's going to be hell to pay."

Two nights after the adventure in the cave, Doc and Sheri were off to St. Georges, a thirty-five minute drive to the other end of the country, to have dinner with his daughter and son-in-law, Debbie and Tom Morrison. Tom was old Boston and it showed. Debbie was Florida from the tips of her usually bare feet to the freckles on her nose. Yet they complimented each other well. Tom had proven himself in Doc's eyes during Debbie's rescue, so the bottom line was, Doc was pleased with his daughter's choice.

Tom was at the grill when they arrived and after hugs and kisses from Debbie, Doc walked through the 200-year-old Bermuda house to the back deck to join him.

The house was white plastered limestone inside and out, like all Bermuda houses of its vintage. Inside, the steeply pitched roof was supported by cedar beams, and a sailor would have immediately recognized the keel and frames of a ship's hull, upside down. The only difference was that instead of having hull planks nailed to the frames, stone slabs, plastered together, made this inverted hull just as watertight as a well founded vessel. Gutters channeled precious rain water into a large cistern which was the only water supply. The house had rented furnished and some of the precious pieces were of hand-rubbed island cedar. Treasures indeed.

Tom and Debbie had just returned from a three-and-a-half-week much delayed honeymoon. They'd visited Tom's folks in Concord, Massachusetts, and explored New England, which was very unlike the Florida panhandle where Debbie had grown up. The colonial history and beauty of New England, even with bitter March winds, charmed her instantly. March snow introduced her to skating and skiing. They also toured the seaports and museums and enjoyed Tom's family history as retold by his grandparents and an amazing collection of uncles and aunts. Debbie heard stories of Emerson, Hawthorne and Thoreau, and of the "shot heard 'round the world," as if the first shot at Concord's old rude bridge had been fired just last month, and the town's three most famous residents, along with the famous Alcott daughters, still lived just a block from the town square.

Sheri listened politely as Debbie told the stories of her New England adventures with enthusiasm. The stories were interesting, but when was Debbie going to get to the good stuff... how were things with her Navy job and Tom, her new husband?

But as Debbie finished one story and began another, Sheri began to worry. Debbie wasn't one for nervous chatter. What wasn't she telling? But before Sheri could get to the bottom of it, Tom and Doc came in with the meat platter and the dinner began.

While they ate, Sheri watched the way Debbie kept looking at Tom and smiling a coy little smile.

"Of course," Sheri thought to herself and grinned. If she was right, Doc was going to croak. She looked at him and winked. It was one of those teasing, "I-know-something-you-don't" winks that always drove him crazy. He had been watching Debbie and Tom and was not totally oblivious to the fact that something was going on. Sheri's wink nailed him between the running lights and now he knew for certain some kind of sinister plot was at work. And, he knew it was time to exercise his parental right to know what the devil was going on. He held up his hand, stopped the conversation and demanded an explanation.

Debbie looked down at her plate and bit her lower lip to keep from laughing. Then with her head still down, she rolled huge little girl eyes up to look at Tom.

"I knew you were going to do this to me," Tom said shaking his head. Then he looked straight at Doc and said, "Sir, I'm terribly sorry, but it appears I've knocked up your daughter. Now, I'd really like to do the right thing about this, you understand, however, my family is real uptight about mixed marriages. So if it's possible for us to just come to some gentleman's arrangement...."

Debbie's jaw dropped, "Mixed marriages...do the right thing...gentleman's agreement...Tom Morrison, you blue-blooded snob, you'll be lucky to live through this dinner. What do you mean, 'mixed marriage?'"

"It's obvious, darling. I'm from Boston. I'm NASA, you're Navy, I voted for Bill and you voted for old what's his face. Obviously any child of ours would be culturally schizophrenic. It's a genetic molecular collision. The results could be devastating. We'll have to send it back."

"Like hell we will! Let me tell you who's going to get sent back."

Doc and Sheri looked at each other in amazement.

"Do you do this often?" Sheri asked.

"Only when he's being a jerk," Debbie laughed. She got up and kissed Doc. "Congratulations, Dad. You're going to be a grandpa. The baby's due in mid-November. We just found out for sure this morning."

"A grandpa," Sheri teased. "My goodness, he's well preserved for a grandpa. Who would have guessed?"

"I'm in shock," Doc laughed. "That's wonderful, honey." But in his mind, the word was hitting him as hard as a well hit racket ball. *Grandpa, whop. Grandpa, whop...whop, whop, whop, whop, whop. Oh shit, I going to be a grandfather. Whop, whop.*

Sheri gave him an evil look that let him know she had just read his mind. "I was right. Look at him, he's having an anxiety attack. Relax, grandpa, you've still got a few good nights left. Very few perhaps, but we'll cherish each and every one as if it were your last. That make you feel better?"

"Hardly. Thanks for nothing."

Debbie served desert and as the conversation about babies and honeymoons and grandfathers slowed, Sheri livened things up with the adventures in the cave. She told the tale with a humorous bent until Debbie suddenly snapped to attention realizing what she'd been listening to for the past three minutes. Debbie's face flushed with anger and Sheri could see a storm on the immediate horizon.

"Sorry," Sheri said under her breath when she realized the seriousness of her *faux pas.* "Guess this wasn't the time."

"It's not your fault. It's his," Debbie said. She got awkwardly to her feet, glaring at her father.

"You just can't let it alone, can you, Dad? You're going to keep on sticking your nose where it isn't wanted until it gets you killed. The Navy's going to raise hell with me because you went back down there against their orders. Did you think of that? Did you think what might happen to all of us if you actually found proof that *Blackwolf* sank that little freighter, or killed the Secretary of State and someone in the Navy covered it up? You're so anxious to point fingers and prove you're right, you've forgotten about us."

Doc made a church roof of his finger tips and rubbed his chin against the steeple of his index fingers. "If Behrmann's still out there," he began thoughtfully, "he needs to be stopped.

What if I'm right and Behrmann did it? Who will their next target be?"

"It doesn't have to be you, Dad. It doesn't have to involve us. Please, just leave it alone." She was sobbing now and that hurt, but he wasn't giving an inch.

"Debbie, listen please. When Vietnam started there were a bunch of good old boys in Washington who thought they could get away with anything. That's what this smells like to me: another private little war with its own little toys. The Navy had Behrmann build that sub and we know it wasn't designed to study deep water sponges. What do you think this is really about?"

"Getting even for Vietnam and a terminal case of testosterone poisoning, that's what it's really about," she snapped back. "All these years you've been mad at the politicians over that damn war, and now you think you've got a chance to get even." She pushed away from the table and ran from the room. Tom excused himself and followed her.

Doc slammed the table with the flat of his hand, swore and stood as if bewildered. They had not fought like this since she was ten and wanted to join the Marines.

"Jerk," Sheri said, shaking her head and laughing softly. When she looked up at him, it was with a sad smile. "Go talk to her, tell her you're sorry. You're her family and she wants a live grandpa for the baby, that's all. Tell her you love her and that you'll be careful. Then let's go home. Don't think I've ever gotten it on with a grandpa. I'll get the oxygen kit from the boat and we'll go howl at the moon."

The next morning as Doc sat at the galley table aboard *Kratos* with a sketch pad attempting to recreate what he remembered of Jason's map, Lieutenant Mike Berry called from the base.

"Got some intel for you," Mike said. "I bumped into a friend at the officer's club last night. He was on one of the destroyer escorts screening for the Secretary of State's yacht when it exploded. What I'm going to tell you is classified so you keep it under your hat. The scuttlebutt in the wardroom is that we had one of our subs operating there which got a tape of another sub leaving the scene."

"I knew it! *Blackwolf*!" Doc said.

"Sorry. Not even close. They think it was one of the new Russian diesel electrics. Like the ones Iraq just bought from them."

"Iraq has Russian subs?"

"At least a half dozen. The Germans and Russians are both building high-tech diesel electric boats. Very quiet, long range and they're for sale to the highest bidder."

"I had no idea...that might change things a bit."

"It might. I thought you'd want to know."

"Mike, wait...is there any way you can find out what kind of torpedoes the Russian boats use?"

There was a pause and then Mike laughed. "You don't give up, do you?"

"Not a chance."

The Bermuda Police Office in Hamilton is a small building full of gray metal office furniture and stalwart officers in blue uniforms with long hose and short pants. The waterfront building is located in a lovely park next to the Royal Bermuda Yacht Club and overlooks Hamilton harbor. Doc had asked for a meeting with Inspector Ian Cord, and now paced the inspector's crowded office as he presented his case. Paul Singleton, retired Royal Navy combat diver and charter boat captain, sat quietly in the corner.

"Look, Ian, they've got no reason to come back to Bermuda. We know that. What we didn't have before was any idea of where they might be headed, but now I think I do. Paul, did you bring those charts?"

Paul, seasoned and solid, Doc's friend for many years, nodded and handed over the chart tube. Doc opened it and rolled out charts of the Cayman Islands on the Inspector's cluttered desk. Then he showed them the sketches he'd done of Jason's map. The sketches were close enough to be very convincing. Ian nodded agreement.

"And I take it you want to go after them? Take the boat to the Caymans and do a little fishing?"

"That's precisely what I want. I've thought about it a lot.

Colonel Sandy Andrews, my old boss when I worked for the agency, was a lot of things, but he hasn't got balls enough to be a renegade. And, if I'm right, he must have still been on the agency payroll and chances are *Blackwolf* and Behrmann were too."

"But why?" Paul asked. "We all agree they were up to something. Something a lot bigger than junk from old shipwrecks."

Doc nodded. "And now our adventures in Behrmann's cave have convinced me that they're still afraid of what we might find. I think we have every justification to go on looking. I have this terrible feeling that if we don't find out what Behrmann's up to, we're going to be reading about it, whatever 'it' is, on the front page of the Royal Gazette and wishing to hell we'd stopped him when we had the chance."

Ian pushed back in the swivel chair, put his hands in back of his head, and stretched his neck from side to side. Like Doc and Paul, the Inspector was a warrior. Tall, lean and swarthy with the strength and reflexes of a rugby player half his age, he had proven himself a valued ally. Doc waited. Now when it counted most, he knew Ian would make the right choice. For a man as dedicated to his job and his code as Ian was, the right choice was the only option.

The Inspector exhaled deeply and turned to Doc. "So, what will you need for this trip, mate? I can get you petrol, firepower and a little expense money, but remember, the last armada launched from Bermuda was sent to sack Washington, not to save it. Stir up a fuss, mate, you'll probably bloody well end up caught on your own hook.... And my pension will be yesterday's news."

Doc waited until he was sure they were alone in the museum's conservation lab to tell her. He hoped the old stone walls would be strong enough, like a grenade trap, to contain her response.

Sheri's hands were on her hips, her head tilted to the side with her eyes target-locked on him. "Sounds lame, Doc. You'll have all the fun and I'll be humping tanks down some mile-long pier and diving with overweighted tourists who trash coral and can't tell angelfish from flounder. Lisa and Mark need me here. Archaeology is interesting. If you don't want me with you..." a short pause here, accompanied by an awful scowl, making certain her feelings of rejection were being clearly communicated. "If you don't want me on the boat, I'll just stay here. Send me a postcard."

Inspector Ian Cord had been right. Bermuda was a small island with lots of eyes and ears. The adventure in Behrmann's cave had proven that the someone was watching Doc's every move. *Kratos* would be an easy target in open ocean. Better not to take the risk of having Paul or Sheri on the boat. Doc was pretty sure Jason's map had been of the Cayman Islands. And why tear it out of the sketch pad if it wasn't important? Doc's plan, if you could call it that, was as simple—safe and simple. But it meant they would be apart for three weeks...so, as he had anticipated, she didn't like it. If the whole truth were told, he didn't like it much either.

She folded her arms across her chest and her chin dropped slightly. Her voice softened just a little. She was shifting tactics and he wondered what the barrage would be. He didn't have long to wait.... "I think all you really want is to have me waiting in some cheap motel so you can have your fun when you get done playing secret agent."

"Just for the record, there are no cheap motels in Grand Cayman, but are you telling me that wouldn't be sufficient motivation? I thought I was doing fairly well in the homework department. Now there's a real kick in the shorts." A smile caught the edges of his mouth and eyes. "Well?" He put his hands on her waist and lifted her to eye level "Well?"

"Higher, lift me higher. I want you to look up to me for a change."

"There?"

"Much better. Almost as good as if you were on your knees."

"Well?"

"Well, hell, of course it would, but don't you leave me stranded on some beach and go off and get yourself killed, Grandpa."

"Oh, my back," he said feigning a sharp pain and dropped her. "You're right, I'm much too old to be lifting a load like you. Been hitting the Little Debbie's again?"

"Bull, that's bull and you know it. Let's go for a run and I'll show you who's a load. Come on, how 'bout a quick ten k, Grandpa, to Somerset and back? Loser cooks and cleans the galley."

"Don't suppose you'd settle for a swim?"

"No way! Your feet are as big as my fins. This is an affair of honor. I want to watch you crawl."

"Have another Little Debbie. I'll get my shoes."

CHAPTER 3

In the isolated lagoon of a remote mountainous jungle island, Karen, blonde, beautiful, tan and very pregnant, swam nude beside archaeologist Jason Richardson in the clear, shallow water. She talked to him, teased and laughed. He played along, but remained silent. Jagged pink scars led from below his right eye up into his hairline, and he let his long brown hair fall across his face to hide the ugly marks. Jason, brilliant young Ph.D., ex-director of the Bermuda Maritime Museum, and once handsome enough to have been a paperback romance cover model, had not spoken a word since the submarine crash.

When the disabled stolen tourist submarine he'd converted into an underwater pirate vessel hit bottom, a heavy radio had come smashing down, disfiguring his face and giving him a severe concussion. He was rescued from the sunken sub by Doc Holiday, only to be taken hostage aboard *Blackwolf* by Behrmann, his deranged grandfather. Perhaps it was better that Jason was silent, safely brain damaged and therefore no longer a threat. Had that not been the case, Behrmann would certainly have killed him in one of his frequent fits of rage.

For months Jason had needed constant care. Karen was by his side night and day. His nurse and protector, she had shielded him from his grandfather's wrath by keeping him out of the old man's way. They spent their days in the lagoon or exploring the island. And when *Blackwolf*'s crew were there, she kept Jason occupied, as far from them and their business as possible.

Karen looked back across the lagoon at the bungalows which were their base. On the covered porch of the main house, she saw Colonel Andrews and Captain Behrmann. Andrews was watching them through binoculars. Uncomfortable as the object of his attention, she urged Jason to swim with her into deeper water across to a more secluded cove. Behrmann was a pest, fondling her whenever she mistakenly came within his grasp. But, she could handle him. Andrews was the dangerous one. As the colonel recovered from his gunshot wound and became stronger, his intentions toward her became more overt but she wanted no part of him. Bill Roberts and his wife, Petra, Behrmann's daughter, were her only hope. So far Petra had always been there at the right minute to protect her from both of them. But if Colonel Andrews ever became strong enough....

Andrews lowered the binoculars as Karen and Jason swam into deeper water. He turned his attention to Behrmann who was standing behind the lounge chair where Andrews spent the majority of his time. He was glad to be able to breathe these last few weeks without a bloody cough and able to sit up long enough to catch a glimpse of Karen from time to time.

"Any word yet?" Andrews asked.

"Soon. My brilliant son-in-law is still working on it. Trouble a three-year-old could handle has him befuddled as usual."

Andrews laughed but said nothing. It was better to stay out of Behrmann's family feuds. Behrmann was the captain—clearly in charge. However, without Petra Robert's care, Andrews knew he would have never recovered from the nine millimeter hole in his chest.

Behrmann took the binoculars and found Karen and Jason. "She should wear something, a bathing costume, or something. Those boys are young, full of fire...there will be trouble."

"Why spoil a good thing? All she's interested in is Jason and a perfect tan. She has both. Why should we give up our simple pleasures? When they get here, just order them to leave her alone."

"Ha, I could give you the same order...if you were their

age, would you listen? Talk to her or there will be trouble."

"You're the one she thinks of as her kindly old grandfather. You tell her. She doesn't like me much."

"Ya, ya, I'll do it. The boys will be back soon. Then she must dress...until then she can wear whatever she wants. I wouldn't want to spoil your fun. Too old, ha! If it weren't for Jason, I'd show her who's too old.... Look at them, like four-year-olds in a sand box." He put the binoculars down and scratched his beard. "You should thank her, you know. Without her sitting up nights watching you when Petra was too tired, you might be under the sand now, not relaxing on it."

"I've been dreaming of thanking her every night for a month."

"You must be getting better. Don't touch her, that's an order," he scowled. "Don't touch her." The old man stared hard at Andrews, scratched his beard again and then went back up the trail to the waterfall.

In the cave Bill Roberts was wiring the terminal to a new satellite tracking dish antenna installed on the mountainside. The cavern, well hidden behind the thundering waterfall, smelled of sulfuric acid from the solder. Roberts had his wife holding the cables while he fused them into place. Behrmann watched for a moment, said nothing and then crossed the timber gangway onto *Blackwolf*'s gleaming deck. He turned, stared at them again and then dropped through the main hatch, crossed the control room and then the small galley, entered his stateroom and closed the door.

He checked his watch for the third time as he opened his desk and unlocked the center drawer. He removed an envelope and read the instructions. He slapped the desk with the envelope, looked at his watch again impatiently and glanced quickly around the snug but immaculate stateroom. He picked up a fountain pen he'd had since the war, tapped on the pad rapidly then ran his hand through his thinning hair. "Too old," he chuckled. "After her baby is born, that young frau might get a big surprise."

Roberts knocked at his cabin door and said, "Let's try it again. I think I found the problem."

Behrmann nodded without speaking. He was intolerant of technical errors, especially Roberts's errors. He treated his son-in-law with cold disregard when in a good mood. At other times Roberts was the target of disdain and open hostility. He tolerated him only because Petra might refuse to cook if the captain ever satisfied his burning desire to keelhaul this ungrateful ingrate his daughter had so unwisely allowed to father her children.

Behrmann took his notebook and quickly made his way to the main hatch. On deck he paused to look around the cavern. It was much smaller than the Bermuda base, but more secure because no one would ever imagine it possible to get a sub, even a small one, inside it. They had been hiding here for the past six months, slowly building the support systems they needed to convert the cave into a first class covert base. But they were desperately short-handed and underfunded, and the work was very slow. Perhaps now, after the success of their last mission, their circumstances would finally improve.

Behrmann stepped confidently across the crude timber gangway as if he were going to a Nazi staff briefing. At nearly eighty, he still had a commanding presence—barrel chested, short, Teutonic neck, heavy arms and piercing eyes. He was the kind of officer who could force his will on a crew without once referring to a regulation book. The captain climbed the steps to the ledge on which Roberts had assembled the new communication station.

Roberts sat at the computer and completed the link. "We've got it! We're in," he said with excitement and relief. He stood and stepped away from the console, giving Behrmann his seat.

Behrmann nodded, sat and after checking his notebook entered the passwords. The message was short and quickly unscrambled. *Blackwolf* had orders again, and Karen would need clothing more quickly than he had thought. The strike team was already on its way. The waiting over, Behrmann felt young and strong as the excitement pumped adrenaline through his veins.

CHAPTER 4

Grand Cayman from the air looks smaller than Bermuda and appears much less densely populated. Both observations are correct. It is much smaller and has less than half of Bermuda's population. And where Bermuda is a chain of lush green hilly little islands connected by quaint stone bridges, Grand Cayman is a single island, brown and flat. Just arriving are the million dollar homes for which Bermuda is known, the manicured golf courses, gardens, lawns and gleaming yachts which make Bermuda one of the most elegantly beautiful places on earth.

But what Grand Cayman lacks in cosmopolitan flair and *Homes and Gardens* appeal, it quickly makes up for with world-class beaches and diving, gleaming condos, comfortable hotels and an international finance community which rivals Switzerland. Five hundred banks call Grand Cayman home, and investors from all over the world employ their services.

As Sheri's plane descended for its final approach, she briefly glimpsed the blue buildings and tanks of the turtle farm on the north shore. The plane banked left and now she could see Seven Mile Beach, lined by hotels and condos, and the dive boats anchored in topaz-clear water along the wall a few hundred yards offshore. A minute later they were over George Town and she could see the Holiday Inn where she would be staying. She remembered the restaurants, dive shops and friends she'd made on her last trip here three years ago. She wondered how many of them might still be working on the island. The plane banked left again, this time over Eden Rocks and the hospital, then it leveled to land.

The Cayman Air pilots earned their wings with a smooth landing and when the rolling stairs were alongside, she was quickly on her way through immigration and customs. A talkative cab driver took her from the airport into town. Just outside the airport they were passed by a small yellow submarine on a flatbed truck. It turned off the highway by the airport and disappeared behind a blue metal building.

"That's one of them little subs takes tourists from the cruise ships down eight hundred feet," the driver offered. "They found some big old ship down there. My sister knew a boy worked on them things. Kept trying to get her to go for a ride, but she wasn't about to go down there with him. What on earth would she do if he got her down there? Ain't no walking home from the bottom of the ocean if that boy decides to run out of gas."

Sheri smiled and glanced at her watch. It was 2:30 and her appointment was at 4:00. Plenty of time to shower and change.

The Professional Association of Diving Instructors (PADI), the training agency she belonged to, had helped her arrange three interviews, including one which sounded really promising. In fact, the listing had come to PADI the same day she'd called and the job description sounded as if it had been written for her. Almost too good to be true.

The cab dropped her at the Holiday Inn on West Bay Road. She was still thinking about the sub she'd seen on the truck and thinking she should check them out. How better to catch a sub than with a sub? She'd have to tell Doc about them.

An hour later she stepped from a second cab at the newest and largest high-rise on Seven Mile Beach. She was wearing a new business-like white skirt and jacket over a coral silk blouse. The outfit looked great. Doc had hardly recognized her in it and that pleased her. He needed a little to worry about—just deserts for not letting her go on the boat.

She wondered about wearing heels and decided they were a bit much. After all these were the islands and she was a scuba instructor not an MBA, but now standing in front of this place, she wondered if heels might have been the right choice after all. She certainly didn't remember anything this ostentatious on the beach three years ago. It was stunning. Fifteen stories of emerald green glass against a rich gold superstructure. A large crane and a dump truck were parked on a side lot, but the building looked completed. The sign announced the place as Morgan's Landing, and one could become a one bedroom owner for as little as nine hundred thousand dollars. Cayman Island currency or U.S., she wondered as she paid the cab and then crossed a pastel tubular arched steel bridge over a green marble moat with fountains. If the architect's intent had been to create the illusion of crossing over into a different world, it certainly worked.

Bronze statues of larger-than-life pirates greeted her at the bridge's far end. They guarded the elegant emerald green glass doors etched with proud full-rigged sailing ships. Inside a wide green marble floor led past six bronze cannon in British carriages to a receptionist's counter of hand-rubbed exotic hardwood. The counter's face was lapstraked like a ship's hull with bronze rigging above and open gun ports with protruding bronze cannon below, giving authority beyond the norm to the very professionally dressed girl behind the rail.

"I should have worn heels," Sheri said to herself, now self conscious that she was underdressed.

The counter was flanked by green marble and gold winding staircases to the second floor balcony. The ceiling was four stories high with overlooking balconies on each floor. Flags and ship's guns decorated each balcony. Magnificent was the only word she could think of to describe it. Errol Flynn as Captain Blood might come swinging out of the rigging at any minute. She stood in the middle turning slowly, taking it all in and wondering how one would go about keeping it all dusted.

She was still looking up when she nearly stumbled into a tall, beautiful Chinese woman in the most gorgeous blue silk dress Sheri had ever seen.

"I'm so sorry," Sheri began.

"No dear, it's 'so solly,'" the woman laughed. "Welcome to Morgan's Landing. I'm Ms. Kee. What brings you to us this afternoon?"

"I have an appointment," Sheri smiled. "It's about the ad

you placed with the PADI placement service for a scuba instructor."

"Excellent," Ms. Kee said. "I'm afraid I was expecting someone in cutoffs and a tee shirt. You present yourself quite well. That's very good. Please, come to my office and let's get acquainted."

Sheri guessed the fourteenth floor office suite to be at least nine hundred square feet overlooking the ocean. Decorated in green leather, bronze marine life sculpture, and a marble desk, it was no less elegant than the entrance. Ms. Kee asked her secretary to bring tea and when it was served from a sterling tea service into fine china cups, they got down to business.

"We've not had a scuba instructor here before, Miss Benson, but since so many of our owners and guests are divers, we thought it might be good, from a liability perspective if nothing else, to have a professional on staff. I've interviewed several of the locals, but frankly, I was hoping for a bit more. Now I'm glad I waited. Your references are excellent. A dual major in history and marine biology, as I recall, and you've directed archaeological projects in Bermuda. That's excellent. Would you like to do some of that here? Mr. Morgan, our owner, is passionate about shipwrecks. He's sponsored expeditions all over the world. Make sure to tell him about your work."

That's not quite what my resume says, Sheri thought, *but perhaps it's close enough.* "Thanks, I will," she answered. "But isn't the government here really strict, like Bermuda?"

"Don't worry about that. Mr. Morgan has friends. Permits are no problem. There is one other thing, as you might imagine—we do a good bit of entertaining here. As lovely as you are, I'm sure Mr. Morgan will invite you to join our staff of hostesses. Perhaps we could even work you into sales. That's where the real money is in a place like this. But for now, would you be willing to learn the ropes and help us out with parties and give tours from time to time? There would be extra pay and tips, of course. Some of our guests can be very generous."

"Sounds like fun, as long as...well you know, as long as there are limits." *Why did I say that*? Sheri thought. *Surely this isn't that kind of place. What a dummy.*

"Of course, dear...of course, there are limits. Whatever

you're comfortable with, that's all."

"Your ad said you have your own dive boats. May I see them?"

"Only one has been delivered so far. The other should be here in two or three weeks. The compressor and a ton of equipment just arrived. Sort of like Christmas down there. Come, I'll show you. Then we'll find Mr. Morgan...he has the final word, but don't worry. I'm sure you are just what we need and he usually goes along with what I recommend." She reached forward and brushed Sheri's hair with the back of her fingertips.

"Obviously a very smart man," Sheri laughed.

"At times," Ms. Kee's dark eyes flashed a smile that implied more to the story than she was telling.

Sheri watched in admiration as the tall woman turned to lead the way. That dark blue silk dress, high slit to show slender legs, must have cost a fortune. Her spike heels clopped on the high gloss green marble floor. *Hope they pay their instructors enough to dress like that. Doc will croak.*

"Ms. Kee," Sheri asked as they clopped up the stairway to the second floor, "we haven't discussed my salary."

"Yes, of course. You'll have a small suite here, that's thirty-five hundred a month, meals in the restaurant, for yourself and no more than one guest, please. That's another thousand or so; a car, probably a jeep, but the limos are available most of the time. I hate driving, don't you, and shall we say seven-fifty? Is that enough to start?"

"With all that, sure, I can make seven-fifty a month work, at least for a start."

"A month, oh no, dear, I meant seven-fifty a week. You will have other expenses: clothing, make-up. We have an image, you know. After you see the shop and meet Mr. Morgan, we'll get you an advance and then you and I are going to do some serious shopping. We might do a little something with your hair while we're at it." She gently pulled Sheri's already short hair back a little straighter. "Yes, that gives me some wonderful ideas," she winked and smiled.

Sheri followed Ms. Kee to the dive locker at the lower side of the pool. Their dive store was still in boxes and the stacks were huge. *Unlike the Dockyard Museum, these folks obviously aren't worried about spending money,* she thought. *Well, Doc, after all my fussing, looks like I've walked into the deal of a lifetime. So where the hell are you?*

Karen saw the boat first. She and Jason had climbed to a mountainside plateau where she could sunbathe without the discomfort of Colonel Andrew's binoculars. Besides the privacy, the view was spectacular. On their right was open ocean for as far as they could see and on the left was the lagoon below. The climb was tiring for her, but Petra had said she should get lots of exercise for as long as she was comfortable doing it. So here they were, almost every day now for the past two weeks, high above the lagoon nearly half-way up the mountain.

The old schooner was a sight under full sail and headed directly toward the cove. Then just outside the surf line it turned into the wind, dropped sail, turned again and motored toward the inlet. She pulled on her shirt and shorts, took Jason by the hand and headed down the trail to tell the captain.

The boat was entering the lagoon by the time they made the climb down. Petra called to them from the bungalow's covered deck. The captain wanted them out of sight while the crew was ashore. They were to stay in their room and that was an order. That was disappointing, but the captain got very angry if she didn't do what he said and so she quickly took Jason to the room they shared. Petra brought them food and they spent the afternoon watching from behind her curtains as the men made several trips from the schooner to the shore with heavy crates.

There were four men: two, the Roberts's sons, were young and blonde. Everyone was happy to see them. The third was dark and had long hair. He looked very strong and he reminded her of the drug smugglers who had kidnapped her in Bermuda and she knew she wouldn't like him. She couldn't see much of the fourth except that he looked older. She pulled back into the shadows as they approached the bungalow.

Jason was drawing again, if you could call it that. She lifted one to examine it. The lines were clean and the colors bright. In red was a football shape pierced by a fat spear or perhaps a missile. She felt anger in Jason's work and suspected there was a meaning she was missing. She put it in the folder with his other work and smiled. He tilted his head and studied her and as always said nothing.

It took what remained of the day to unload the schooner. The men made dozens of trips rowing to the sailboat and back with two large red and black inflatables. The schooner was big—nearly a hundred feet—and typical of the inner-island fleet on which islanders depended until after World War Two when most of the sailing fleet was replaced by surplus military vessels. The boat was easily seventy-five years old and not well cared for. Scum and barnacles fouled its wooden hull, the sides were streaked with rust stains and the sails were tattered and patched. Still, her classic lines would put a smile on any sailor's face and for a neglected old scow, she was still dry and solid.

It was hot in the room and Jason grew restless. He wanted to swim and when she refused he became sullen and pouted. But this time he obeyed. He sat on the floor beside her and watched the men working for a while. Then, when he saw the dark, long-haired man, he withdrew to his bed, covered his head with a sheet, and hid.

That night Petra brought their dinner and a bag full of new clothing. She said the men would be leaving soon on the sub, but she and Colonel Andrews would be staying. Karen had hoped they would take the colonel with them and never bring him back. But, Petra added, the schooner had brought wonderful things to eat as well as new clothes. The food sounded good, but why did they need the clothes? Not if the strangers were leaving.

It was nearly dusk when the captain slipped into her room to say goodbye.

"We'll be gone about three weeks this time, child." He was holding her hand. Jason was glaring from the corner.

"This is a treasure hunt and we're going to be rich as kings and queens. Will that make you happy?"

"Once I thought the only way I'd ever be happy was to be rich. But now I only own one shirt, and I'm the happiest I've ever been. So I guess you don't need so many things when life is simple and good."

He ignored her wisdom and hugged her, and when he did his hands explored beneath her one and only shirt. Her arms hung limp at her sides and she looked away. Jason became upset and began throwing things as the old man scowled at him.

"Well, if not for you then at least nice things for your baby," Behrmann said and moved away. He glared at Jason, kissed her coldly on the cheek and was gone.

When the last of the heavy crates were unpacked and the stores and equipment loaded on the sub, the new men set to work assembling the components of a remotely operated vehicle. The ROV was too large to be carried in the sub and would ride in a cradle on the bow. They set up lights powered by the sub's generator and worked well into the night bolting the modules in place on the cradle, connecting and sealing wiring harnesses, and finally installing the storage drum for the umbilical in a special compartment in the sail.

Toward daybreak the ROV began to resemble a large spider, and by noon that day the spider had come to life, responding to commands from within the sub received through the umbilical. By that evening the ROV, named *Black Widow,* and the sub were ready to put to sea.

Petra Roberts was anxious to talk to her sons, but that would have to wait. With the ROV assembled and tethered to the deck, the last job was to deflate the inflatables and store them in deck compartments beneath the shell outside the pressure hull. Then they exchanged hasty goodbyes, the sub's hatch was closed and the four new crewmen stood in the control room awaiting the captain's orders.

Behrmann watched the monitors and guided the sub to the center of the cavern mostly with the bow thruster. He nodded at Roberts who issued the computer commands to flood the ballast tanks. The sub began a slow, carefully controlled descent. The natural light faded quickly on the monitors and he turned on the flood lights.

"Not too fast...slow us a bit. We must make certain we have compensated our trim for the lovely passenger on the bow, ya, the computer has done it. Now we start the turn. We'll have to drop the bow to come about, make sure everything is secure and no one moves forward or aft until we are back in trim, understood? Ready now, drop the bow six degrees, reverse turbines, now drop her another six."

Glass shattered in the galley as a coffee mug fell from the counter. Behrmann swore but did not lose his concentration.

"Now we come to starboard, forward port, reverse starboard, bow thruster half power starboard, half power...just like threading a needle," he continued.

"The computer has found the laser track, come to zero eight five degrees and we're down and out."

"Zero eight five," Roberts responded.

"Ya, ya, I see it."

"I hope we don't ever have to do this in a hurry," the youngest Roberts boy, Martin, laughed nervously.

"It's why we are safe here," Behrmann answered. "Even if someone found out about these caves, no one would ever believe we could get the boat in here. The diameter of the tunnel is tighter than the length of our hull. It can only be navigated at this steep angle. For anyone else it would be impossible. See, there is the entrance."

Blue green light appeared on the monitors. By pulling back on the zoom lenses to wide angle, they were able to see the sub's bow as Behrmann dropped it a third into the narrow entrance.

"Now, reverse and drop the stern, we go out tight to the bottom. Watch the stern camera monitor. Slowly, very slowly until we are in trim, then full power to keep us straight against the current as we come out. Ready? Bow angle?"

"Down ten degrees."

"Ya, full power until we clear, watch the monitor." The sub lurched forward without scraping and when they were in the safety of the dark water, Behrmann reduced power and the oldest Roberts boy, Randy, took his turn at the helm. "Take us to three hundred feet, secure lighting, set our course on the auto pilot, keep a close eye on the monitors, and then let's eat. All this excitement makes me hungry."

His crew cheered. They would go north out of the Cayman Trench, and follow the Yucatan current east to the Gulf Stream which would speed them further north, two hundred miles off the South Carolina coast.

CHAPTER 5

I can't believe what I paid for this dress and I only got to wear it for an hour, Sheri thought as she changed. She put on a blue-green swimsuit with matching flowered skirt which Ms. Kee had gotten for her as a welcome aboard present. She checked the mirror with an approving smile. The suit fit like it was painted on and for what it cost, it could have been. It might take a bit to get used to her new shorter hair, but Ms. Kee had insisted and Sheri had to admit the woman had exquisite taste and was exceedingly generous as well. "Not bad for a redneck Georgia," she laughed and left her suite to meet Ms. Kee in the foyer.

The guests had arrived and after the poolside reception, they were going for an evening sail on Mr. Morgan's boat. Ms. Kee came to the second floor balcony and called her to come up. "There's something up here you need to see," Ms. Kee said and opened a locked double door marked private. The suite was green marble and spacious, like hers, but much larger. This one was neo-classical following a bacchanalian theme with erotic nude sculpture, gold leaf everything, and hand-carved, dark walnut furniture. There was a large bed and dressing area, and a second set of double doors leading to a bath suite.

The octagonal bath suite had three showers with ornate, gold-framed clear glass doors. In the spacious room's center were four Roman salons arranged about a sunken marble tub large enough for ten. Twenty-five feet above the tub was a skylight and vent of cut glass which filled the room with prismatic rainbows of golden sunlight.

"Why would one need three showers in a private bath?" Sheri asked with a playfully innocent smile.

"It's not unlikely that sooner or later one of our guests might invite you up here," Ms. Kee said as she put her hand on Sheri's shoulder. "This isn't part of your job.... I wanted you to see it so that you wouldn't have any surprises later."

Sheri stood wide-eyed imagining what might go on here. *Perhaps it's that kind of place after all,* she thought and swallowed hard. *But at least I don't have to play if I don't want to. That's what she meant by whatever I'm comfortable with. Well, I don't think I'm comfortable with this. Not if what she's telling me is what I think she's telling me.*

Ms. Kee took her hand and laughed. "Don't be so shocked, dear. Not everyone plays by the same rules, you know. Other cultures have been sharing baths for centuries. Now if you can gather your wits about you, let's go down to the party."

"Do you....?" Sheri began and then blushed.

Ms. Kee raised an eyebrow and smiled, "If I chose to, yes. But then it would be my business, wouldn't it? Just as if you choose to, then it would be your business. Two rules: make sure that if you come here, it's your choice and only your choice. Second, what happens in this room stays in this room. What you might see or do here is never to be discussed even with other staff members. You understand, I'm sure."

An orange inflatable was the shuttle from the beach to the boat. Sheri looked over the others waiting at the beach. Most looked like they had just stepped out of *GQ* or *Esquire.* On their way out to the boat, she asked Ms. Kee who the men were.

"Business associates of Mr. Morgan—commodities brokers and bankers mostly. One or two in the oil business. All Americans. Interesting group. Very competitive. Very successful. That's why Mr. Morgan hires them."

Most were already aboard the sixty-five-foot ketch when the women arrived. The little inflatable bobbed them through the low surf across emerald water. As the dinghy passed the traditional high stern of classic yachts, Sheri saw the name *Bluebird* gracefully lettered in blue and gold.

Their host, Jack Morgan, helped them up the ladder and introduced them to the guests still on deck. "Get whatever you want from the bar and have a look below while we get the sails up," he suggested with a warm smile.

"Be happy to help up here," Sheri answered.

"You sail?"

"Never on a lake this big, but enough to know a sheet from a halyard and when to duck."

"Good for you. I had her built in Maryland and brought her down myself."

"She's more than I'd ever want to handle alone."

"Not bad actually. Her rig is both self-reefing and furling. All the winches are electric. I enjoy going solo at times. Helps clear the mind. What do you think of your new job so far?"

"The perks are certainly impressive," she laughed. "But when will we start diving?"

"Late this week. I want to check out that new pontoon boat and there's a project waiting for us on the edge of the wall. But I'm buried until Thursday or Friday. You married?"

"Not officially, but..."

"He on the island?"

"No."

"Then you're single. It helps to have these things clearly defined."

"It's not that clear. I live with someone—he's bringing our boat down."

"Oh."

He turned his attention to the boat. A crewman with "Doug" embroidered on his shirt dropped the mooring line, automatic winches raised the sails, Morgan trimmed the main and Sheri worked the ginny until it filled without luffing. The boat healed slightly and slid smoothly forward through the clear water. Sheri secured the ginny's sheet and dropped back down into the cockpit.

"College sailing crew?" Morgan asked.

"Right, Georgia State, Atlanta. Lake Lanier. Not exactly a sailing mecca, but we had a lot of fun."

"That where you met your sailor?"

"No, that's where I met my ex. He liked to give orders, shouted a lot."

"Should have been keelhauled."

"You think he wasn't? Told you he's my ex."

"Ready about," he commanded softly.

"Ready about," she repeated and pulled the ginny's sheet from the jam cleat and cleared the winch.

"Hard alee," he shouted and the boom crossed to the port rail.

"You're shouting," she cautioned and took several wraps around the port winch. With a quiet whir it tightened the line until the sail filled.

"I'm the captain," he laughed.

"It's good to have these things clearly defined," she answered as she used the electric winch again to trim the sail. The air was light and it filled lazily. She played the sheet as best she could and then secured it with just a whisper of luff. Morgan nodded his approval then brought the bow west to catch the southern air. As they crossed the edge of the shallows and the wall, the water turned from milky green to deep blue. When they passed out of the lee of the island's north end, the sails filled and the big boat healed smartly to port.

"I love the sounds she makes, that little luff in the main in air like this, the chime of hallards in the masts, the hum the shrouds make in a blow, little moans of pleasure, like riding a horse you know loves to run and you feel her tug at the reins. She's telling you, come on let's go, give me my head, this is going to be fun."

She found herself staring at him. It was his skin. He had a perfect tan and there was not a blemish, not a wrinkle nor a line to show for his sixty years. Perfect teeth. *No one is born with teeth like that—his father must have been a dentist. Maybe both parents were dentists.* Their eyes met and he tilted his head but said nothing. She realized she was staring, held captive by the coldest penetrating gray eyes she had ever seen. She shook it off and he smiled. "I'm ready for something to drink now. May I bring you something?" she asked.

He asked for a fruit juice blend; she went below to get it. The stairway into the cabin was blocked by a slightly drunk, young brunette in a peach chiffon cocktail dress. "If you're done with him for a while, honey, you won't mind if I give it a shot, will you?" Without waiting for an answer she pushed past, spilling part of her drink on Sheri's new swimsuit in the process.

Sheri entered the cabin and got a wet towel from the bar. Her suit was stained with fruit juice and needed to be soaked. Ms. Kee joined her behind the bar. "That was hurricane Stephanie. She's an accountant Jack brought down from Atlanta. What a mistake. Just stay out of her way. She's about to blow herself out, thank goodness. Try club soda on that. Come on, I'll find you something else to wear."

Tiffany lamps filled the cabin with soft light and gave it the look of a turn-of-the-century saloon. The couches were red satin and behind the bar, the reclining nude in the painting looked a lot like Dorothy accompanied by faithful Toto. Behind her Scarecrow was enjoying an après cigarette. *At least someone has a sense of humor,* Sheri thought, and turned her attention to the bulkhead opposite the bar. It was hung with enough diplomas to fill a dentist's office. She could read Ohio State on one, the magna cum laude gold seal and the Phi Betta Kappa key plainly visible, but the others were in Latin. She tried to remember if it was Harvard or Yale who still did that, or perhaps both?

There were several photographs, men in camo uniforms and berets, and one with each of the past three presidents. Our boy Jack gets around, or so the hero wall would have one believe. Ms. Kee came out of the owner's stateroom with a robe and called to her to come and change.

Sheri was on the way when the boat lurched as if they had struck bottom. Guests fell to the floor and Ms. Kee landed hard. Sheri ran in to help her, but through a starboard porthole, saw the peach chiffon dress going over the side.

"You okay?" Sheri asked Ms. Kee.

"Oh, that hurt, but yes, I think so."

"I need to go topside. I think our southern belle just went for a swim."

"Go, I'll be alright."

Jack Morgan was laying in the cockpit with blood on the back of his scalp. Sheri knelt beside him and without moving him, checked his pulse. Then the boat lurched again as the keel struck bottom a second time and Sheri was thrown across Morgan. He moaned. She scrambled to her feet and grabbed the helm, swinging the boat toward deep water.

"I need some help up here," she shouted. "We're running shallow and that woman fell overboard." Morgan tried to get to his knees.

"You stay flat," Sheri snapped. "And don't move your neck."

"You're shouting," he answered feebly and collapsed back to the deck.

"We need help up here," she shouted again. This time a guest appeared in the hatchway. "Find Doug. We've got to start the engine and get the sails down," she shouted. "We're in trouble here."

The boat touched bottom again, hurling the guest back down the ladder and swinging the boom across the cockpit in a dangerous jibe. Sheri dropped just in time, amazed that the boom arched so low to the deck. The wheel spun brutally from her hands and she waited until it stopped to grab it again and bring the boat around. This time she tied the wheel and released the main sheet from the jam cleat. Then she did the same with the ginny. With the sails luffing loudly, the boat lost momentum but pitched badly in the swells. Doug appeared in the hatchway and she screamed at him to get the engine started while she hauled enough of the foresail to get some steerage back.

Doug got the engine started, brought the boat into the wind and hit the switches to bring in the sails. A guest came up the ladder and said there were others injured below. Sheri sent Doug below and pressed the guest from the ladder into service looking for the peach dress and the dangerous shallow reef patches while she remained at the helm. *I should have thrown a buoy,* she thought, *so we'd have some point of reference. It couldn't have been more than a couple of minutes.* She checked the compass and started counting. When she had counted to a hundred and twenty, she swung the boat back on the reciprocal heading and started counting again. They were dangerously close to the shallows when the call came from the bow. "There, over there in the surf...that looks like her."

Sheri shouted for help and put the first man up the ladder at the helm. "Watch the compass. Hold west until Doug gets back up here. I'm going after that girl. Doug will take the wheel and get you back safe and sound. Mr. Morgan needs a doctor.

See that there's a ambulance waiting and send a car back up the beach for me. Got it?"

"But I've never..." the bewildered guest began.

"It's all right. Doug will be right back," she answered and without waiting for more of an argument, she threw the life ring overboard, dropped her skirt and dove in after the life ring. She pushed it ahead of her and kicked hard toward the surf. She covered the twenty-five yards in record time but found nothing. She rode through the surf and into the calm water inside the shallow reef. Pulling herself up on the ring, she tried to look down into the water. The sky was bright and the visibility excellent. Then she saw a light spot on the bottom, about fifteen feet below her.

She took the life ring's lanyard, held it in her teeth, did a surface dive and kicked hard to the bottom. At first she could see nothing. She hit the sand before she saw it and turned in a circle, looking, reaching out. Nothing, she shot back to the surface for air.

She looked down again...nothing. *She must have drifted. Which way? Toward the beach, of course,* Sheri thought. She swam back into deeper water, pulled herself up on the ring and saw the light spot on the bottom again. She dove for it, kicking down with strong powerful strokes. This time she identified the light spot. It was a rock pile complete with black sea urchins. She jumped back and swore when her hand hit one and was instantly turned into a pin cushion. Frustrated and out of breath, she swam back to the surface.

"He throw you over too, honey?" Stephanie hailed her from the life ring. Blood oozed from a wound in her scalp and her dress was in tatters. She clung desperately to the ring, choking and sobbing as she spoke. "I swam underwater so they wouldn't see me. He tried to kill me. We've got to get away." She gasped for breath, passed out and sank beneath the surface.

Sheri dove after her, following her down into the cool darkness.

CHAPTER 6

Prior to his violent death, the result of a carefully coordinated team effort organized, coached and led by Doc, drug smuggler Esteban Maldias, the late owner of *Kratos,* had realized the need for extra fuel storage aboard his vessel. Her normal cruising range, with twin turbocharged 871 Detroits, had been extended from six hundred and fifty miles to over eight hundred.

After the Bermuda government confiscated the boat and consigned it to Doc's care, he added an additional two hundred-gallon plastic fuel bladder on the stern deck. Following a brief yard period in Bermuda, Doc and Mike plotted a course for Charleston, South Carolina. The seven hundred-mile run took forty-five hours and they averaged sixteen knots. The seas were moderate for spring and the air cool. He alternated six-hour wheel watches with Lieutenant Berry who had taken a month's leave to make the trip. They soon adjusted to the noise and vibration of the turbos, and were able to sleep comfortably, waking only when the engines changed pitch or the sea wind sent a wave from a new direction. She was a good boat and Doc was happy to be at her helm, back in the gently rolling open sea.

They would pick up the inner-coastal canal at Charleston, or run close enough to shore to avoid pushing against the Gulf Stream. After a short stop in Miami and another at the Naval

Station in Key West, the last leg would be a five hundred-mile run from the Dry Tortugas around the west end of Cuba and then straight south to the Caymans. Mike was in the engine room changing oil in the generator. *For a big boat sailor and officer, he was learning fast. By the time this was over he might even be a decent cook,* Doc smiled to himself. He enjoyed the irony of life's little pranks especially when they were pranks of his own creation.

"How deep?" Martin Roberts asked his father. They were sitting at the small galley table aboard *Blackwolf.*

"Eight thousand feet, that's why it's taking them so long to work her," Bill Roberts answered.

"How much gold?"

"Literally tons of it—dust, bars and thousands of pioneer mint coins. California miners bringing their fortunes home to the East Coast. Imagine the stories that gold could tell. It's ironic, as if old Mother Earth wasn't ready to let it go."

Bill Roberts finished his coffee and returned to the control room. He left the others watching a single monitor, now displaying sonar imaging, as *Blackwolf* descended slowly into the cold darkness. They were four thousand feet deep and still dropping.

"How did you find it?" asked Dennis Johnson, the long-haired, tattooed man. Johnson had been a graduate student in ocean engineering with Martin and Randy at Texas A&M. He was the designer of *Black Widow* and a world class chess player. He sat now with a computer chess board contemplating his next moves. As usual, he was winning.

"With the NASA satellites and the computer net in Bermuda. Dad had the location even before *Benthic Explorer* found it, we just didn't have any way to work it until *Blackwolf* was ready, or until you decided to bring *Black Widow* to the party."

"Won't they be surprised when they get back out here and discover we've picked her clean, right under their noses," Martin's brother, Randy, laughed. Captain Behrmann's voice over the public address system, known to all sailors as the 'bitch box', called them to the control room. On the monitor green sonar lines outlined the image of a large wreck.

"Check, and mate," Johnson said and turned off the game.

"Do you ever loose?" Martin asked.

"Why would I want to do that?" Johnson asked, sincerely puzzled. He was still trying to answer the question when they reached the control room.

"Welcome to the benthos, the dark closet of all nightmares. Home of *Chacaradon megleadonus*, granddaddy of the great white, a hundred feet long with teeth big as power saw blades and just as sharp. And the giant squid, *Architeuthis*, the only creature besides man vicious enough to attack the great whales, or sailing ships for that matter." Bill Roberts's eyes were wide with excitement as he welcomed them. Captain Behrmann watched the monitors and digital displays with a scowl.

"And resting place of nearly half the precious metals ever extracted from the fillings of Mother Earth's crumbling mandibles," Roberts continued.

"Is that what we are, demented dentists come to steal the fillings from dear old mom's teeth?" Martin laughed. "Come on, Dad, that's pretty morbid even for you."

"Well, it did have a poetic ring, didn't it? I was on a morose roll there, like Edgar Alan Poe, 'Quoth the raven, nevermore.'"

"Look, there's the wreck," Johnson said pointing to the monitor.

Blackwolf moved slowly fifteen meters above the black bottom. In her powerful lights they could see a debris field—parts of the ship which had fallen away as she settled into the bottom. Bottles, cooking pans, pieces of rigging, and deadeyes, which had served as blocks for shroud lines, stared at them as ghostly sentries. Both sidewheels and the stack remained in place, and the center section looked amazingly intact. There was no doubt about her identity. She was the *Central America*, big as life.

"Her captain's name was Herndon, from a prominent Fredericksburg, Virginia family," Roberts continued his narration. "He's still here somewhere. They put up a memorial for him at the Naval Academy in Annapolis. There were five hundred seventy-eight passengers and crew—only one hundred fifty-three survived. Must have been one hell of a storm," Bill Roberts said.

"Or too much gold," Behrmann laughed. He was following the sonar image to the main portion of the wreck. "No one has ever been down here. The salvage crew, they worked her from the surface with a robot, but no one has ever seen her like this."

The port side of the stern rose as a wall. Above them loomed the ship's funnel and parts of the steam engine's machinery. Doors leading into the first class cabins hung open and a portion of the main cargo hatch cover had caved in.

"Looks like they haven't gotten into the main hold yet. Whatever they've recovered so far must have been out in the open. Let's have a look at the starboard," Roberts said.

"Ya, we go to starboard."

They lifted and crossed over the mid-section. At the mudline there was a series of holes six feet square.

"Their robot must be able to operate burning bars. Those cuts look fresh...I'll bet they haven't gotten inside yet," Randy Roberts said, trying to sound authoritative.

"Can you imagine how tedious this must have been? Sitting up there, bobbing like a cork in all kinds of weather, trying to keep on station while their robot works down here taking this wreck apart an inch at a time. No wonder they've made such little progress," Martin said.

"This looks like a good place to start, Captain. *Black Widow* can get in any of those holes. Let's see what they've left for us." Johnson's eyes were wide behind thick round glasses as he turned on his computers.

"Ya, we rest here."

He set the sub down easily in the clay about twenty feet from the wreck and shut down the engines. Johnson began eagerly flipping switches to power up the ROV.

"*Black Widow*, are you awake?" he asked the computer.

"Yes, Dennis, I am awake and I acknowledge your voice commands." The computer's voice was a sultry alto, not at all mechanical and only slightly overstated.

"Just a precaution," Johnson said dryly. "I added a little job security. She won't play without me."

"How 'bout a systems check, *Black Widow*?"

"All systems are fully functional and I am ready to begin."

"Good, then let's start. Show me what you can see."

Four small monitors responded, giving a view of the sub and the wreck. Johnson sat back in his chair, hands folded in his lap and continued the dialog with the computer. The spider's body contained a pair of thrusters in a sphere capable of 300 degrees rotation. Upon command, she lifted from the deck with her six arms retracted and flew to the wreck. Before landing she lowered six narrow legs with pads at the base of the last four and tested the bottom. The bearing strength was enough to support her weight and the thrusters were still.

The front legs were multi-function telechirics with cameras in the palms for close-up work. A basket carrying an assortment of tools rested beneath the abdomen, and below that were coils of flexible magnesium burning bar. The oxygen required would be provided through the umbilical. The ROV could operate either tethered or independently, but without the tether the duration of operations was limited because the batteries couldn't support the huge power demands for long.

Johnson continued to talk as if in casual conversation and his talented creation responded perfectly. *Black Widow* approached the largest opening which led into crews quarters. It was cluttered with debris. With cutters in its telechiric "hands", the spider set to work clearing the passage, reducing timbers to inoffensive rubble until it reached the cabin door.

It opened the door, pulled it from the hinges and pushed it out of the way. Again using its strong arms, it went sideways on the bulkhead, retracted its back legs and pulled itself through.

"If we need to, we can cut a larger opening, but let's see what we've got first," Johnson said. The others watched, fascinated with *Black Widow*'s agility and dexterity. In the passageway were the clothing of two passengers—little remained of bone or tissue, but a glint of gold caught the camera's eye. *Black Widow* carefully extracted a gold pocket watch and chain and put it safely in her abdominal pouch.

"Our first treasure," Johnson said with a grin.

"Ya. Go on, don't waste time here...go to the holds."

At the end of the passageway the hatch opened into the forward hold. There were chests and barrels, most of the wood gone and the contents spilled everywhere. But closest to the keel, where it was placed to help stabilize the ship, were rows of heavy chests secured with rusting locks and bound with steel straps.

Black Widow cleared her way to the first and snapped off the locks. Wood crumbled into sediment as she lifted open the lid. When the silt cleared they were staring at ten rows of three-inch-wide by three-inch-deep, eighteen-inch-long gold bars, stacked four high. Cheers went up from the excited crew.

Black Widow lifted the first bar from the box.

"How much does it weigh?" Johnson asked.

"Disregarding Archimedes's principle or considering it?" came the sultry response.

"Give me the surface weight, please."

"Five hundred and ninety-seven point eight troy ounces."

Martin ran the math in his head. "That's sixty pounds per bar times forty bars, that's twenty-four hundred pounds per case...."

"A market of three hundred and fifty per ounce, that's roughly two hundred nine thousand three hundred dollars per bar times forty bars per case...holy shit, that's eight million, three hundred seventy two thousand dollars per case, times how many cases?" Randy asked, looking up from his calculator.

"According to the manifest she was carrying over three tons of gold." It was Rudolph Geist, the fourth new crew member, who spoke. Tall, military lean and postured, with gray hair cut very short, he spoke with the voice and look of authority. He moved from the hatchway, stood behind Behrmann and rested his hand on the captain's shoulder. "Now all we have to do is bring it up. And when this gold has served it's final purpose, it will be worth many times what you have calculated, Randy. Many, many times."

Rick Franklin, the weathered and wiry first mate and senior technician of the salvage vessel *Benthic Explorer* stared at the flat head on his warm beer and then looked over at the woman again. She wasn't especially young or that attractive, and for that matter neither was he. But on your last night in port, one would do well to remember the wisdom of a sign he'd seen in a bar, not too different than this one, twenty years and a million sea-miles ago: “True beauty is only skin deep and a light switch away.” He finished the beer, pushed away from the table and approached. She’d been waiting. She traced her finger over the sub tattooed on his left arm. It was a hot night and a really cold beer would hit the spot. Sure, she was willing to try another bar. What the hell?

He guided her off the stool and down the street. How long would he be in town? Ship’s leaving tomorrow? Too bad. Oh, you’re on that big salvage boat; one going after all that gold. What the hell, honey, there’s still ten hours ’till sunrise. “Cum’mon baby, tell me ’bout all dat gold an ledz ’ave uz a time.”

Black Widow lifted two bars from the eighth crate and placed them in its abdominal pouch.

“Ten bars. That’s it for this trip. Don’t want her stuck in the mud,” Johnson said. Again, using verbal commands, he brought the ROV out of the wreckage.

“Satellite is coming into range. I’m going to send up the wire line antenna and check the mail,” Bill Roberts said as he sat down at his computer and typed in the commands.

The mechanical spider crawled to her nest on the sub’s deck and began unloading the pouch into external bow cargo holds. Johnson stood and yawned. Job security had its downsides—he’d slept only six of the past thirty hours and was ready for a break.

“Trouble,” Roberts announced as he read the printout from the unscrambler. “*Benthic Explorer* left Charleston two days ahead of schedule. She’ll be out here tonight.”

“We need at least two more days,” Behrmann growled. “Tell Geist his men were supposed to keep them in port. Tell him to do something,” Behrmann ordered and turned to Johnson. “Can’t you go faster? There must be something.”

“I’m stealin’ as fast as I can, boss. Nobody told me getting rich was going to make me old before my time.”

Kratos’s twin diesels purred contentedly at twenty-two hundred rpms. They had droned the same tune, sync’d in reassuring monotone for the past 600 miles from Bermuda. They were now 100 miles off the Carolinas, headed for Charleston. The lights of a large cruise ship headed to the Caribbean faded in their wake as the boat flew through dark glassy night seas. Doc was in the tower, his favorite spot on the boat. The night air was hard on his face, heavy with humidity and greeting him with the force of a thirty-knot wind. On the port dolphins were running with the boat. They cut phosphorescent trails through the dark water as they sped in and out of the bow wake or chased each other back and forth under the hull. Ancient mariners would have recorded the event as a good omen at the beginning of a voyage. Doc agreed.

Cloud cover, from the small squall they'd encountered earlier, dissipated and the night sky brightened with celestial light from billions of stars. "How easily we miss the measure of the infinite and its overpowering beauty," Doc remembered writing in a freshman English theme, "when we focus only on the momentary flickering of our own insignificant candles." It sounded profoundly philosophical at the time. He smiled as he recalled the sophomoric platitude, reflecting that the boy who had written it had not yet collided with the realities of babies, mortgages, or combat.

Still, on a night like this, high above the purr of the diesels and rush of the wake, suspended in the tower above the dark sea and nearly touching the sky, it was impossible not to reflect on the measure of the infinite. Even the pragmatic old warrior, often forced to focus with laser-like intensity on the realities of babies, mortgages and combat, was not immune. A falling star blazed across the southern sky and appeared to dive into the night sea. Perhaps the star had been only a high leaping dolphin filling the sky with a trail of star dust. Or, perhaps what appeared to be dolphins playing in the bow wake were really.... Perhaps he'd had too much coffee and it was time to call Mike to the helm and get some sleep.

On board *Benthic Explorer*, Rick Franklin listened intently to his headset. There was no doubt, they had company. Eight thousand feet beneath them something large was moving on the wreck, something large and mechanical, which made whirring sounds as it moved, and scraping and dragging noises as it pulled away debris to get to the gold...gold, which by court decree belonged to *Benthic Explorer.* They were being robbed by pirates right under their keel. Rick turned on the side scan sonar, watched as the stylus printed the familiar outline of the wreck and then swore as he saw the hard target that didn't belong there. He tore the paper from the side scan sonar and ran up the compartment ladder shouting to the captain.

Roberts pulled off the headset and nodded his head affirmatively. In the vast expanse of the dark sea, *Blackwolf* was no longer alone.

"We need another five or six hours just to get the rest of the bars," Johnson said. "And there are still thousands of loose coins right here. There could be more in other compartments."

"Can they see us?" Geist asked.

"No, not *Blackwolf...*perhaps the robot when it moves, only if they're really high tech."

"Never underestimate your adversary," Rudy Geist said as if quoting from a training manual. "We have to assume they have the best equipment available. But even then we might be able to stay and finish, and be gone before they get their ROV deployed." Geist said.

"Possible but doubtful," Roberts answered.

"The real question is not if they can see us," Behrmann said. He sounded aggravated with his crew's trivial concerns. "It's what they can do if they know we're here. I'll tell you, nothing...they can do nothing. They're a research and salvage ship, built in some backyard bayou. If they get in our way, I'll deal with them. Keep working."

"Thank you, Captain, for those reassuring words," Johnson said under his breath.

"What?" Behrmann demanded.

"Nothing, boss," Johnson answered, looking over his thick glasses with an impish grin.

"Don't call me boss. I was highly decorated as a U-boat captain before you were even born. I built this boat and you will address me as Captain or sir, is that understood?" Behrmann snarled.

"Yes, sir, Captain sir," Johnson answered with a left handed salute. His grin faded to a glare.

Behrmann turned his back in anger.

"Easy," Geist cautioned. "He hasn't slept in two days."

"There is no excuse for insubordination."

Roberts had withdrawn to the safety of the headset. He adjusted the volume and background filter levels and listened intently. "I think they're deploying an ROV."

"Speakers," Behrmann snapped.

On the sound system they could hear the whine of a large winch and the eggbeater whir of thrusters.

"Do something," Geist said in a commanding tone to Behrmann.

"Right...we move back and wait. Mister Johnson, return your toy to our bow and secure it."

Johnson complied without comment. Randy Roberts was now standing beside him to give moral support. They watched *Black Widow* cross from the opening in the wreck's hull to the sub and listened as the sound of the ROV's thrusters grew louder.

"Hurry, damn you! We must move!"

Randy cautioned Johnson not to answer. *Black Widow* climbed the hull and settled into her nest.

"We're ready, sir," Randy answered for him.

"Blow the water ballast...get us up."

"It will be slow, we've got quite a load," Roberts said.

"Just do it!"

"Something's wrong...line pressure's at 5,000, but the tank's not dumping. I'm running a computer check."

"I don't believe this shit," Johnson swore.

"Get out! Leave now!" Behrmann screamed at him.

"Computer says a valve's stuck."

"Run the damage control program. Have the computer find which valve it is," Geist demanded.

Roberts worked frantically for a moment then nodded. "It's forward, port side, number 5."

"Ya, Ya, we find it. Randy, get the tools. The valves are in the diving locker. This has never.... Come on, let's go!"

They quickly worked their way forward to the diving locker. The compartment smelled of smoke and a red alarm light was flashing.

"The computer didn't tell us...this could have been serious," Randy said.

Martin lifted the deck grate, gaining access to the valves. "It's this one," he said pointing to the smoking servo motor.

"Looks like the motor's cooked."

"That's not possible," Behrmann growled. "I designed the system myself...." His voice trailed off as he slammed the bulkhead with his fist.

Randy and Martin remained silent.

"Remove the motor and open it manually. Give me that adjustable wrench," Behrmann said, answering the unasked question. He lay on the deck and reached in for the valve. Screaming in pain, he pulled back his burned hand and slammed the motor with the wrench. The wrench flew from his hand and broke a glass-faced pressure valve on the recompression chamber.

"Let's get some ice on that," Randy offered.

"Ya, ya, ice on the outside, whiskey on the inside...I'll be alright," the old man growled and held his wounded hand.

"We got to fix this quick and get out of here. Get Martin... I'll tell you what needs to be done. Tell your father to shut down everything, put us on batteries. No need to advertise our position. Hurry, boy."

"What the hell is it?" Captain Peterson asked as they studied the monitor from the tiny probe dropped from the hovering ROV. It would take three hours to get to depth, however, the arrow-shaped camera probe could be dropped much faster. Now they were getting their first look at the intruder.

"Looks like something out of Jules Verne, but why aren't we able to read it on sonar?"

"Could be jamming us...could be made out of something that absorbs our signal, Captain. She looks pretty high tech."

"She know we're here?"

"Have to be asleep not to."

"You sure you heard them working?"

"That's what I heard, alright. They shut down their ROV when they heard us coming."

"So why don't they run?"

"We're still an hour above them, over a half mile. They probably haven't picked up our camera yet. Hell, it could belong to anybody. The Navy kept NR-1 secret for years. She's about that size, is the smallest nuclear powered sub, has a manipulator arm and wheels to roll across the bottom. Hell, we could be looking at her baby sister. I wouldn't put anything past those guys these days. That gold would buy them a lot of peanut butter."

"Let's make a few phone calls. Keep an eye on her, Rick, but stay clear. Don't start anything until we get a read on what we're up against."

"You bet. I'll be right here."

CHAPTER 7

The instrument console of *Kratos* looked as if it had been designed for an intergalactic starship, not a forty-five-foot sportfisherman barely capable of thirty knots. There was a reason, of course, and now it became apparent. The high tech console, added before departing Bermuda, concealed sophisticated communications equipment. A red light flashed and an alarm buzzer sounded, indicating an oil pressure failure on the port generator. Like most sportfishermen, however, *Kratos* carried only a single generator positioned between the big turbo-charged Detroits. Mike came running to the wheelhouse awakened by the alarm.

"Take the wheel, hold due west."

"Got it."

Doc stepped to a fuse panel and unlocked the cover. He flipped the switches in proper sequence, opened the panel and removed a hand held VHF. There would be only one person calling on this radio.

"Hello, Inspector Cord. What on earth are you doing up at this hour?" Doc said.

"A friend of your Lieutenant Berry just called from the Naval base. He overheard a very interesting radio message on the satellite net. Take down these coordinates."

"Hot stuff," Captain Peterson said as he dropped down the ladder into the ROV control center. "They patched me into the Pentagon to some hot shot in the SecNav's office. He said it's either Russian or German, and armed to the teeth. Might even be the boat that sank that yacht with the Secretary of State on board. What was that...five, six months ago? They're sending help from Charleston, but that's going to take a while. They want us to haul ass out of here. All they said was if we've got any video or audio tape, they want it. Want to compare it to some audio tape they got when that yacht blew up."

"Hot damn. So what are we going to do?" Rick asked.

"I can tell you what we're not going to do. We're not going to run and let that bastard have our gold without a fight. That's what we're not going to do. Get the ROV back on deck then get the engineers up here...we need to come up with a battle plan."

"What's going on up there?" Geist asked Roberts.

"Their ROV is hovering a half mile above us. They dropped a television probe about fifty feet over the main hatch."

"They've seen us?" Geist said.

"Every freckle." Roberts twisted in his chair, holding his stomach. A carton of milk sat by the console and the wrappers of Maalox tablets littered the deck.

Geist's jaws tightened, but he kept his professional composure. He went forward to the dive locker. Randy and Martin were working beneath the deck grates while Behrmann, now frantic, yelled orders.

"No, no! Not that way! Counter clockwise to loosen it... don't you know anything? Our friends up there won't wait for you to learn right from left. We'll be blown out of the water while you fumble."

"Easy, Hans, no one can concentrate with you screaming at them like that," Geist said in a firm, controlled voice and put his hand on Behrmann's shoulder.

Behrmann shook it off and turned in anger, but when he recognized Geist he held his retort.

The boys worked in silence looking at each other in fear. Randy got the bolts loose and they lifted the burned out motor out of the way. "Now what?" Randy asked.

"Now take that pipe wrench and see if you can gently open the valve. That's counterclockwise, gently now. It's a Monel shaft, not steel."

"Don't do that. Loosen the packing gland, make sure the shaft is cool and then lube it with silicone," Johnson said from the hatchway.

"Get out. If you come in here again, I'll shoot you." Behrmann snapped and pulled a Luger from his belt.

"You crazy old fool! You'll kill us all!" Johnson shouted back and left the hatch.

"What do we do?" Randy asked Geist.

"Follow my orders...open the valve." Behrmann was still waving the gun.

Randy tightened the pipe wrench on the valve shaft and pushed gently. The shaft snapped and the pieces clattered to the deck.

"You idiot!" Behrmann screamed, pointing the Luger at Randy. "Gently. I told you do it gently."

"That's enough, Hans, the boy did his best. The heat must have weakened it. Put the gun away," Geist commanded. "Go get some rest, you're exhausted. Go, rest, and think about what we must do next."

"But the..."

"That's an order, Captain. I'll call you if we need you."

Behrmann left the diving locker, repeating to himself, "But I designed it. I designed it. It has to work."

Randy took several deep breaths and dropped back against the plumbing. "He's crazy. He will kill us all."

"No, son, he's just exhausted. Martin, wait until he's in his cabin, then lock the door." Geist handed him a key. "He just needs rest. It's alright. I'll talk to him."

"Yes, sir." Martin took the key and followed his grandfather.

"Go find Johnson, Randy. Let's see if he can get us out of this mess."

"Yes, sir," Randy paused. "Sir, may I ask a question.... You don't stand watches, you have the keys...and my grandfather obeyed your orders.... Sir, who are you?"

"That should be *Benthic Explorer*—she's in about the right place," Mike said looking up from the radar. The blip was still thirty miles away. "Shall we call them?"

"No. Wouldn't want to tip our hand if Behrmann's got his ears on."

They continued to stare into the darkness. A half hour passed before Mike spoke again. "There, dead ahead." Twenty minutes later they were close enough to make out the lines of the salvage vessel. Bright lights shone on her stern as men worked on deck. They were recovering their ROV, *Argo.*

Doc waited until the large robot was aboard then secured *Kratos* along *Explorer*'s port side. After requesting permission to go aboard, he and Mike were met at the rail by Captain Peterson and escorted to the sonar room.

"The Navy said they were sending help. You're not exactly what we expected," Peterson said.

"We're not exactly from the Navy," Doc answered and quickly told the story of his past dealings with *Blackwolf* and Captain Hans Behrmann. "Just let me see your video tape and we can get to the bottom of this right now. At least then I'll know if I'm just a lot paranoid and a little crazy, or if our friends in Washington really are up to their old tricks and the sub down there is really *Blackwolf.*"

"That's quite a story, Doctor. But I wonder if we shouldn't check you out before you see this tape?"

"That's logical but harder than it sounds. The Navy doesn't know I'm here and if I'm right, I'm the last person they would want to see your tape. The Bermuda government can't acknowledge sending me to you—that would mean admitting they were eavesdropping on the Navy's response to your call. Look, Captain, all I want to do is see that tape. Then if you want me off your ship, I'm gone like last week's pay."

"But your story...it's hard to believe that..."

"Captain, were you in Vietnam?"

"No, too young. But I think I know what you're going to say. This could be like that movie *Air America,* couldn't it? Like the CIA using the war as a cover for running drugs. Do you think that was true?"

"Show me the tape. That's the answer to your question," Doc said. He was losing patience.

Captain Peterson nodded and Rick hit the VCR's play button. There was only dark gray light and then the outline of the sub became visible with the robot spider nested on the bow. Doc clenched his jaws. "There is no evidence," he said half aloud. "Those lying bastards."

"Then I take it that's the sub...that's *Blackwolf*?" Peterson asked.

Doc nodded slowly, "That's her alright. You've been here three hours and she hasn't moved? Then something's wrong. If she were operational, Behrmann would have sunk you by now."

"What? You're kidding."

"Sorry, I wish I were, Captain. Behrmann is real paranoid about leaving witnesses. You've seen him and that's all the justification he needs to blow you out of the water. How much gold is still down there?"

"Three tons or more, a billion dollars at least."

"That's enough...three tons. I wonder if the greedy bastard's stolen more than he can carry. But, that's too easy and Behrmann's a better engineer than that."

"So..."

"Smart thing would be to head for home, unless you're carrying depth charges."

"But that's our gold."

"And it's your ass if he comes after you. We've seen what his torpedoes can do."

"Torpedoes! Damn the torpedoes, that's our gold!"

"Actually, Captain, the line was 'damn the torpedoes, full speed ahead,'" Mike offered. Captain Peterson was not amused.

"There must be something we can do," he responded.

"Well, sir, if you're not leaving, then we better do something before he does. Have you got any explosives aboard, or a conservation lab with solvents or strong acids? Or how 'bout a real big minnow net?"

"Looks like somebody tried to go to the moon with the lowest bidder," Johnson said, shaking his head. "These valves weren't designed for this kind of depth. No wonder the old man is pissed."

"What are you saying?" Geist asked.

"These would be fine in a normal sub diving to a thousand feet or so, but not at eight thousand feet. We tried these on *Black Widow.* Pressure warped the housings and froze 'em."

"So what did you do?" Geist said.

"Pulled her up and changed valves. It's the only way."

"And for us, what can we do?"

"Lighten the boat and hope we can break mud suction."

"You mean the gold. You're talking about dumping half a billion dollars."

"I'm talking about a ton and a half of ballast and being alive to steal the rest another day," Johnson spoke as if the entire discussion were academic.

"There must be another way."

"Probably so, but if you don't mind, I'm going to get some sleep while you figure it out."

"One more question. How long will it take?"

"What difference does it make? We're not going anywhere until it's done." Johnson pulled himself up from the bilge and left the compartment.

"There might be another way," Roberts offered as Johnson left them. "What if we can get the lift we need from outside the sub?"

Sheri dragged Stephanie up on the beach and banged on condo doors until a young woman in a terry robe answered. After the ambulance arrived and Stephanie was loaded, Sheri sat exhausted beside the gurney and watched the EMTs check vital signs and start an IV. In the hospital emergency room the staff cut away Stephanie's blood-matted hair and the chiffon dress, then covered her in clean warm blankets. After checking for other injuries, they cleaned and stitched the head wound. Halfway through the stitching Stephanie woke and was sober enough to feel the pain. Gone was the drunken swagger. Now she was obviously frightened and other than an occasional sob, was very quiet.

"Bleeding from scalp wounds always looks a lot worse than it is," a nurse told Sheri. "Don't worry, your friend will be fine. Suppose you could tell the policeman in the reception room what happened? He needs a report for his office. One other thing, I think your boss, Mr. Morgan, just came out of the emergency room. He sounds awfully worried about you both. Go on now, we'll take good care of your friend."

Stephanie heard the nurse and tried to sit up. She reached for Sheri and pulled her close, whispering, "Don't let Jack in here, please. Don't leave me alone with him...promise, please."

"Sure," Sheri answered, and for the first time wondered if Stephanie had told the truth about what had happened on the boat. Perhaps there was more to her request than not wanting Jack to see her without makeup.

Jack Morgan greeted Sheri as a long lost relative and sat close beside her while she gave her statement to the police. He encouraged her and put his arm around her.

"Just one other thing, Miss. You certainly did a heroic thing going after her like that, and Mr. Morgan told us you probably saved his boat as well. I'm sure the paper will want this story. There was something bothered me though. One of the boys in the ambulance said he heard Ms. Smith say she was pushed off the boat. She say anything like that to you?"

"She was pushed," Morgan interrupted, "by the boom when we hit the reef. It hit me at the same time. That's why I've got these stitches." He turned his head so that the officer could see the short neat row of needlework in the back of his scalp.

The officer nodded politely. "Certainly, Mr. Morgan, but..."

"Yes, what is it, officer?"

"Well, sir, you know our waters pretty well. How did you end up there in the shallows? Your big boat, she must draw quite a bit of water."

"The young woman who went overboard had been drinking. She works for me and there have been some problems. Quite frankly, we got into an argument and I...I guess I wasn't watching the helm. Next thing I knew we were in the shallows."

"An argument?"

"Yes, about her drinking and her behavior with my guests. Talk with any of them. Like I said she's been having some problems. But don't worry, it's nothing we can't handle. If necessary, we'll help her find a treatment center back in the States. She's a valued employee. Not one we want to lose."

"Yes, sir, well, thank you for being so candid. I hope things work out for her. Sorry about your accident, Mr. Morgan, and good night to you, sir. Thanks for your help, Miss."

When the officer had gone Jack Morgan took two deep breaths, exhaled deeply and turned to Sheri. "Good. That's over. Now, there are two more things. I need to know everything Stephanie said to you or anyone else, and there will be no reporters and no story in the paper. I'm sorry, but we just can't afford that kind of publicity. You understand. Ms. Kee is taking care of the press right now. She'll have something for you in the morning. Sleep as late as you want. When you get up meet me in the office. If you're ready to go now, you can ride back with me, or I'll send the car back for you."

"They said they could get these urchin spines out of my hand as soon as they finish with Stephanie."

"Just call, the car will come." He turned and was gone.

"Miss," a nurse called from the doorway as Jack Morgan vacated it. "Your friend is asking for you. Could you come and sit with her?" Stephanie had been moved to a private room. She was crying like a shivering, frightened child. "Is he gone?"

"Yes." Sheri was holding her own sore hand, not in a mood to play nursemaid to a whining drunk, but she saw real terror in Stephanie's eyes. She sat next to the bed and Stephanie reached for her hand. "Not that one, please. It's still a pin cushion." Sheri tried to laugh and offered her left. Stephanie took it as if reaching for a life ring.

"He tried to kill me and he will try again. You've got to get me out of here."

"What are you talking about? The boat hit a coral head and the boom pushed you overboard. It was an accidental jibe, that's all. You'd had quite a bit to drink, remember?"

"You don't understand," she sobbed. Her breath was strong enough to melt cast iron. "Oh, get me something...I'm going to be sick again."

Sheri found an emetic basin in the bedside table and got it to her just in time. Stephanie retched violently, nearly filling it and covering Sheri's hands at the same time. When the wave of nausea had passed, Sheri emptied the basin and washed it in the room's private bath. "Honey," Sheri began as she returned, "if you're sure it wasn't an accident, you don't want me in here. You need one of those big Caymanian cops."

"Can't talk to them," Stephanie sobbed. "Can't trust anyone."

"Then why me?"

"You saved me. And someone has to know what's been going on here. Look, just listen for a minute, okay? I was an investigator for the U.S. Customs, and was working undercover to investigate Morgan. You must have wondered where all his money came from."

"You were undercover, like a spy?"

"Just listen. Morgan showed up down here with a ton of money and our office got curious. So they set me up to meet him. I got enough of a look at his books to know he could write one on creative accounting. He's a player, honey—big arms deals, stocks and bonds, commodities, oil. That condo and his holdings here are just the tip of the iceberg. His daddy was a big oil man in the Middle East, but he lost it all. Jack had to drop out of grad school and join the military because daddy couldn't pay his tuition. So he didn't get his start with family money like he says. And believe me, honest colonels don't make the kind of money it took to bankroll an operation like Jack's. He's as dirty as they get."

"You sure?"

"Absolutely. We were this close to an indictment and then things happened. Wait, I'll tell you, but could you get me something to drink? My mouth tastes awful."

"Sure, I could use something myself." She started to get up, but Stephanie pulled her back.

"Don't leave, honey, just call the desk. Please don't leave."

"Yeah, sure." Sheri found the call button and pushed it. "Okay, they're coming. Now tell me the rest."

"Jack hired me—that was part of the plan—but I was really undercover like I said. Well, he got suspicious and I think they drugged me...." She paused, looking for words as a young nurse came in to answer the call button. They asked for soft drinks and the nurse left.

"What do you mean?"

"There was a party in the hot tub room. They took videos. I would never have done anything like that. I swear it. But there it was on tape. Well, I had to tell my boss. I couldn't risk having those tapes come out in court. So the government dropped the case. They said it was my fault. I'd blown my credibility as a witness."

"Then why didn't you leave?"

"I tried, but Jack brought me back. I think he's afraid...."

"You might make trouble?"

"Sure, even if the government doesn't indict him, I could still go to the press. Jack Morgan would make one hell of a story...."

"So why didn't you tell someone?"

"Well, stuck here with not much to do, I had plenty of time to think, you know, and I started asking myself questions. Like, what if the reason I was put on the investigation was so that I would blow it? I'd never been on anything like this. The more objective I got, the more I could see it. They set me up to fail. I wasn't sent here to convict him, I was sent to protect him."

The door opened again and the nurse returned with the drinks.

"So you were a sacrificial lamb, a virgin for the volcano?" Sheri said after the nurse left.

"Close enough." Stephanie managed a faint smile.

"Then why would he try to kill you now? You're not a threat anymore, are you? And wouldn't you be much more protection to him alive? Killing you might muddy the water."

"There's more. He's up to something. Something big. A lot of government people and even some scientists have been here for meetings. The dragon lady knew some of the lab rats, you know the guys in the white coats and gray beards. She sat in on their meetings, but I didn't find out what the meetings were about. Jack locked the place down tight while they were here. He doesn't trust me anymore. But, he won't let me leave...and now this."

"Bigger than all the stuff you said, the arms deals and stuff?"

"Yeah, much bigger...people at the condo...all the communications and computer stuff in his office. He's got his own satellite, you know. He's the only guy I've ever slept with who has his own satellite. What the hell does a banker need with a satellite?"

"You were sleeping with him?"

"Yeah, of course. Me and half the women on this island. How do you think I got the job in the first place? But listen, honey, we've got to get out of here, off this island, right now."

"That's good...you can't even walk and neither one of us has any clothes. Don't you think we should get a good night's sleep and talk about this again in the morning? Say, after you've had some coffee and a little time to think?"

"You think I'm nuts or still drunk. I don't blame you, but believe me. Jack was trying to throw me overboard when the boom hit us both. I couldn't tell the cops. They'd just think I was drunk and then I'd never have the chance to get away from him. I'm sorry you got involved in this mess. But I'm not drunk and I'm not crazy, but sure as hell my life is on the line here and I have to get off this island tonight. Promise you'll help me, please."

"Okay, I'll do what I can. If you're right, I can't risk going to your room. You sit tight and get yourself together, I'll bring you some of my clothes and a credit card or two. Maybe you can check on flights, ok? I'll get back quick as I can. What the hell, this job was too good to be true anyway."

"What about your hand?"

"Looks like it will have to wait until you're on that plane."

Sheri called for the limo. While she waited, she tried to pull the urchin spines from her hand. They crumbled, leaving the tips well embedded. The pain kept her focused and even though she wondered if she should risk helping Stephanie, for some reason not readily evident she believed Stephanie was telling the truth. And the good life at Morgan's Landing was now tainted. Life had certainly gotten complicated in the last three hours. She'd help Stephanie get off the island and then start looking for another job. *Doc, where the hell are you? That old song is right...a good man is hard to find.*

Ms. Kee was waiting in Sheri's room. "How is your hand? Are you all right?"

"Sore as hell," and that was the truth.

"I'm sure you are hungry and exhausted. I've ordered food. Take a hot shower, eat and then sleep as long as you want." Sheri nodded. This wasn't going to be easy. Ms. Kee opened a bottle of wine and poured two glasses. Sheri took a sip. It was good and she took the glass with her to the shower. She soaked in the hot water until her head cleared and she was refreshed. When she opened the shower door Ms. Kee was holding a thick robe for her.

"You are very beautiful," the woman said as Sheri stepped into the robe.

"Thanks," Sheri answered with a little hesitation, but she accepted her refilled wine glass and headed for the neatly turned down bed. *This might be another real good reason to change jobs,* she thought.

A sterling silver soup and sandwich tray was waiting by the bed. Sheri allowed herself to be tucked in, still wearing the robe, and ate heartily while Ms. Kee sat beside her asking questions, mostly about Stephanie, and gently worked around the edges of what Stephanie might have said. Sheri lied, saying Stephanie had slept most of the time. She wondered what she would have to do to get Ms. Kee out of the room so she could get her things and get back to the hospital. Then her vision began to blur.

The last thing she remembered after collapsing back into the overstuffed pillows but before slipping into a coma-like sleep, was Ms. Kee taking the soup spoon, bending over her pillows and gently kissing her good night.

"What do you mean, get lift from outside the hull, Dad? You plan on hiring a crane?" Randy Roberts asked his father.

"Pretty close," came the serious reply. "When we were trapped on the *Nautilus*, your Uncle Jason's sub, the crew from the *Oceanic Explorer* attached lift bags to her hull to help get us up."

"I still don't get it."

"Our inflatable boats could be our lift bags. *Black Widow* could tie them on. We should be able to calculate how much lift we'll get and my guess is if we have to dump any of the gold, it won't be much."

"Good, Bill," Geist said. "And once we're up, we'll fix that valve and be on our way, a half billion dollars richer."

"But won't the boats explode as the gas expands when we start up?" Martin asked.

"All we'd have to do is cut slits in the bottom of the boats for dumps...it's simple. And everything we need is out there. We just have to make it work."

"Now all we need to do is make more coffee...."

"And wake Johnson up," Martin finished his brother's sentence.

"They're moving...something's going on down there," Rick Franklin shouted up the ladder to the bridge. Doc and the captain were quickly beside him. "They're still on bottom, but they've started their engines and a compressor. Sounds like that ROV is back at work too."

"Any chance we can get a look?" Doc asked.

"In about an hour. *Argo* won't be at depth 'till then," Captain Peterson answered.

"What did you come up with to catch those guys?" Rick asked.

"First we disable its propulsion, then blind it, and then negotiate," the captain answered confidently.

"Sounds like the old 'once you've got 'em by the balls their hearts and minds will follow' strategy," Rick laughed. "Think we can we pull it off?"

"If I can't convince you to leave, then we'd better," Doc answered quietly.

Sheri's head was splitting and her mouth felt dry. As her eyes began to painfully focus she saw Ms. Kee sitting beside her bed, reading. Sheri raised her arm to check her watch. It was eleven-thirty and the sun was shining.

"Stephanie," she blurted as she tried to sit up.

"Stephanie's okay, Sheri. That's why we let you sleep. Her doctor's released her this morning and she is just fine. She left the island about an hour ago, but she left you a note. Don't worry, everything is fine. Now, what can I get for you?"

"It's not virtual reality, but it's not that far from it either," Dennis Johnson explained as he put down the coffee mug and slipped on two gloves which appeared overgrown with thin red and white wires. "When an activity is too complex to command verbally we still have these as a fall back." As he spoke he raised his hands and *Black Widow* mirrored his actions. He rotated his wrists, and opened and closed his fingers. Again, the ROV's response was perfect.

"When I put these on in combination with the voice-activated commands and focus only on these monitors, I sort of become *Black Widow*. It's like looking at your hands in a dream and then realizing it was you seeing it all through someone else's eye sockets. Like a double reverse out of body experience. That make any sense?"

Martin laughed and nodded.

"Well, we're ready. What's first?

Bill Roberts had a task list ready. It began with removing the inflatables from their lockers and securing them to the hull. Once in place they would be inflated with the external scuba tank filling hose. Randy and Geist were in the dive locker, checking the valves and compressor to make certain they could deliver enough pressure to overcome the four thousand-pound bottom pressure and still fill the boats.

"Can you see what they're doing, Rick?" the captain asked.

"She's not close enough yet—just hang on another minute. There, there she is. Look, they're working on the bow of the sub. There's that big spider-looking ROV...mean machine. Man, look at that thing! Looks like the spider from hell, don't it?"

"Get closer...I still can't tell what they're doing," Peterson said.

"Yes, sir."

"Go easy. Don't want them to see *Argo*," Doc cautioned. "That's good...what have they got out on the deck?" He watched for a minute and then they could see the port side inflatable start to rise from the deck.

"What do you think?" the captain asked.

"Looks like they've got a ballast problem and need more lift."

"They've got our gold!" Captain Peterson swore.

"We've a choice to make," Doc said. "Go for the props or go for those bags. If we go for the lift bags we might force them to unload the gold. But if he unloads and surfaces, you won't want to be anywhere in the neighborhood. He can outrun us and he can damn sure blow us out of the water. But if we can cripple him before he surfaces, we might have a chance to ram him before he gets a shot at us."

Captain Peterson agreed. "Let's stick with our original plan. Rick, try to blind side 'em with *Argo.* Set her down on low and then come in under her stern. Maybe we can get in the back door while they're worrying about the front."

Rick maneuvered the *Argo*, the flying boxcar, into position and then dropped her to the bottom. Then using the manipulator arms, he lifted the end of a length of the *Benthic Explorer's* anchor chain and moved in closely to the starboard wheel. It was a slow process, but when he finished the chain was wrapped between the propeller's blades and then around the rudder behind it. Rick produced a large shackle from the work box and the mechanical arms slowly linked the ends of the chain.

"Yeah, let's see him get out of that," the captain said.

"Let's hog tie the other wheel before he gets those bags inflated," Doc said.

As Rick maneuvered the ROV away, he bumped the sub with the lower skid frame. He swore and powered *Argo* away from the hull, making a forceful landing on the port side.

Inside *Blackwolf* Bill Roberts felt the jolt. "What was that?"

"What?" Martin answered.

"Something hit the hull. Switch the monitor and get a look at the stern."

"Not now," Johnson said. "Let me finish this tie down first."

"Something hit the stern. Let me have one monitor long enough to get a look."

"Okay, okay. Take the monitor. Martin, hold my mug so I can get some coffee, will you?"

Martin obliged as his father switched the main monitor and turned on the stern camera. "We have company. Take a look at this, right now," he demanded.

"Shit!" Johnson growled. "What do they think they're doing?"

"Do something," Bill Roberts shouted, his voice up an octave.

"Keep pumping the air. I'll get rid of that asshole. Give me back the monitors," Johnson said and when he had them, he quickly completed securing the last tie down on the starboard boat.

"This is going to be fun. Just watch," he said and started the thrusters which lifted *Black Widow* from the deck and flew her, octopus like, to the stern. *Argo* had the second chain in place and was starting to shackle the ends when its cameras caught *Black Widow* in flight.

"Shit," Rick said. But his years at sea supported him well. He kept his head and kept twisting the pin into the shackle until *Black Widow* was almost to *Argo*. Then at the last possible moment, he hit full thruster power and raised the much larger ROV up into a collision with the spider. Following through on the initial surprise, Rick put full power forward in an attempt to crush *Black Widow* against the sub's hull.

The nimble arachnid, however, was able to avoid the fatal blow. It darted to the side then attacked again while Rick was trying to reverse the momentum of his foiled attempt. *Argo* crashed into the sub's hull. Rick tried to quickly raise his ROV again. The collision shook *Blackwolf* and her bow started to rise from the mud.

Argo's cameras picked up the cloud of mud as the sub started to rise, but Rick had lost contact with *Black Widow*. Rick rotated his cameras in desperation trying to find the spider.

"The sub's coming up," Captain Peterson shouted.

"Where the hell's that spider?" Rick yelled, trying to hear himself think above the confusion and panic in the compartment.

Doc turned to Mike who had remained quiet throughout the debacle. "Fire up *Kratos* and get her clear...I'll stay. This doesn't...well, you know. Good luck." He turned, grabbed the chief engineer by the shoulders and shook him to get his attention. "Get your lifeboats over the side," Doc said loudly enough to get the frightened man moving. "Do it now!"

The chief ran to the back deck to follow his orders.

The captain's glazed expression passed and he was back in the game. "What now?"

"Keep perpendicular to her and maybe we can ram her before she can launch at us. And if that chain works, maybe she won't be able to turn."

"Got it. I'll stay at the wheel."

Black Widow was riding on the top of *Argo's* skid frame. Johnson was out of his chair and got on top of the desk. He'd assumed *Black Widow's* position atop *Argo* and in a low crouch, he examined *Argo's* electronics cables and black boxes through the monitors. Then with the animation and enthusiasm of a three-year old, he reached into the mass of cables and began gleefully and methodically ripping them from their receptacles. "Checkmate," he shouted and laughed. "I win, you die." Then he looked up to see the other crew members staring at him with wonder and amazement.

Rick's monitors died and he knew the fight was over. "Winch her up," he ordered through his headset to the deck crane operator, but there was no one at the controls. The frustrated chief was screaming orders and the men were arguing about how to deploy the two little rectangular web-bottomed life boats.

Doc jumped up the stairs into the wheelhouse. "Put out an SOS and a call to the Navy in Charleston," he ordered the First Mate. "Give our location and tell them we're under submarine attack."

"We're what?" the man said, looking at Doc as if he were crazy.

"Do it!" the captain snapped and the man reached for the radio.

A large boil of bubbles formed off the port beam and then two orange inflatable hulls broke the surface followed by *Blackwolf*'s sleek bow.

"There she is," Doc pointed. "Give her everything you've got."

Captain Peterson pushed the throttles to full speed. *Benthic Explorer* lumbered forward and then turned abruptly to port. It rolled as if straining against an anchor.

"What the hell?" the captain swore.

"It's *Argo*—her umbilical is holding us. I'll check," Rick shouted as he went out the side door.

"I'll back down and have another run at it. Maybe we can break the cable." The captain hit full reverse, and suddenly the port engine locked up and died. "We backed into the cable. Oh my God...now we're a sitting duck."

"Try to restart the engine and ease her into forward, just for a few turns. Maybe you can unwrap the cable. I'll have a look and call you from the crane's radio," Doc said and followed Rick out the side door.

Captain Hans Behrmann found the spare key to his stateroom door in his desk, and exploded into the passageway, Luger in hand. When he entered *Blackwolf*'s control room his eyes were wild with rage. "How dare you lock me in my cabin," he stormed. "This is my boat. This is MY boat," he repeated, "and this boat and its crew live and die at my command. Is that understood?"

"Yes, Captain," Geist said, looking at the gun and contemplating the possibilities. "This is your boat. We only wanted you to rest undisturbed. I take full responsibility, and I apologize, sir."

Behrmann leveled the Luger at him and clenched his jaws.

"Don't, Grandfather. He was trying to help you. You were exhausted," Randy pleaded.

The monitors caught Behrmann's eye and he saw the *Benthic Explorer* struggling to free itself from *Argo*'s umbilical. Behrmann waved Bill Roberts out of the command seat with the Luger and eased the joy stick forward. There was no response.

"What's wrong with the engines? What have you done?" he demanded.

"While we were inflating the boats, they used their ROV to foul our wheels...we have no propulsion."

"Idiots," Behrmann snorted. "We still have the bow thruster and the torpedoes." He activated the thruster and swung the bow perpendicular to *Benthic Explorer*. His eyes burned with hatred and he laughed loudly as he flipped up the red safety covers on the torpedo firing switches and with the joy stick, locked in the target on the main monitor.

"You can't!" Martin cried. "They're civilians...they're unarmed. They can't hurt us." Martin lunged at him and the Luger fired, missing the boy but stopping him in his tracks.

"I am the captain...I decide!" Behrmann screamed at him as he hit the switches, firing both bow torpedoes.

Captain Peterson saw the bubbles as the torpedoes left the sub and knew what was coming. With his one functional engine, he tried to maneuver out of destruction's path and then he saw the white sportfisherman running full speed on an interception course with the deadly missiles.

Mike, steering from the tower, ran *Kratos* directly into the path of the torpedoes and then turned her broadside. He waited as the fish sped toward him. He turned to look at *Benthic Explorer* and saluted. Seeing Doc return the salute from the ship's stern deck, he turned back to check the torpedoes. Mike saw them coming, exactly on target, then watched in amazement as they passed beneath his shallow hull and raced on to their original target.

Without warning the sub's machine guns opened fire on *Kratos*. Mike hit full throttles in an evasive pattern, trying to get out of range. The torpedoes slammed into the salvage vessel's side, splitting her in half, and sections of torn, twisted metal flew high into the air.

Mike braced himself in the tower as debris showered down on *Kratos* and ricocheted off the high aluminum fishing tower. When the roar of the deafening blast passed, he heard the screams of wounded men. Dropping below into the cabin, he used one hand to place a call on the hidden red telephone and the other to ease *Kratos* forward toward the wreckage.

The Navy had already scrambled two fighters and dispatched a Spruance class ASW destroyer when they received the first call from *Benthic Explorer*. They assured Mike help was on the way as he tried to communicate over the racket of the hellish gunfire from *Blackwolf*.

"When?" Mike shouted.

Behrmann began firing on the survivors, but he had not yet found the range. Mike saw the men waving desperately from the water. He signed off and raced into the line of fire to pick them up.

Blackwolf kept firing. Without forward power she couldn't come closer, but when Behrmann found the range *Kratos* took several hits. Mike hit the power and tried to draw the fire away from the wreckage and the few survivors. Behrmann took the bait, tried to track him and kept laying down heavy fire even when his targets were doubtful. Then Mike heard the jets. They made their first pass for observation a hundred feet off the deck, then climbed, rolled and came back with guns blazing.

Mike couldn't tell if *Blackwolf* was hit on the first pass, but the fighters quickly changed the game. *Blackwolf* quit firing, her hatch opened and two crewmen ran to the bow and cut loose the rubber boats. The jets returned, flying slower this time and laying down heavy fire. But again it was impossible for Mike to see if they were hitting anything. The sub's crewmen ran back to the hatch as the jets both launched rockets. Huge explosions dropped Mike to the deck and blocked his view. Water thundered down on him, hammering the boat so hard it took out the cabin windows. When the spray finally quit falling and Mike could see again, the sub was gone. Had the jets blown the sub out of the water, or simply given her time to escape by firing short? Mike couldn't tell. However, for now his immediate concern was to pick up *Benthic Explorer*'s survivors and find Doc.

CHAPTER 8

Stephanie's letter was short and to the point. She thanked Sheri for saving her, apologized for her drunken paranoia at the hospital, and promised to call in a few days from the States. She had talked with Jack Morgan and the misunderstandings had been cleared up. Now everything was lovely. All she needed was a rest and to get it, she was going to spend a few weeks back home in Atlanta.

Sheri leaned back into the overstuffed pillows, took note of how intently Ms. Kee was watching her, and then read the letter again. When she finished, she kept her face passive, folded it and replaced it in the powder-blue envelope. She laid it beside her on the bed's lime and peach quilt. *I wonder,* she thought, *if Stephanie's still alive.*

"So you see, dear, everything really is alright, just like I told you," Ms. Kee said. "And I have something else for you, from Mr. Morgan." She handed Sheri a second envelope. Jack Morgan's note was brief:

"Sheri, glad to have you onboard. Thanks, J.M." Enclosed was a check for ten thousand dollars.

"I can't...," Sheri began.

"Money is always an awkward way to show appreciation. Mr. Morgan thought that since you are new with us—just getting started, you know—well, the check would help with wardrobe expenses and the like. I told him that was a good idea, so if you don't take it, I'll be the one who looks bad. Take it, darling...if you decide not to cash it, you can always frame it and hang it on your wall," she laughed.

Sheri forced a laugh and sat looking at the check. It was the most money she had ever held at one time. And it was tempting. She laid the check on the quilt beside Stephanie's letter. *Where was Stephanie, really? Stephanie had been scared-sober enough to know what she was saying at the hospital. And, where the hell was Doc? He hadn't called in over a week.* Sheri didn't buy the letter, not for a minute. She looked back at the check, then looked up and forced herself to smile at Ms. Kee.

Two thousand feet deep in the Gulf Stream, Dennis Johnson contorted his face in superhuman concentration as again using the gloves, he commanded *Black Widow*'s movements to remove the chains binding the sub's propellers.

"Hurry, you idiot! We're sinking!" Behrmann yelled.

"Then finish fixing the ballast control valve and leave me alone," Johnson retorted. "I can't work any faster with you yelling, Captain, sir."

Behrmann's face flushed red. He swore that he would kill Johnson as soon as the boat was safe, but for now he turned his fury toward Geist and the Roberts boys who were forward frantically trying to replace the faulty valve. On the surface during the attack, they had been able to remove and replace the damaged valve. However, the repairs were leaking and the ballast tank was still full.

"We've got to get that gun away from him," Randy said quietly as they worked.

"Yes," Geist answered, "but carefully. It was only luck he didn't hit Martin before."

"Help me, will you? This is as tight as I can get it by myself and it's not tight enough yet," Martin said. He was on his back in the alleyway, lying in three inches of water and trying to tighten the short pipe nipple enough to withstand five thousand psi leaks.

"I can't believe he sank that ship. Those men, they didn't have a chance," Martin grunted between turns on the wrench. Randy lay down on the deck to help him. "The whole world will be hunting us for that...and...and there was no reason for it."

"In his world it was an enemy vessel. He might have gotten a medal," Geist said.

"But his world was destroyed by that kind of madness. It was crushed."

"Not all of it, not by a long shot. There were dreams of a second effort. The ones in South America...."

"But they were just dreams—that could never happen," Martin declared with the certainty of youth.

Geist said nothing.

The search for *Benthic Explorer*'s survivors continued well into the night. Of the crew of forty-six, only twelve were found. Captain Peterson and First Mate Rick Franklin had gone down with the ship, perhaps for a last first hand look at the *Central America* or to speak with Captain Herndon in person. Doc was the last of the twelve found. He was burned, battered and bruised like the others, and like the others, maintained that all he needed was a cold beer and good night's sleep and he would be fine.

Kratos was in need of repair. The turbo on the starboard diesel had been hit by the sub's machine gunfire and was beyond repair. Now she chugged along on one engine, crawling the rollers and wallowing in the following sea. The other survivors had been airlifted to shore by the Coast Guard. Doc's dislike of helicopters and the possibility of a cold brew, made completing the trip with Mike an easy choice.

Halfway through the beer, Doc began to worry about the grief he was going to get from Inspector Cord about the damage to *Kratos*. After finishing the first beer, he had the perfect answer: Tell Ian the truth. Lt. Mike Berry was driving. Send the bill to the Navy.

Mike cringed when Doc delivered the resolution to the dilemma. "I don't want that big moose blowing his bagpipes at me, Doc. Come on, help me out here. I sort of stuck my neck out trying to help...if anyone noticed."

"You are not allowed to get killed on my watch and that's an order. Got it?"

"Aye, aye, sir. Anything else?"

"Yes. Thanks for trying. As usual, your efforts were magnificently motivated even if disastrously ineffective."

"What a bunch of crap."

"Yes, and that's why I'm the captain. Carry on...I'm going for a second and final beer. Want anything?"

"Sure, I'll take a beer."

"Not on watch, you won't. Look at the damage you did cold sober."

It took twenty-three hours to reach the Charleston Naval Yard on one engine, and Doc was surprised to find reporters and television crews waiting as they limped to the dock. The survivors had been talking. Two of the more aggressive reporters were on the boat even before the spring lines were secure.

"Which one of you is Berry, the Navy guy?"

"I am," Mike answered uncomfortably.

"The guys in the hospital said you tried to block that sub's torpedoes with your own boat, and then you went into the line of fire to get them out. That true?"

"Guess so."

"That makes you quite a hero. Want to tell us about it?" The reporter was young and eager.

"Not much to tell, not really." Mike felt old and tired.

"Come on, Capt'n, give us a break. We've been waiting for you guys for a hell of a long time."

"Well, we don't know anymore than you at this point. I'm sure the Navy will give you a statement as soon as..."

"Don't give us that, Capt'n. Come on, give us something we can use. What about that sub? What can you tell us about her?"

Mike was now staring at three television cameras. He looked over his shoulder to Doc for guidance. Doc's glare was all the guidance he needed.

"It's only lieutenant, not captain, and look guys, I'm not the one you want. This is Doctor Joh...." He was interrupted by an elbow in the back and when he turned again, Doc was gone.

“Where have you been? Why haven’t you called like you promised?” Sheri began when she recognized his voice. “Doc, a lot has happened here and I need you. A girl disappeared and there’s something spooky going on here. I left messages for you, like we agreed. But you didn’t answer. Doc, that’s not fair....” She started crying. “I’m scared. I don’t want to be here alone. Doc, are you there? Doc?”

“Easy, girl. I’ll be on the first flight. Now start at the beginning and tell me the whole thing. First, where are you and who was the girl?”

He listened carefully and patiently. Her voice strengthened and then he could hear the excitement as she retold the story of rescuing Stephanie and the events that followed. Then she told Doc what Stephanie had told her about Jack Morgan and life on the other side of the rainbow. When the tale was told, Doc cautioned her to be careful until he arrived and promised to call again as soon as his flight information was confirmed. As an afterthought, he suggested she go have a good meal and then watch the evening news.

“What channel?”

“Probably won’t matter. See you tomorrow. Love you.”

“Love you too, bye.”

She heard him hang up the phone and dropped the receiver to her lap before returning it to the nightstand. She was just starting to feel better when from her lap, she heard the second click and then a dial tone.

The crowd had left the boat by the time Doc returned from the phone booth on the pier. Mike was sitting in the galley, finishing his first beer. Two others were standing at attention, waiting. Doc took one and popped the top. “Sheri’s in some kind of trouble in Grand Cayman. I told her I’d be on the first ight out.”

“Better call her back. Inspector Cord called on the red one. Secretary Anderson is on the way. Wants to meet first ng in the morning.”

“Damn, she sounded scared, Mike. I need to go....”

“The inspector didn’t sound good, Doc. You need to be e.”

“How early?”

“0700.”

"Then I can still catch an early flight. I'll call her."

Sheri was in the shower when the phone rang the first two times and didn't hear it. He called a third and fourth time just after she had taken his advice and gone out to dinner. She had waited until late because she wanted to go alone. She caught a cab to the Lone Star, a Tex-Mex hangout for local dive instructors. There was a crowd gathered around the television—that was unusual because people come to Cayman to escape what's on the evening news. But she didn't give it too much thought and asked for a table in the main dining room, away from the noise of the bar.

She ordered a beer and fajitas, and looked back toward the bar, trying to figure out what the shouting was about. The crowd was getting loud about something. Then whatever it was ended and they returned to the normal routine of comparing tourist stories and loading liquid carbohydrates in preparation for the next day's diving.

She turned her attention away from the bar and was looking around the full dining room, wondering if any of the sunburned faces could be from Atlanta, when a tall, bearded instructor, well known on the island, came to her table from the bar and introduced himself. He was John Bentley, charter captain and part owner of a dive operation with locations in three hotels.

"Heard about what happened on that sailboat. You did real well."

"Thanks. Want to sit?"

"Sure, for a minute. There's a winsome willing tourist waiting, you understand," he laughed and nodded toward a leggy Texas redhead glaring at him from the bar. "Actually, I've been wanting to talk to you. You're going to run the new dive operation at Morgan's Landing, right?"

"Yes. I guess so."

"There's a rumor that Morgan's dredging in Great Bay is screwing up the viz on the North Wall. The local court handed down injunctions to stop him until the biologists have a look, but we heard he's ignoring the court order and has the dredges working at night. Like no one is going to notice after dark. You know anything about that?"

"No, this is all news to me. I've only been here a couple

days."

"Well, he has a lot of pull with the suits at Government House, and the Dive Operators Association thought maybe he pulled a few strings to get around the injunctions. You know, like under-the-table strings. A lot of folks are really pissed at him. Be careful out there. You don't want to end up in the middle of something ugly, especially when none of it was your fault. Might be a good thing to let one of us know if you get wind of what he's up to. If there's nothing to it, that's important too. No use reefing for a blow if you're sailing in clear skies."

"Sure, I'll do it. No one has the right to do that."

"Well, the meter's running. She flies back to the cactus patch tomorrow. Thanks, and see ya 'round, right? And oh, watch the fajitas...they're deadly."

She watched him go back to the bar and get a Texas-sized lecture on the way real gentlemen treat their ladies. His redhead was obviously ready to leave, but on the way out he spoke to a waiter. When they were gone the waiter brought Sheri a beer and told her that her dinner had been paid for, including the ice cream she would need for desert. Sheri thanked the waiter and then asked if he knew what the excitement in the bar had been.

"Yeah, really weird, man. This treasure-hunting boat off the Carolinas blew up. Lots of people killed. Survivors claimed they were like torpedoed by a submarine. You believe that? Some dudes in a fishing boat tried to help. Their boat got all shot up and one of 'em got hurt. Really weird, man, like out of a war, you know? Strange shit. How 'bout another brewski?"

Ms. Kee was waiting when Sheri crossed the bridge to the condo's foyer. It was late, but getting out had been the right thing to do.

"You should have told me you wanted to go out. I'd have gotten you the limo. We were worried."

Worried that I might try to leave like Stephanie? Sheri thought. Instead she politely said, "Sorry, I really needed some time. It's okay, but I didn't mean to worry you. I'm really fine now, honest."

"I'm glad to hear that. Then you'll be able to dive with Mr. Morgan in the morning. He's really looking forward to it. Can you have things ready about ten?" It wasn't really a question.

"How many divers?"

"Just two, I think. Josh, our maintenance chief, will go to watch the boat while you're down. Okay?" That wasn't really a question either.

"Oh, my friend is coming tomorrow. Will it be alright if he stays here?"

"With you?" That was a question.

"Yes. He'll be bringing our boat later. This will be just a short visit."

"Yes, of course. You must be happy he's coming."

"Yes," she realized as she thought about it. "Yes, I'm very happy. Good night, Ms. Kee."

"Just one more thing, dear...what is your friend's name?"

"Doc," she froze for a moment wondering if Doc would be using a different name as he had in Bermuda. "Doctor John Holiday," she said and tried to muffle the Holiday. Then she turned and went quickly up the winding emerald green stairs to her suite.

A message on her telephone voice mail said Doc would be arriving by four, not exactly first thing in the morning, but better than not coming at all. *Well, now at least they know someone will be here looking for me...someone who's not afraid to kick butt and take names if anything happens to me,* she thought as she turned on the television and tuned in CNN. She watched for an hour, but she was tired and wanted to sleep. She rested her eyes a moment but then bounced back when she heard Mike Berry's voice and saw his round face and little-boy smile fill the screen.

Doc was standing behind him looking tired. There were bandages on his hands and arms. He was wearing dark glasses even though it was well after sundown. *Flashburn,* she thought and remembered her experience of watching Behrmann's torpedoes sink the *Rose.* She could see broken glass and bullet holes in *Kratos* and she shook her head. *Ian's going to be pissed.* Then the clip was over. She turned off the set, turned on her side and tried to sleep. Her body was in park, but her brain was still in drive. *At least Doc and Mike are alright, but the Navy would have a devil of a time trying to deny this one. What about Behrmann and the sub? What about Jason and Karen? Poor Karen, wanted it all and look what it got her. It wasn't good to be that hungry*...then Sheri remembered the check in her dresser. *What am I going to do about Jack Morgan's ten thousand dollars?*

Is that check supposed to keep me quiet about Stephanie? And was Stephanie telling the truth about Jack Morgan? And, what about the things John Bentley had said about Jack? God, do I really want to dive with Morgan in the morning alone?

She tossed from her side to her back, pulled up her favorite dive scene—a manta gliding effortlessly above a deep reef—and tried to free her spirit to ride with him. She took several deep breaths, exhaling slowly and matching her breathing to the slow rising and falling of the manta's ten-foot wings. Better. She felt her head and neck relax. More breathing. She was beginning to see the reef through the manta's eyes. *Doc was okay and this would be her last night alone for a while.* Good feelings as she held that thought. *Breathe and glide, almost there.* But the reef and the manta faded as Stephanie's frightened face returned to haunt her and kept her from sleep.

After a brutal sleepless night it was a relief to get up from her tossing and turning. It was barely daylight when she pulled on a tank top, shorts and running shoes and headed for the beach. She had too much respect for her ligaments to run on the soft white sand, but the cool, clean air, the gentle surf and a good long walk would clear her mind and focus it on the demands of the day.

She stopped on the pool deck to do some stretching and then started north, up Seven Mile Beach toward the turtle farm. The new aluminum twin-hulled dive boat was anchored next to Jack Morgan's sailboat, *Bluebird.* Further down the beach toward town, dive boats were going out with early morning charters. But other than the eager divers, she had the beach and the ocean to herself. She breathed deeply and picked up her pace.

She could see two small turtles in the shallows, not much larger than dinner plates, swimming inside the first sand bar. Once teeming with turtles, the island was named La Tortolas by the buccaneers who came looking for water, turtle meat and a safe place to bury their loot. Henry Morgan, the most famous buccaneer, had a castle and lived like royalty, eventually becoming Lt. Governor of Jamaica. The castle still stands, and with five hundred banks chartered on the island, so does at least one to the traditions the pirates began. *Henry's castle didn't hold a candle to Jack's condo,* she laughed to herself. *I wonder if Jack plans to become a politician like old uncle Henry.*

She walked for an hour, past the place she had dragged Stephanie up on the beach, and back again. *I need a plan. I need a sample of Stephanie's writing...I need to call her family in Atlanta, I need to stay alive 'til Doc gets here, I need to find out if what John Bentley said about Jack was true. I need a good night's sleep. I need to lay off the fajitas.*

There was no one in the condo restaurant except staff. They were friendly as always and welcomed her to fresh coffee and pastry. She settled for coffee and went down to the pool and across the deck to the dive locker. The dive locker doors were double French with Cape Cod windows. It was hard to tell the glass had been smashed until she nearly put her hand through the hole.

She pushed open the door and surveyed the damage. Her displays had been pulled down and wet suits slashed, regulator hoses cut and buoyancy compensators stabbed. It looked as if there wasn't a functional piece of equipment left in the shop. However, then she found her own gear bag, sitting neatly on her desk, unopened, with a note written in magic marker on the pink fabric. "Go home." No profanity, no damage to her gear, just a warning to get out. She found the phone under a pile of equipment catalogs and called security.

Jack Morgan came running, followed by Josh, the elder Caymanian security officer, and Ms. Kee, in a stunning green silk robe.

"How bad is the damage?" Morgan asked first. He got a dirty look from Ms. Kee and changed the question to an obligatory, "Are you alright, my dear?"

"Sure, they were gone by the time I got here."

"News travels fast on a small island, right Katherine?" he said and strained to laugh. Then as he got a good look at the shop, he shook his head with frustration and anger.... "What a mess. Whoever did this is going to be damn sorry. Get it cleaned up, Josh. And I want a list of everything that's damaged. Everything, got it? We'll make sure our friends get their attitude adjusted and then some. Protests are one thing, but now they've crossed the line."

"Mind telling me what's going on?" Sheri asked.

"After we eat. This is no way to start the morning." Morgan ordered breakfast served poolside. He didn't drink coffee, but when juice was served he began, "I spent most of my working life, after I retired from the army, as an economic advisor to the government." His breakfast of bread and fruit arrived, but he let it sit while he went on. "What that term 'advisor' meant was that I helped the army and then the government handle...sensitive is a good word...sensitive negotiations. Ones that were too hot for the politicians to handle. Like when we wanted our hostages back from Iran. My father was an oil man in the Middle East so I had some background dealing with those people.

"Then it was decided that I should open up shop down here. That it would be easier to do business here. Our friends would feel more comfortable on neutral ground and this place has good connections as an international finance center. Plus on a small island it's easier to keep track of what's going on...."

"That's very impressive—international finance, working for the government and all, but why did somebody trash your dive shop?" Sheri asked bluntly.

"This island has unique investment opportunities. Because of its rather liberal philosophy about investments, it occurred to me that it might make a wonderful safe haven for investors who wanted to stay a bit closer to their capital. The island was lacking in accommodations suitable for that clientele. So for starters I built this place and at the same time bought a large parcel on Great Bay. That's where the real money will be made. Not condos, but villas. Villas built for royalty. Say seven million and up. Twenty million gets you indoor plumbing. Thirty million, a heliport and secure satellite link. Security and privacy are the keys...and...well now to answer your question. Some of the locals are against construction and more outsiders coming to live on the island. Tourists they like. But residents make them nervous. Especially residents with the kind of money I'm talking about. They're afraid the island will change. Afraid they might have to wear shoes or something."

"Will it change?"

"Of course it will. Change is inevitable. And these fools had better learn to like it. Because...well, just because it's going to be good for them."

"So the reason the dive shop was trashed is that the locals don't like what you're doing to their island?"

"You have a real way with words," he chuckled. "They don't like what I'm doing to the rather large chunk of the island which they were delighted to sell me, a postage stamp at a time at outrageous prices, not to mention the construction permit fees and the contributions to the school fund and the hospital fund and the campaign funds of half the derelicts on the island. They have bled me every way a man can be bled, and now they are trying to stop me with some bogus environmental nonsense. Fortunately, I have friends, or they might have succeeded in stopping our work altogether. That would have been very costly.

"The problem with environmentalism," he went on after taking a bite of toast and then sending the plate back because it was cold, "the problem is that nobody can afford it. Recycled paper costs more than new. Oil, cleaning chemicals, automobiles, plastics, all are cheaper if you can just use them and then throw them away. To live in an environmentally balanced world might raise the cost of living two or three times. This condo's a good example. There are no outfall lines dumping our sewage anywhere. We have our own tertiary treatment plant and even our gray water is recycled. But it costs more. Lots more. Most of the world simply can't afford it. No wonder the mermaids Henry Hudson reported in New York haven't been seen for a while. Four hundred million gallons of raw sewage hits the Hudson River everyday. Millions of gallons go down the Mississippi, and the U.S. is supposed to be an advanced, wealthy nation. What about the really poor nations? If Manhattan can't afford sewage treatment or trash recycling, can India, or China, or....? The other problem is people think they can have their cake and eat it too. You can't make an omelette without breaking eggs.... Well, you're a smart girl. You know this already."

"No, I don't. Not really. Please go on."

"In Florida and New England there's a problem with lobster—the yearly catches keep getting smaller and smaller. Years ago there was good research suggesting the reason was the legal size is too small. It may be legal to take them before they've had a chance to make more little lobsters. But rather than increase the legal size, commercial fishermen blame divers. Divers don't have much political clout so that's easy, and a war is on."

"But in the long run, won't that wipe out the lobster?"

"Sure, just like abalone in California and red snapper in the Gulf of Mexico; but you and I will be retired from politics by then so it won't be our problem. You can have eggs or..."

"An omelette. Okay, that part I understand. So why did someone trash the dive locker?"

"Let's go diving and see if you can figure it out."

"The old man must be nuts," Secretary of the Navy Andrew Stillwell Anderson said, shaking his large head with such vigor that the folds of skin beneath his chin shook too, reminding Doc of an overweight turkey. The meeting was in the airport bar and Doc was anxious to get it over and get on a plane to Grand Cayman.

"Stealing the sub was one thing; but, sinking that civilian...I had hoped that if he wasn't destroyed in Bermuda, we might still find him and convince him to give us back the sub. We were willing to make a deal. But it's too late now. The planes got him, I'm sure of it. I saw the combat film...direct hits. There's no way they could have survived. But just in case, we've got two boomers out looking. They've got orders to kill on sight."

Doc had heard Anderson sing this tune before. *We had a problem, but it's all over now.... If this is the best he can do, I'm outta here. Let's cut the bull and get down to the real business.* "What about us, Mike and me?" Doc asked rather impatiently.

"You had no business being here in the first place. In the second place, you've made me look like an idiot after I told the President *Blackwolf* was destroyed in Bermuda."

"I do recall mentioning then and also after the Secretary of State was killed, that Behrmann's sub was still operating," Doc said wanting a little vindication.

"I'll give you that, Holiday. Perhaps you were right after all." Doc's vindication came but begrudgingly. Anderson unwrapped a cigar and chewed the end without lighting it.

"Alright then, let's say that earns me the right to play one more hunch. Don't take us out yet," Doc said. "Here's my logic. First, Behrmann's a tough old bird and until you show me his tail feathers, I have to believe he's still out there. Second, you were looking for him before and couldn't find him. What makes you think your luck is going to improve now? My guess is he's sophisticated enough to evade anything you send after him. Evade, that is, until he gets tired of playing your silly games and blows one of the President's boomers out of the water. How's that going to play in the White House, Andy?"

The Secretary was searching for his lighter, but stopped and put down the cigar. Doc had connected with that one.

Doc continued, "Third, let's assume you're right and he is nuts. The harder you push, the more desperate and dangerous he'll become. How many torpedoes has he got? What are you going to tell the President if Behrmann decides cruise ships are really troop transports and tankers are hauling supplies to the Normandy invasion?

"If the map we found meant anything and he is hiding in the Caymans, a small boat outfitted with good equipment and a little firepower would draw a lot less attention than the sixth fleet. Keep the Navy looking, but don't take us out of the game. We might be your ace in the hole."

Secretary Anderson gave up looking for the lighter, looked at Doc and Mike, wondering if someone were going to offer him a light. No one offered. He looked away and one of his two aides went looking for matches. He wasn't a happy camper. None of this ever should have happened, and now he was under the gun. *Holiday was right, of course. Little did Holiday know how close he was to stumbling on the truth about Blackwolf. And that would be more dangerous than actually finding the sub.* On the other hand, Holiday's luck hadn't been that good and at least back on the payroll, Anderson could keep track of his whereabouts. "You never give up do you, Holiday? Alright. You can play out your hunch. But I want a report daily, understood? We'll outfit your boat and you can keep Lieutenant Berry. But, dammit, I want to know where you are every damn minute.

And one more thing. Your mission is strictly recon and not a damn thing more. Under no circumstances are you to engage that sub. That's the deal."

You bet your ass, Doc thought. *If I get that sub in my sights, Behrmann gets a one way ticket to the big Nazi reunion in the land across the River Lethe. I'm sure he and the fuhrer will have a lot to talk about. Anderson's been lying about the sub all along and was probably lying about the combat film now.* Doc was sure of it and sure the honorable Secretary of the Navy was not to be trusted. So the question now is, *Can I use Anderson without trusting him? Hell, yes. It's time to turn the tables.*

"Fair enough," Doc answered. "Daily reports, no problem."

The Secretary nodded knowing full well Doc had no intention of keeping his end of the bargain.

"By the way, does the name..." Doc fumbled in his pocket for his notes and his reading glasses, "Jack Morgan ring any bells? I think he was army, probably retired now. He's some sort of banker in Cayman."

"How do you know Morgan?" Anderson answered, obviously surprised.

"I asked you first," Doc said. He caught the Secretary's start at the mention of Morgan's name.

"Jack Morgan was a wiz kid—part of army intelligence, top level strategic planning. Still carries the rank of bird colonel, or perhaps even general in the reserves. I see him in Washington from time to time. Whatever he does he must be good at it because he serves as an advisor to the Army chief of staff. I think he remains active in the diplomatic sector. Why do you ask?"

"Diplomatic sector? You mean he's a spook?"

Anderson was uncomfortable with the question. "Let's just say he is extremely well qualified to serve his country in certain delicate political arenas. And for those services, he is extremely well rewarded."

"He's a high-paid spook. Spooks are spooks. Thanks for the info," Doc said. *Once a spook always a spook, just like my old buddy Colonel Sandy Andrews. Hmm...I wonder.* But he decided not to tip his hand any more than he already had. If Andrews was working for Anderson, some cards are better left face down until the pot's right.

"Who knows, he may have outgrown that stuff."

Fat chance, Doc thought. He lowered his chin and looked over the top of his half-frame reading glasses at the Secretary who immediately glanced away. *Right. He's a spook and a big one to boot. I hate spooks. Now what the hell has Sheri gotten us into?*

Karen woke before dawn and found Jason kneeling beside her cot, holding her hand and looking very concerned. Her eyes were wet and her sinuses full, like they always got when she cried. It must have been a dream. She wiped her eyes and smiled at Jason. He smiled back, sat back on his cot and reached over to her. She took his hand and squeezed it. "I'm okay. Let's try to go back to sleep."

Jason pointed to her stomach.

"No, it wasn't the baby. Everything is alright...the baby's fine. Now let's sleep." She squeezed his hand again, released it and turned on her side. Through the window she could see the cove and clear night sky with it's bijillion stars. The drone of the air conditioner kept her awake. She would have preferred to sleep with the window open, but poorly fitting screens and plenty of bugs made that impossible. The room was stuffy and she was uncomfortable.

She closed her eyes, tried to sleep but ended up wondering about her dream. In that mental state somewhere between sleep and awareness, she began to see it again. She was in a garden with high crumbling stone walls covered in lush vines. The garden was full of children but there was something wrong—the children were all silent. Even those who cried had no voices. In the garden's center was a shrine. There were flowers beneath it and flat stones for seats around a large reflecting pool. At the edge of the pool stood a tall white statue of the Madonna and Child.

Karen was drawn to the statue and as she approached, she could tell it was very old. It was cracked and broken, rust stained and streaked. Birds had contributed to the desecration quite generously as well. The cumulative effect was grotesque.

The Madonna's face looked old and the features of the Child were nearly obliterated, as the marble proved insufficient to withstand the ravages of time, nature and neglect.

Karen's heart was heavy as she studied the statue. She struggled with the weight of her expanded girth as she attempted to sit on one of the flat stones at the edge of the pool. It was on kneeling that she saw the reflection of the statue in the water.

However, unlike the ravaged reality of the ancient statue, the image in the pool was radiant. It was the face of a beautiful young woman with graceful hands and slender arms holding a happy, laughing child. Looking into the pool's deep water was like looking at the afternoon sea reflecting golden sunlight on gentle ripples. Karen shaded her eyes and tried to change her angle to the light so that she could see better. When she did she could see it was filled with gleaming coins, catching the sun and sending it back in a thousand directions. Suddenly she was no longer alone. Along with her own reflection, seated at the pool's edge, other faces looked back at her from the water. Startled, she looked behind her, but there was no one. When she looked back in the pool, however, she was surrounded by sad-eyed, silent children dressed in rags.

A breeze sent a ripple across the water and when the image was restored, Karen realized that the Virgin had moved. From the depth of the pool she looked up at the children, then looked directly at Karen. Then as if recognizing an old friend, the Virgin smiled and reached up her hand. In it was something for Karen. It caught the light and was blinding. Karen squinted her eyes and then as the Virgin turned her hand, Karen could see she held a golden Spanish escudo like the one Jason had given her a lifetime ago.

There was something else besides the woman's radiance. Rather, like the coin she held up to Karen, she and the child in her arms were solid gold.

This time when Karen awakened, she remembered all of the strange dream. She saw before her the golden Madonna in the water, reaching out to her, and the sad, sad faces of the silent children.

Josh, a big, good natured Caymanian, helped Sheri haul her equipment to the beach and lug it aboard the boat. Morgan was late so she had time to set up the rigs and check everything before he arrived. Finally he came across the sand, smiling grandly and carrying two large green canvas bags.

Josh lifted the bags aboard and then helped push the pontoon's bow off the beach.

Morgan took the wheel and headed north toward the wall. "I came here the first time years ago—my junior year in college I think. I had lived with my father in the Middle East and traveled most of Europe. But there was something about this place—I was sure that one day I'd live here. Funny how things work out, isn't it? Anyway, the trip was with just three of my student friends. I'd heard about the treasure of Henry Morgan which Collier, one of his captains, had supposedly hidden here. Even when Morgan caught up with him and tortured him, Collier didn't talk. The legend is well known on the island, and Collier's Point is named after him. Anyway, my friends and I came here looking for that treasure. At least that's what we told our parents," he laughed. "Mostly we drank and tried to pick up the local girls. We probably would have had more luck finding the treasure. Parents had seen horny college students before and were adamant about keeping their girls away from us.

"That was about forty-five years ago...things have changed a bit since then. I didn't come back until twenty years later, but my first dives were right here. Not a bad way to start. The walls look just the same. Perhaps the visibility was a little better then."

As he talked he began unpacking the green bags which looked to be veterans of the Great War. Sheri's eyebrows raised to new heights as she saw what he intended to wear diving.

"The big changes of course have been in the lifestyle of the locals. It was just an oversized sand dune then. Mostly they fished and turtled. That was it. They were damn glad to get a few tourist bucks, let me tell you. But today...well, it's a different generation. These people don't remember what it was like before we came, we the ex-pats, I mean. We built this island. Without us it would still be a swamp and a sand dune, nothing more. Perhaps we should just leave for about ten years and let them go back to eating turtles and coconuts. I think we'd find life a little easier when we came back. I bet we wouldn't hear so much of this environmental nonsense then. They'd just be damn glad to have our money under any circumstances."

He was holding an orange horse-collar buoyancy compensator, the oldest Sheri had ever seen. It had an inflator bottle at the bottom. Next out of the bag was a weight belt made from an aircraft seat belt, then an army knife in a leather sheath, brown gum rubber fins, a rotting black rubber mask with side windows and a capillary-type depth gauge. He laid out the equipment and lastly pulled a pair of heavy leather work gloves out of the bag.

"I have a regulator and a BC ready for you on this tank," Sheri said and pointed to one of the rigs she had salvaged from the dive locker. He looked distrustfully at the new equipment.

"Thanks, but I better stick to what I'm familiar with. All I need's the tank and regulator. I took mine into town to get it checked and they are having a hard time finding hoses."

"Hoses...two hoses as in double hose regulator?"

"Sure, I like it because you don't have bubbles in your face and it doesn't scare the fish. I've never used one of those," he said, pointing to the single hose with octopus and instrument console. "You better show me what all that other stuff is for."

No wonder you wanted your own dive boat, Sheri thought and tried not to laugh. *No one on a real boat would let you on board with that junk. Wait till Doc sees this stuff. He'll probably want to buy it!*

The other bag contained plastic Nalgene collecting bottles. Morgan set them out and checked the hand-written labels before removing the tops, stuffing them into two large green mesh collecting bags. He handed Sheri some slates divided into grids with the names of several fish across the top in Latin.

"You recognize these?" he asked and started putting on his gear.

She read *Chromis cyanea, Chromis multilineata, Thalassoma bifasciatum, Clepicus parrai, Halichoeres garnoti, Bodianus rufus, Bodianus pulchellus*, and about twenty others. "Most of them," she answered. "Blue chromis, brown chromis, bluehead wrasse, creole wrasse, yellowhead wrasse, spanish hogfish. What's *Bodianus pulchellus*?"

"Spotfin hogfish."

"See many?"

"No, like the spanish, they're good eating. Don't last long."

"How about *Canthidermis sufflamen*? Isn't that the big ocean sunfish? See many of those?"

"Once in a while, usually out in deep water. Ready?"

She had not started putting on her tank yet. "Just a minute," she said and turned to pick up her tank. "What are we going to do..." before she could finish she heard a splash and he was gone. Sheri was left on the deck still holding her tank. Josh held it while she put it on and admonished her to be careful. She wondered if she needed to read between the lines. She studied him for a moment, didn't find what she was looking for, thanked him, pulled on her fins and mask, and did a giant stride entry. Once in the water, she gave an okay to the boat. She checked her computer and watch, dumped most of the air from her stabilizer jacket and started down after Morgan. She had made only one equipment modification for this dive: she'd added a second knife in a concealed sheath inside her stabilizer jacket.

She guessed the visibility at a hundred feet and he was nearly at the limit of it. She dumped the remaining air in her stabilizer jacket and dropped, feet first in a rapid descent. It was her first dive in nearly a month and it felt great. She dropped past coral heads and sponges, trying to remember their Latin names. *Porites*: the finger corals, and the brain corals: *Diploria*, *Colpophyllia*, and two kinds of *Montastrea*, one with large cups and the other with small.

And then there were the sponges. She remembered the hours and hours of memory work and how she had wondered how learning the Latin would help her be a better dive instructor. She still wondered. She checked both knives—the one in the usual leg scabbard and the new one—at least six times during the descent.

Morgan was a strange duck. She felt better about him now. He was more human out here on the boat, but she realized she had yet to understand him. *What were they doing out here and what was it about Jack Morgan and his world that made her feel so uneasy? And, those eyes, those cold gray eyes—on the rare occasions when he laughed and his eyes sparkled, it was like seeing sunlight through shattered glass. But that night in the hospital or the morning the dive shop had been broken into, his eyes had been as cold as steel. What kind of a man is he?* she wondered. *And why did he bring me on this dive?*

Morgan found what he was looking for. He was wedged into the bottom, hanging onto a brain coral head, *Diploria strigosa,* she remembered, and was pointing to a long brass pin driven into the wall with a number one stamped on its head. He pointed across the face of the reef and she could see other pins. They formed a large grid pattern. He gestured that they were in the lower left corner.

Sheri trimmed her buoyancy to hang motionless above him and checked their depth—a hundred and seventeen feet. She watched him take the first of the Nalgene bottles from the bag, find its cover and seal the first of the water samples. Then he handed her the green mesh bag and pointed to four more pins going up the face of the wall. Four empty bottles remained in the bag. She got the message and ascended to the pin at one hundred feet. She kept an eye on Morgan working below her as she found the bottle labeled one hundred, shook it through the water to remove any air and then firmly sealed its lid.

Morgan was changing bottles in a sediment trap. A stainless steel frame about the size of a truck tire held three wide-neck bottles. He closed them with lids from the green bag, removed them from the frame and replaced them with clean bottles. He pointed to a second frame about twenty yards away, gave her a wave and headed south along the wall face.

The sun was higher now and more color was visible on the wall. Huge red and orange sponges, and very large purple sea fans and other soft corals caught the light in gentle and silent beauty. A yellow trumpetfish passed her and then a pair of shy queen angels. Morgan was hard at work on the second sediment trap. She ascended slowly to the eighty-foot pin and sealed the third water bottle. She checked her console...plenty of air and time according to the computer. She waited for Morgan to ascend.

She was just saying to herself that he might be the worst diver she had ever seen when she saw him come trudging up the wall carrying the six wide-mouth sediment bottles. He was swimming very hard because of the drag of his load and his horse collar buoyancy control device was still totally deflated. He was too close to the wall and was kicking the tops of the soft corals.

That's it, she fumed. *I've got to do something or there won't be a gorgonian left alive on this reef.* She hung the water bottle bag on the brass pin and swam down to get him. He was breathing hard when she approached and looked relieved to see her coming. She smiled, took the bag, hit her auto inflator to put two short blasts of air in her jacket and led him up to the eighty-foot pin.

Two thirds of his air was gone when they arrived, but there was still time to get the last two samples. She gave him time to catch his breath, then they ascended to sixty feet, gathered the last two bottles from the trap she'd been working on and returned to the permanent mooring anchor. Sheri ascended slowly and did a safety stop at fifteen feet for three minutes. Morgan, however, went directly to the boat and was waiting, lounging on the bow with a beer when she surfaced. He made no effort to help her with the heavy mesh bag or her equipment. Josh came forward to give her a hand.

"Great dive, huh?" Morgan said from the couch. "We've got time for a beer before we go back down. You don't mind, do you? One or two give you enough carbs to stay warm the next time down."

She looked at Josh who shook his head to caution her.

"No thanks," she said, choosing her words carefully. "I think I'm warm enough already. Say, why don't you show me how that old horse collar is supposed to work? Don't think I've ever seen one quite like it. And then let's talk about the next dive after I work out our surface interval on my tables. Did you happen to notice how deep you were or how long you were down?" she asked and picked up the computer on his regulator console.

Doc had been waiting at the condo for over an hour when Ms. Kee greeted him and confirmed that Sheri was on a very important dive with Mr. Morgan and wasn't expected back until late afternoon. "Why don't you have a good lunch and go for a swim," she suggested.

He took her advice, ate a light lunch, then took his Randall dive knife from his suitcase, wrapped it in a towel and went to the dive locker. The door was still broken. He found mask, fins, snorkel and compass in the wreckage, looked for a spear gun but came up empty. He laid the equipment by the pool with the towel hiding the Randall and went back into the condo and took the elevator to the top floor.

When the door opened he found himself in the middle of a high tech communications and computer center. Several people stared at him through the heavy glass walls and he guessed immediately that swim suits were not the uniform of the day on the top floor.

He smiled politely and walked on thick emerald green carpet to the south end of the corridor. Through the dark green glass he could see across twenty miles of ocean or more. He counted eight dive boats along the edge of the wall. Three were pontoon boats, but only one had a an emerald green canopy. He took a careful bearing on it with the dive compass, estimating the distance to be a mile and a half. *Well, the lady did say take a swim. Might as well make it a good one.* Jack Morgan was a spook and in Doc's book that meant Sheri had no business alone on a boat with him. Especially not after the way she'd sounded on the phone last night.

He swam on his side with strong kicks. The fins never broke the surface and he did not use his arms, except that his right was extended to help keep his body stretched straight and streamlined as he powered through the shallow water. *Why would Sheri have gone diving alone with someone she had been so afraid of just twenty-four hours before...unless she had no choice?*

Sheri was trying to be tactful, but it hurt. She wanted to tell Morgan he would never pass a beginning openwater course, or that he was the worst thing to hit the water since red tide, but he was her boss and according to what he said and the vintage of the junk he was wearing, he had been diving before she was born. So she held herself under control and tried to find non-combative ways to talk about the situation. He listened to her questions and suggestions, but never acknowledged he had a problem.

On the second dive they would replace more of the sediment trap bottles.

"These bottles are supposed to collect particulate and let us know what's in the water," he began. "Problem is there's no base line study and no lab here qualified to analyze this stuff. But that isn't stopping the dolphin huggers from claiming they have absolute proof my construction is screwing things up. That's hogwash. So to defend myself—I'm shipping these samples to the best labs in the States. Got to build a case of my own, one we can go to court with. The judges here are the problem. They render decisions based on emotion and politics rather than on the logic of the island's long term benefit. Fortunately, my friends were able to convince the court to hire a team of big league environmental consultants, my consultants, of course.... It's simple really...the solution to pollution is infinite dilution. You heard that? It's not that there's too much crap...there's just not enough water," he laughed and his eyes were cold and ruthless. "They can't blame me because the ocean's too small, and besides, six months after the work's done nobody will ever remember what this fuss was about anyway."

Sheri bit her tongue to keep from saying what was on her mind. She turned her attention to their equipment. She insisted they stay within sight of each other, surface together and make a safety stop on the way up. He agreed, telling her not to worry—he would look out for her. Again she choked back her reply, but only until he was underwater. Then she swore at him with language that made Josh, the old Caymanian, blush.

The next set of sediment traps were slightly north of the boat. She swam until she saw him on the bottom, then began her descent. He was standing on two coral heads and photographing anchor damage on a third. She swore again as he looked up and she signaled him to get off the coral. He shook his head as if he didn't understand and pointed in the direction she was to work. She shook her head in frustration, gave an okay, found the trap, and began sealing and removing the Nalgene jars.

The water was thirty-two feet deep, warm and clear. The sediment trap was nailed to a dead coral head at the edge of a rather picturesque sand pocket. She saw five types of coral she could name and at least six others she wasn't sure about. There were a few fish, yellowtail snapper, wrasse, damsels, two small peacock flounder, and both princess and stoplight parrotfish, which were busy biting hunks out of the coral and reducing it to sand.

It didn't take long to remove the five jugs, seal and bag them, and start back to the mooring line. On her way she heard a boat engine in the distance and turned her head, trying to hear with one ear and locate the source. The boat sped directly over her. She was deep enough not to be in any danger, but she was sure there was a dive flag flying from their pontoon boat and this speedboat had no business coming so close to the flag. She could see twin screws and a blue bottom race past. She turned toward the departing boat and failed to see the loop of stainless steel cable lined with heavy monofilament leaders and big hooks the boat was dragging.

A two-inch, stainless steel snapper hook caught her shoulder, embedded deeply and ruthlessly jerked her toward the surface. She screamed with pain and tried to bring her leg up to reach her knife but could not overcome the force of the water. She exhaled forcefully and reached for the second knife, but the pain in her arm was so great she was paralyzed. She fought to stay conscious and tried again for the knife. This time she found it and pulled it free.

She was being pulled on her back like a downed water skier who forgets to let go, and couldn't reach the line behind her shoulder to cut it. Then something grabbed her foot. She looked down and saw Jack Morgan. He had her by the ankle and was trying to pull himself up with one hand. In his other hand was the rusty, leather-handled, field knife. The additional weight on the embedded hook was merciless. She screamed in pain, lost the regulator, and kicked with all her strength. She caught Morgan in the face with her knee and he let go. But in her panic, she dropped her knife and flooded her mask. The pain was the worst she had ever experienced. She was choking and couldn't find her regulator.

Then suddenly she was free. Someone put the regulator back in her mouth and hit the purge, she coughed and gasped and got a breath. She grabbed her mask and cleared it. The first thing she saw was Doc's face and his big Randall dive knife. He was breathing from her octopus and Morgan was swimming beside them. She pointed to the surface, but just as they started up they heard the boat coming back. Doc pointed to the bottom and they swam down as fast as they could. She had been pulled toward shallow water. There was nothing below them now but sand and a few low profile coral patches.

They hit bottom just as the boat roared over. This time she saw the hooks coming. She had been caught by a cable running between two downriggers with razor sharp hooks on weighted monofilament leaders hanging every six inches. The downrigger weights were dragging close to the sand. Doc took several deep breaths and released the octopus. He began exhaling slowly and as the boat approached, he lunged forward with a powerful dolphin kick and caught the port downrigger line. The cable jerked him forward. He managed to wrap his arm around it and his reward was a fresh wound as the cable cut into his flesh and blood clouded his view. But he held on and began sawing the cable connecting the two outriggers just below the port weight with the Randall's serrated back blade. The strands parted, one at a time. When he had cut the last strand the heavy weight fell toward the bottom and he followed it down.

His brain was screaming for air, but he had to keep the weight off the bottom until the precise moment. He guided the weight toward a ridge of limestone rock, released it, blew the rest of his air and kicked to the surface. The boat was stopped dead in the water when the weight caught between the rocks. The two occupants were smashed forward against the cabin bulkhead and the down-rigger pulley and reel were ripped from the transom and came flying back across the water.

Doc watched the two men picking themselves, battered and bleeding, off the deck. They were too far away to identify so he waited. One of them had binoculars and was looking back toward the deeper water. Doc started a leisurely surface swim toward the wall. He felt bubbles break against his chest and looked down. Sheri and Jack Morgan were following beneath him. Morgan was helping her and he waved a thumbs up to Doc. Doc returned the signal and continued to swim. He wanted a look at the men in the boat.

He heard the engines rev and the boat went into a sharp

turn. They had spotted him and were on their way under full power. Doc let them get close before making his first dive. Unfortunately, all he could see was the boat's hull. The boat roared over him, circled and came back slowly...now they were hunting. He needed air and wanted to get a look at the men in the boat, but not enough to risk surfacing and getting shot. He was twenty feet down and Sheri was thirty feet below him. He kicked down to her and got the octopus. Green blood oozed from her shoulder. The hook was in deep. She didn't look good and the pain must be really something. He checked her air...she was nearly in the red: five hundred pounds wouldn't last long.

He motioned Morgan to come closer. Morgan had more air, but not much more. Then Doc noticed the horse collar and the inflator bottle. Doc motioned for Morgan to hand it over and at first all he got was a blank stare. Doc held up the Randall. Morgan came to his senses and quickly slipped out of the vest. Doc put it on and tried breathing from the bag. It wasn't the best air he'd tasted, but it was better than breathing water. Then he put his hands together in the shape of a hull, asking where their boat was. Sheri pointed toward the wall and they began the swim.

The attack boat was still circling above them. Suddenly two violent explosions shook them. "Grenades," Doc shouted, but all that came from his lungs were a garbled bunch of bubbles. His head hurt and he was disoriented. He forced himself to concentrate on listening for the boat. He couldn't hear it and wondered if it was gone, or if the ringing in his ears was just so loud he couldn't hear anything else. He did a quick 360, but there was nothing above them. He surfaced, saw the pontoon boat a hundred yards away and the sportfisherman disappearing to the north. He dove down to Sheri and Morgan, slid his hand under Sheri's good arm and lifted her gently to the surface. As they got closer he could see two dark legs dangling from between the hulls. Josh had gone over the side and had hidden between the hulls.

Doc surfaced at the bow and cautiously checked the deck. It was empty. "Get on the boat and help me with Sheri," he told the two men. Morgan was the first up the ladder. Josh followed and after he removed Sheri's equipment, they carefully lifted her aboard. "Now get on the radio and get us some help," Doc ordered.

"New boat, no radio yet," Josh answered. "Or you can sure bet we'd have had some help by now."

"You see anything, Josh?" Morgan asked. He was out of his equipment and strutting like a man looking for a fight.

"Sir, all I see is the bottom of this here boat. They come by so fast and so close I thought we was going turtle over, so I got me in the safest place...yes, sir...I went right in that water, sharks and all."

Doc was bending over Sheri. He made a clean slice with the Randall and the hook was out. And so was Sheri. Doc stopped the bleeding with direct pressure and held her while Morgan drove to shore to find a phone and an ambulance.

The cove at the base of the mountain was several hundred yards across and very deep. The beach around it was steep, heavily overgrown and difficult to explore. But Petra had encouraged Karen to exercise, and even though she was beginning her eighth month, she and Jason swam or took long walks every day.

Jason would patiently lead, sometimes going ahead to find the easiest paths and then returning to be her guide. *Blackwolf* was still at sea so they set out on their daily adventures with great abandon. Jason's strength was returning and his eyes were quick to catch everything around him. And while he still did not speak and his behavior was still childlike around the others, Karen knew. She knew he was not the dim-witted reprobate he seemed to be. Now if only he would talk to her.

The morning sun broke over the mountain's rim just as they finished eating. Karen cleared the table. As usual, they had eaten on the bungalow deck overlooking the lagoon. She told Petra they were going for a swim, then she and Jason walked down to the water's edge.

Colonel Andrews was fishing and said, "'Morning, beautiful," as they passed. There was something about the way he looked at her that made even a simple greeting sound sinister.

"He's getting too healthy for his own good," she said to Jason when they were out of the colonel's hearing. "He needs to get off this island and find himself a woman. He scares me.

I'm glad I look like I swallowed a watermelon. If I weren't this big, I think he would be a problem."

Jason smiled.

"And I float like one too," she laughed. "Come on and laugh. I know you can. Come on."

He turned his eyes away and she knew she had gone too far. It was enough that she knew he understood her. The rest would come in time.

They swam in slow easy strokes. It took about twenty minutes to cross the cove and when they reached the bank, they rested. Two days ago they had discovered a new trail. Unlike some they had explored, this one looked like a real trail, like someone else might actually have used it to get through the heavy vegetation and up the mountain. Karen sat by the water enjoying the sun while Jason went climbing up the new trail. He was gone nearly an hour and Karen began to get worried. When he returned, he appeared so excited she forgot all about the scolding she had planned for him and followed him carefully up the steep trail.

The undergrowth was thick, at times forcing them to crawl. But it had been a well-worn trail and was fairly easy to follow. It ascended gradually along the water's edge for three hundred yards before cutting up to a small plateau in the side of the mountain. The last hundred yards winded her and she wanted to sit and rest, but Jason was adamant that she keep going and when they reached the second plateau, she understood why.

The view, in a world of spectacular views, was breathtaking. A waterfall cascaded down from the rocks high above into a freshwater pool. Set back against the mountain side, nearly hidden by the lush flora, was a crumbling wall made of large blocks of hand-cut island sandstone.

They were high enough that they could see over the rim of jungle that surrounded their cove and also see for miles across the deep green water. She realized they must have doubled back on the narrow trail and were now on the mountain, somewhere above the cave and hidden pool which served as *Blackwolf*'s hiding place. The trees and steep sides of the mountain had kept this place hidden from their view even though they had been exploring the area for months.

The remnants of the vine-covered wall were eight feet high and extended sixty yards. Centuries of vine growth now formed a trellis of tropical flowers in reds, yellows and violets. Their fragrance was intoxicating. Jason brought her a yellow one, placed it by her ear and compared its color to her blonde hair. Then he encouraged her to get up and they explored the length of the wall. There was no opening in the lattice of vines and after covering its length twice, Jason began climbing.

From the top of the wall he could see the foundations of one large building and several smaller ones. He lowered himself into the courtyard and went cautiously forward. There were stone steps leading to the entrance of the largest building and wide metal bands lay across the threshold. Long ago they had held together timbers for heavy doors. Jason stepped across them and went in. The stone walls smelled musty and the floor was covered with rotting timbers from the ceiling and shattered clay roof tiles. He picked up pieces of the tile and examined them with the intensity and understanding of the trained archaeologist he had been, prior to his accident. The tiles were blackened by smoke and heat. He rubbed away the soot and scraped the surface with his fingernail. They were fired red clay.

He replaced the tile and moved forward. The room was twenty feet wide and sixty feet long. The far walls remained at nearly their original height of sixteen feet. The ceiling had been steeply vaulted and the wall opposite the entrance remained intact. He worked his way forward, picking his steps carefully to avoid the rubble and broken glass. He saw the long tapered necks and conical bases of a half dozen hand-blown dark glass onion bottles.

The front of the building was shrouded in darkness where portions of the roof beams still supported rows of tiles. It was a precarious arrangement, and looked as if it should have all come crashing down a century ago. There was an altar beneath it, and on the floor on either side of it, marble statues lay face down, shattered and etched by time and the salt air. Jason picked up what remained of a once-graceful marble hand. When he turned it over, there was a square spike driven through its palm.

He jumped when a bird screeched and flew from a high

perch. Kneeling, he looked in under the sagging beams. He could see a window shaped like a cross in the stone above. It was now filled with a nest and the remaining occupant made it clear his company was an intrusion. He jumped again when he heard Karen call his name.

"There's a way in under the vines. I made it without climbing."

He nodded.

"It was a church, wasn't it? Looks like a very old mission church."

He nodded again.

"Show me."

He shook his head and pointed to the broken glass and tiles on the floor and to her bare feet.

"Alright then, let's have a look outside."

He agreed and took her hand.

The yard inside the wall was not as overgrown as the outside. They crossed an open space to the remains of four small buildings or apartments built against the wall and sharing common center walls like horse stalls. The first was a kitchen. Shards of majolica earthenware littered the floor—bowls and plates of thick, fired ceramic, boldly decorated with wide lines of blue in primitive patterns. Iron pots lay rusting on the stone floor and barrel hoops testified to the presence of food storage. The open hearth was in the side of the building and flowers grew from the ash in its base.

Only low profiles of walls remained of the other three apartments. Pieces of iron, badly decayed were collected in one room. Jason examined several. Were they weapons, tools, stock waiting to be formed? It was impossible to tell. Perhaps that was the answer—a blacksmith shop with scrap iron waiting to be remanufactured into usable tools. However, he was able to identify one piece: a bullet mold still containing a lead ball half an inch in diameter.

The next artifact to catch his eye in either of the other rooms was the bowl of a clay pipe. He picked it up and pretended to smoke it. Karen laughed. The lipped bowl was small, not quite an inch in diameter and it angled forty-five degrees out from the stem, not perpendicular like the larger, later pipes. Also, the heel was flat, not spiked. He put the pipe back where he had found it and they walked on.

In the back of the courtyard on the left side of the crumbling church, they found five open graves. The grave stones had fallen or been pushed over and the graves themselves, which had been cut into the soft stone, were now occupied only by dirt and dead vegetation. Something caught Jason's eye. He dropped into one and carefully scraped the dirt away from a small object. Karen couldn't see what he was doing, but when he came out of the grave, he was holding several dark glass beads and a small gold cross.

"A rosary...how beautiful! Do you suppose we could find it all and put it back together? What a wonderful treasure."

Jason nodded, dropped back in the hole and dug further. There were many beads. He counted thirty seven and looked at her wondering if that were enough.

"Not yet. There should be at least five sets of eleven, one Our Father and ten Hail Marys in each set. The Our Fathers are the big ones. Keep looking. I'm sure the rest are there."

It took over an hour to find the last three. Jason climbed out of the hole and stood on the edge like a conquering hero, then he dropped to his knee before her and presented the last of the beads. She rolled them into her shirt and tied a knot to hold them. Then they started back toward the front of the church.

"What could have happened here, Jason? Why would those graves be empty but something as beautiful as this rosary be left behind? Even grave robbers would have taken this, don't you think?"

Jason nodded in agreement. They were nearly at the front of the church when he noticed something unusual about the church wall. Three and a half feet up from the ground was a row of baseball sized holes in the soft stone. He looked, then motioned for Karen to wait. He went to the stall with the scrap iron and returned with a sharp pointed piece of broken metal. He dug into the stone and a few moments later showed her what he had been digging for: lead musket balls.

"Oh no, you think people were shot against that wall? That's terrible. It's a church, for God's sake. Who would shoot people at a church?"

He shook his head.

"Let's get out of here. Terrible things happened here. I don't like this place."

He nodded and led her toward the wall. They walked past the steps leading into the church then Jason motioned for her to wait. He walked around the back of the church where they had not yet explored. When he returned for her, he was as excited as when he had first found the wall.

"I'm tired, Jason. I want to swim in the waterfall pool and rest before we start down. What is it?"

He motioned emphatically for her to follow him. She got up slowly and walked behind him. The surviving high wall of the church joined the much higher, vine-covered face of the mountain to form a rectangular courtyard. In the center was a small pool and in back of it, cut into the face of the mountain, was a shrine. At the base of the shrine, laying face down by the pool were the decaying remains of a large marble statue.

Karen caught Jason by the arm to steady herself. A chill passed through her before she spoke. "I've been here before... in my dream. The marble statue was up there, and I saw her reflection in the pool, but when I looked closer it was different...." She stood behind him and quickly told him the rest of her strange dream.

"Oh, Jason, nothing like this has ever happened to me before. I'm really frightened."

Jason moved forward. She clung to his arm and followed as if hiding behind him. When they got to the pool's edge she looked down, but there was no golden Madonna in the depths as there had been in her dream. All she saw in the bottomless pool of crystal clear water was her own timid face looking back at her from behind Jason's shoulder.

She shuddered and said again, "It's just like my dream. Just like it, except for the golden statue and the children. It has to mean something. Hold me, please, I'm so afraid."

He put his arm around her and held her close.

Behrmann had been at *Blackwolf*'s helm for twenty hours. He had ordered all of the crew, except Bill Roberts, out of the control room, and he had not spoken to Roberts for several hours. He was, however, carrying on an interesting dialog in

German with an unseen mentor.

"They all think I'm insane, but they don't understand. We are only safe if there are no witnesses. That's all. It's a simple rule, really. Why don't they understand? It's because they don't remember the war, that's why. You won't let me explain, but if I could everyone would understand. Even the ones who go down, they would understand. It's the only way. The world will thank us. Any really sane person can see that."

Roberts watched. He only caught fragments of what the old man was saying, but they were enough to scare him badly.

In the galley Geist, Johnson and the Roberts boys were gathered at a mess table talking in low voices. The PA two-way speaker was covered with a pillow.

"No," Geist said again, "we can't kill him. He's the only one who has gotten the boat in or out of the cave and he's the only one who can operate the hydrogen peroxide generators without blowing the sub to kingdom come. We need him and that's the bottom line."

"You may need him, man, but can you trust him? That's the issue. I'm telling you, he's more dangerous than a hurricane. There's nothing on this boat we can't do with just a little time. He is the first problem we have to solve, then we worry about the rest," Dennis Johnson said and slammed his fist into the table.

"And another thing," he began again, "just what is this mission? I thought we were going out to pick up a few hundred million in California gold and that was it. That's what I hired on for and we did it. So what's this 'mission' crap?"

"This was only a test...our real mission hasn't started yet. You can quit now with a couple million or stick around for the real payoff, more than you can imagine." Geist's eyes glowed as he spoke. "The boys know. They can tell you."

"It starts with Dad's professor at Texas A&M, Ben Travis," Randy began. "He spent thirty-five years as an archaeologist looking for the greatest treasure ships in the world. Ever hear of the *Santa Rosa, Santa Catalina, Grosvenor* or *L'Orient*? The *L'Orient* alone was carrying 25 tons of gold. The *Santa Rosa* had 26 tons. The *Santa Catalina* had 22 chests of diamonds and other gems."

"Come on, Randy," said Johnson, "lots of folks have spent

their lives looking. It's finding that counts."

"That's where my dad fits in," Martin said. "He was a senior computer and satellite scientist with NASA. Ben Travis did the research and dad found the wrecks, with the NASA satellites. They found the *Central America* years ago, but like some of the others, she was too deep to go after at the time."

"Until *Blackwolf*," Johnson said, "and *Black Widow*."

"Exactly. Now we have everything we need, but..."

"But Travis changed his mind at the last minute. He had a fight with Jason and he never liked Grandpa Behrmann, so he gave something to someone else. It's the key to the vault, sort of. It has the only location of the sites."

"But couldn't your dad...?"

"No, he found thousands of sites. Ben was the only one who knew which was which, and maybe Jason."

"Well, Jason's no help. What about Ben Travis?"

"He had a heart attack and died."

"Goodbye, gold. End of mission. I'm going home."

"No, we know who has the key, and we're getting it back," Randy said.

"If the kindly old Nazi in the control room doesn't kill us all first."

"There is one person who he'll listen to, who he trusts."

"Who?"

"My mom, and she's at the cave. If we can just keep him calm until we get there, she'll know what to do."

"Who is the other guy at the cave, the one who was shot?"

"You don't need to know that and it's better if you don't ask," Geist answered.

"What the hell does that mean?"

"Just what I said. But let me give you a scientific explanation. It's an inverse relationship, like Boyles Law. The less you know about him, the more likely you are to reach old age. Got it?"

"Yeah, and I suppose that's true about you as well. I don't suppose you'd like to explain who you are or what you're doing down here?"

"How brilliantly perceptive of you, Mr. Johnson. No, I would not. But don't worry, you'll have the answers to all your questions soon enough."

CHAPTER 9

Two white stretch limos were unloading a group of white-suited, turbaned guests when Black Jack Morgan's Mercedes pulled into the emerald green glass condo's circular drive. Ms. Kee and her very surprised staff were greeting the unexpected guests, and she looked anxiously toward Morgan's car as if pleading for help.

"What the....?" Morgan swore. He parked, checked his appearance in the rearview mirror and with an anxious, yet unhurried, measured stride, went to greet his uninvited guests.

Doc and Sheri had ridden back from the hospital in the Mercedes back seat and Morgan left them without a word of explanation.

"Who are these guys?" Doc asked.

"Don't know."

"I need to call Mike and check on the boat. Let's go up to your room and then we'll get something to eat."

"Be careful of the phones here. I think someone was listening to our last call."

"Interesting. What else?"

"Get me upstairs and out of these clothes."

"You're wounded and I'm starved."

"You've got a lot of homework to catch up on, and you need to get started before my painkillers wear off. Then we can eat. I really missed you."

"Thanks, I missed you too."

It was sunset when he left her sleeping with a note on the overstuffed pillow beside her. He guessed he'd return before she awakened, but didn't want her to worry. The cab took him toward Rum Point, to the northwest of George Town. In back of commercial fishing docks by an aging warehouse, he found what he was looking for: a favorite restaurant from a visit to the island years ago, a cold beer, and a very private phone.

Sheri had been awake for an hour when he eased open the door and tried to slip back into the bedroom.

She turned on the nightstand lamp and sat up in bed. "Well, I'm sure you weren't out chasing women after this afternoon, but would you mind telling me where the hell you've been? You swim to Cayman Brac for that sandwich?"

"Yep, and I brought you back half. It slowed me down a little having to keep it dry and all." He handed her the bag from Burger King and began undressing.

"Doc, that's a damn lie. There's no Burger King on Cayman Brac."

"Really? Then where do you suppose this whopper came from?" he grinned as he slipped into bed and turned off the light.

They slept late, and when they awoke, Doc changed the dressing on her shoulder to check the drain. Then he taped a plastic pad over the dressing so she could shower.

"Sorry you won't be able to dive for a while. There are some great spots on the wall I'd love to see again, and I haven't been to the *Balboa* in years. Are there still big grouper that eat out of your hand?"

"Sure, there's one over two hundred pounds...must be fifty years old."

"That old? Amazing," Doc teased.

"Yeah, but rumor has it he's still great in the sack."

"Wonder if he's a grandfather?"

"Probably hundreds of times. Where were you last night?"

"Let's talk about it later. Go take your shower and we'll have breakfast by the pool." He swatted her hips, turned her around and headed her toward the shower.

"Wash my hair. It hurts to raise my arm."

"You buy breakfast? Grits, eggs and salsa?"

"Deal."

It was another perfect day in paradise. Not a cloud in the sky and the ocean flat calm. They sat under a beach umbrella overlooking the calm royal blue sea and ordered breakfast. The waitress fussed over Sheri and wanted to know all about her injury. Josh came with an anxious look to check on her too.

"Who are the Arabs?" she asked him.

"Big money boys, and trouble. Something's going on upstairs. They had us set up the big conference room last night, move a bunch of computers and TV's around. They're having a meeting this morning. One of those satellite meetings where they talk all over the world. Big shots, you know," he laughed.

"Morgan didn't know they were coming?"

"No way...he puts on the dog when those boys come to town. Ladies and all, you know."

"You mean the fun palace on the second floor?" Sheri asked.

"Sure, that's the one. But not this time. They're all real serious this time. Well I'm glad to see you up this morning. That was some excitement yesterday. You folks enjoy the morning. I've got to fix the big umbrellas up on the eighth floor pool deck again. Every time we get a little wind them big umbrellas go flyin'. Had to chase one a half mile down the beach last storm we had. Got some new weights...should hold 'em. Can't have no little breeze carrying away the guests," he laughed.

They exchanged friendly smiles and he was gone.

"What's on the second floor?" Doc asked as the old man ambled off.

"Amazing. It's a green marble party suite—big hot tubs, couches, music, lighting, video on the ceiling, everything. Stephanie told me about the parties and Ms. Kee took me up there...fantasy land for big kids."

"Really?"

"Sure. You didn't think I'd just sit on my butt and pine away waiting for you, did you? This place really swings...come on, Doc." She realized he had not appreciated her joke and took his hand and gave him an "I'm sorry, I was only kidding," smile then quickly changed the subject. "Tell me about the sinking of that ship and Mike. I only saw parts of the story on cable news."

He was still telling the story when Ms. Kee came to their table. "Doctor Holiday, Mr. Morgan would like you to join him for some fishing tomorrow morning. Breakfast at five, if that's convenient. He told me to tell you he has some information about your submarine. Do you have a submarine, Doctor?"

"No, we're still looking."

Sheri chuckled and Ms. Kee wrinkled her forehead in a perplexed look.

"Fishing?" Doc looked at Sheri and smiled. "Please tell Mr. Morgan I'd be delighted."

"Just as long as it's not bass fishing," Sheri said and they both laughed.

As soon as Ms. Kee left, Doc turned to Sheri and asked, "How does Morgan know we're interested in subs? You didn't...."

"Not a word, Doc, I swear...not a word to anyone."

Blackwolf and her cargo of stolen gold made the passage quickly from the Carolina coast averaging better than thirty-five knots even submerged and pushing against the Gulf Stream. She crossed the Hatteras Abyssal Plain, slipped silently between Cuba's east end and Hispaniola, passed north of Jamaica into the deep waters of the Cayman Trench and continued west toward the Yucatan Peninsula. Captain Behrmann returned to the helm when they were an hour away from their island base. The crew gave him a wide berth, for his mood shifts were ranging from moderately ugly to overtly hostile, except for the quiet times: the hours he spent talking to himself, isolating the others, leading them to believe that he was completely mad. They waited for some sign, what new tricks would the old man unleash on them this time?

Behrmann checked the Sat Nav and course plotter before standing behind Bill Roberts and running down a checklist of the sub's systems.

"Report?" the old man asked.

"We picked up active sonar once or twice. Navy's looking for something. We stayed far enough out that there was no chance of them getting our scent. That's all."

"Yes, they're looking, but not for us," he laughed and Roberts smiled. "I'll take her now," was all he said.

Roberts nodded and stretched up from the helm seat. Behrmann set a coffee mug on the console and slid into the thickly padded leather seat. He checked his watch against the digital display on the course plotter, typed co-ordinates into the computer and hesitated. The engines changed pitch slightly, then the sub began a starboard turn. As she did he blew a fraction of the ballast and she began to rise. The deepest known depth of the trench was over twenty-five thousand feet, well beyond the designed crush depth of *Blackwolf*'s plastic hull. They had been cruising comfortably, safely, at six thousand feet, except of course for the shallows passing through the Bahamas. Now they would see sunlight again. Behrmann glanced up at the three-dimensional sonar screen. They were at fifteen hundred feet and beginning to close on the wall. He turned on the television cameras and the lights.

At nine hundred feet they could see the wall. Randy and Martin moved closer to their father and the monitors. Johnson had tactfully retreated to his bunk while Geist remained seated at the chart table, content to watch the show and keep out of the old man's way.

At four hundred fifty feet the sonar alarm told them they were rising beneath an overhang. Behrmann nodded, turned off the alarm and eased them away from the wall. As they rose above the ledge at three hundred feet Behrmann turned on the floodlights and bathed the wall in fantastic color. The reds and oranges, purples and blues of elephant ear sponges six to eight feet across, and tube sponges ten feet high lined the wall. The wall was undercut with canyons, as if a great dragon with massive claws had tried to climb up from the abyss and in its struggle cut deep into the clay. The scars dropped away into darkness.

Behrmann leveled the boat at two hundred seventy feet and checked their heading.

"We pick up the laser track in eight minutes," Roberts offered. He was the first to break the silence.

"Ya, I can still read," Behrmann answered and gave him a condescending glare.

Roberts nodded and checked their heading and speed again. The boys were glued to the monitors, watching the increasingly abundant marine life. Roberts waited for Behrmann to reduce speed in preparation for the turn, and when he did not, Roberts risked censure again. "Beg your pardon, Captain, but we're eight knots over our turning speed. The computer should have cut our..."

"I have the boat. The computer is only an aid...I know what our speed is. Thank you."

Roberts got the same glare. He glanced back at the course plotter. "Hans, we're going to miss our turn unless..."

Without warning Behrmann reversed the engines, slamming the sub to a dead stop. Books and charts slid to the floor. Roberts was thrown from his chair and Martin went quickly to help him up.

"We're turning on my mark," Behrmann said arrogantly. He had his coffee cup in one hand and toasted Roberts who was still on his knees. "Mark."

They could feel the torque as the sub shuddered its way through the turn. Johnson, thrown from his bunk, staggered into the control room rubbing a bruise on his head.

"What the hell...?" Johnson grumbled.

"Glad you could join us, Mr. Johnson...the scenery's spectacular. Please have a seat," Behrmann laughed and Geist cautioned Johnson not to respond.

"Was that it?" Roberts snapped. "You just wanted to dump Johnson out of his rack? Why didn't you just go after him with a firehose? What's wrong with you, Hans?"

But before he could get an answer, the narrow entrance to the cavern loomed in front of them and Behrmann reversed thrust again to cut their speed.

"Look out, Hans!" Roberts shouted as the sub's port bow careened off the cavern's side. "Full reverse! We can't make it. FULL REVERSE!!"

"*Halt's maul*! Shut up!" Behrmann growled and twisted the joy stick trying to correct his mistake. The sub continued to grind against the limestone and hard clay. Behrmann shouted at them again, "Everyone to the stern...we've got to get her bow up. Hurry, the current's got us. We'll be pinned. *Mach schnell*!"

The crew ran through the narrow passageway to the engine room and were thrown off their feet as Behrmann's prediction came true when the current slammed their starboard side against the cavern entrance. They heard rocks falling on the hull. The boat shifted, rolled, righted itself and then everything went deadly silent. They had lost the engines.

"Stay. Get a damage report," Roberts told them. "I'll go back to the control room."

"Careful, Dad. Remember he's got that gun," Martin cautioned.

Roberts eased forward hearing the thundering against the hull as the unstable bank continued to give way. Behrmann was still sitting in the helm seat, all the monitors were dark and he was staring at the Luger in his left hand.

"What happened to the engines?" Roberts asked cautiously.

The old man ignored him and held the gun to the light.

"Donitz himself gave this to me," the old man said. "Hitler gave them to him and he presented them to me. Three hundred officers at the ceremony. There were two, you know, but I've lost one."

"Yes, I remember. What about the engines? How are we going to get out of here before the whole seamount falls on us?"

"We're not." Behrmann pulled back the Luger's slide and chambered a round.

"What?"

"I've thought it through. This is a good place. They'll never find us here. My secrets will be safe. That's all that counts." He was looking down the barrel now.

"Now wait just a minute! What about the rest of us? What about your grandsons, what about Petra, what about me?"

"I can take care of you first if that's what you want. If you don't have guts enough to do it yourself? Petra is strong. She will take care of the others." He turned the gun towards Roberts. "Well?"

"Petra won't know. She'll try to find us and that will bring the others. Your secrets won't be safe. Holiday will see to that. The only way you will ever be safe is to kill him first."

"He's telling you the truth, Captain." It was Geist in the hatchway behind Roberts. "Holiday is dangerous. The secret of your wonderful engines will never be safe until he's been dealt with. We have to surface and deal with him first."

"Holiday has my other gun, the one Donitz gave me," the old man said as if coming out of a trance. "Three hundred officers were there just to honor me. We have to get back my gun."

Martin appeared in the hatch behind Geist. He was covered with oil. "The props are jammed with rocks and we've got rudder damage. We'll have to dive to clear them. Everything okay up here?"

Behrmann nodded affirmatively and Roberts exhaled a sigh of relief.

CHAPTER 10

Jack Morgan was a congenial host at the subdued breakfast the next morning. Although his meetings had gone on well after midnight, he looked as fit and rested as ever, immaculately groomed, nails buffed and not a wrinkle beneath his slate gray eyes. The six fishermen ate quickly but well, conversing mostly in English with only an occasional comment in Arabic usually followed by laughter. Morgan was obviously as comfortable in their languages as with his own. When someone made a comment in French, Morgan answered in kind, then looked at Doc and smiled. Obviously, anyone not multilingual was a lesser being.

Arrogant bastard, Doc thought and returned the smile. Military language schools had left him comfortable in Vietnamese and French. Latin was the basis for all classical literature studies, after which Spanish had been fairly easy. *So, parle'vous all you want, asshole. Just remember, paybacks are a bitch.*

The four Arabs were comfortably dressed and signs of last night's hostilities were calmed by the smooth oil of diplomacy poured over deep and troubled waters. Doc was introduced as Sheri's visiting friend. That was all. No mention of academic credentials, combat ribbons, or forthcoming grandchildren. His identity was important only as the older friend of the lovely young diving instructor. The mention of her name brought smiles, which made Doc even more uncomfortable, and then, the others, satisfied that he was not someone to be concerned about, politely resumed talking among themselves. Doc listened but caught only the names of large European and American companies and gathered the discussion was about international finance and the oil market—topics in which Doc had little interest. He turned to Jack Morgan, who had not mentioned a word about yesterday's attack. This was not the time or place for Doc's questions and so he waited; perhaps Morgan had invited him so that they could talk on the boat.

They took the stretch limo to the Grand Cayman Yacht Club. Jack Morgan drove and invited Doc to share the front seat. It was a short ride up Seven Mile Beach, past the entrance to Governor's Creek and beyond to the yacht club road. Real estate signs announced Morgan's Harbour. Jack nodded when Doc asked.

"The plan is a hundred estates, villas actually, on canals," Morgan answered. "Plus condos for domestics and the like and a boat basin. All the amenities of course; it will be rather exclusive."

"Canals that have to be dredged?"

"Yes, I'm afraid so. When I started I was assured permits would be no problem. Now that we're millions into the project the government is trying to pull my permits."

"Politics?"

"Politics and greed, of course. Just because this looks like paradise don't think it hasn't got its share of problems. Like many other islands, the locals act like spoiled children. They demand control without responsibility, wealth without work, and respect without education or experience. Cayman for Caymanians," he said disdainfully. "If they get what they're asking for and the ex-pats leave, Cayman will be a welfare state in six months and a ghost town in two years."

They parked in an unfinished parking lot. Morgan stepped out of the limo and pointed to a 52-foot Hatteras with a high aluminum tower and twin fighting chairs. Sleek and fast, she was all fishing machine. The mate had warmed up the engines and set up the boat. As soon as the lines were off, they negotiated the narrow cut into North Sound and were flying across the shallows that would end at the North Wall, some of the most spectacular diving on the island.

Morgan was at the controls in the tower. Doc joined him while below, the mate baited lines and helped the guests get ready.

"Not going to fish?" Morgan asked.

"Perhaps later. I had questions about yesterday. Sheri was nearly killed. We need to talk about that."

"The boat that tried to kill me...or Sheri and me, to be exact, was found adrift early this morning. Stolen from the Yacht Club yesterday. There was blood on the dash and a broken tooth. Shouldn't be hard to find out who lost it. Anyway, the owner's mad as hell about the damage to his downrigger. Wants us to pay for it."

"What?"

"It makes sense to him. You're the one who broke it and he doubts that the boys who stole it have that kind of money. Don't worry, I made him happy. This is a small island, Doctor. I'd rather pay him than have him looking for a way to get even. Besides, if we want to find out what really happened out there, we're going to need all the friends we can find."

"Shouldn't think you'd have any trouble finding friends, especially if you're that willing to buy them."

"Business is business. Look, I know who you are and why you're here, so cut the crap. I can help you. Come to work for me. Find out who was driving that boat yesterday and get them off my back. There's a lot at stake here, and this is not a good time for me to be dealing with a mob of irate fools."

"I'm not really looking for a job, but I'll look into it."

"Doesn't work that way. I can't afford to have you snooping around unless you're on my team. The last thing I need right now is you getting into trouble and causing me more unfavorable publicity. You can see that, can't you?"

"I understand."

"Doctor, don't waste my time. Twenty-five hundred a week, expenses and my protection. You become chief of security, you and Sheri move into a penthouse up top. Yes or no?"

"Like I said, I'm not really looking for a job, but I intend to ask a few questions. Thanks. Sheri and I will be happy to move out if you'd prefer."

"What is it that you want, more money?"

"No, money's not the point. It's...well, maybe it's time for me to fish awhile. A little fishing is a great way to sort things out."

Morgan shook his head and then begrudgingly nodded. Buying Doc would have been the easy way. Plan B was not nearly as friendly. Doc went down the aluminum ladder to the deck and slapped the mate on the shoulder.

"The big ones are just waking up and I feel lucky. Where are we going anyway?"

"Twelve Mile Bank. It's some of the best marlin grounds in the islands," the darkly tanned, well built younger man answered. The crossed arrows over a dagger on a gold necklace identified him as Special Forces. Doc noticed, but chose not to mention it.

"Good fishing, really? I'm surprised I've never heard of it."

"It's a seamount, like the West Texas Flower Gardens or the Middlegrounds south of Tallahassee. This one is about three miles wide and five miles long. If it were a dry mountain, it would be over ten thousand feet high. Comes up to within a hundred feet of the surface and the big boys like it there."

"Sounds like great diving," Doc said.

"We don't dive there. Like I said, man, big pelagic sharks go there to feed and breed. And you don't want to get in their way."

The mate handed Doc a gut bucket, a waist strapped rod holder and pointed to a rod on the starboard rail. "Try that one. It's got a Jamaican pink and white artificial. We've had good luck with them out here."

Doc thanked him and eased the rod from the gunnel and checked the drag. Not too tight, the reel clicked as he pulled out a short length of line. He nodded and was putting the rig back in the rail's rod holder when it bent double and was nearly ripped from his hands.

"Strike!" Doc shouted.

The mate repeated his shout and Jack Morgan eased back the throttles.

"Set him, set him!" Morgan shouted from the tower and Doc leaned back on the rod with a mighty jerk.

"He's running," Doc said. Line was ripping from the reel.

Doc tightened the drag and when the line stopped playing out, he began working the fish. The other fishermen brought in their lines and the mate stood by Doc's side watching and coaching.

"In the old days you'd have fought him from a chair with a much bigger rig," the mate said. "But hell, man, anybody can catch fish with big tackle like that. If you get this one to the boat, you'll have earned her. Looks like one hell of a fish by the way she's bent that rod."

Doc smiled and pulled back feeling the strain and then reeled in line, working the fish toward the surface. It was a powerful fish, not easily turned, and before long Doc felt pain in his back and upper arms and knew that the mate was right. If this fish came to the boat, it would only be after one hell of a fight.

"Breathe," the mate told him. "Breathe and get a rhythm working or she's going to wear you out."

"She?"

"Yeah, the big ones are always female."

"What's the record?"

"Local record was five hundred eighty-seven pounds, but who knows, yours might beat it."

Doc laughed and the Arabs began talking among themselves. After a short conversation one of them said in excellent English, "Doctor, if you get tired, I would be happy..."

Doc smiled, thanked him and declined the offer.

Suddenly the line went slack.

"What?" Doc asked the mate.

"She's coming up. Take in line as fast as you can and keep the rod tip down. If she beats you, she'll throw the hook."

Doc nodded and cranked the reel like a grinder on a world class racing boat. The fish broke water in an explosion of sunlight, spray and energy. The Arabs shouted their approval and cheered Doc on.

"What a horse," the mate said. "Bet she's over six hundred pounds. Concentrate man. Keep that line tight, but not too tight. Don't let her break off."

The magnificent fish climbed into the air, twisting and turning, throwing her head. She seemed to hang there indefinitely, glaring at the boat with softball-sized black eyes.

She crashed back into the water only to explode upward again, repeating her acrobatics to the amazement of the crew.

"Mr. Holiday," the Arab began again. He had moved close, too close and Doc wanted him out of the way. "I would be most grateful to help you bring in that fish..."

"That's a hell of a fish, Holiday. Think you can handle it?" Morgan yelled down from the tower.

"You going to offer to help me too, Jack?" Doc grinned.

"Nope, it's your fish, but I'll give you ten grand for it and put your name on a plaque under it on the clubhouse wall. How's that?"

"Twenty thousand," the Arab who had first offered to help countered. "And I'll save you the trouble of bringing it up. Twenty thousand if you give me the rod right now." He stepped forward and held out his hands for the rig.

"Now wait a damn minute, Faud. This is my boat; he works for me and that fish is going on the clubhouse wall." Morgan started down from the tower and the mate went to the stern controls, leaving Doc alone to contend with the fish, Faud and now an angry Jack Morgan.

The magnificent fish broke water for a third time, now much closer to the boat. Sunlight flashed from the rich blue-green luster of the monster's broad back and she hung in the air glaring directly at Doc. There was something in those cold black eyes that touched him. Something that communicated the answer to everyone's problem.

He braced himself against the rail, made certain the rod butt was secure in the gut bucket and then with his right hand, dropped the lock-back hunting knife from its inverted case on his belt. He snapped open the blade with one flick of his wrist and before any of them could move, he cut the line. The marlin crashed back into the water and was gone.

Jack Morgan stood in the middle of the deck dumbfounded. The veins in his neck were bulging. Faud laughed as if he had won—as if his only reason for wanting the fish had been to keep Morgan from getting it.

"Now boys," Doc said, "back in Bermuda, where marlin go one thousand five-hundred pounds, that little lady was barely a keeper. But since I caught her, it was my call to set her free. But I do thank you, Jack. That was one hell of a fight. And there's just one more thing: I don't think your job is for me, so Sheri and I will be moving out as soon as we can find another place."

"No! No, you won't," Morgan snapped and then caught his anger. He cooled and started again. "That won't be necessary. You cost me a fish, but I'm not mad enough to lose Sheri too. She's a valued employee, so you are my guest for as long as she still wants you around."

Doc glanced at the mate who was still at the stern controls. When Morgan climbed the ladder back to the tower, the mate looked up at Doc and nodded. A moment later Morgan called Doc to the tower.

"I have some information for you, Holiday. But after what you cost me down there, I don't know why I should still help you."

"It was only a fish, Jack. Hardly worth getting an ulcer over."

"Is that what you think? Let me tell you something, Holiday. When you deal with those guys, everything counts. Screw the fish...you cost me a lot of face down there and they won't let me forget it."

Doc nodded, but said nothing.

Morgan hesitated a moment as if still deciding whether to talk, but finally said, "The sub you're after isn't *Blackwolf*. It may have looked like Behrmann's boat, but it was Russian built and operated by the Iraqis. It got away with a couple of tons of gold and the Navy came up empty handed. They've called off the bottom search and are deploying a strike force to hunt her. Your boat, or rather the Bermuda government's boat, is still in the yards. They had to replace the starboard engine and the work will take at least another week. Lt. Berry is doing well. He's been spending his evenings with a young blonde ensign from supply."

"I'm impressed."

"And, I'm disappointed. You made a bad call, Holiday. You're chasing a white whale when you could be making a fortune with me. Just be careful, friend. There's no catch and release in this game." He turned his back and the conversation was over.

Blackwolf's digital clock displayed four zeros. Behrmann looked at his watch. He stretched and yawned as he got up, picked up his coffee mug and walked abruptly toward the forward hatch. "You have the boat," he said to Bill Roberts as he disappeared down the companionway. Roberts heard more debris hit the hull as the old man closed his stateroom door.

The rest of the crew gathered quickly in the control room. Roberts turned on the television monitors and they surveyed their precarious situation. They were resting on a ledge just inside the cavern entrance with large rocks jammed between the propeller blades and the protective cowlings. They could see large fissures in the cavern walls above them with massive stalactite-like formations ready to come crashing down at any minute.

"Think *Black Widow* could get our props cleared?" Geist asked Johnson.

"Not now. She's not responding to her activation codes. Probably knocked loose some wiring when we crashed.

"Any other ideas?" Geist tried again.

"We could dump the gold and try a buoyant ascent," Randy offered.

"Without the engines, we'd hit the walls for sure and that could set off one hell of a landslide," Roberts answered. "That big stuff looks awfully unstable."

"If we can't go up, then let's try to back off this ledge," Johnson said. "Add enough water ballast to get her sliding out backwards."

"Might work," Martin said, trying to sound more knowledgeable than his years allowed. "If we drop off the shelf, we could get neutral and drift with the current until dark. Then we can surface and clear the props. But how deep is it here just in case we have problems?"

"Over twenty thousand feet," his father answered.

"It's not that much of a risk as long as those control valves don't crap out again," Geist said. "I'd say check those valves and then give it a go." He looked at the others and they all agreed. Randy and Martin went to stand by the ballast control valves, Roberts went to the helm with Geist, and Johnson went to the ballast control panel. In order to raise the bow, Johnson blew the forward tanks and flooded the stern tanks. The bow rose, but the were still stuck.

"What now?" Geist asked Roberts.

"I'll try the bow thruster, maybe it will break us loose."

Roberts began working the bow from side to side with full power on the thruster. At first there was little movement, but then the soft bottom began to shift and clouds of sediment exploded from the bottom. Then the sub began to quiver. Roberts increased the arc of the bow's movement and then they felt her start to slide. She slammed into the cavern wall and sediment and soft rock fell from the overhead, setting off a massive slide.

"Here we go," Roberts shouted as the sub was caught in the momentum of the slide. She rolled violently on her side and slid stern first toward the end of the ledge at three hundred feet. The television monitors went dark as they were engulfed in a river of sediment and debris. They could hear the hull scraping against stone as they dropped deeper and deeper. Johnson tried to crawl back to the panel, but he'd been thrown across the compartment and lay pinned beneath the navigation table. Seeing Johnson's predicament, Geist half crawled and half slid down the deck to help him. The control room lights flickered and went out as did the monitors. Roberts was shouting to Johnson and Geist to dump the ballast, but could not hear his own voice over the grinding against the hull. Suddenly there was a loud explosion followed by a thundering of air rushing from the sub, and then she rolled completely over to starboard. She hung there upside down for a moment, dumping everything that wasn't nailed down, before righting herself with a painful groan. When the roll stopped she was resting on her starboard side. Everything was silent as the emergency lights came on. Behrmann had crawled to the helm and had the computer back on line.

"What happened?" Johnson moaned from beneath the navigation table.

The monitors came on and some of the lights, but there was nothing to see but black water. The digital Fathometer was scrolling numbers so fast they couldn't read them.

"We're off the ledge," Behrmann answered. His voice was cool as ice. "But we're sinking much too fast.... There's the problem...the starboard tanks are flooding," he said looking at a flow chart on the computer screen. "Blow those tanks dry again, find the valve that failed and isolate it. We need all the buoyancy we can get with our extra cargo."

As he watched the monitor, his fingers flew at the computer keyboard. He sat erect in his chair, lucid and in perfect composure. "It's for the boys," he said in answer to Roberts's unasked question. "I've decided it's not necessary for them to die for our failures." With that he pulled the joy stick back and eased on the power. The engine alarms sounded and the turbines shut down.

"Props still jammed," he said philosophically. "Still it was worth a try. The boys may not get another chance after all."

Roberts shook his head in amazement and then turned his full attention to the valves. The collision must have caused a solenoid to activate the ballast control valves. He went to the manual control panel with Johnson and began closing them. The first closed easily, but the next was more difficult and the third nearly impossible. Johnson gave him a hand and they were finally able to close it. They worked with their hands on the valve wheels, but their eyes were transfixed on the Fathometer's display. A minute passed, a second and then a third. The numbers still scrolled past too quickly to read.

"It's not working!" Johnson yelled. "The tanks aren't holding pressure." They left Geist at the helm and worked their way back to the engine compartment where Randy and Martin had found a ruptured air line on the main high pressure compressor.

"The big tank shifted when we rolled," Randy said. "The brackets weren't designed to take the weight upside down. Thank God it vented outside the hull or it would have blown our ears."

"What can we do?" Roberts asked.

"Jury rig some plumbing. Plug the dump valve. Is there any way to replace that line?" Martin said.

"We're dropping fast. Whatever we're going to do, we need to start now," Johnson said.

Martin had a battle lantern and was following the lines with the light. He looked and pointed at a length of stainless steel tubing which came from the main compressor line. "We could use that high pressure line to blow the tanks if we can tie it into the system," he said, pointing over his head. "We might have the right size fittings in the dive locker. That air line's small...it will take a while, but I think it's our best chance."

"Good plan," Johnson said and sent Randy running for the tools and Roberts to get the parts they would need. It didn't take long to complete the refitting work, but when they turned on the air nothing happened.

"Look the flywheel shaft is bent! Must have happened when the tank shifted," Johnson said. "We don't have enough air pressure to blow the tank. What the hell do we do now?"

"Use the scuba compressor," Martin answered.

At the helm, Geist watched the Fathometer's numbers scroll quickly past: six thousand six hundred feet, then six thousand nine hundred, then seven thousand.

Behrmann returned to the control room. The old man was disoriented and talking to himself or to the boat.

"How deep did you design this hull for?" Geist shouted at Behrmann to get his attention. The display zipped past seven thousand five hundred feet.

Behrmann read it with academic indifference. "The hull will take the pressure, that's not the problem."

Johnson and Geist returned to the control room.

"The compressor's working," Roberts said hopefully. "As long as we don't drop deeper than the pressure of scuba tanks, we should be alright."

"How deep is that?" Geist asked.

"Three thousand psi or about six thousand feet."

"Too late. We're almost at eight thousand now." Geist shook his head.

Behrmann looked up. "The scuba compressor will deliver five thousand psi. Reset the unloader. There is still time," he said.

"You're right, we'll try it," Roberts nodded and hurried aft to the engine compartment to tell his sons.

"Wait a minute," Johnson said. "Where are we going to get the air for the compressor to compress? Won't we be creating a vacuum in here?"

"No, we have plenty of pressure in the port tanks and if we need more we can use the oxygen the perhydrol generators create. That's no problem," Behrmann explained. "The problem is that we are so heavy and have no way to dump the gold. If we drop below ten thousand feet we won't have enough air pressure to blow our water ballast. We will just drift. Nothing more we can do." It was the first civil thing he'd said to Johnson since the beginning of the cruise.

"Your sub and its engines are brilliant, Doctor," Johnson answered, his voice soft and calm. "This will work. It just has to."

The old man looked away and said nothing.

"How deep are we now?" Johnson asked.

"Eight thousand one hundred feet." Beherman replied.

"Close," Johnson said almost under his breath. "It's going to be very close. "

They watched the Fathometer in silence. They were all sweating and the hull continued to creak and groan as the boat sank deeper. Johnson took the helm and monitored the gauges on the starboard buoyancy tanks. Little by little they were displacing the water. But they were still to heavy.

Johnson began timing their descent on his digital watch. "I think we're slowing down a little." He began counting aloud, timing the intervals between the Fathometer's slowly changing numbers.

"Yes, but we're still dropping," Geist said.

The display changed from eight thousand four hundred to eight thousand five hundred fifty. "Two minutes, forty-one seconds," Johnson called out. eight thousand seven hundred fifty became eight thousand nine hundred feet. "Three minutes, seventeen seconds."

No one else spoke.

From eight thousand nine hundred feet to nine thousand one hundred fifty took four minutes, twenty two seconds.

"Nine thousand feet," Behrmann said. "Two miles down in a hull made from recycled milk jugs. Just imagine." Thirty minutes passed and they continued to drop.

At nine thousand six hundred feet the sub rolled vertical. Back in normal trim she seemed to be fighting for her life. At nine thousand seven hundred feet they seemed to hang.

Behrmann looked old and very tired. He stumbled as he stepped away from the control console and Roberts moved to catch him. He shook off Roberts's hand and said quietly, "You have the boat. There's nothing more...." His voice trailed off and he left the control room.

The display remained unchanged. Johnson looked up from his watch and said, "Forty-five seconds."

"We're drifting...we're nearly two miles deep. We're trapped and we're drifting," Roberts said, his voice breaking as he wiped a tear from his eye.

They all stared at the digital display in silence.

One minute passed and then another.

Ten thousand one hundred feet.

"My God, we're still sinking. We're done for," Roberts said looking ghostly white and holding his stomach. The hull groaned again and the desolate crew stared at each other and then looked back at the Fathometer and waited.

"Ten thousand fifty feet," Geist exhaled deeply, "No, we're on our way back up."

CHAPTER 11

Doc had been putting together notes on the 'accident' and asked Sheri about the warning she had been given at the Lone Star. "So, what do you know about this John Bentley?"

"He's six one or so, late thirties, dark hair, good looking beard, attractive, great buns. The usual C.S.I."

"What?"

"Sorry, that's Cayman Scuba Idol," she teased.

"What else? Where's he from?"

"He was with someone else, but he bought me dinner. Oh, he's from the States. Maybe Florida."

"Dinner?"

"It was a nice touch. He didn't stay. A redhead from Texas had him on a short leash. It was just a lavish romantic gesture, a totally spontaneous act of affection."

"Okay, I give up. What's the message here? Have I been remiss in lavish romantic gestures? It's only been..." He looked at the Rolex. "Four hours. Is it time for another spontaneous act of affection?"

"No, and it's not just sex I'm talking about. It's romance too. Anyway, I'm hungry. If you're so interested in Bentley, hurry up. He's probably there, waiting for us now. Don't forget your notebook, grandpa."

"That's doctor grandpa, to you, Martha. And if you hit me with another grandpa jab, I'm going to turn you over my knee."

"I'll look forward to that the minute we get home. Now come on, we're goin' to be late."

The Lone Star was crowded with locals in tee shirts and shorts, and tourists in sunburns and exhaustion. Parents with tired children waited at the door for tables. Doc and Sheri went past them to the long bar. John Bentley was at the rail surrounded by younger instructors and divemasters. Most of the island's dive operations were represented. It was obvious Bentley was popular with this crowd and was looked upon as an old Cayman hand and someone you could trust.

He waved to Sheri and pulled them into his crowd. Sheri got a hug, Doc an introduction. "I'm usually called JB, Doc. But I answer to most anything," he said, giving him a solid handshake followed by a matched set of iced beer bottles.

"I'm sure glad you're alright, girl," Bentley said. "I want to hear all about it. But wait 'till we move to the dining room. Can't hear a damn thing in here. I got us a quiet, intimate table," he winked at Sheri.

"Where's the redhead? You remember, the one with the legs all the way up to those tight little white shorts?"

"Dallas, thank God. That was so good it made me think twice about coming up for air. If you don't, you know you're going to die, but if you do, you just might miss your only chance to get to heaven."

Sheri choked on her beer. Drinking, laughing and breathing were more than she could handle. The moment was saved only by the waiter announcing their table was ready.

Their booth was in the far corner of the restaurant. Bentley sat where he could watch the room, Doc and Sheri were hidden from view. The room was loud but tolerable—loud enough there was no danger of their conversation being overheard.

"Doc, I have you both at a bit of a disadvantage," Bentley began when the waiter had left with their order. "And, I want to get us started off on an even keel." His hands were folded down on the table and when he opened them a small leather wallet remained. Doc picked it up, put on his half-frames and opened it. The ID and badge identified John James Bentley as a senior agent with the United States Customs Service. Doc closed the wallet and slid it back across the table and waited.

"Ian Cord and I worked together when I was stationed in

Bermuda. He told me what happened to you in Bermuda and asked me to look after you here. I have to apologize for not doing such a great job so far, but I promise not to let you out of my sight again. He also told me to tell you you're getting a bill for the repairs on your boat. Afraid I can't help you there," Bentley laughed. "One other thing, I'm strictly undercover, so please...." He looked at them both for affirmation.

"No problem," Doc answered.

Sheri was wide eyed. "You mean all your years of living large in the islands you..."

"Got the government to pay for. Not bad for a country boy, right?" He smiled a charmingly mischievous smile. "Now let's start with your friend Jack Morgan, alias, Black Jack Morgan III, perhaps the last of the great pirates in these latitudes. Morgan was a colonel in army intelligence, probably assigned to CIA Special Ops. Here's a Cayman history trivia question, Sheri, for the next round of beer: who was the 'Knight of the double-cross?'"

"Easy. Sir Henry Morgan, governor of Jamaica."

"And do you remember why?"

"Because after he got into power, he turned on his old shipmates and supposedly cheated them out of their share of the take after the infamous Panama raid. I read Michener, now pay up."

"Smart girl, and such a great bod too. Not from Texas by any chance?"

"Just order the beer," she laughed.

"When Morgan came down here ten years ago, his cover story was that he was a bad boy banker from the Midwest who cleaned out a couple of savings and loans and now had money to burn. In those days folks down here didn't ask where your money came from as long as you had lots of it. But it was my job to find out, so I started an investigation. And boy, did I get a surprise. Turns out Morgan was really connected in Washington. Perhaps all the way to Pennsylvania Avenue—at least until the last election. And he was strictly hands off...didn't exist as far as my local office is concerned. But you know how it goes, the higher the fence the more you want to know what's on the other side, so for the next few years we watched him while his bag men came and went and his little nest egg got bigger and bigger.

"Then things here changed. The locals got tired of the scum that were bringing in all the dirty money and decided to start cleaning house. In fact now they are so touchy about it they didn't even want *The Firm* filmed here. I heard they even got the script changed to take out a scene where a Caymanian official takes a bribe...now that's power! Anyway, the change in attitude towards Morgan and his kind threw him a curve. But like the Chinese say, crisis and opportunity are one and the same. So he bought that land on Seven Mile Beach, put up the condo and opened his own bank in the attic. We heard he may even have gotten the agency to foot the bill. And, speaking of spooks, you wouldn't believe the surveillance system that place has got. Sound and video in living hot pink."

"Oh no, you mean...?" she said.

"That's exactly what I mean. You're never alone at Black Jack Morgan's house."

"Thanks for the warning," Doc said. "Go on."

"There's a lot more going on there than just a nice vacation spot for overworked government employees. Now that he's in the banking business, Morgan has quite an assortment of interesting international guests—on both sides of the fence. We've gotten wind of arms deals, money laundering, influence peddling, you name it. But so far, we've got nothing tangible enough to take to court. He even has his own communications satellite. Now, what do you make of that?"

"Is there a purpose to what he's doing, like the money Ollie North raised for the so called freedom fighters?" Doc asked.

"Tough question, Doc. We know he hates the current administration, but that's not a crime. Hell, I don't much care for those clowns myself. From what we've seen so far, he's just a greedy bastard making a ton of money any way he can, and so far no one's called his hand."

"But it smells," Doc said.

"Exactly. All my instincts tell me he's as dirty as they come. But so far, we haven't been able to nail him. And big players cause big problems, which I don't need. So, we're not sticking our necks out even a little bit until I'm sure we've got him cold. Perhaps discretion really is the better part of valor, at least until the deck is stacked in our favor for a change."

"What's the story on the Arabs?" Doc asked.

"I've only got bits and pieces on that, but here's another interesting theory about Jack. Several years ago, before the Gulf War, Jack spent time in Iraq. And, as we know, Iraq bought a lot of surplus U.S. military hardware. Now, in those days, Saddam was our pal. Remember the Iranian hostages and the Ayatollah? Our revenge was selling Saddam the arms for the eight years of fighting between Iran and Iraq which followed, and we didn't much like Kuwait in those days either, because the the Kuwaitis kept lowering oil prices, which hurt our oil industry. There were rumors, remember, that the reason Saddam destroyed the Kuwaiti oil fields and refineries was that he had assurances from us that we wouldn't interfere.

"Now my question is, what if he had more than just assurances? What if someone, someone like Jack, encouraged that attack to solve our problem with Kuwait and then double crossed Saddam?"

"That would certainly answer the question I've had about why Saddam has such an attitude toward us, wouldn't it?" Doc said.

"Yep, and eliminating two major competitors certainly didn't hurt our oil interests. Fascinating theory, isn't it? Too bad we can't prove any of it."

"That sure sounds like our friends at 'Christians in Action' looking out for our best interests," Doc said. "You got anything that ties him to the agency?"

"Doc, if it walks like a duck and quacks like a duck.... Look, in hearings a couple years ago the CIA admitted building a three hundred and twenty million-dollar office building in Crystal City—right in the heart of D.C.—and no one discovered it for six years. Some of the military are pretty upset about closing the bases. A lot of guys lost their rice bowls. And what about the beltway bandits? You think for a minute the military support contractors are going to give up their spot at the hogtrough without a fight?"

"What are you saying?"

Bentley leaned forward and lowered his voice. "I've been thinking about this. That Gulf War was the best thing that could have happened to the military. A great victory, just at the right moment. If Bush had been re-elected, it would have been all the justification the administration needed for a massive build up of the military. However, when the next three elections didn't go their way, they needed an action plan. And, just like the agency putting up that office building, they operate on their own agenda with apparently all the money they need even in spite of the cuts. So what if they started using that money to go political, maybe with someone like Morgan helping them? How much clout could you buy for three hundred million, or for two or three billion? Enough to swing a presidential election? Maybe. Jack's got the money and Jack's got the friends. In short order, we could be sharing the fate of most third world countries—puppets and pawns of an all powerful military."

"And they could easily build a condo on Seven Mile Beach or a billion dollar submarine that Congress never heard about," Sheri said and the men nodded agreement.

"There was a woman..." Sheri began.

"Stephanie Smith, the accountant from Atlanta," JB answered. "She was mine and that was my fault. I got too curious. It was a mistake. A year and a half ago an old friend from our office in D.C. showed up here unannounced. He was checking up on Morgan for some interested party in Congress. He said there were concerns in Washington about what Morgan was up to. Apparently, a big power play was in the works and my friend wasn't on Morgan's team. I agreed to help and we started talking about what we might do to get the goods on old Black Jack. It didn't take us too long to come up with a plan. About the time he put our plan into action, my friend was killed in a plane crash...there were questions, serious questions about the accident. I decided to go ahead with my part of the plan, which was to put someone inside the condo, and we moved Stephanie into Jack's life.

"Unfortunately, Jack was too slick for her. He drugged her and gave her to his friends in the hot tub room. They had quite a party and the video turned out real well. That was that. You know the rest. Now she's gone. Not a trace. Don't doubt for a minute that Black Jack plays hard ball."

"Oh, Stephanie...." Sheri said. "I was afraid, but I wanted to believe she was...well, you know."

"Yeah, we'd all like to believe that."

"And what about Sheri's so-called accident?" Doc asked.

"Locals who were pissed about what Jack's doing to the reef. That's all. But it's damn good you made that swim, Doc."

"I want a look at that boat. Any problem?" Doc asked.

"Tomorrow night quick enough? One other thing, don't change your behavior at the condo. They'll pick it up fast."

"But the cameras..." Sheri said.

"Just look on the bright side, princess—royalties, distribution rights, major film offers."

"Lovely," she said with disgusted resignation.

"That's the spirit. Just pretend you're working for the government, where the shitty things we're forced to do to others is what makes it all worthwhile."

Doc laughed a grim laugh appropriate to Bentley's grim humor. "Back up a minute to what you said about locals and the reef."

"Right. Morgan bought up most of the buildable land in Great Bay. He's building ten million dollar villas on canals he has to dredge. The run off is screwing up the water quality on Seven Mile Beach and The North Wall. The watersports association got together and hired a biological research team to prove it. Morgan tried to buy the biologists off, but when that didn't work he began screwing up their research."

"By switching the collecting bottles so that there wouldn't be anything in the bottles they retrieved for analysis?"

"Right. They were sure he was doing it, but they hadn't caught him in the act until yesterday. That's when things got out of hand."

"That lying scumbag told me those were his research stations and that he was collecting data to defend himself against a bunch of greedy politicians. What a story! I've never met anyone like him. Everything he does is a lie," she said. "We've got to do something." She turned to look at Doc for confirmation. He was staring at the cable cuts on his hands, and opening and closing his right fist.

"I wonder if Morgan could have anything to do with *Blackwolf*?" Doc said. "On his boat today Morgan mentioned the sub and Behrmann. Told me I'm sniffing down the wrong rabbit hole, but I'm sure he was lying. Morgan and my old buddy Colonel Andrews are two of a kind, and this is exactly the kind of operation that snake Andrews would be involved in. It's a long shot, but I wonder..."

"*Blackwolf*? What's that?"

"A sub that the Navy had a German scientist build. The inventor worked out the onboard manufacture of hydrogen peroxide fuel from sea water. Brilliant, really...the only exhaust is breathable oxygen. She disappeared during her sea trials. The inventor stole her and hid her in Bermuda. That's were Sheri and I got involved. The Navy says the sub was destroyed in Bermuda eight months ago, but I saw her a week ago off Charleston. And, we think she might be hiding somewhere in these islands."

"And you think Morgan might be involved?"

"It's a long shot, but it sure wouldn't surprise me. Not with everything else you think he's involved in."

"I know how we might find out," Bentley said. "When I sent Stephanie undercover, we were going to try to get a look at Morgan's bank book and find out what he uses that satellite for. Satellites talk to submarines. Who knows? We might still pull it off. You're already on the inside. Want to play?"

"Won't be easy. He sure as hell doesn't trust me," Doc answered thoughtfully.

"The best ones never are," Bentley said and winked at Sheri.

"Even the redhead?" Sheri asked.

"Easy? She damn near killed me. And I can't wait for her to do it again."

"On the subject of beautiful women," Sheri said, "what's the story on Ms. Kee? You got anything on her?"

"Good question. I'll see what we can come up with. You hear anything interesting?"

"Stephanie said there was a meeting of scientists. She called them 'lab rats,' and she said Ms. Kee knew them."

"Interesting."

"There are some things we'll need," Doc said, still absorbed in more serious contemplation.

"Name 'em." Bentley answered. His eyes were bright with boyish excitement, or perhaps it was fiendish glee tainted with a little righteous indignation. Doc caught the look and grinned. Life was about to take a nasty turn for Colonel Black Jack Morgan, and obviously Cayman scuba idol John Bentley intended to enjoy every minute of it.

CHAPTER 12

Roberts was still dazed by their close brush with death and he stammered as he tried to speak. "At, at, at this rate it will take us hours to ascend."

"I don't think so," Geist corrected. He was standing at the navigation station with Johnson. "We'll gain momentum, just like we did during the dive. And if we can't get those ballast control valves working, we'll blast to the surface out of control. If we come up under the ledge, we're in big trouble."

"You got it," Johnson said. "Take a look at the sonar."

As Geist had predicted, they were coming up directly under the long undercut side of the mountain, created when the sea level was nearly a hundred feet shallower than at present. Roberts scrambled to the helm seat and tried the bow thruster. Nothing.

"Try to reverse it," Johnson shouted.

Still nothing. Only a clunk as the prop hit the rocks lodged in its fairing.

"*Black Widow,*" Roberts shouted back. "Try her again."

Johnson climbed to the console, turned on the power and waited. Nothing. Then he scratched his head and turned to check the junction boxes. *Blackwolf* rolled violently as she bounced off the mountainside. The crew were again hurled across the compartment, falling over control stations and landing hard. The chart table, however, remained in place, tied to a stanchion with Johnson's belt. Johnson quickly rebounded to his feet and returned to *Black Widow*'s control monitors. He wiggled cords and connectors and suddenly his monitors powered up. Through the ROV's cameras he could see a large coral head, half the size of a pick-up truck, wedged into the bow thruster tunnel.

"That must weigh a ton," he whistled.

"Can you do something?" Roberts asked.

The sub hit the mountain face again, grinding against the rock overhangs and gouging the soft sonar-absorbing plastic skin covering the pressure hull. Inside the sub they could hear the soft plastic being skinned away. Then she rolled clear and began gaining momentum. Her stern rose higher and the Fathometer began rapidly scrolling the numbers. Behrmann appeared in the hatchway looking confused and disoriented. He had the Luger in his belt. Martin was just behind him.

Johnson was shouting verbal commands at the monitor, trying desperately to bring the huge robot to life, but she refused to respond.

"Maybe I can do it manually," he said as he ran to his bunk and came back pulling on the gloves he had worn during the fight with *Benthic Explorer*'s ROV, *Argo.* They were bulky, each sprouting a hundred plus tiny telemetry wires.

"Marty, get on my computer. There's a menu called self-abuse. Open it and then enter what I tell you. Somebody help me with these. I'm all thumbs."

Johnson rattled off one command sequence after another and at the same time shouted directions to Randy and Geist who switched leads on his circuit boards. On the sub's main monitors they could see that they were dangerously close to colliding with the wall again.

"Plug the red leads into that one," Johnson shouted, glancing over his shoulder at the monitor and pointing to the bottom row of cable plugs.

"You've got it!" Martin shouted back. In the monitor he could see *Black Widow*'s right front leg mimic Johnson's action.

Johnson used the mechanical arms to release the spider's locking pins and secure a stainless steel tether. Then operating the winch in the spider's torso with one claw and grasping the sub's hatch cover in the other, he began lowering the ROV toward the jammed bow thruster.

Suddenly Johnson screamed in pain as sparks arched across the back of the gloves. He lost his concentration and the spider dropped from the deck.

"Sponge for me!" he screamed. "My damn sweat's shorting the circuits."

Randy pulled off his shirt and dropped to his knees beside Johnson, sponging his brow and arms. Johnson found the winch controls again and even though he was still being burned by the electrical shorts, he managed to hold on while the winch reeled the ROV back to the bow.

"Range?" he shouted.

"One hundred yards, maybe less," Roberts shouted back.

"Can you do it?" Geist asked.

"Damned if I know. You want to try?" Johnson answered without looking up from his monitor.

"There, there. Got you, you son-of-a-bitch," Johnson shouted as he clutched the coral head. He grasped it with both claws and held on like a scared cat.

"There will be no profanity in my control room," Behrmann thundered. "That man is on report. Get him out of my sight!"

"Hans, shut the hell up!" Roberts snapped.

The old man drew the gun and struck Roberts across the back of the head. As Roberts dropped, Geist and Randy jumped the captain. The Luger fired before Geist could twist it from the old man's grasp and the bullet shattered the stern camera's monitor. Johnson dropped to protect himself from the flying glass and tried to roll clear. When he did, *Black Widow* mimicked his actions and the coral head fell clear of the bow thruster's shroud.

"Use the thruster! Get us away from the damn wall! NOW!" Johnson shouted.

Martin ran to the controls, grabbed the joy stick and brought the thruster to full power. The sub twisted violently but kept rising toward the ledge. Johnson checked the monitors again. Just beneath *Black Widow* he could see a large rock outcropping. He released the winch's spool and let the ROV free-fall toward the rock below. He held his breath and jammed on the brakes just before impact. Then he let the ROV drop and with the steel claws, dug into the rock bottom. He locked the winch and gritted his teeth. The steel umbilical stretched taut, tighter than the E string on a good guitar, but it held and in a final violent lurch, the sub was saved from crashing into the ledge above.

Johnson lay on the deck, glaring wide eyed at his monitor. The rock he was holding was crumbling. Through the tiny cameras in the palms of the claws he could see fracture lines beginning.

"Somebody better do something. We're not out of the woods yet."

Geist still had Behrmann pinned against the deck, and Roberts was on his hands and knees, blood trickling from his scalp wound. Randy was down as well, covered with glass from the blown monitor.

"The bow thruster's not enough. We need the engines," Behrmann said calmly.

"No shit. What else did you learn in school today?" Johnson snapped and immediately regretted it. Behrmann gave him a look that had a slow, painful death attached.

"How deep are we?" Martin asked, pulling himself up the navigation table to get to his feet.

The Fathometer showed 306 feet.

"We could lock out and try to clear the props. That's probably our best shot."

"What happens if we lose our anchor?" Roberts asked. He was still down.

"We'll at least have a chance. We could surface and try to swim it," Randy said hopefully.

"Not if you're down more than a couple minutes. The decompression..."

"Listen," Johnson cut him off, "I can't hold us here much longer. Martin's right. It's slim, but that's all we've got and that's not going to last long. Do something and do it now, or we're dead meat."

"He's right," Martin said. "Let's go, Randy."

"Wait, we haven't checked the recirculators. It will take an hour..." Roberts called after them. But he was too late. The boys were headed to the diving locker on a dead run. Roberts staggered to his feet and went after them.

Martin was pulling on a wet suit and Randy was reading the tables for setting up the recirculators. In two minutes he adjusted the unit's onboard computers to control the oxygen and helium partial pressures they would need, checked the pressure gauges, soda-sorb canisters, and computer canister seal, then replaced the top shroud and locked it down by twisting the cam lock's handles.

"That's it. Put the tools in the lock and let's get wet."

His father helped him into the lock-out chamber, closed the inner hatch and opened the valves. Roberts watched through the small acrylic port as water rushed in, and returned the okay signal Martin gave before opening the top hatch and climbing up to the sub's deck.

The water was clear and warm. There was enough light to see several hundred feet, but what he saw was of little comfort. The sub's port fins and rudder had been mangled. And the cowling, designed to protect the propeller, was now smashed against it. Randy climbed out of the hatch, also surveyed the damage and looked at Martin who shook his head.

In the distance a pair of spotted eagle rays passed and Martin was momentarily distracted by their beauty. Randy shook him and pointed to the damage. Martin nodded, picked up the tool bag's strap handle and together they dragged it to the stern. Randy paused to clear his mask, checked the computer display on his wrist and then opened the bag. He removed a wrecking bar and a large stillson wrench and set to work trying to pry away the fairing. It was hopeless. He pointed toward the surface and then opened his hands toward his brother. There was still time. They could decompress with the oxygen in the closed circuit recirculators and swim to the beach. They were good swimmers and he was sure they could make it.

Martin shook his head angrily. He wanted no part of what Randy was thinking. He left his brother and swam back to the lock. He had an idea of his own. There was an intercom in the lock for use during decompression. Martin climbed in, blew down the water, and called to his father.

"We need a burning bar. We've got to cut away the fairings." As he spoke he felt the sub jerk on its anchor. Johnson was losing his grip.

Randy waited outside the lock, wondering what was going on. The long minutes passed and he began to worry. It felt like an eternity and twice more he felt the boat lurch as Johnson struggled to hold them from crashing into the rock above. Then the hatch opened and Martin re-emerged. Martin closed the hatch, waited and then opened it again. This time he passed up a pair of heavy jumper cables from the engine room and a half dozen pieces of heavy pipe filled with welding rods and wrapped in duct tape. He signaled Randy to take them to the stern. Martin swam quickly to the bow and returned with the hose they used to fill the inflatables. He found the fitting he was looking for, connected the hose and signaled to his brother for one of the four-foot pieces of pipe. After cutting the fitting off the end of the hose, he stuck it on the end of the pipe and handed it to his bewildered brother and smiled an exaggerated, irritating smile. Next he connected one end of the jumper cable to another deck fitting and the other end to the length of pipe. Then from the bag he produced a pencil detonator connected to a short length of fuse and Randy's favorite sunglasses. He gave his brother that irritating smile again, handed him the detonator, held the sunglasses up and proceeded to break off the arms. Randy grabbed for him and missed. Martin waved the glasses, removed his dive mask, did a quick 360 and when he was again facing his brother, he was wearing the broken glasses inside his mask.

Now Randy was getting the picture. Martin pointed toward the Monel shaft of the starboard propeller and gestured for Randy to pound on it three times with the stillson. Randy handed over the pipe and hose and went for the wrench. He slammed the shaft three times and the signal was returned. The air hose went rigid and bubbles blasted out the end of the pipe. Martin had his hands full just trying to keep control of it. Randy knew what to do next. He pulled the ring on the detonator, laid it on the deck and backed away. Fifteen seconds later the fuse ignited and Marty pointed the blast of bubbles toward it. The oxygen ignited with a deafening blast and now the end of the pipe was burning white hot and spewing sparks and fire like a mini volcano.

Martin made his first pass at the crushed fairing and the high density plastic melted away in globs. He worked until the pipe had consumed most of its own length and was too hot to hold. He nodded to Randy who pounded on the shaft again and the fire went out. Martin quickly replaced the pipe and gave Randy a second detonator. He examined his work while he waited for it to fire. This rod should do it; the prop was nearly cleared. The fuse lit, Randy pounded on the shaft and they were back in business. Hanging onto the rod was like trying to hold down a two and a half-inch fire hose single handed. He wore gloves, but slag and sparks burned through his wet suit. Still he refused to allow his concentration to be broken, even when the rock crumbled between *Black Widow*'s mechanical claws and the sub started rapidly rising.

Randy felt it and then looked up. He grabbed Martin's arm and pulled him clear of the deck. The burning bar was jerked from Martin's hands and whipped through the water like a fire-headed snake. They watched in terror as the sub rose past them toward the ledge. Then they heard the whine of the engines and a horrible grinding as the propeller tore through the remains of the cowling. They had saved the sub. *Blackwolf* leveled and eased away from the wall stern first. They could see *Black Widow* still hanging from the cable start to climb back to her nest. With both engines and the bow thruster working, they might get home after all.

Randy checked his wrist computer and began the ascent to their first decompression level. It would take a while, but the water was warm and clear. He wondered if he and his brother might be better off risking the bends and the swim to the ironshore beach, rather than return to the insanity of their grandfather's plastic submarine.

CHAPTER 13

Jack Morgan cleared his throat and clenched his teeth in anger. He pushed the thickly tufted green leather chair back from the boardroom table, got up, and adjusted the air conditioning for the third time in an hour. The room was already freezing, but the air was rank with cigarette smoke. The damned Kuwaitis smoked like chimneys and he wondered if he would ever get the smell out of his favorite Armani jacket. He swore at himself for having worn it in the first place.

Faud was the most dangerous one. The wiry Arab refused to speak English in these meetings as though it was beneath him. However, on the boat he had demonstrated a comfortable mastery of the language. His file said he'd been a brilliant political science student at Cambridge. Now he directed his constituents with nods and glances from those coal black eyes and they understood. And now the others following Faud's lead were circling like a pack of wolves, growling and snarling like they'd done for the last two years.

"You cannot ignore us any longer," Hassid, the balding diplomat, was saying. His fingers flashed diamonds and gold, and he reminded Morgan of a New York shoe salesman—too smooth, too slick, too oily.

Faud's eyes flashed and Hassid slammed the table with his palm to get Morgan's attention. Jack looked and forced a patient, paternal smile. He had listened to their anger and fear until he was bored with it. But listening first was part of the game. Let them rant and rave and get their nickel's worth. Morgan's turn was coming. The situation was stable. Saddam had played right into his hands and now it was time to collect.

"My friends," Morgan began. He was cool and unruffled—Maverick couldn't have done a better job playing this hand. "We promised you we would put an end to the madman and we will. We promised that your borders would remain safe and they are. But surely you didn't think that we would attack without provocation, that our government could rain down the terrible fire of vengeance without just cause? Until now we have been held back by our need to have the support of the United Nations and in order to convince them..." He paused to make eye contact with Faud. Cold black eyes stared directly back. Good, it was working.

"In order to convince the United Nations of the righteousness and necessity of our cause, we had to wait as patiently as a cobra for our simpleminded enemy to drop his guard so that we might strike."

Then Faud stood and glared directly at Morgan. For the first time in all Morgan's dealings with him, Faud spoke in perfect British. "You play a dangerous game, Mr. Morgan, to starve Iraq with sanctions and use us as the bait in your trap. However, that is not my concern. You made a deal on behalf of your government. You have been well paid and we expect you to deliver. And to do so promptly. What happens with the United Nations, or your president or Mickey Mouse is of no concern to me. Keep your bargain. Do you understand?"

"The waiting is over, our plan is brilliant, and I promise the revenge you seek will shortly be within your grasp. As to using you as bait? No Iraqi troops crossed your borders and the madman has once again shown the world he is worthy of extinction. I am keeping my bargain. Our ships and planes were there and our bombing missions were very successful—in spite of the temporary political inconvenience of our current administration. I am keeping our bargain, and the contract will be carried out to the letter."

Faud nodded. "Our borders were not crossed, that much I will concede. But you have not fulfilled your contract. And I must tell you that if you do not, there will be consequences.

We are here to learn when and how you intend to accomplish your mission, because every day that passes in which the rape of our women, the deaths of our brothers and the destruction of our holy land goes unavenged brings us more shame. And so, the time has come for you to feel the anger of our discontent."

Blackwolf cruised the dark shallows while Martin and Randy did their best to repair the damaged rudders and diving fins. The eastern horizon was changing from gray to soft pink when they closed the hatch, slipped quickly out of their dive gear and into the chamber to complete the rest of their long decompression. Johnson brought *Black Widow* back to her docking pad and secured her in place. After Geist and Roberts sedated Behrmann and restrained him in his bunk, they were ready to attempt the tunnel. Roberts was at the helm with the rest of the crew tensely gathered in the control room.

The pounding they'd taken in the rock slide had destroyed three of the four external light banks and half the cameras. Navigating the entrance tunnel was going to be like threading a needle by braille. Roberts found the laser track and after two aborted attempts, was able to hold course against the current. At the moment they needed to raise the bow Martin and Randy flooded the diving locker, just forward of the engine room, and using countering engine torque to compensate for the mangled rudder, they got the attack angle necessary to ascend in the narrow passage.

It was an exhausted and bedraggled crew that crawled from the main hatch that morning. Petra Roberts went immediately below to care for her father, still sedated and restrained. Colonel Andrews listened with amazement to the story of the voyage and there was hardy laughter and rowdy backslapping when they opened the cargo holds to examine their hard won booty. Andrews and the Roberts boys lifted double handfuls of the gold coins and let them stream through their fingers. Johnson picked up a single coin, examined it briefly, replaced it and started to work assessing the ROV's damage. Then Colonel Andrews returned from the schooner with a case of beer. Toasts were made and oaths were sworn and no work was done until the beer was gone.

Karen and Jason kept out of sight, watching from behind the curtains as usual, trying to guess what was happening as the crewmen came and went from the cave past the bungalow to the dinghy in the cove. The homecoming celebration was brief. The beer and exhaustion of the trip soon took their toll and by mid-day Geist was the only crew member still on his feet. Jason watched him leave the cavern with Colonel Andrews and in spite of Karen's protests, slipped from their room to follow them.

"What about the old man?" Andrews began when he and Geist were well clear of the cave.

"Behrmann's not just a loose cannon, he's a one man Spanish armada," Geist answered. "He tried to destroy the sub and take all of us with him, then thirty seconds later everything is peachy keen. More than once, I thought he was completely gone—absolutely nuts and that he was going to kill us all—and then in the rock slide, there he was at the helm, cool as a cucumber, normal as hell. Twenty minutes later he was a raving lunatic again, probably didn't know his own name."

"So what now?"

"Haven't called in yet. But my thinking is, it's time to tidy up and move on. That sub's a mechanical disaster. We lost buoyancy control. Bad valves. Damn lucky we made it back. Johnson said they were cheap replacements for what should have been used. Just like something he would do. Can't go to the moon unless you're using the lowest bidder and doing it half-assed. And we sure as hell can't take her into Philadelphia Naval Shipyard or back to Groton for repair. My recommendation is that we load the gold, unload the liabilities, and get the hell out of Dodge."

"When are you going to call?"

"Tonight's satellite pass is about 2200 hours. It's a wonder that works. He must not have had to pay the bills while it was being built."

"Didn't you know? We stole it from the Russians. They think it lost power. We just gave it a new signature and changed it's orbit. Damn fine piece of work."

Jason held his breath in the cover of the lush ferns as Geist and Colonel Andrews passed. When they moved down the path to the cove where the schooner was anchored, he slipped quietly behind them and watched Geist row the inflatable across the lagoon and come alongside the schooner which was draped in camo net close hauled into the trees along the stream bank.

Jason stuck a short branch upright in the sand and marked the outline of its shadow. When the tip of the shadow had grown longer and had moved two inches in its clockwise arc, he moved quietly along the trail until he was certain Andrews could not see him and then slipped into the water.

"It must have been Jason," Andrews fumed. "He's the only one we didn't have working in the cave. The girl couldn't have done it. Not in her condition."

"I must be getting old," Geist said. "Hell, I didn't hear a thing. He got the guns and the radio right out from under my nose and I didn't hear a damn thing. Now that's scary."

"You are lucky he didn't take your scalp while he was at it. Now we've got to get those weapons back. That's what's scary."

"Excuse me, Colonel, sir. Were you asking me to go unarmed, chasing a demented boy child who's got enough firepower to re-write history at the Little Big Horn? I'll pass on that; thanks a hell of a lot."

"For once you might be right. Maybe we should just take the gold and get the hell out of here. If Jason's gotten any of his memory back, he probably doesn't like us very much. While we're loading the gold, why don't you have a talk with the girl? You might get lucky."

"I might get my ass shot off is more like it. What do you want me to tell her, 'Honey, please bring back our guns so we can wipe out the lunatics on this island including your halfwit boyfriend?' Come on."

"You didn't make admiral thinking like that. Put all those years of experience and the millions our taxpayers spent training you to work and do what you do best."

"What's that?"

"Make up some bullshit and subvert the innocents. How did we ever get into this mess?" Andrews said shaking his head.

"You sold the boss on the idea of building that sub and then helped the old man steal her, that's how," Geist laughed.

"And somewhere along the way you even sold me. We were going to get rich selling them to the Israelis and Saudis, remember? Can't let the Germans and Russians have the whole market to themselves."

"Yeah, I remember," Andrews chuckled. "But that was before Herr Behrmann got his peroxide plant to work. That screwed the whole deal."

"Who could have figured that one? The old kraut really did it, and instead of winning the Nobel prize for engineering he ends up living in a cave hunted by every navy in the Western Hemisphere. Just one of life's little jokes, I guess. I like what Bernard Shaw said, 'God, if you'll forgive the little jokes I've played on thee, I'll forgive the big ones you've played on me.'"

"Life's little jokes? I had no idea you were such a philosopher."

"Oh hell, yes, that's why I have this job, because I'm such a great philosopher. Now get your ass back there and find that girl. I don't want to have to explain how we lost those weapons. The boss doesn't have much of a sense of humor."

It didn't take long to find Karen. She was washing her hair in the waterfall. The colonel waited, enjoying the view until she finished and was on her way to the bank. As he stepped out of the trees, she stopped in her tracks and covered her bare chest with her hands.

"Good morning, honey. You're looking real fine this morning."

"Give me my towel."

"Sure, honey, no problem." He teased her with it for a moment and then tossed it to her. She glared at him and wrapped herself in the towel.

"What do you want?" she asked him with disgust.

"Seen Jason this morning?"

"No. I wanted him to swim with me, but he's not here. Do you know where he is?"

"No, but listen. There's something I need to tell you, something important. You helped me when I was sick and I guess I owe you for that. Just stay and listen to me for a minute, please."

She didn't trust him and he knew it. She tilted her head, studying him, and kept her distance.

"It's alright, I'm not going to touch you or hurt you. That's what I wanted to warn you about. I'm leaving today, and I figured I owe you, so here it is. Karen, you and Jason have to get off this island. The captain is very sick and if he ever figures out that Jason isn't really...well you know, brain damaged, like he pretends, the captain will kill him, honey. I know."

"What?" So he knew that Jason was pretending. She wondered if the rest of them knew it as well. "Why would the captain want to hurt Jason?"

"It's a long story, a family argument I guess, but take my word for it, the old man will kill him, and there's another thing. I heard them talking about your baby."

"My baby?"

"You don't think they're going to let you keep it do you?"

"What do you mean? Of course they will." She wrapped her arms around her stomach as if she felt a sharp pain.

"Karen, they don't want you to have that baby and that's the truth. You think Petra is going to help you? I promise you that if she gets her hands on that baby, you'll never see it again. She wanted you to kill it when we were all still on the sub, remember? They don't want you to have that baby, honey. Not even if it has Jason's blue eyes. You think about it."

She remembered overhearing Petra talking about the baby and what Andrews was saying terrified her.

"What can I do?" she asked. Now she was frightened and crying.

"Jason took some things from the boat. Tell him to bring them back and we'll take you with us. You'll be safe and so will your baby. Good doctors, good hospitals, everything. I promise."

"What about Jason?"

"No problem, as long as he brings back the things he took. Same deal, best doctors, everything. And tell him not to worry about the law. We can fix it. He won't have anything to worry about. Now you go find him. We're leaving this afternoon, after we finish loading. I doubt that we're coming back, honey, so it's now or never. I'd hate for you not to come with us. But I can't take you without Jason and what he took, understand?"

"I understand. I'll tell him." She turned, still holding her stomach and hurried back to the cove. She doubled back on the trail so they wouldn't see where she had gone, waited until she thought she was alone and eased back into the water. She swam along the stone wall with easy strokes, trying to be as quiet as possible, to the small beach where they had found the trail up the mountain.

It was a steep climb, and her heart was pounding and her vision blurred with tears. She was short of breath and had to stop several times to rest. She had followed Jason the last time and had not studied the trail. She made wrong turns that ended abruptly and she had to double back. Finally, she could hear the waterfall and she worked her way up to the plateau and the deep pool. Jason was not there. She called to him, guessed he couldn't hear her over the noise of the water so she went to find the crawl space through the vine trellis into the mission.

Jason was sitting by the reflecting pool with his sketch pad. He had beautifully recreated the garden shrine as it would have been three hundred and fifty years before. The white marble Madonna looked down from her place of honor in the mountain vestibule on a group of happy, laughing children playing by the pool. Two priests sat by the pool talking and watching the children. What could have disrupted the beauty and tranquility of their world? Why were there bullet holes in the wall and empty graves?

Karen sat down beside him and put her hand on his arm. "Jason, do you love me?" she began.

CHAPTER 14

On board *Blackwolf* Petra stood vigil by her father's bed in his stateroom. He had slept well in a drug-induced respite from the stress of his crumbling world. She had not. Through the long night, childhood memories of the terrible last days of the war and their escape from Germany haunted her. She and her older sister, Jason's mother, waited anxiously for any word of their missing mother. Still hoping her mother would come through the door at any moment, she remembered seeing her father with the dark haired woman who cared for them. She felt her anger when she saw them touch, and remembered how she cried when she discovered they were sleeping together. It was then that she knew he had taken her mother from her forever.

Now she sat beside him, syringe and vial in hand. She could end it now, or simply prolong his peaceful rest while the world he created crashed in flames around them all. She heard men talking in the galley and saw Randy pause by the splintered door.

"How is he, Mom?"

"He'll be fine, honey, don't worry. He'll be just fine. How's it going?"

"Faster than I thought. We're nearly finished."

She looked down at her father, stroked his hair and shook her head sadly. It was over. His spirit was broken and he would not last much longer. The dark horseman was coming for him, but she would not be its instrument. He would not die by her hand.

"Colonel Andrews promised to take us with them, Jason," Karen pleaded. "And the baby will be born in a real hospital with good doctors. I'm not afraid for myself, but it's our baby and I want it to be born where it will have the best chance."

Jason stood and took her by the hand, helping her up. He walked with her, holding her hand, to the church wall where the musket balls had carved several deep holes in the soft stone. He put her hand in the largest hole, touched her chest and then his own, and mimicked the pain of being shot. He was not doing so to entertain her. She understood.

"Why? Why would they kill us?"

He pointed to his eyes and then his forehead.

"Because of what you saw and what you know? What is that?"

He looked at her with frustration, trying to imagine how to explain. He led her back to the reflecting pool, picked up the sketch pad and began to draw. First there was a ship on the horizon and then *Blackwolf* in the foreground. She identified the sub and encouraged him to continue. He drew a torpedo leaving the sub and then drew flames and debris erupting from the ship, then drew X through it.

"The captain sank a ship? Why, why would he do that?"

He shook his head and began sketching again. This time he added a flag to the stern of the sub, an American flag.

"You mean the government used the sub to sink the ships... the captain was working for the government."

Jason was perplexed again, then he drew several large dollar signs.

"He did it for money? If he got the money, why are we still here and why are we in hiding if he was working for the government?"

Again he shook his head and then pointed down the mountain to the cove. He quickly drew an army beret with an eagle on it.

"The colonel? What about him?"

He nodded and then made the motions of dealing cards.

"The colonel made a deal. They are working for the government, sinking boats, for money? That doesn't make sense. If he made a deal with the government, why are we in hiding?"

Jason hesitated, thinking, and then beneath the colonel's hat he drew a western bandana pulled up like a mask, and then mimicked an outlaw pointing a gun and a victim putting up his hands.

"You mean the colonel's a crook?"

Jason nodded.

"And they know you know it and they're afraid you'll tell? That's why you don't want them to know you are getting better?"

Jason took her hand and nodded again.

"But you were part of it. Weren't you their friend?"

He nodded, then pointed to himself and put his hand up like a stop sign.

"You were, but you stopped."

He nodded.

"I remember, when you took the *Nautilus,* that wasn't part of their plan. You were going to take the little sub and leave, right?"

He looked at the ground, avoiding her eyes and nodded again.

"Oh, Jason, no wonder you wanted them to think your mind was gone. But I think they know. The colonel told me. He said the captain would kill you if he found out. Is that true?"

Jason nodded again.

"Can you tell me why?"

He rolled his eyes and rocked his head from side to side, then began sketching again. He drew a treasure chest overflowing and then a rough map covered with small x's.

"A treasure map. The captain wants it and you have it?"

He held up one finger and nodded and then two fingers and shook his head.

"Sorry, I know, one at a time. So if you don't have the map where is it?"

He quickly sketched two snakes entwined on a staff held by a stick man wearing a cowboy hat.

"Medical cowboy?"

He encouraged her to keep trying.

"Doctor cowboy?"

He rolled his finger in a circle and then her eyes widened.

"Doc Holiday, the guy who was with Sheri in Bermuda, only he told us his name was Harrington. He has the map? Where did he get it?"

Jason pointed at himself and smiled, and then made a giving motion toward her.

"There was a treasure map and you gave it to Doc Holiday. No wonder the captain would kill you. I heard them talking about a cup. What does that have to do with this?"

He pointed again to the map and then formed his hands like a chalice then pointed again to the map.

"The map is in the cup? And Doc Holiday has the cup. Okay, now what did you take from their boat?"

He got up, went to the church and returned with the guns. He laid them on the ground between them.

"Are there more?"

He shook his head.

"Good. Throw them in the pool."

His eyes widened and he grabbed for the guns. He pointed to her stomach and to her heart and then at the cove.

"No, I don't want you to protect me, not by killing. There has been enough. Whatever happens to us will be what we deserve. Throw them in the pool."

He studied her and realized he had never seen her so resolved. In her hand was the rosary. She was pulling the beads through her fingers one at a time as if gaining power from them. She looked directly into his eyes and waited.

Slowly he picked up the guns and threw them into the center of the deep pool. He sat back down beside her and took her hands.

"Jason, I love you," she said matter of factly. "Whatever happens now is out of our hands and that's the way I want it. I remember who we were and how we got here. Yes, and I know you were leaving without me and you probably would have let me die on that boat with Maldias, that's why nothing after that mattered. And if we both hadn't been hurt, we never would have gotten another chance. A chance to find out what real love is. You just showed me your love when you threw those guns in the water. If I never live to hear you say it, I will always know that you love me and our baby."

She opened her arms to him and he came close. She felt his tears on her neck and knew she had done the right thing. She held him away so that she could see him. His face was streaked with dust and tears and the creases of the scars on his forehead. She kissed him, put down the rosary, then cupped her hand into the pool and gently washed his face with the sparkling water and dried it with her shirt.

"Come," she said and led him to the vine-covered wall. They crawled through the hole in the churchyard wall, climbed the rocks by the waterfall's pool and looked out across the dark blue-green ocean. Far below, the inflatable dinghy motored to the old schooner. The crew climbed aboard and shortly thereafter the schooner motored across the cove toward the narrow inlet. They lost sight of the boat as it passed between the walls of the cove's narrow entrance, but soon it appeared again under full sail driving through the gently rolling swells gracefully heeling on a port tack.

Jason encircled Karen in his arms as they watched the boat grow smaller and smaller until it seemed to vanish into the sea.

The day after their dinner with Customs Agent John Bentley, Doc and Sheri heard from him again. Things were set for a visit to the boat which had been trolling for Sheri and Jack Morgan. It was early evening when they drove through downtown George Town, past the banks and jewelry stores to Airport Road and then north toward Rum Point. The night air was heavy with the promise of rain and large drops began falling as they arrived at the fishing docks. The boat had been found adrift and towed in by fishermen. Bentley went to the door of the white frame dockmaster's shack and pounded on the door. He got the gate key from the sleeping guard and permission to board the boat.

"Funny thing," said Bentley, "the owner hasn't come round to pick her up. I think he's scared to death Morgan thinks he was in on it. Can't say that I blame him. Morgan doesn't seem to have much of a sense of humor."

There was still blood on the cabin hatches, and as the rain

fell some washed across the white deck and out the port scupper. The hatches weren't locked and they went below into the cozy cabin. More blood.

"Anybody sample that and check for prints?" asked Doc.

"Yeah, should have reports in a day or two. The samples were flown out."

Doc started looking and Sheri asked, "What are we looking for?"

"Everything," he replied.

They began taking the cabin apart. Doc pulled the cushions off the dinette and the bunk and started to toss them out of the way when Sheri noticed zippers on the edges and began checking.

"Oh no, damn it, no..." she said crying and handed a pair of peach underpants and a diamond earring to Doc. "They're hers. I remember the fuss she made about losing the other one in the water. And look at the monogram, SS—Stephanie Smith. They are even the right color for her dress."

Doc took the panties and looked. "No blood, not torn and the earring is pinned to them. What the devil was she doing on this boat?"

"Looks to me like she was a hostage," Bentley said. "And she left us a trail. She was telling us the same guys kidnapped her and then attacked Morgan. Good work, Sheri. If you ever need a job..."

"Thanks."

"Now, wait a minute, that doesn't make any sense," Doc said. "Keep looking. There's got to be something more. What if she left those because she knew we would come to check out this boat and she wanted us to know she's alright? That makes better sense, doesn't it?"

"She did leave a note," Sheri said and pulled an ink-stained scrap of paper from the cushion. "Only it looks like it got wet and the ink ran. See?" She handed the paper to Doc who held it up to the light. Most of the message was washed out, however, only the salutation to JB remained along with the first line. "I'm okay and will contact you as soon as..." and that was all.

"Well, I'll be damned," Bentley swore. "I was convinced Morgan's men got her, but that sure looks like her writing."

"Do you suppose she might still be on the island?" Sheri asked.

"Yes, and if she is, I think I know where. The question is, can we risk trying to get to her? I wouldn't be at all surprised if Morgan is having us followed. We might lead him right to her."

Doc looked at the note again. "I wonder what she was waiting for...what she was expecting to happen when she wrote, 'as soon as.' As soon as what?"

"As soon as she was certain she was safe...as soon as she was off the island? Or was she expecting something else?" Bentley echoed Doc's questions.

"Did she think something might be happening to Morgan that would make it safe for her to surface?" Doc asked.

"She knew we were planning to take him down," Bentley said. "But that was weeks ago. That plan went on hold when she disappeared."

"What if we still could take him down?" Doc asked.

"If only there were some way for us to get into that surveillance system and into his computers," Bentley said. "That might be the only way we're ever going to get answers to any of this."

"Could you get a court order?" Doc asked.

"Not a chance. He's got a better pipeline to the locals than we do."

Doc scratched his chin again and then raised his right eyebrow and smiled. It was an evil smile.

Sheri looked at him and her eyes got wide. "Doc, I know that look. What are you thinking?"

"Oh, it's just a simple little plan. But perhaps one of my very best. Cunning, ruthless, and more fun than a sorority house panty raid."

Summer lightning flashed across the sky followed by an earthshaking rumble. She jumped and Doc held her safe in his arms.

"A panty raid?" Sheri said laughing. "Here we go again. Did you bring me the Smith and Wesson? We want the girls to know we mean business!"

John Bentley studied them for a moment before joining in their mischievous laughter. "We're off to see the wizard," he sang as the rain thundered down on the deck above them and lightning danced across the water to his song.

In the height of the squall, an old schooner motored to the pier just ahead of them. Crewmen in yellow oilskins and down easter headgear secured the lines and then disappeared below decks.

The storm was trying to be more than just a twenty-minute summer squall so Doc suggested they make a run for it. They were halfway down the pier when lightning flashed again like stadium lights turning on, and thunder followed less than a second behind.

"Too close," Sheri shouted. "Just like the mountains at home."

"Yeah...good storm. Glad we weren't out on that old tub," Doc said, nodding toward the schooner. "They must have had a ride. By the way, great tee shirt."

Her soaked white shirt was now clinging and mostly transparent. She covered her breasts with her arms and gave him a dirty look. On the schooner her plight had not gone unnoticed. From the main cabin ports, the boys cheered the lightning and what it revealed.

"What's the matter with you?" Geist asked Colonel Andrews. "Afraid of a little blow? I thought you liked this sailor stuff."

"You know who that was on the dock?" Andrews said. "That's the little bitch who was with Doc Holiday in Bermuda. What the hell is she doing here?"

"Don't you know?" Geist laughed. "She was invited."

"That Jeep belong to the condo?" JB asked them as he pulled into the parking lot beside it to drop them off. The squall passed on toward Little Cayman, leaving the pavement steaming and the air heavily laden. Sheri was shivering, even wrapped in the towel she'd borrowed from Bentley.

"Yes."

"Better assume it's bugged too. Careful now and remember, this is hardball. Goodnight."

They got out of Bentley's Toyota and climbed into the Jeep. Doc drove north past the brightly painted stores and hotels until he found a pay phone. Sheri got out of the Jeep with him. "Who are you calling at two in the morning?"

"Tom and Debbie. I want to check the mail, and I've got another idea."

"Not at two in the morning, Doc. Get serious."

He touched his lips with his right index finger and pointed back to the car. She nodded and he placed the call.

They talked for half an hour. Tom knew a little about computer transfer of funds, a service mainly provided by a New York City firm called CRISP and another in Culpeper, Virginia, SWIFT. Both networks were highly secret and well protected. And both moved millions internationally each day. Doc wanted to know if Tom could use the NASA communications network and satellites to monitor transactions from Morgan's condo.

"Interesting," Tom answered. "And probably impossible. Give me twenty-four hours and I'll get you in. We do the impossible quite often around here. One of these days we might even send a man to the moon."

Doc talked with Debbie. She and her pregnancy were getting along fairly well. Was he going to be back before the baby was born? Yes, of course. That was still months away.

Doc thanked them and let them go back to sleep with the admonition not to discuss anything related to their call with anyone and not to call the condo.

They rode silently for a another mile to a public beach and got out to walk and talk.

"I don't want JB or anyone to know Tom is helping us. We don't want them involved if this blows up in our face."

"Sure."

He smiled and laughed again. "This is going to be fun."

"Does it involve making explosives out of cleaning solvents or high altitude night jumps into the middle of a jungle?"

"Not this time. This is going to be a piece of cake."

White cirrus clouds were blowing across the night sky now as the storm moved north and the stars shone brightly above them. Moonlight drenched the beach and now the air was crisp and clean.

"What time is it?" he asked.

"Three."

"Want to swim?"

"Sure, the ocean will warm me up and maybe this stuff will

dry." She slipped off her shirt and shorts, hung them on the mangrove trees and crossed the narrow strip of sand to the water. Doc quickly followed her. They swam out through the surf into calm deeper water and were soon in each others arms talking softly, rising and falling with the rhythm of the swells. The eastern sky was turning pink when he carried her up to the Jeep. She was still pulling on her clothes when they arrived back at the condo. They showered together and were getting into bed when the phone rang. Jack Morgan invited them to join him for an early poolside breakfast.

"Have you seen the morning paper?" Morgan asked as they crossed the pool deck to his table. The storm had cleared the morning sky and the uniformly perfect weather had returned. He was casually dressed in shorts and sandals and sat at a table set for four. Ms. Kee stood to welcome them. She kissed Sheri and took Doc's hand warmly. They were the only early risers and had the pool deck to themselves.

Morgan had turned on his charm again. Doc was cautious.

"Exciting news today," Morgan said and handed Sheri and Doc each copies of the local paper. "With your background in archaeology, Sheri, this should interest you. Looks like Captain Humphreys and his crew really hit pay dirt. Although I must say, I'm very surprised."

The front page photo showed the grinning captain and his crew holding gold chains, coins and bars, standing on the treasure-laden deck of the research vessel *Beacon*. The story was the captain's narrative of the years of searching and final discovery of the "big pile," the main artifact deposit of the Spanish treasure galleon, *Nuestra Señora de las Maravillas*, Our Lady of the Marvels, which, according to the article, sank in January of 1656 carrying a treasure worth nearly two billion dollars.

The article recounted how the history of the sinking was first discovered in the Spanish archives by Sir Robert Marx who compiled 1,200 pages of reference work before searching and finding a portion of the bow and some treasure in the early seventies. Difficulties with the Bahamian government forced him to hand over the treasure and abandon the site.

Later, Captain Humphreys was able to reach agreement with the government, and for a fourth of the take, was able to work the wreck with the government's blessing and protection. The search began in 1986 and after seven back-breaking, financially exhausting years, the crew and their investors were finally going to get the payday of the century. The article went on to describe the find: twenty silver bars; forty of the original fifty-eight bronze cannon worth thirty thousand each; gold and silver coins; and twenty priceless emeralds, two of which were over one hundred karats and could easily bring a million dollars. The article concluded by saying that the crew was confident they would shortly find the rest of the mother lode, including a four hundred-pound solid gold table encrusted with diamonds, emeralds and rubies, and a life-size, solid gold statue of the Madonna and Child known to have been part of the treasure.

Doc scanned the article quickly. "What is it that surprises you?" he asked.

Morgan had several leather bound books on the chair beside him. "What do you know about Henry Morgan?" he asked and held up a copy of Alexandre Exquemelin's, *Bucaniers of America,* written in Dutch in 1678 and translated into English in 1684.

"Just what Michener wrote in *Caribbean,*" Sheri answered.

"Exquemelin was Morgan's surgeon and is about the only historical witness. He wrote very unfavorably about the captain once he was off Morgan's ship, safe ashore in England. Morgan sued the good doctor's publisher and won, but still there is a ring of truth to most of it. Exquemelin describes Morgan's raids on Spanish towns looking for treasure, the mass murders of the Spanish, including priests and nuns. Rape, torture—you've heard the stories."

"Sure," she said. Doc nodded.

"Well, consider this: the *Maravillas* went down in 1656, just a few years before Morgan came into power as Admiral of the Brethren operating out of Jamaica. He captured and tortured thousands of Spaniards. Don't you think he would have known about a treasure that big, right in his own backyard? William Phips was all the way up in Massachusetts and he knew enough to sail to Hispaniola in 1686 and take a treasure off the wreck of another galleon, the *Conception.* So far so good?"

"Okay, go on," she answered.

"Years ago I read about the Madonna in one of Clive Cussler's novels and she fascinated me, so I hired a researcher to look for her history in Spain. He found some old church records with this story. The Spaniards were terrified of Morgan and when the *Maravillas* went down, they sent salvage crews immediately. They found her and were able to recover some of the guns and a portion of the treasure which they sent back to Spain. But, the leader of the salvage party was deeply religious as were most of the Spanish, and when the Madonna came to the surface he was awe struck and vowed he would return her to the Mexican village in which she had been worshipped as the patron saint. So he stashed some of the treasure, the statue and the four hundred-pound gold table encrusted with jewels in the hold of his best ship and sent her on her way back to Mexico. But something happened and the statue never made it back to Mexico. Nothing appears in the record for years until a dying priest writes an account to his bishop, and my man finds it three hundred years later—not in the Spanish archives where everyone else is looking, but in the Vatican papers in Rome.

"Somewhere in the islands is a mountain with a sacred spring. Supposedly it had healing power and the Spanish built a shrine there. The caravel carrying the Madonna and Child gets caught in a storm and ends up on the reefs of this island. The priests take it as a sign from heaven, salvage the treasure, haul the statue up to their shrine and burn the remains of the wreck to hide it from the *luteranos*, the Lutherans. Namely my long lost relative, Uncle Henry.

"Somehow, however, Uncle Henry hears about the wreck and sends his men to find it. They raid the shrine. The priests have done a good job hiding the statue and when Morgan's men arrive, they find nothing. So they start torturing the priests, but no one talks. They rape and beat the women, and still no one talks. Finally, they start splitting the tongues of the children. Still no one tells them what they want to hear. In frustration and anger, they destroy the mission, execute everyone and leave.

"Years later, an ex-slave of Morgan's is dying and confesses the story to a priest who, years later on his deathbed, violates the secrecy of the confessional...well, you know the rest."

"And you think the priest's story was true?" Sheri inquired.

"Yes, for a couple reasons. The Spanish were unbelievably honest, and the priest would have nothing to gain by lying. Next, the site of the *Maravillas* has been worked for years by two of the best salvage crews in the business, using the best equipment available. And now they're about to find the main pile right where they've been looking all this time. Good story, but I don't buy it. And I want to find out what's going on. If this is a scam, it could hurt the island."

"What do you want me to do?" said Sheri.

"Our library on the top floor has got everything in print on this. Have a look and then see if you can determine if anything they bring in is from the *Maravillas.* My bet is this is a stunt to raise more money. Why don't they have pictures of the Madonna along with the rest?"

"The article says they anticipate finding her. They don't have her yet," Doc said.

"I know what they said," Morgan snapped. "I just don't buy it. And one other thing, Doctor Holiday, I understand that last night you visited the sportsfisherman which attacked us."

"That's true. I asked a local instructor to drive us out there."

"I think you should be more careful. If you insist on refusing to follow my advice, at least leave Sheri out of your meddling; I don't want to see her hurt again. That's all for now. Sheri and I need to discuss rebuilding the dive shop and that doesn't concern you. Don't you have a whale to catch or something? Have a nice day, Doctor." He glared at Doc, waiting for a reaction. Doc took two deep breaths, smiled without speaking, nodded and left the table. Now that his plan was in place he needed to stay at the condo, at least for a few days more.

He had turned and taken two steps when Morgan said, "Oh, Doctor, I almost forgot...." Doc turned and Morgan handed him a bill from the restaurant. "I believe this is yours. Sheri's meals are included in her employment package. Yours, however, are not. I'm sure that there's no problem. It's just that when we ran your credit card...well, we also ran a credit check—company policy. Your card cleared, but I wouldn't count on using that one much longer, Doctor. Not unless you plan on paying down that balance fairly soon. Sorry." He smiled and waited.

"No problem," Doc said and took the bill. He turned again and left the pool. Sheri was glaring at the table unable to meet Morgan's gaze. "Charming fellow, your doctor, Sheri. I do hope he decides to stay," he said laughing.

CHAPTER 15

Two aging tank trucks painted with large red letters spelling out "Cayman Water Company" rumbled through the guarded entrance of a high-fenced tank farm. The trucks pulled into an old warehouse and when the doors closed behind them, Rudy Geist stepped from the first wearing a tattered pair of white coveralls and white rubber boots. He carried a clipboard and asked the young Caymanian guard to let Mr. Morgan know they had arrived.

"He's on the way, man. The gate called when they let you in."

Heavy doors, like those in a cold storage vault, opened at the end of the warehouse and Morgan appeared. Behind him a forklift followed.

"Everything go alright?" Morgan asked.

"Yeah, except for that storm last night, and the surprise of seeing Holiday at the dock. He still here?"

"Yes, and the girl too. There won't be a problem as long as you stay away from the condo. He doesn't get far from her skirt and I've made sure she's got plenty to keep herself occupied. Where's Andrews?"

"In town. Andrews feels he has a score to settle with the girl, the one with Holiday. I think he's just been on that island too long. I sent him into town with enough money to get his attitude adjusted. He needs to mellow out."

"Good. Well, let's see what we've got. I've been waiting a long time for this. Wish to hell I could have been with you."

Geist looked at him and raised an eyebrow. *Only an idiot would have wished himself along on that cruise,* Geist thought, but said nothing.

The gold was packed on pallets and the forklift went to work unloading them. Large freezer doors at the end of the warehouse opened, revealing an elevator which lowered them several floors to a catacomb with several glass fronted vaults. Morgan opened electronic locks with a key and the heavy glass panels withdrew into the ceiling. This vault and several of the others were empty. But some contained guns and ceramics, mostly from Bermuda.

Geist had seen it before. "Still empty, I see."

Morgan nodded. "But not for long, once I get that chalice. Damned ticklish though. Holiday is a hard one to figure—little or no interest in money even though he's nearly flat broke. It will take a different kind of leverage to get what we want, and the girl may be the answer. So don't let Andrews do anything cute. We can't afford to lose our ace in the hole. When the time is right, I don't want to have to waste my time with a middle-aged Travis McGee with a penchant for lost causes. How much gold did you bring?"

"About two tons of bars and coins. Not bad considering the salvage company had a big headstart. If they'd gotten any luckier, we'd have never made it off the bottom."

"Forty thousand troy ounces at four hundred dollars an ounce, sixteen million if we melt it down. However, taking a guess at the numismatic values, sixty to a hundred million, I'd say. Not a bad night's work."

"Better than the Navy," Geist answered.

"How's the old man?"

"Not good—loony tunes most of the time. Too dangerous to keep around, if you ask me."

"We still need him, so don't get any ideas."

"Maybe not for long. Johnson thinks he can handle the sub. Perhaps even figure out how the old man makes the fuel. But he's asking questions. I wanted to check with you before giving him answers."

"He came highly recommended. Send him to me later today." As he spoke, Morgan opened the first box and lifted out a handful of flawless, double eagle, twenty-dollar gold coins.

"Pretty. We won't have any trouble moving these, not like Jason's precious gun collection, or those stinking four hundred-year-old Spanish olive jars. Frankly, I don't understand why anyone with a brain would waste their time on that junk. But gold...well now, gold is a different story. Too bad there wasn't more of it for Jason to steal in Bermuda."

"Yeah, too bad," Geist answered. "How are your meetings going?"

"Kuwaitis are mad as hell. Too bad Saddam went north instead of south. No one gives a shit what he does up there, but let him get close to the oil and we'll have carte blanche to level the whole damn country. So we dropped a few bombs and took out an airfield or two. Big deal. If we don't take him out soon, Faud's going to start dropping a few bombs of his own, just to remind us we made a deal and he expects us to keep it. There's just too much at stake. I've set things in motion and we're going to need the sub.

"You'll love this one, Admiral. It's absolutely brilliant. Two birds with one stone. All the justification we need to solve our little problem and then some. And there won't be a damn thing the White House can do to stop it. In fact, that's the real beauty of it. The prick's going to see it coming and there won't be a thing he can do. It's even better than when we convinced Carter to go after the Iranian hostages and then sabotaged the mission. Don't you just love politics?" he laughed.

"Especially the way you play," Admiral Geist answered.

"We were followed last night," Doc said. "And I think someone's on my tail now." He looked from the phone booth toward a man in a small white car who looked immediately down at a newspaper.

"I'll get one of my guys to..."

"Don't bother, JB, just listen. My welcome is wearing thin. If you still want to see his bank book, we need to get moving. Here's what I have in mind...."

He finished the conversation and walked on to the dive shop at the Holiday Inn. The walk was over a mile. He passed the beach where he and Sheri had spent the night, yawned and smiled. He was trying to remember if he'd ever made love in a Jeep before. He laughed when he thought about someone monitoring a bug in the Jeep. That tape would bring top dollar. Sheri was something else. He was a lucky man, if she didn't give him a heart attack before his next birthday.

"Karen, wait please. We need to talk," Petra called after her as Karen slipped out the kitchen's back door with a bag of food. Karen hesitated and then turned to face her.

"What's wrong?" Petra asked. "You haven't spoken to me since the schooner left. What's happened?"

Karen studied her and hesitated. "Why did you want me to abort this baby?" she asked. Her hands were on her hips and she had a resentful, fearful look in her eyes.

"Remember, you had been seriously hurt and we didn't know if you would be strong enough to carry the baby full term. And because..." She hesitated, looking intensely at Karen, then blurted out the rest, "because it might be the child of that horrible man who raped you—Maldias."

"And now, what about now?"

"You made a choice, Karen, it's much too late for that now."

"Colonel Andrews said you would kill the baby and that the captain would kill Jason." She was still tense, ready to run.

"That's a lie. I love you. You are my family now, just like my sons, like my sister's son, Jason. We are going to leave here together and forget all this. We'll find a beautiful island, like Bermuda, and have a real house and a school for your baby. It will be alright, you'll see. I promise you, no harm will come to your baby, Karen...on my life, I promise it."

"What about the captain and Jason?"

"Papa is very sick and he has done some terrible things, but that's over now. We won't let him hurt anyone ever again."

"I want to believe you. You've been good to me, but I'm so afraid. What if the schooner comes back, what then?"

"It's not safe to travel on the sub anymore; we need them to take us to our new home. It will be alright."

"No, it won't. Jason heard them. They want something from the captain, something about the sub. When they get it, they're going to kill us all. Jason took their guns and I made him throw them away, but they will bring more. Be careful, Petra, don't trust them." She turned and pulled open the door.

"Jason told you that? He can speak?" Petra said as she stepped back toward the stove, stumbling on a wooden potato crate. "Oh my."

"No, he can't speak yet, but he will, and he understands everything. He knows the captain sank a ship and killed a lot of people. That's why he's afraid. I have to go now. Jason will worry if I'm gone too long," Karen said before sliding past the screen door and hurrying toward the lagoon.

"Oh no," Petra said. "Oh no, Papa, what have you done?" she repeated over and over while rocking back and forth on the crate. "What have you done?" She tried to choke back her sobs with her anger, but all she could do was cry.

Bill Roberts came up the back steps as Karen was leaving. She ran past him without speaking and he hurried into the kitchen to find Petra. She heard him coming so she stood and wiped her tears. "Can you pilot the sub? Can you get us out of here?" she asked her husband.

"She needs major repair. We have nothing to work with, no tools, no replacement parts. We'd never make it out of the cave."

"But if it was an emergency—life or death—isn't there something you could do?"

"You're not listening. The steering was destroyed and the valves which operate the ballast control don't work. We were damn lucky to make it back at all. Taking the sub out now would be suicide. Do you understand, or shall I say it again?"

"Yes, but couldn't you fix it? Not like new, but just enough so we could escape?"

"Perhaps, with the right tools and enough time."

"Then do it. We have to leave before Colonel Andrews comes back. Jason overheard them planning to kill us."

"Jason...?"

"Yes, Jason. He's been pretending because he's afraid of you all. Karen said he can't speak yet, but his mind is clear. Karen did it...she brought him back. Now we have to leave here."

"But, where...?"

"Back home, back to Bermuda. Make a deal with the government: give them back the sub, give them papa, give them anything they want, but get us out of here before those awful men kill us. I'll go and find Karen and Jason. They can help."

"Back to Bermuda? Do you know what will happen to me back there? Do you care? I didn't want any part of this, and you drove me crazy to help your father. My life is gone...I'm a traitor to my country...I'm an accomplice to murdering at least a hundred men and now you don't want to play anymore. 'Oh, Bill let's go home...you can go to jail and I'll go to high tea at the South Hampton Princess.' It's a little late for that now, dear wife."

"If we stay, they will kill us all, after they beat what they want out of you and papa. We have to leave."

"We'll go, but we'll go south, hide the sub and then...hell, I don't know. You go back to bedpans and I'll get a job fixing toasters. My God, what's happened to us? Half the world is trying to kill us and all I ever wanted was to dive a few wrecks and save a little history before teredo worms and dry rot got us all. How did it get so out of control?" He was talking to himself now. Petra had gone to search for Karen and Jason.

Doc lifted his arm to check the time again. The luminescent hands of the old Rolex were dim. He turned its face to catch the moonlight through the window.

"It's three thirty, Doc," Sheri said. She turned toward him and pulled closer. "Do you miss the old green couch in the museum hostel? That's where I'd look for you when I knew you weren't sleeping. Remember how we used to sit and talk all night?"

"No, I don't remember talking all night. What I remember is sitting beside you watching you sleep and wondering, how can she be so beautiful when she sleeps and such a pain when she's awake?"

"Thanks pal," she said, and bit his chest. "Promise you'll be careful tomorrow. None of this is worth your getting hurt again."

"I promise, and you keep your head down and do what you're told. No heroics. Got it?"

"Yeah, I got it."

Daylight began a little after five and he doubted that he'd slept at all. He turned toward her and studied the softness of her neck and the short curls of her blond hair. He kissed her bare shoulder gently and slid from beneath the sheet. After his shower, he would wake her and they would walk on the beach and go over the plan one more time. He stood by the window and looked out over the ocean. It was calm and the sky was clear. It would have been a good day for fishing.

At seven-thirty they came in from the beach to the restaurant by the pool. Jack Morgan was there with Faud and one of the others from the fishing trip. They were in serious conversation. As Doc and Sheri walked past his table, Morgan said good morning to Sheri and introduced her to the men. She didn't like the way they looked at her.

"And you remember her friend, Doctor Holiday. The doctor is looking for a white whale. Make certain to let him know if you see one. It is a white whale, isn't it, Doctor Holiday?" Morgan taunted.

"White as virgin snow, Jack. They're very rare, you know, almost as rare as honest diplomats or developers who don't screw up the environment. Gentlemen?" he smiled and nodded to Morgan's guests who were chuckling. Then he guided Sheri across the pool deck to a more private table.

"My, my, you're a bit testy this morning, aren't you?" Sheri laughed when they were seated. "I take it that means we won't be staying here much longer."

"It means I've had about as much of that guy as anyone needs. And if he wants to get cute, he'd better take a whetstone to his wit or he's going to be sitting in the corner wearing a tall pointed hat," Doc said. Morgan was still glaring at him. Doc smiled and waved to the Kuwaitis who were still enjoying their laugh at Morgan's expense. Morgan quickly turned his chair to put his back toward Doc.

"I think you're starting to get to him."

Doc checked his watch again. "Not for another forty-seven minutes. Which gives us just enough time to have a magnificent breakfast and savor the impending demise of Black Jack Morgan."

The entire Grand Cayman Immigration and Customs force arrived at exactly nine and the television crews were right behind. Cameramen stormed the lobby. Officers pushed their way to the front of the reporters and flashed warrants and badges at terrified desk clerks. Jack Morgan came running into the foyer and was told immigration had gotten a tip that the Kuwaitis were actually Arab terrorists wanted by Interpol and were under arrest.

Morgan flashed white and then deep red like an angry, frightened octopus. He tried to block the officers' entrance and found himself being arrested.

Doc and Sheri came through the lobby on the way to the elevator just as two large Caymanian officers were pinning Jack Morgan to the wall. "Thanks for breakfast, Jack," Doc said in passing. "Have a nice day." They got out of the elevator on their floor and waited until the immigration officials had a chance to sweep the top floor. U.S. Customs Officer John Bentley was waiting when they arrived.

He nodded, pointed to the surveillance cameras and passed his finger across his throat. Then he pointed to his ear and turned both hands palms up in front of his chest. Doc nodded. They would not speak.

Two technicians, flown in for the occasion, were hard at work replacing cables. The replacements came with extra added attractions harder to spot than splices or jumpers.

Doc and Sheri sat at one of the computer terminals and opened the book of notes he'd gotten from Tom. He got to a main directory, found operating files and opened the one labeled AUTOEXEC.BAT. Sheri headed for Morgan's expansive office. There was an impressive collection of first edition works by Defoe, the narrative of Drake's adventures and then the volume Jack had shown them on his long lost Uncle Henry. As Doc had instructed, she looked under, behind and in between the books until she found what she was looking for. Inside the file drawer of Morgan's desk, she found a remote control. When she pushed it wall panels opened and she looked into a private room. There were two computers, three large-screen monitors and stacks of CD disks filed chronologically. And sitting beside the first computer were a half dozen disks from random dates. She touched nothing and backed out of the room to get Doc.

Doc had closed the computer file and was on the floor helping the technicians pull cables when she tapped him on the shoulder. He jumped and turned with a look that made her jump back in fright, especially when she realized how quickly he'd drawn the Randall. He smiled and followed her.

He immediately recognized the room for what it was—a surveillance center and library of video disks. They waited for the techs to make certain the room was free of cameras or bugs before entering. Doc quickly turned on a computer and monitor and picked up a disk labeled December 20,'95. The recording was of the executive playroom. There were nine people in the room, two couples on the Roman salons and the rest in the tub. Sheri recognized Ms. Kee in the tub talking to two men. On the salon in back of the tub was a woman astride a reclining man, arching her back and throwing her head from side to side as if riding a mechanical bull.

"Wait a minute," Doc said. "Who does that look like?" He pulled up a menu across the top of the screen and selected zoom and pulled down on the couple.

"That's Stephanie. The guy looks like that congressman—the one who got caught with his fingers in the Savings and Loans cookie jar. He was on the news last night...something about deregulating banks. This is hot stuff, X-rated Congressional videos. My, my...I wonder if we are in those somewhere too?"

"Probably, but there isn't time for a screening now. We'll have to come back later." He checked his watch and was about to close the disk when an overweight middle-aged male, wearing nothing but a smile, entered the tub room with two much younger women in matching attire. The trio slipped into the water and the girls were immediately atop their companion, laughing and splashing.

"Does that surprise you?" Sheri asked.

"No, but it sure as hell disappoints me. But I guess I should have known. It explains a lot, doesn't it? Not that there's much we can do now that we know."

He closed the program and turned off the computer. He wanted to take the disk, but knew its absence would alert Morgan so he replaced it on the stack and they went into the larger office. After Sheri showed him the remote switch, he closed the bookcase panel and they left the office.

The two computer technicians rolled down their sleeves, put their jackets back on and hung badges from their lapel pockets. Then they escorted Doc and Sheri to the main lobby to join the others. Morgan and his staff had been taken to Government House along with the Kuwaitis. Now officers with clipboards were checking passports, and asking questions before allowing the remaining guests to return to their rooms. Doc and Sheri answered their questions and were released. Ms. Kee was the only staff member allowed to remain, and she was apologizing profusely to the guests, assuring them the incident was all a terrible mistake.

"She's right about that," Doc said. "It was a terrible mistake that began when they built this place. Come on, let's go for a dive. I don't want to be around when your boss gets back."

"Do you think we should?"

"Afraid of losing your wonderful job?"

When they were alone on the condo's dive boat headed to visit the tarpon at Bonnie's Arch, she asked, "What happens next?"

"Hopefully he got enough of a scare that he'll act before he thinks to check the hardware. If he panics enough, he may show us where the skeletons are, and if we get really lucky, Tom may be able to monitor his transactions and get his security codes. I don't know how hard those cables will be to find, but for now we're in. I wonder how many more faces we'd recognize if we could get a look at the rest of those disks."

"Oh, it's the faces you're interested in?"

"I wonder how your boss and his friends are making out with immigration. That will be a show worth watching. The arrogant bastard."

"Catch the mooring line and tie us up. You need an attitude adjustment dive. Come on, I'll introduce you to the famous deep diving, twelve-foot Cayman alligator."

At the Caymanian Immigration headquarters, Jack Morgan had a difficult time maintaining his composure. He called his corporate attorneys who wanted nothing to do with Libyan terrorists, but came anyway. He also called the American Counsel, who was conveniently off the island on holiday. John Bentley monitored Jack Morgan via the cell's surveillance equipment and talked with the chief immigrations officer, a stout British chap named Teddy.

"There's going to be bloody hell to pay when we turn him loose, JB. I hope to hell your tip was not some racist prank. That could do real damage to our working relationship. Your next big time consulting job may be at a school crossing."

"We'll know soon enough. Just hold them as long as you can. Washington is working overtime on this and your guys will be heroes if we get lucky. With all that money, somebody's got to have dirty fingernails. Now it's up to us to find him."

"Morgan's a cool one...must know he's on camera. I thought he might react...give us something...you know. You'd think this was just a walk down the beach."

There was a knock on the door and an attractive uniformed Caymanian woman entered. She slid into the seat next to Bentley, leaned close and whispered, "This must be your lucky day. Why don't you come outside with me?" When they stepped into the hallway, she said, "You aren't going to believe this, but we hit pay dirt. Two of those guys are wanted for questioning in England and the States. They were involved in the BCCI scandal and Interpol has been looking for them for ten years. They may even have been the bank for some terrorist activities."

"What? Talk about a shot in the dark. The most I was praying for were New York parking tickets. What does Washington say?"

"Bad news...let them go. We're to tag them, of course. D.C. wants to know what holes they crawl back to. My government gets the credit, of course. I think we're going to declare them persona non grata. It will look good in the news."

"What about all the work I went to setting this up? I swear, getting credit for a bust takes more work than making it. Except in your case, of course."

"Is this a set up for more of your sexual harassment, JB?"

"Just for the record, it's not harassment as long as you keep saying yes, darling. Thanks. I'll tell Teddy about our bad boy bankers. See you about nine?" He winked at her. She gave him a dirty look and then smiled and nodded, but blocked his attempt to pat her behind as she turned to leave.

"Your American SWAT team tactics need restraint, Officer Bentley," she whispered, "or you're going to get me fired. And make it ten. I gotta get my kid to bed."

"Teddy, my lad, there's good news and bad. What's your pleasure?" Bentley said as he slouched back down in the steel folding chair.

"Oh shit, JB, don't tell me we screwed up. I don't want to work the airport again."

Jack Morgan slammed his desk phone back down on the receiver, picked up his glass and turned to Ms. Kee. "Washington is denying any knowledge of it. They're saying it was a local op. That's bull. It was the White House, I'm sure of it. What a stupid stunt. I know what they're up to. Well, it's a little too late, boys. All you did was piss me off and now you're going to learn that's a very foolish thing to do."

The six-foot-long silver tarpon were waiting in the natural alcove created by the stone arch. The water was sixty feet deep, warm and clear. *It's hard to remember how really beautiful they are,* Doc thought as they approached the school. He guessed there were about twenty, suspended motionless, facing into the gentle current. Their sides looked armored, like polished sterling plates fused together in a chain mail coat, catching the sun and reflecting a rainbowed hue as the waves passing above bent and refracted the light rays across their glistening bodies.

Sheri took his hand and motioned toward the bottom of the alcove. They moved down slowly, trying not to disturb the fish. On the sand below them was a cement alligator. Doc chuckled and gestured to Sheri: Where had it come from? What was it doing here? She shook her head. Who knows? It's just here. Enjoy it.

It was good to be back in the water. Like his late two- and three-mile night swims in the Georgia State pool, he came up the dive ladder feeling his soul had been refreshed. He set his rig on the deck and went back to the ladder to help Sheri. She hung the water bag from the bimini frame and washed the salt from her face and hair.

"Need any help?" he offered.

"What'd you have in mind?" she smiled.

"Apparently the same thing you do by the looks of things," he said.

A tone sounded from the hand-held radio JB had given them. She pulled it from her dive bag and handed it to Doc. "Just a cold shower, that's all I had in mind," she teased. He turned on the radio and answered with a gruff hello.

Bentley told him about the Arabs and then added, "We need to meet, tonight about midnight. Come down to the beach across from Fisheye. And be careful. Our little escapade hit pay dirt and Morgan is fit to be tied. Make sure you're not followed."

CHAPTER 16

Black Jack Morgan sat alone in his office eight stories above Seven Mile Beach, sipping Jack Daniels from a half empty bottle and staring through the emerald tinted glass at the last rays of sunlight dissolving into azure blue water. His ketch, *Bluebird*, rode easily at her mooring, dwarfing the other boats anchored off the beach. Morgan raised the bottle in mournful salute when the last glimmer was gone and took a long drink. He was way past feeling the burn as the liquor hit the back of his throat and then his empty stomach. He was a long way past a lot of things. He closed his eyes and let the booze saturate his rage and soothe his exhausted spirit. He'd replayed the events of this disastrous day a dozen times, imagined that everything he'd been working for during the past ten years was about to explode in his face, and then, by some miracle of bureaucratic stupidity, the locals called off the dogs, released Faud and the others without any explanation or apology, shoved them out the front door of Government House and left them standing on the street corner, madder than a bunch of wet tomcats.

The Kuwaitis had taken the incident as an outrageous insult. As far as they were concerned, they had made a deal with the U.S. Government to avenge the outrage of Saddam's attack. Jack Morgan had brokered that deal and cashed the check. The fact that the wrong man was now in the White

House was not their problem. A deal is a deal. Now it was up to Morgan to deliver or face the consequences.

Morgan had never seen Faud that angry. He and his associates had gone directly from Government House to the airport, and didn't even bother with their things at the condo. "Someone will come," that's all that was said. Their jet was waiting, and zip...they were gone. *Someone will come alright! Not another word spoken. None needed. Message received. Someone will come. Enjoy the sunset, Jack, we're sending someone. Someone for you. Someone for your president, someone for your whole damn country.*

There was another problem. *How much had the customs agents, or whomever they were, really found? Were his communications networks still secure?* His team would be working round the clock until they had the answer. And the clock was ticking.

He surveyed his office: the heavy emerald glass tables on gold pedestals, the rich carpet and leather couches, the models of his developments at Rum Point and the marina at Morgan's Landing, the financial compound that would replace the ramshackle houses on the south side of town, and his masterpiece—the villas surrounding North Sound. They'd be well underway, perhaps half done or more, if it hadn't been for the damn environmentalists. His eyes came to focus on the phones on his desk. *Useless and threatening. Not to be trusted. Not until they were secure, and how do you call the phone company when your phone is dead?* He laughed, but there was no humor in it. He spun his soft leather chair to face the painting behind his desk. The head and talons of a large bird of prey appeared to burst through the canvas in full attack. The eyes made it work. Not cold dead shark's eyes sheathed for blind attack. The eyes of the huge black hawk glowed like embers in a blacksmith's forge. *You could feel their heat. The hawk comes, eyes wide, seeing everything, full of deadly fire, diving for the merciless kill. That's how it was. That's how it would be.* He raised the bottle and renewed his oath.

How? How in the hell, after all the precautions he'd taken, after all the precautions they had all taken, how had they been tumbled by a bunch of third rate island cops? Then, of course, there were other possibilities.

He raised the bottle again and realized that his vision was blurring. He could no longer read the Latin on his MBA diploma.

In the States, the feds might be stupid enough to try a stunt like this, but not here. Here, money and privacy were respected. Here, money has no personality, no politics. Here, money is money, no questions. That's what had made the island perfect for his operation.

He stared at the bottle but didn't lift it. *So if Government House hadn't planned this, and assuming for the moment that the President's team was too stupid to have pulled it off, then who? Who would have the balls for a stunt like this? The dolphin-hugging environmentalists? No, they just broke things and left nasty notes. This had a different feel. A malevolent dry humor feel. More sophisticated, but still sophomoric: a college prank with an ironic note attached. Holiday! Of course it was Holiday. Perfect. Nice try, you s.o.b., you think I don't know about Agent Bentley? You think I can't solve his problems anytime I want?*

Too bad, Holiday. Only one chance in the majors. No catch and release, remember? Now you get stuffed and hung on my wall instead of the damn fish. You and that horsefly Bentley. He raised the bottle and finished it. Then in a blind anger, he hurled it at the construction models.

Doc and Sheri avoided the condo for the rest of the day. After a quiet dinner at The Lobster Pot, they walked the beach, swam, walked more and waited. Agent John Bentley emerged from the mangroves shortly after midnight.

"Come sit here, out of the light," he said quietly.

JB looked cautiously back into the mangroves once and then again, as if he'd heard something, before speaking.

He's spooked, Doc thought and it was very much out of character for the usually carefree customs agent.

"We hit pay dirt," JB began. "Two of the Kuwaitis have their fingers in some very hot pies. The one called Faud was wanted for bank fraud in London. He was part of BCCI, but it gets better. He may be bank rolling the build-up of a terrorist group in the States. So far, we don't know why or when, but there's a team to watch, and he's the coach."

"Is Morgan in on it?" Doc asked.

"Our guys don't think so. In fact Morgan may even be a target," JB answered. "It may be that Morgan's double-crossed them somehow. Whatever Faud's up to may be paybacks."

Doc chuckled, "Then maybe you should let him go. I think I like the guy already."

"We did. We let him go."

"What?"

"Had to. Orders. Hot orders. We tagged them, just like we were told and turned them loose."

"Too bad..."

"Oh, it get's better. Morgan knows it was us."

"Us? As in the all of us?" Sheri asked.

"Yeah. He called a friend of mine in Washington. Hell, he called everyone I know in Washington. Madder than hell. He wants my head or maybe it's my ass. People started calling me, warning me. Morgan has friends on the Hill. There's going to be trouble."

"What now?" Doc said.

"Damned if I know. He could get nasty. Oh, one other thing. He shut down his computers and hasn't used the phones all day. Did the calling from his car phone with some high tech scrambler."

"Smart," Doc said.

"Yeah, and if he finds those bugs, I may become a full time scuba instructor...in Siberia. Looks like we've stirred up a hornet's nest. There are two more things you need to know. We ran prints on all of them including Ms. Kee, Sheri. And it's not Miss Kee, it's Doctor Lin Kee. Top secret clearance with D.O.D. She was a project scientist on Office of Naval Research grants at the University of Massachusetts, Amherst. Our dragon lady was a high level geneticist working on something called novel agents. That mean anything to either of you?"

"No," Doc said. "But if Morgan was interested, it's worth looking into. What else?"

"I've made arrangements for you and Stephanie to..."

"Stephanie?" Sheri began, but a twig snapped in the mangrove behind them. JB coughed and fell across Sheri, pinning her to the sand. Doc flattened beside them. The air was deathly still and Doc turned his head trying to get a fix on the movement in the scrub. Someone was there moving on all fours, carefully, patiently.

Sheri reached for him. He motioned for her to be still,

but saw that she was trying to hand him Bentley's gun. He stretched toward her and took it. Bentley still hadn't moved and when Doc took the gun, he understood why. It was covered with blood and so were Sheri's arm and hand. Doc crawled closer and felt for a carotid pulse. Nothing. Agent John Bentley was dead.

Doc rolled him off Sheri. She was choking back sobs and shaking.

"You hit?" Doc asked softly.

"No."

"Good. Find his keys."

In the brush something moved again. They both flattened to the sand. Doc looked toward the sky. The moonlight was bright enough to silhouette them if they moved, but there were clouds moving. If they could get just a moment of darkness....

"Found 'em," Sheri whispered.

Doc nodded. More movement in the brush. This time to the left. *How many? Were they flanking? Setting up a crossfire?* His instincts were screaming to get the hell out of here, but in the game of ambush, the first to move loses. He squeezed Sheri's hand and waited. Movement again both to the left and right. Behind them was the white sand beach, an open field of fire for twenty yards to the water and then they would have another fifteen yards before the water was deep enough to protect them. *Too far. Ahead at least two gunmen well hidden in the brush. Moving closer. How many more in the parking lot? Can't go forward or backward. What about....*

There were three large palms growing in a tight cluster ten feet away.

"Give me his belt and start digging," Doc whispered.

She was too terrified to argue and they set to work. Doc watched the clouds. They would only get a few moments of total darkness. It was a real long shot.

In the mangroves Andrews inched forward again. He could no longer see Geist, but that wasn't the problem. The problem was the mangroves were so thick he couldn't see anything else either. And his rabbits were too smart to run. Stalemate. He'd have to get closer. He flattened and picked his next hand placement and then the next. He heard Geist moving a few meters to his left. *The admiral is a little old for this game,* he chuckled. *Hell, aren't we all?* He pulled forward and then paused to listen.

Nothing. Holiday was smart, and he was dangerous. *But why prolong it? The ex-SEAL was smart enough to know the situation was hopeless. Why not just run for it and let it end? Isn't that what I'd do? No way in hell. I'd do just what Holiday is doing. Try every trick in the book and write a few new ones if necessary.*

The moonlight was gone. He looked toward the sky. The cloud cover wouldn't last long, but suddenly it was darker than the inside of a magician's hat. The perfect time for rabbits to jump and run. Geist must have thought the same thing. He heard the admiral moving quickly toward the beach, making too much noise. *What the hell, Bentley may not have even been carrying. Too long in the islands and you start thinking you're bulletproof, just like the Brits. Still, I'll let him get there first.* He eased forward a few feet, swearing at himself for the noise he made. Ten years ago he wouldn't have disturbed a mosquito. Now he could see the sand patch where Bentley had been sitting. *No body. Nobody. What the hell?*

Andrews stepped boldly from the brush onto the beach and swore. He walked to the spot where Bentley had been kneeling and looked at the sand.

"You missed. How the hell could you miss a shot like that?" Geist accused him,

"I don't think so," Andrews answered as he stepped into the clearing. He knelt on the spot where Bentley had gone down and ran his fingers through the sand. Then with a cruel smile he pulled a long bladed fighting knife and with the heel of his palm against the hilt, began plunging it through the soft the sand.

Geist stepped back looking distrustfully at the ground around them, expecting Doc to erupt from it at any moment. "It's over, Holiday. You can still walk clean if you come up now. Don't make us hurt the girl. Damn it, come on out." He was poised, ready with his gun, but there was no answer.

Andrews kept working until there was the sickening sound of ribs breaking and a single "whoosh" as air escaped from a thoracic cavity.

"Which one is it?" Geist asked, still at the ready.

Andrews was digging. "It's the customs agent. Told you I

got him."

In the distance car doors slammed and they heard laughing.

"Cover him back up and let's go," Geist snapped.

"Yes, sir, admiral, sir," Andrews answered. "What about the others?"

"You see them?"

"No."

"Any suggestions?"

"No."

"You like it here enough to homestead?"

They heard the laughter moving down the path to the beach.

"Screw you," Andrews said mostly under his breath and kicked sand back over Bentley's body. Geist ignored him and they slipped back into the mangroves just as two couples appeared on the beach and ran toward the water.

Doc waited until Geist and Andrews had withdrawn. And then he waited longer. Eventually a third figure rose from the mangroves and then a fourth. They looked up and down the beach from the cover of the mangroves and then backed slowly away until they were out of sight. Doc watched them head for the parking lot from the top of the palm tree. When the next cloud blocked the moonlight, Doc used his belt and Bentley's to climb down the same way he'd gone up. He dropped to the sand, quickly uncovered the upper half of Bentley's body and lifted it enough to let Sheri escape from beneath him in the shallow two-man grave. Sheri trembled in his arms. "It was Colonel Andrews, wasn't it?"

"Yes." He brushed the sand from her face and hair.

"Then Morgan is involved with Behrmann and *Blackwolf.*"

"Looks like it."

"And if Morgan is working for the government, like JB thought, that means..."

He held his finger to her lips and pointed toward a couple walking toward them on the beach. The clouds had passed now and the moon was very bright again. In the water the other couples were playing keep away with someone's swimsuit. Doc took her hand and they began walking toward the water. They kept their backs to the couple behind them and waded into deeper water.

Sheri was calmer now and there was an angry determination in her voice. "Why didn't you shoot them?"

"Timing is everything. It's Morgan we want. Andrews will be easy when we've got Morgan." Doc looked back to the beach. The couple behind them were now at the trees. The girl screamed.

"What are we going to do, Doc?" Sheri asked.

"Swim...just relax and swim. We'll think of something."

He undid his belt and ran it through the trigger guard of Bentley's small .38. On the beach the three couples gathered around Bentley's body. They shouted and pointed toward Doc and Sheri, but no one wanted to run down the beach after them. Doc and Sheri swam for half an hour until they could see Morgan's ketch and the condo's pontoon boats. They swam beneath the pontoon boat and rested, hanging on to the deck beams.

The condo was lit like a fortress. Doc could see armed men walking the beach and most of the lights were on inside. It didn't look inviting. As they watched, Josh, the friendly maintenance chief, walked across the beach carrying two fuel cans and set them in an inflatable. Then he spoke with the two men guarding the beach and went back to the hotel. He returned shortly carrying two more five-gallon cans.

"It's for the sailboat," Sheri whispered. "There was water in the marina's diesel, so now Morgan has Josh keep a special supply for *Bluebird* which is filtered before they take it to the boat. He's a real fanatic about that boat."

"Good, let's borrow it."

On the beach Josh finished loading the inflatable and shoved off. Doc waited until the small boat was tied at *Bluebird*'s stern before leaving the security of the pontoon boat.

He took several breaths, exhaled deeply after each, then dropped beneath the surface and swam fifty yards submerged before surfacing beside the sailboat.

How does he do that? she said to herself before following him. She had to surface twice to cover the same distance. When she came up the third time she had gone past the stern so he pulled her into the darkness behind the boat.

"What now?" she asked still trying to get her breath.

"I'll lift you up."

He dropped beneath the surface again and dolphin-kicked himself high enough beside the boat to get a hand on the spray rail. Then he turned so that his back was to the hull and whispered, "Come on, I'm getting taller by the second."

"How?"

"Grab my neck and step into my hand, then stand and I'll boost you up."

"You're going to hang on with one hand and lift me with the other...this I've got to see."

"Hush."

To her amazement, she was suddenly boosted aboard. She kept low and at Doc's instruction, moved forward out of sight. Josh's inflatable was tied on the beach side and the cabin door was open, but he was nowhere to be seen.

Doc pulled himself aboard and waited, expecting to see the big Caymanian emerge from the cockpit. Nothing. Doc pulled the gun from his belt and eased, head first, down the companionway ladder. The boat was dark. He crouched by the navigator's station, gave his eyes a moment to adjust to the light and listened while he waited. There was movement in the master cabin, aft of the companionway.

He eased forward and tried the door. It opened effortlessly and in the cabin, he saw a red-lensed flashlight pointed at a compartment beneath the deck. Josh was sitting with his back to the door, examining something in the hidden compartment.

"Josh," Doc said quietly. "Josh, go easy. It's Doc Holiday."

The light went out and the big man rolled across the deck in the darkness.

"What you doin' here, Doctor? This here's no place for you."

"I might ask you the same question. Do all maintenance men carry red filtered flashlights? A friend of ours, a customs agent named John Bentley, has been murdered. Morgan's men did it and they're after us too."

"JB is dead?" The red light came on shining directly into Doc's eyes.

"You knew him?"

"He was my friend."

"We need your help, Josh. We need to get away."

"Not on this boat. You won't get two miles. Morgan's got fast boats, and guns, man. Enough to start his own navy."

"Then what do you suggest?"

"You sure it was Morgan's men killed JB?"

"I saw them. One was someone I used to know, a Colonel Andrews."

"Andrews, CIA? I thought he was dead."

"Not dead enough," Doc answered.

Josh chuckled and lowered the light. "You knew him, that's for sure. We got to get you off this boat, man, and away from here quick. Morgan is worried. He's going to run."

"What did you find?"

Josh stepped forward and pointed the light into the hidden compartment. There were ten bales, each a foot thick, of stock certificates sealed in heavy plastic. "European bearer bonds. Good as cash, better than gold. Smallest worth a hundred grand. Most are more."

"A hundred million, two hundred, three hundred?"

"Who knows?" Josh dropped to his knees and replaced the flooring. "Come on, we got to go."

"What now?"

"I got more fuel to haul. He's afraid to take her to the marina. Want's her here where he can watch her. Can't say I blame him with ballast like that. They are watching me. I'm just supposed to be checking the oil and that don't take but a minute. I need to make another fuel run and while I'm on the beach, I'll try to find out what's going on. You'd do better to just keep swimming, Doc—as fast and as far as you can."

"It may be too late for that."

"Then wait here and keep out of sight. We'll figure something when I get back."

"I trust you, Josh, and so does Sheri..."

"It's alright, man, we're on the same side. Sit tight. I'll be back."

The old man went back up the companionway and climbed over the side into the dinghy. Sheri watched him go and then dropped into the cabin. Doc was at the nav station checking out the radios. He turned one on and changed the channels. He talked quietly for a moment, waited and then spoke again. He turned off the radio and turned to Sheri.

"We need to buy some time. Morgan has his loot aboard and he's ready to run. Josh will be back shortly. You keep an eye on things and stay out of sight. I've got a couple things to do."

Doc slipped back over the side, submerged, swam back to the pontoon boat and quickly cut the rubber fuel lines. From there he swam to the only other boat, the tow boat for parasailing, a large twin inboard Donzi. Then he heard the inflatable's outboard fire and start the high pitched drone of a small two-cylinder engine. He dropped beneath the hull, swam to the stern, and cut free the stern mooring line. On the second dive he tied the line in a figure eight through the blades of both propellers and as an afterthought, pulled off his tee shirt, wrapped it around one of his deck shoes, and crammed both into the exhaust. He used his other shoe as a ram until the first was lodged well out of sight. Then he rested for a moment, submerged and returned to *Bluebird*'s port side just as Josh was securing the inflatable to the starboard.

The big Caymanian was hoisting the fuel cans aboard when Sheri said his name quietly from the cockpit.

"Missy? Is that you? Lord bless me on Sunday morning, I've been mighty worried 'bout you, child. What the devil you doing out here?"

"There's trouble, Josh. John Bentley's been killed."

"I know. Doc told me. Police sayin' you did it. You and Doctor Holiday."

"You don't believe them, do you?"

"Course not, Missy, but it would go bad for me if I got caught helping you. You understand. I got a big family, they need me and I need this job."

Doc pulled himself back aboard and lay in the shadows. "What's happening on the beach?" he asked.

Josh turned quickly. "They're lookin' for you everywhere, man. They say you kilt JB. But I don't believe it. None of it." He stopped short, looking at the beach. "We've got trouble now. They want me back on the beach. They must have seen you."

The two men on the beach were waving frantically and shouting at him. Josh waved back at them as if everything were alright and then ducked below, where Doc was on the radio again and Sheri was watching the beach from a porthole. Soon more men were lugging another inflatable down to the water.

"Here comes trouble," she said. "Josh, if you need to go back, it's alright. We understand."

"No. Like Doc said, it's too late for that now. You get the mooring lines off, I start the engine."

Sheri ran forward and dropped the mooring lines while Josh was at the helm, trying to start the diesel. It coughed twice and then fired with a burst of water and black smoke. As Doc finished his radio call, he pulled the .38 from his belt and handed it to Sheri. "Keep an eye on things," he said and looked towards Josh.

Sheri nodded. Sirens whined on the highway and she saw flashing lights pull into the condo's parking lot. "This doesn't look good," she said quietly.

"Josh, do they keep weapons aboard?" Doc said from the companionway.

"I don't know, man. I'm not like what you'd call a frequent guest." He was looking over his shoulder, watching the men walking the inflatable through the shallows. Four men and they were holding weapons up, trying to keep them dry as they walked the boat through the gentle surf. Men in uniforms were now on the beach pointing toward the ketch and shouting into hand-held radios. Josh shook his head. *What chance did they have? The ketch couldn't outrun anything.*

Doc popped back up at the base of the companionway. "Sheri, come down and look. Flare guns, anything we can use to slow them down. Also turn his scanner on. Let me know if you hear anything exciting. Hurry!"

The inflatable had headed for the Donzi. Josh had the sailboat's throttle wide open and was headed north toward the Turtle Farm. If they could make it around the point, they might ground the boat and run. He heard the Donzi cough and then die. One more try was followed by loud swearing and then two men jumped back into the inflatable. The inflatable's outboard engine snarled to life and the boat was hot on their trail. They could hear bursts from a small caliber full auto as the man in the bow opened fire well out of range. Doc came back on deck, sat beside Josh and waited.

Bluebird crossed into darker, deeper water. They were over the edge of the wall now and the swells were ocean swells, long and rolling. Doc dropped down the first steps of the companionway ladder and took the flare gun and six flares Sheri handed him. "I'm afraid that's it. What else can we do?" she asked.

"Load the fuel back into the inflatable. We don't want it on our decks and maybe I can hit it with this," he said holding up the flare gun.

Josh dropped to his knees behind the wheel. They heard rounds popping through the rigging. Doc grabbed the last of the fuel cans, stabbed holes through it and tossed it into the inflatable. Then he cut the painter.

"Good idea," Josh said.

"James Bond...I think it was *Dr. No* in 1963 or maybe *Thunderball.* You remember?"

"I remember. It was *Thunderball.* Great flick."

Doc looked up over the gunnel and saw the gunner's boat closing fast. He steadied himself and fired the first flare. High and away. They kept coming hard and fast, and were nearly beside Doc's fire ship when the second flare hit it. The explosion lit up the night sky. Both rubber boats vanished in the blast. For a moment everything was deathly still and then they heard both the Donzi's twin inboards bark to life.

Sheri came to the companionway. "Something's up. Morgan is on the radio yelling at them not to shoot at us. He wants them to go back to the beach, but they must not be listening. They're not answering."

Doc looked back just as the Donzi powered around the burning fuel and opened fire with a heavy caliber weapon. He saw the orange muzzle blast and saw a tracer leave its comet's trail through the rigging. Doc shouted at Josh to change course, but it was too late. The next volley tore into the hull and the diesel died in a last belch of black smoke.

"Poor *Bluebird*'s a dead bird unless you've got more tricks up your sleeve, Doctor," Josh moaned.

But Doc was helping Sheri up the salon ladder and didn't hear him.

"We're taking on water," she coughed as he took her arm and pulled her to the cockpit. "There are a half dozen holes the size of baseballs. Any ideas?" she asked, coughing some more.

Doc looked around in desperation and ran his fingers through his salt and pepper hair. "Where's the Navy when you need them the most?"

The Donzi was alongside now, about fifty feet off the port beam. They were calling with a hailer for *Bluebird*'s crew to show themselves. Josh stood up waving his tee shirt and Doc looked at Sheri and nodded. They climbed up slowly from the cockpit deck, but lost their footing as the boat healed to port. She was sinking fast.

"You think Jack will fire me for this?" Sheri laughed nervously. "There go all the autographs on his ego wall."

The Donzi came closer, still yelling through the bullhorn for them to stand.

"We can still swim for it," she said and waited.

"No need," he answered. "The Sixth Fleet has finally arrived."

Out of the smoke and darkness *Kratos*'s gleaming white hull suddenly emerged towering over the Donzi.

Doc stood and in a commanding voice yelled, "Put down your weapons, put your hands on your heads and get on your knees or we will blow you out of the water."

There was laughter over the bullhorn and an obscenity or two, but Mike put a stop to the frivolity with a short blast from the mini-gun. The crew abruptly turned to face the lights and when they saw the competition, quickly did as they were told.

Mike kept them in his spotlights as he came alongside *Bluebird*. "Shall we break out a salvage blanket and the pumps?" he asked as Doc and Sheri climbed up the dive platform. Josh was just behind them.

"No. Call it poetic justice, call it my bad attitude, but somehow I think it's time for this bird to fly the coop. Let's just get the hell out of here. By the way, who's driving this tub?"

"It's an old friend of Sheri's I picked up along the way. Come on, I'll introduce you."

In the wheelhouse Stephanie turned to greet them. Mike took the helm and left the Donzi in their wake. When Josh entered the wheelhouse he stared at Stephanie as if he were seeing a ghost.

"Girl, what are you doing here?" Josh demanded.

"JB called about three hours ago and told me to meet him at the fuel dock. He said I had to get off the island right away and he'd made the arrangements. We were going to the airport by boat and then we were to fly back to the States together, but he didn't show. Do you know what happened?"

Sheri stepped forward a bit uncertain. Stephanie opened her arms and greeted her with a teary-eyed hug.

"John Holiday," a voice boomed over the radio. "This is the Cayman Islands Police. Attention, John Holiday, surrender immediately. You are under arrest for the murder of U.S. Customs Agent John Bentley. I repeat, you are under arrest for the murder of Agent John Bentley. Surrender now, before there's more bloodshed. You have a woman aboard."

Doc looked toward the radio with a perplexed look and started to speak.

"Oh no," Stephanie sobbed, "not JB."

"It was Morgan's men," Sheri said. "They tried to kill us too."

"You can't go back there, Doctor," Josh said. "Morgan has men everywhere. You'd never get to the real cops, the honest ones, and even if you did, I don't know how long they could protect you."

"He's right," Stephanie said, drying her eyes. "Let's go. I won't have a chance if Morgan finds me. Neither will any of you."

"Where to?" Mike asked.

"How's your fuel?" Doc asked.

"Not good. I'd just pulled into the fuel dock when I got your call."

"North side of the island, in Great Bay. We can hide in the groves 'til we see which way this storm blows," Josh answered.

"Done," Mike said and without waiting for Doc to answer, he pushed the throttles to the firewall and the turbo cats snarled again. Within minutes the emerald green lights from the condo and the police with their radios were lost in their wake.

It was still early when Mike came knocking on their stateroom door with coffee. Doc was awake instantly, but with the comfort of the bed, the softness of the plush carpet when his feet hit the deck, and the garishness of the ceiling mirrors, it took a moment to remember where he was. Sheri moaned and turned toward him. Kissing her as he covered her with the sheet, he pulled on his shorts before opening the door for Mike and the steaming mug. "Bentley called Ian yesterday. He was desperate to get you off the island," Mike began as they moved to the salon. "Ian told him I was on the way, then called me back and told me to pick you up at the fuel pier, but Stephanie was the only one there."

"Right, Bentley was killed before he could tell us about the arrangements he'd made. Too bad, he was a good man. Sorry to lose him. But anyway, thanks. Thanks for everything. Your timing couldn't have been better."

"I got underway quick as I could after you called last week. The base did everything they could to keep me there. I finally had to go AWOL. Hope Anderson can square it or I'm in for some serious brig time. They'd assigned me to a bunch of boatswains mates, can you imagine?"

"I can imagine they might have taught you a lot."

"Actually they did. That's the only reason this tub is still running. Tom called... said he'd gotten into Morgan's computer and that Morgan has started moving money. Big money. He thought you'd want to know."

"I thought none of our phone taps worked," Doc said rubbing his jaw and stretching.

"That's what Bentley thought too," Mike said.

Sheri joined them still wrapped in the sheet, but with a mug of coffee.

"You're going to love this one..." Mike went on. "Tom told me Morgan was too spooked to use the phones or the computers in the condo. So he took a laptop with a modem and hooked it up to his car phone. Tom nailed him with the satellite. And wait till you hear Stephanie's part of the story. She was too nervous to sleep much last night so I heard the whole thing. It's unbelievable."

"Where is she?" Sheri asked.

"She and Josh slipped into Rum Point a couple hours ago. We need groceries and Josh was worried about his family. Should be back anytime."

"Tell me the rest. What happened to Stephanie at the hospital, and why couldn't we find her?"

"Josh took care of that. He called Bentley and they got her out of the hospital. She's been on the island the whole time, staying with Josh's family."

"Okay, but what about her stuff on the boat, her earring and panties?" Sheri persisted.

"That whole thing was a screw up. The break-in at the dive shop too. Stephanie knew that Morgan was way out of bounds and that you were going to be in a lot of danger, Sheri, so she did two things. She told Josh's two sons what was going on and asked them to try to warn you. So they broke into the shop and left you that note. Then when she heard about the attack by the environmentalists, she left you a note on the boat."

"But unfortunately, the cushion got wet, the ink ran and we couldn't read it."

"Right," Mike said. "The note was another attempt to warn you to leave."

He was interrupted by the whine of a small outboard. The dinghy was returning.

"Get dressed," Doc said and opened the hidden compartment in the nav station. He handed Sheri the Smith and Wesson and stuck a Beretta in the back of his shorts. Sheri returned to the cabin and the men went on deck. Mike had pulled the boat in tight to the trees, laid the tower forward over the bow, and covered her with mangrove branches. He had repositioned the rotating radar antenna on the highest point and a remotely operated video camera as well. It reminded Doc of Operation Gamekeeper on the Rung Sat River and he nodded his approval.

Stephanie was in the dinghy's bow accompanied by two men in their early twenties. The older was handling the outboard.

"Josh stayed. He thinks there's going to be more trouble and your boat isn't big enough for his whole family. Said he'll slip back out tonight if there's any news," Stephanie said.

"These are Izaak and Benjamin, Josh's sons. He sent them to help. There are still nine more at home."

When they were all aboard and the groceries stored, Izaak and Benjamin returned to the deck to stand watch. Stephanie handed Doc a newspaper. His picture was on the front page.

"You're not bad looking for a fugitive," Sheri teased as she refilled his coffee.

"What about Morgan?" Doc asked Stephanie. "Can you tell us what the devil's going on? What his business with the Kuwaitis is? And what all this is about?" he said, pointing to the paper. "My boss is expecting a phone call and I'd sure like to have some answers before I call him."

"Well, the big news is Jack Morgan is gone. His plane left the island just after midnight."

"And no one tried to stop him?"

"They don't want him, Doc. They want you."

"What about the rest...what are your pieces of this puzzle?"

"You know that the condo was a front, set up as a cover for his so-called banking operations, right?"

"That's what JB told us."

"Well, it was a black op from the beginning. Besides his so-called diplomatic mission, he's into money laundering, brokering arms deals, and something to do with oil. He's been building quite a network of political friends. He has serious political intentions."

"He wants to be president?" Doc asked a bit surprised.

"No, he wants to own one. This one's cramping his style."

"That figures," Sheri laughed. "He owns a satellite, why not a president?"

"And it was well on the way to happening until they hit a snag," Stephanie agreed.

"The Kuwaitis?" Sheri said.

"Right. Morgan made a deal to deliver Saddam's head on a platter and got big money up front. He was going to irritate Iraq to the point that they would do something dumb and we would have justification to retaliate. But Saddam cooled his jets and the plan didn't work. Now they have to try something else."

"How do you know this?" Doc asked her.

"From the security tapes. Morgan watched the disks at night in our bed and made notes."

"How romantic," Sheri laughed.

"Is that it?" Doc asked.

"Unless you want a list of the congressmen and senior staff officers who are on his team. That gets pretty exciting."

"Absolutely. We need to know what we're up against and

whom. That list could be powerful stuff."

"Powerful enough to get us all killed," Stephanie answered. "But, just remember, without those CD's I can't prove anything, and my credibility is blown, so they will never use me as a witness. All you get from me is hearsay from an unreliable witness, and you can't go to court with it."

"I still want the list. It's easier to trap rats if you know where they live. I think my grandfather said that."

"Okay, I'll do my best."

Stephanie started her list with Sheri's help, while Mike checked the perimeter and Doc used the satellite linked phone to call his daughter and son-in-law in Bermuda. He talked with Debbie and Tom for nearly an hour. Then armed with a new game plan, he used the red phone again to call Inspector Ian Cord, head of the Bermuda Marine Police.

There was a long pause after Doc explained their current situation, his suspicions about Morgan, and what John Bentley had learned about the Kuwaitis. Next, someone had to contact the Navy and smooth things over for Mike. The complexity of their situation was such that they needed more help than Inspector Cord could give. After further discussion, they agreed Doc should call Andy Anderson, Secretary of the Navy.

Doc sat for a few moments making notes and then placed the call. It took awhile to get through the layers of staff, but finally the Secretary was on the line. From the beginning it was apparent that Anderson was not a happy camper. Doc followed his notes carefully explaining his suspicions about Morgan. He discreetly made no mention of the video disks at the condo.

"You actually saw Andrews?" Anderson said. His tone was very skeptical.

"Yes, sir," Doc answered. "He killed a U.S. Customs Agent, John Bentley, and would have killed both of us too."

There was a long pause before Anderson asked, "And who else saw him?"

Doc's face began to flush as he answered. "No one on our side, sir."

"So the only proof that *Blackwolf* survived is that you think you've seen Andrews, who you thought had been killed, is that right?"

"Sir, it was Andrews. And that's further proof that *Blackwolf* survived and is somehow connected to Jack Morgan. We thought you should know. That's all. Now it's up to you to decide what to do with what I've told you. You can ignore it...again. Or you can send us help and we'll try to get to the bottom of this mess. Either way, we felt obligated to keep you informed. After all, it was your submarine." He winked at Mike who had just come into the wheelhouse, and who looked up at Doc in disbelief, then smiled and gave a hearty thumbs up.

"Very well, Doctor Holiday. You have discharged your obligation. You'll be hearing from us soon," Anderson replied and the phone went dead.

"Every cop in Grand Cayman is looking for us, Doc. Why not piss off the entire U.S. Government as well? I wonder how long it will take him to get the Sixth Fleet looking for us?"

"They won't have to look far. Tom's satellite's infra-red camera will pick us up on the next pass and my guess is, Anderson had this boat tagged while you were in dry dock. He didn't ask where we are because he already knows. So the next question is, what do we do next? Abandon the boat or get ready to defend ourselves?"

"Against what?" Mike answered. "There's no military base here and the Marine Police ran their only boat up on the rocks two or three years ago. Government House refused to get it repaired. Thought they'd teach the cops a lesson."

"What about Morgan's men? They didn't look shy or retiring to me, and they've got boats and guns."

"And a healthy respect for LAW rockets," Mike countered. "No, I don't think they want any part of us. At least not yet."

"Then we sit and wait. We wait to see what Anderson does and see who comes after us first. But, damn it, I hate waiting."

CHAPTER 17

Three hours after sunset, Mike saw a blip on the radar moving slowly through the swamp. He called Doc who had been cleaning their tiny arsenal. "I've got the gain pretty high. It could be damn near anything: a wooden boat, a swimmer, an animal."

They had covered the windows to black out the boat. At the cabin door, Doc said, "Kill the lights...I'll tell the boys."

Mike cut the switch and Doc slipped out onto the deck. Benjamin stood and nodded.

"Where's your brother?" Doc asked quietly.

Benjamin pointed to the trees just at the opening to the larger canal. Izaak waved and Doc waved back. It worried him that he hadn't seen the boy when there was still plenty of moonlight.

"Good. Company coming, from there." He pointed toward the south.

"Could be Dad," Benjamin said.

"Could be anybody," Doc cautioned and looked out into the darkness again. His night vision certainly was not what it had been twenty years ago.

Soon an old wooden dory with a quiet little outboard came into sight. It carried a single passenger. When Benjamin recognized his father, Doc slipped back inside to check the radar again.

"There's trouble downtown," Josh said as he got on the boat. He turned down the beer Mike offered, but took a Coke. It had taken him two hours to crisscross Great Bay and the network of canals leading into the heart of the mangrove swamp.

"You know Morgan has left the island?" Josh began.

Doc nodded.

"Well, two of my daughters work in the banks. Somebody's movin' a lot of money...got the suits all excited...."

"What the hell are you doing here, Josh?" Doc asked abruptly. "You could tell the police we kidnapped you, that I had you at gun point and forced you to drive the boat. Your family shouldn't be involved in this."

Josh was a big man with the look of an ex-pro football player, strong shouldered, thick calved, his nose broken once too often. His face went dark and his eyes narrowed.

"You forgettin' whose island this is Doctor Holiday? I don't remember invitin' you to come down here and fight my fight. Men like Jack Morgan, with their big money and their big important ways, been comin' to my island for years treatin' me and my people like we was dirt." He shook his head with anger and disgust, paused as if he were done, thought about it a bit longer, then having decided there was still more that needed telling, began again. "These islands was a simple God-fearing place when I was a boy, Doc. People was honest, lived by hard work—fishin', building boats and working the other islands for trade. My father had a fine boat. Sailed all the islands, even to Florida. Was a respected man. Sent me to college. First in the family to ever go. Wanted me to see it, you know? See what it was out there. Bring the best of it back. Leave the worst of it alone. Wanted me to be a respected man like he was. Be somebody like he was.

"But then the money come, you know? And suddenly we was house boys and boat boys and kitchen boys on our own island. You think my sons goin' to listen to me talk 'bout what livin' should be when they see what the money does? You think they care 'bout anything 'cept getting that money so they can have what the white boys have? It ain't right, Doctor Holiday, what the money men done to my island...to my people. This was a God-fearin' place where hard workin' men had respect.

What Morgan done and his kind done, it ain't right."

"That why you were searching Morgan's boat? Is that why you know Colonel Andrews?" Doc said.

"Andrews been comin' here for years, just like Morgan. They had big important business and then they'd charter our little boat, that's all. They'd drink and they'd talk. Don't matter what the boat boy hear. Who he is anyway?

"I had my reasons for wantin' to know what he had stashed on that big sailboat. Now we know. But I wasn't doin' no stealin' if that's what you're thinkin'. Ain't no stealin' in Josh."

Doc nodded. "You want to tell us your reasons?"

"Can't do that now, Doc. But like I said, I'm on the right side and so are my boys. That's why we're here. You didn't kill John Bentley and we'll help you stay alive until we can prove it."

"Alright, I guess that's good enough for now. Now what were you saying about the banks? Customers coming in to make big withdrawals?"

"Naw, nobody comes to these banks, Doc. It's all done by computer. No tellers like the old days."

Doc nodded and Josh took another pull at the Coke.

"My girls said the transfer orders came through their computers just like normal, but when they tried to find out where the orders were coming from they drew a blank. Then when they tried to freeze the transfers they couldn't. Someone had taken over the computers and was cleaning out big accounts. You know, like the computer was haunted or something. My oldest girl said it was real spooky, like tracing an obscene phone call to a vacant lot. You know, ain't nothin' there. The house and the phone burned up years ago."

"Morgan and his private satellite."

"Gotta be," the old man said and finished the Coke.

"One more thing, Josh. What do you know about the scientists who came for a meeting? Ms. Kee knew them."

"I remember. Strange lot, never went outside. Spookier than most of the government types, real edgy if you know what I mean."

"Okay, how many and what do you know about the meeting or where they were from?"

"There were three meetings about six months apart. Real

secret. There were seven or eight of them, came on private planes, landed after dark and left the same way. Top security—I mean nobody was supposed to know those folks were ever on the island. I think they was from New England. The accents and the clothes, like college professor types, dressed all wrong, you know...sort of geeky."

"But you didn't find out what they were talking about?"

"No, sir, not a peep. They was real quiet, that bunch."

"Okay, can you remember when the meetings were? Especially the last one?"

"Yeah, that's easy. It was between Christmas and New Year's. They stayed three days. Like I said, none of them ever went outside, like they were afraid of a little sun. You never saw such white folks. Funny."

"Interesting...maybe they didn't want to explain the sunburn when they got home. Thanks, Josh, that helps."

Doc waited until the wheelhouse was empty before using the radio to call Tom. He plugged in the scrambler Tom had built into the laptop Debbie had given him, placed the call through an intricate phone net to an electronic mail bulletin board, and then started typing.

Yes, Tom answered, he'd been able to follow what Morgan had done. The amounts of money transferred were now being counted by billions not in hundreds of millions. Enough to bankrupt a small country.

"But can't they stop him?" Doc typed.

"Perhaps, but he's got all the right access codes. So, as far as the computer or anyone else knows, it's his money. With those codes he can do whatever he wants with it."

"Could you duplicate what he's done? Could you monitor his transactions and re-route his deposits?" Doc asked.

"That's hot.... But each computer has its own signature, even if we could..." Tom paused again and Doc waited. When the rest of Tom's message appeared on the screen, Doc chuckled and nodded his head. "That's it. That's what I want to hear."

Tom had written, "Can you get us into his computer center?"

"Get on the first plane," Doc wrote back. "We'll have it figured out by the time you get here."

"I just left."

Doc chuckled and closed down the program. Having a plan was better than waiting empty handed. Sheri was sitting out on the deck. Grabbing a beer, he cut the lights and slipped out into the darkness to join her. The mangrove swamp was alive with the calls of frogs and birds, and the splashes of feeding fish.

"Well, if it isn't my favorite fugitive," she smiled and kissed him.

"You left out the grandfather part. Which leads me to assume fugitive now has greater harassment potential than grandfather."

"Well, let's just say it has new harassment potential. I may have worn the tread on the grandpa bit a little thin. Especially since we still have a few months to go. But, no problem," she concluded cheerfully. "As long as I hang around you," she said and kissed him again, "there will always be wonderful new opportunities bulging with potential."

"Now there's a thought that makes life worth living," he said.

It was a little before dawn when the red phone rang. Doc was on watch, sitting in the helm seat as he watched the radar and worked on his third mug of coffee. He caught it before the second ring.

"Good morning, Mr. Secretary," he said calmly.

"'Morning, Doc. You ever sleep?"

"Not much last night. How 'bout you?"

"No, I was with the Joint Chiefs and the President most of the night."

"And....?"

"We still aren't certain what Morgan's up to. No one here knows anything about any deals with Kuwait. So whatever they were, the info is in his footlocker, not in ours. And that's the message were going to send to Kuwait. However, this could get real ugly, Doc. There are congressmen involved. Powerful ones on Morgan's side. And we've got no proof he's done anything wrong. Nothing solid enough to justify going after him."

Doc waited, then asked, "What about the sub?"

There was a long silence before Anderson said, "Sorry, Doc,

I tried, but until the Joint Chiefs give the okay, I can't discuss that with you. Anything else?"

"Yeah, I believe so, Andy. I believe there's a whole lot more. Checked your bank balance lately?"

"What?"

Tom's plane touched down with the usual screech on Cayman International's tarmac. He moved quickly through immigration and customs, but there was no sign of either Doc or Mike. It was already hot for mid-morning, so he found a bench with a bit of shade and settled in to wait. It was not unlike Doc to get a bit distracted, Debbie had warned him. Just relax...her father would be there, sooner or later.

Most of the other passengers from his flight were long gone by the time a large, gray haired islander with a newspaper sat down beside him.

"You Tom Morrison?" Josh asked quietly without looking up from the paper.

"Yeah," Tom answered cautiously.

"Doc can't make it. Asked me to pick you up. I'll bring my truck. You bring yourself quick now, okay?"

"What's happened to Doc?"

"Read the paper," Josh said and smiled. "But don't worry. Ain't nothing we can't handle. Take me just a minute. You sit tight and don't talk to strangers. Things a little crazy round here right now."

Doc's picture was again plastered squarely in the middle of the paper's front page. Tom squirmed uncomfortably as he read about the manhunt for the murderer of Customs Agent John Bentley and the ex-Navy SEAL accused of the crime. Josh's old white Toyota pulled up just as Tom finished reading about the daring escape from Seven Mile Beach and the mysterious gun boat which had appeared from nowhere and fired on the condo's security officers.

"Well, what do you think about that story?" Josh asked. He was intently watching the rear view mirror.

"My wife's going to have a baby," came the befuddled reply. "Sure hope I live to see it."

They met at a small boatyard, far enough from the yacht club to be well off the beaten path. Josh was doing a good job of keeping them out of sight. Tom jumped from the truck and greeted Doc with a warm smile and then handed him the paper.

"We didn't get publicity like this in Bermuda," he said. "Next you'll be doing all the talk shows."

They loaded Tom's gear into an official-looking rental van and as they were finishing, Josh asked how Doc intended to get back into Jack Morgan's condo.

"Getting in's not the problem. The question of the day is, how are we going to get out? And I'm still working on that. You got any ideas?" Josh shook his head, looking perplexed as Doc went to use the boatyard's phone. He returned smiling.

When the equipment was loaded, the four of them huddled in the back of the van as Josh drove. Tom's official greeting had been short. A pat on the back and a mug of cold coffee. Now they were down to business.

"Okay, here's the plan," Doc said with a grin.

Mike and Sheri exchanged knowing glances. "Oh shit! Here we go again," muttered Mike.

They made two stops along the way, one at a uniform shop for coveralls and a second at the local hardware store. Doc kept careful track of the time and when the streets were suddenly full of police cars and sirens, he grinned at Sheri. She knew that the first part of the plan was working.

They arrived at the condo just after two A.M. and parked officially, just behind the police cars. Unorganized security guards and staffers were helping guests flee from their rooms while fire and policemen tried to bring order to the chaos.

"It's the damn Kuwaitis. They must have been pissed about getting arrested and all," Doc heard one of the security men say. He smiled to himself as he led Tom up the main steps to the emerald green foyer. They were carrying large official-looking aluminum suitcases and had on official-looking uniform coveralls.

They waited until a tall, older man with a distinct military bearing approached the two door guards and exchanged a few words. Then he turned and nodded toward Doc.

"You guys from the bomb squad?" the guard asked.

"Yeah, on vacation with the wife. Washington just called and said you guys needed some help. Hope this doesn't take long...the wife's pissed. It's our anniversary," Doc answered and waited.

"Bomb squad? Would that be pick up or delivery, mate?" the tallest of the men, Inspector Ian Cord, Chief Inspector of the Bermuda Marine Police, quipped. And then before anyone else had a chance to speak, he added, "Good to see you, Mr. Harrington. The men here are still clearing the building, but we should be ready for you shortly. Were you able to find the equipment you'll need in our office?"

"Harrington, John Harrington, Secret Service," Doc said to the guards and flashed the I.D. Inspector Cord had given him in Bermuda with his finger covering the bottom of the card.

"U.S. Secret Service? What the hell are you doing here?"

"Like I told you, I was on vacation, but my office has quite an interest in Mr. Morgan and his recent activities. Have you seen him lately?"

"No..."

"Washington hasn't seen him either. When this is over, I suspect our team will be wanting to ask you and the rest of his men some questions. It would be a good idea for you to stick around."

"Ah, I didn't really work for him, see. Charlie and I are just contract security. Not much we could tell you."

"Then I'm sure you won't mind telling that to our men when they arrive."

"Yeah, yeah sure. No problem." But his nervous laugh conveyed an entirely different message.

"So in the meantime, the islanders don't have a bomb squad and they hit the panic button—and there goes my anniversary party."

"Yeah, too bad," the first laughed. "Say, you suppose Morgan had anything to do with all that money disappearing today? The story is all over the island."

"Bank on it," Doc said straight faced and Inspector Cord rolled his eyes but still kept a straight face.

"Okay, it's all yours. These folks coming out now are the

last. Here, take this radio and just let us know what you need. We'll keep everyone else out of your way. Got any idea how long we'll be here?"

"You mean if there is a bomb and it goes off? Probably not more than a milli-second or two. Not standing here under all this glass," Doc said pointing up. "Now over there, across the street behind those barricades, a man could be here a long time over there."

"Thanks, buddy," the guard answered and quickly transmitted a radio message to the others around the building. Then he tripped as he tried to walk backwards still looking up. Ian caught him, took the radio and helped him on his way.

"Mind if I tag along, Doctor Harrington?"

"It's your funeral, Inspector. But thanks for getting here so quickly. We couldn't have pulled this off without your distinguished British accent. It makes the damnedest lies sound so bloody believable." Then he laughed and shook Ian's hand. They had crossed the foyer and were waiting for the elevator.

Doc used Josh's keys, first to let Mike and Sheri in through a kitchen entrance, and then again at the elevator to access the executive levels. In the elevator, Tom explained why it was so important to get to Morgan's own computer: "You can set up each terminal with its own signature," Tom began. "Without that signature it doesn't matter how good you are, you aren't going to get in. And that's what we're here to do. Get in, and see if we can get back a few million dollars."

"Just as long as there aren't any oil spills. That's where I draw the line, lads. Alright, let's get to it."

The elevator doors opened on the eighth floor. Tom set his suitcase down in Jack Morgan's office, took out his notebook and booted up Morgan's computer. Sheri pulled open the desk drawer and pushed the button to open the secret panel to the surveillance room. The bookcase panel opened, but Inspector Cord stopped to examine some of the titles in Morgan's extensive collection of old books. The Maritime Museum in Bermuda would love to have these, he thought as he followed Doc and Sheri into the video room.

"What are you looking for?" Inspector Ian Cord asked Doc.

"Video disks of Morgan's guests. Some of it pretty hot stuff, I'm told." He winked at Sheri who turned bright red. Doc found the logs and looked them over briefly. Ian helped him search while Mike stood guard in the hall where he could watch the elevators and the crowd below them.

There was a power surge followed by the soft hum of air conditioners built into the floor beneath the huge computer in the next room.

"We're on," Tom said. "Now let's get in."

"Sounds like the lad's on his first date," quipped Ian.

When Doc found the log books he wanted, he tossed one to Ian. "See if you can find Christmas of last year, a bunch of scientists."

Ian nodded and began scanning the book.

"Hot damn, we're in!" Tom shouted from Morgan's desk.

Doc took two of the video logs and went to join him. "Now what?" he asked Tom.

"I wrote a program on these disks to speed things up. Pray they work because if they don't, we could be here for hours. I can't believe he had this much security and then blew it all using a cellular phone. You must have rattled his cage pretty well."

"Don't you just love it...."

"When a plan comes together?" Tom laughed. "Does that make us your A-team?"

"More like a C-minus team so far," Doc chuckled and slapped him on the back. "Look at this," he said pointing to a log entry. "Half the Joint Chiefs were here just last year. How are you doing, Ian?"

"Nothing yet."

"Okay, keep looking and if you come across anything from 98-8-14, grab it."

"What's that?" Tom asked.

"Blackmail material—Sheri and me. A little home video she'll kill to get her hands on," he laughed. "How you doing?"

"The disk is still translating. We'll know in a minute."

"If it works, how long?"

"Six, maybe seven minutes.... That's it, we're in. We're downloading the files we wanted and making the corrected mailing addresses on the transfers. We've got him!"

"Here's your Christmas meeting," Ian said.

Doc went back to the file room and loaded the disk into a

computer drive. There was an argument going on about the delivery date of something the scientists had promised and Morgan was angry. Doc advanced a bit. Now Ms. Kee was in the room and was asking questions about a project at Ft. Detrick. None of them gave her clear answers. Fast forward again. Now Morgan was alone with the oldest of the group—a grandfatherly type with half-frames. This time the discussion was about delivery vehicles and the old man kept insisting that thousand-pound bombs were the safest way. Morgan was shaking his head. He wanted an option which didn't involve an air strike, but the older man insisted it would be too dangerous.

Fast forward again. This time Morgan was pouring drinks. At first Doc couldn't identify who Morgan's guest was, but when the other came forward to accept the drink, Doc recognized him immediately and shook his head sadly. Both men were laughing and they raised glasses in a toast.

"To Project Sverdlovsk," Morgan said, and the other grunted his agreement.

Doc took the disk from the computer and dropped it into his shirt pocket.

Jack Morgan was asleep in the plush bedroom of his lavish Costa Rican mountain estate overlooking the Pacific Ocean when an alarm at a sophisticated security panel went off. His computer turned itself on and then turned on two video monitors. The first monitor scrolled the commands Tom's disk was programming in and the second image was from the surveillance camera in his office. He rubbed his eyes and looked at his watch. It was three A.M.

"What the hell?" he said sliding out from under Ms. Kee's head and arm. He rubbed his eyes and maneuvered awkwardly to his desk. What he saw on the monitor was enough to shock him fully awake. He swore again and grabbed the phone. No answer at the front desk or in the security office. He tried to follow the commands scrolling on the monitor and dial security's mobile number at the same time. After he mis-dialed twice, he put the phone down and pulled a program operations manual from his desk. When he found what he wanted, he entered the command to freeze the screen and allow him to read Tom's entries.

"How in the hell...." He hit the keys allowing the screen to scroll again, but now much slower.

Ms. Kee jumped from the bed and grabbed a robe. As soon as she saw the screen, she grasped his arm as well as the situation. "Where are our people?" she demanded.

"Damned if I know. Here, you find them," he said handing her the phone. She began dialing while he continued entering commands on the keyboard.

"He locked us out. The son-of-a-bitch has locked us out," he said and slammed his desk.

Ms. Kee had found someone to talk to on the mobile phone. They were explaining about the bomb threat as they tried to find the short red headed chief of security.

"Something's up," Mike yelled from the hall. "The security guys are talking to the cops. Here they come."

"The doors have electric locks," Doc shouted back and ran back to the video room. Ian had opened the switch panels and was trying to decide which to throw but there was no index. Doc turned on the computer, found the menu and pulled up the screen.

"They're in the foyer," Mike shouted. The elevator was starting its descent.

"Shall I shut down everything, Doc?" Ian asked.

"Not until Tom's done. We have to hold them off for a while. There, this is what we need." The security screen came up with a menu across the bottom. Doc began locking down the condo. The elevators stopped between floors. Electric locks dropped dead bolts on stairways and all exits.

"How's it going, Tom?" he shouted.

"Two minutes," Tom shouted back.

"Now, how do we get out?" Ian asked.

"Beats me," Doc answered. "I thought that was your department."

"Charming."

"You have to stop them before he finishes loading those

commands," Ms. Kee said calmly.

"I can't. We're locked out."

"Yes, you can. Do it."

He turned to look at her and slowly nodded. He pulled open his desk drawer, removed a small leather bound notebook and began entering commands on the computer.

"Well?" she demanded.

"It's working," he answered and kept typing.

Doc was still at the computer's security screen looking for a way out of the building when the message, "CODE RED AUTHORIZED," flashed on the screen.

"What'd you do?" Tom yelled from Morgan's desk.

"Nothing," Doc yelled back.

A tremor shook the building as the first demolition charges took out six-foot sections of the foundation piling. Doc felt the floor bounce beneath his feet and knew instantly what was happening. A second blast collapsed the structural beam support of the first floor. The floor hung suspended on air for a second before starting to drop.

"Come on," Doc shouted. He stuffed the logbook and disks into his shirt, grabbed the coffee table and hurled it through the heavy green glass window. Then he grabbed Sheri and jumped through the opening. The others followed as Doc shouted instructions. They crossed the pool deck and lunged at the nearest patio table sending chairs flying out of the way. Doc pulled the retaining pin on the huge umbrella base weights. The up draft of hot air from the explosion lifted the ten-foot-diameter umbrella up through the table, pulling the pole from his grasp. He rolled clear, leaped and caught the pole. "Hang on!" he yelled at Sheri and she grabbed his knees just as the umbrella lifted them over the eighth story ledge of the pool deck.

His hands were sweaty and slipping on the smooth aluminum pole. He tightened his grip and began hand over handing his way up it until he found good handholds in the frame. Sheri was hanging on to his knees for dear life. The mass of hot air from the blast continued to lift them as the building dropped one floor collapsing on another until it had completely imploded in on itself with hardly a piece of debris landing more than a few feet from the original foundation.

Doc looked down and could see three other umbrellas airborne beneath him. He pulled on the frame and discovered that he could steer just a bit. He shouted down, "Go for the water," and shifted his weight to bank into a turn. Sheri, much to Doc's amazement, was scared speechless and did not enjoy the ride.

Jack Morgan's monitors went dead. He began the process of re-booting his computer and activated the modem. Ms. Kee waited anxiously behind him.

"Well?" she asked as he began entering the access codes for their account information.

"Is McDonald's hiring?" he asked as he watched the screen display "ACCESS DENIED" beside each of his long list of account numbers.

"I suppose so," she answered and sank despondently into his lap.

"That's good. For a minute there I thought we might have a problem."

CHAPTER 18

As Karen and Jason watched from the mountain plateau by the waterfall and lake, the old schooner dropped anchor in the cove and the two men climbed over her gunnel into the dinghy. Jason put his arm around Karen and she leaned into the protection of his side. She looked up at him with apprehension and he nodded. The old boat and the men she carried were not a welcome sight. Below, at the last pool of the waterfall, Bill Roberts and his wife also waited. Roberts sat in a rocker on the bungalow deck and clutched his stomach as he watched Colonel Andrews and Rudy Geist row the small inflatable to the beach. Andrews, in the bow, gave a friendly wave. Petra, afraid not to respond, waved back. But there was no enthusiasm in it.

"Do you see their guns?" Petra asked as the men drew closer.

"No, but that doesn't mean much. Just remember, they think we have the guns Jason took from them. That should give us a little leverage."

"I hope they don't find the boat. Just a few more days..." she said.

"It was a good idea at the time," he answered. "I'd rather take my chances in a homemade boat than with these sharks on an ocean liner. Too bad we didn't get it finished."

When Colonel Andrews and Geist were halfway up the trail

from the lagoon, Petra blurted out, "Where are my sons?"

"Not this trip, I'm afraid," Andrews answered, stopping a few yards away and looking around for the others. "But don't worry, they're fine and they'll be flying in by chopper to meet us. Look, there's been a problem. We have to take the sub out again. I think we've got everything on the schooner we'll need to fix her: new ballast control valves, repair material for the hull, and new props. Everything," he said, looking at Roberts.

"What's the target?" Roberts asked.

"Well, quite honestly, that's why we didn't bring your sons. We thought you wouldn't want them on this one so we brought Johnson and two more good men. And look, we've come to make a deal. You train Johnson to operate the sub, and when this one's over we'll help you get resettled with your sons, your father, even with Jason and the girl. Safe passage and a new life. Plenty of money, whatever it takes. That's the deal, anywhere you want to go. You have my word on it."

"Colonel Andrews, we saved your life. You owe us the truth. Where are my sons?"

"I swear to you they are safe, Mrs. Roberts. And I swear you have nothing to fear from us."

"As long as we help you," Roberts added.

Andrews glared at him and then nodded.

Josh was waiting in the darkness of the construction fence when they swam into the beach. "We got to go, man. The security guys know it was you. They're already talking to the cops."

Doc stripped off the wet coveralls. Tom, Mike and Ian were just coming through the low surf line. Ian was gasping, but Tom and Mike were stoked, pumped full of adrenaline.

"Come on," Josh said again. "I moved the van. Let's go!"

Across the street, spectators were still coming out from behind trees and cars. Electrical wires were arcing and water poured from broken plumbing in Morgan's hundred million-dollar debris pile. Sirens could be heard coming from town, but not loud enough to drown the sobs and crying of wounded and terrified spectators. Doc and the C-minus team hurried down the beach behind a row of partially completed units, ducked in through a construction fence gate and ran to the van. Grabbing Sheri by the arm, Josh lifted her and plopped her down between the seats as Doc jumped in after her. Slowly, Josh pulled out through the construction site's main gate and turned north, away from the growing crowds, the sirens and the rubble pile.

Only when they had slipped away did Tom and Mike give forth victory yells and postulate on the future of umbrella jumping as an Olympic sport. Sheri, soaking wet and sitting on the floor with a glazed look on her face, was only moderately enthusiastic. Biting her lower lip, she looked up at Doc in the seat beside her, took his hand and held on tight. He squeezed back and stroked her wet hair out of her eyes and winked down at her. The glazed look remained, but slowly an amazed smile beamed through—a smile that said clearly how surprised and overjoyed she was to discover she was still alive. Reveling in that discovery kept the words from coming at least for the moment. Inspector Cord was still trying to catch his breath, but Doc was all business. He turned on the radio and they listened to the reports of the terrorist bombing of the condo as the van wound through the narrow rural highway.

"At least they're not blaming you, mate," Ian commented.

"I'm sure that's only a matter of time," Doc answered. He'd been looking at the wet pages of the surveillance log. "These entries go back two years. Morgan has done a good job of protecting his flank. With these records, he can show he's had meetings with a dozen congressmen, half the military chiefs of staff, and several White House aides there, right up until the election, and then it gets real quiet. Only those scientists from Boston and the Kuwaitis. Man, I wish we could have gotten more of his disks. There's going to be quite a house cleaning if we live long enough to get this stuff into the right hands."

"I wouldn't be going back there anytime soon if I were you, Doc. Not if any of Jack Morgan's security boys survived," Josh offered.

"Yeah, you're right. Poor bastards. Talk about friendly fire...Morgan dropped the building right on top of his own troops. At least all the guests were out."

"I wonder how we did?" Tom said. "If the big computer had enough time to finish the command sequence, I mean."

"We'll find out just as soon as we get to the computer on

Kratos. Josh, has this old tub got anymore energy, or is she as tired as I am?" Doc asked and slapped the van's dashboard.

"You got it, Capt'n, you just hang on and we'll find out."

They drove in silence a short ways and then Josh began humming a familiar tune. Doc recognized it and smiled.

Joshua fought the battle of Jericho, Jericho, Jericho.
Joshua fought the battle of Jericho,
and the walls came tumbling down.

"I'm sorry for those men," Josh said. "But I hated that place. Morgan is an evil man. Like the snake in the garden, he turns other folks evil too. His walls came tumblin' down and I hope that's the last we ever hear of him on this good island."

"Doc," Tom said. "Doc, no one is following us. They saw us leave...they should be chasing us. They should want to ask us a whole lot of questions."

"What bothers me," Doc answered, "is that a lot of problems would be solved for some pretty powerful people if we just got back on the boat, head for open sea, and were never seen again. We've been worried that they might have put a bug or a transponder on board. We may have missed the point entirely."

"Are you saying a bomb?" Sheri gasped. "We slept there last night and they might have put a bomb on board?'

"Then why haven't they used it?" Mike asked.

"Because we have something Morgan wants," Doc said. "Think about it...if Morgan financed the sub, then he knows about Jason's grandfather and their treasure-hunting scheme. He's got the ambition, the men and the means. The *Central America* proved that. Now, what doesn't he have?"

"The chalice?" Sheri said. "The key to all the treasure."

"Exactly! Old Ben Travis may have saved us all when he gave me the chalice. Or perhaps Jason saved us when he gave the chalice to Ben."

"That's good so far," Mike said. "But the congressmen in those videos don't give two hoots about treasure hunting. And if they think we're about to bring a world of shit crashing down on them, which we are, Morgan won't even get a vote and that chalice won't protect us from anything."

"Tom, what do you think?" Doc asked.

"Morgan has moved more money in the last forty-eight hours than all the shipwrecks on record. I agree with Mike."

"Ian, it's your boat. What say you?"

"Let's not take anymore chances. I've had all the excitement I need for one day."

"Then it's settled...we abandon the boat. Josh, we need a place to live. Any of your family in the real estate business?"

The sun was bright as it can only be in a cloudless tropical sky when they reached the dock and set off through the mangroves for the last trip back to *Kratos.* Doc and Ian took the first boat, put Sheri in the second with Tom and Mike and told them to lay back far enough to be able to turn and run if trouble was waiting.

Stephanie was waiting on *Kratos*'s stern with Josh's two sons as Doc approached cautiously, wishing he was carrying more artillery. He peered intensely into the mangrove swamp looking for ambush points. Useless. There could be a hundred men in those trees and not one of them would be seen. "Let's see," he said caustically to himself, "where have I played this game before?"

Josh's oldest son caught the bow line and tied it to a stern cleat. Stephanie didn't wait for them to climb aboard to start saying what was on her mind.

"That's the last time I'm ever going to sit and wait for your sorry asses," she said through tears. "The radio said twenty people were killed...what was I supposed to think? You were out for a beer when the place blew up? What the hell happened?"

Doc pulled her gently and held her without speaking until her sobbing stopped. Then he whispered softly, "It's alright, we made it out okay. Josh is waiting, but we don't think the boat is safe anymore. We're going to get a few things and move to a place Josh knows about."

He put a finger to her lips and motioned for her to hurry. Then he silently set about collecting the things they would need from the gun cabinet and tool chest. Doc had already decided against going over the boat with a fine tooth comb. No use pushing their luck until he had the time and the tools. When they had taken the bare essentials, they slipped back into the inflatables. He locked the cabin doors and said a quick adios. Nice boat, but too dangerous.

Josh sent his sons home with Stephanie while the others loaded the equipment into the van. It took forty-five minutes over back roads to reach an overgrown, abandoned house off the north shore.

"Owner was a friend of mine—lived in the States," he explained as they unloaded. "Used to come every year. Guess he must have died though. Place hasn't been used in four, maybe five years."

There were broken windows and piles of trash and beer cans on the tile floors.

"Kids use it to party, that's all. You'll be safe here until we can figure out how to get you off the island."

They brought in the bags of supplies from the boat and Sheri began cleaning out the trash. Doc asked Josh to walk with him out to the beach. They sat in the shade enjoying a light breeze and Doc began, "Josh, did you ever hear them talking about a submarine?"

"Not that I recall. But you got to remember, ole Josh was not exactly on the board of directors, man. Nobody told me nothin' 'cept fix the shitter and take out the trash. So tell me about the submarine."

Doc told him the story in detail including the hidden base in Bermuda.

"You think when they left Bermuda, they would have been looking for another place like that, with caves and all, to hide the sub?"

"There was a drawing, a sort of map, but it didn't have any caves drawn on it."

"Show me," the old man said.

Doc drew what he could remember of the sketch in Jason's notebook and then waited.

Making a few changes, Josh asked, "Could it have been like that?"

"Yes, I think so."

"Looks a little like a place I sailed by once with my father. Some of the trading schooners still go past. The reason I remember is that my old man said there were big caves there, but nobody ever went ashore because the old timers believed the place was haunted. I'll ask around and let you know."

"Thanks."

"Look, the thing we got to do is get you off this island and that's not going to be easy. You got to lay low until we can figure something out."

"I appreciate your help, Josh. I just hope this isn't all going to come back on you and your family. But there is one more thing I wanted to ask. When was the last time you saw Colonel Andrews?"

"Yeah, I saw your colonel. Real arrogant that one. He was at Morgan's the day JB got killed. Then I didn't see him no more."

"He was at the condo?"

"Naw, Capt'n, he was at Morgan's warehouse. I had to pick up stuff for my boys, drums of floor cleaner, things like that. Your colonel was real rough. His men was unloading a big truck, had pictures of fish on it. But it didn't have no fish in it. Just big old wooden crates. They were using the forklift. Made me wait outside where I couldn't watch 'em. No shade outside and that big old truck ain't got no air conditionin'. Imagine, a man build that big fancy condo and buy a truck with no air conditionin' for the men who keep it. Now, I ask you, what kind of a man is that?"

"What warehouse, Josh? Where is it?"

"Big old bunkers, down by the fish docks and Morgan's water company. You know, the desal plant with the big storage tanks. Looks like an old prison or something. Big fences, guard towers and all. Nothin' there but water. Don't know why he needs the fences and the guards."

"Is that on the water, where the boat that chased Morgan and Sheri was taken? The boat JB took us to?"

"Yeah, that's the place. I've still got my keys, but I don't recommend it. Tell me what you're looking for...me and my boys will check it out for you."

"Josh, if I knew, I'd tell you, but it's just a hunch, that's all." Doc wasn't sure how much to trust Josh, and the idea of sending him after several tons of gold had a few drawbacks.

"Like I said, you need to be layin' low, not out gallivantin' round like some free man. If they catch you, there won't be nothin' I can do to help."

"I understand. But that warehouse may be hiding what we need to get the goods on Morgan. And you are right...why have fences and guards if all he's got out there is water? This island's surrounded with it. Let's go tonight. We'll be careful and if there's nothing, we'll be there and gone like a cloud across the moon."

Doc pulled a mattress from the house out onto the patio deck and was soon asleep, while Sheri sat in a sagging chair beside him. Mike took the first watch and Tom rode into town with Josh to buy supplies. It was nearly dark when Tom returned in a rented white Toyota station wagon.

Hearing the car door, Doc awoke with a start, then leaned back on the mattress when he realized the house was not under attack.

"South Sea islanders believe that you should always awaken a person slowly," he groaned, "because when you sleep, your spirit leaves the body, and you have to make certain to give it time to get home before you get up and go off without it."

"*The Derelict*," Tom said with a smile. "Charles Nordhoff, 1928."

"Yes, but what page?" Doc laughed as Tom offered him a cold beer. Doc set it down unopened.

"What did you find out?" Doc asked.

"I called Barkley's Bank...told them I was a pension fund manager and asked for verification of the wire transfer I'd ordered this afternoon on three of the accounts."

"And?"

"We did it, Doc. I couldn't check all the accounts, but I'm sure we did it. Every nickel they had in those accounts has just disappeared into computer never never land, at least for a few days."

"And Debbie?" Doc asked about his daughter.

"She's great. Says the morning sickness hasn't hit her since I've been gone. Thinks maybe she's not pregnant, just allergic to me. Also, she said to tell you Chaplain Bill Stone's leaving Bermuda. Going to Washington to become the new Chief of Chaplains. President's hosting a dinner for him. A really big deal, I guess."

"Good for him, but I'll certainly miss him, as will a lot of others on the island. I just remembered something. What do you know about the University of Massachusetts at Amherst that might relate to ONR grants—top secret stuff?"

"There were protests and demonstrations there when I was a student at M.I.T. They were doing chemical or biological warfare stuff, maybe both."

"Interesting. Before Bentley was killed, he told us Morgan's aide at the condo, a Chinese woman named Lin Kee, was involved in work on something called novel agents. That mean anything to you?"

"No, but I could make a call or two."

"Good, I think we need to know what that was about."

Josh arrived an hour after dark. They stowed their gear and took both vehicles to the desalination plant.

The road followed the south shore back beyond the airport and finally brought them to a small, old military storage base with high fences and a six-by-six frame guard shack in need of paint for more years than its occupant was old. Josh leaned out of the van window and after speaking with the young man briefly, the gate opened and they were waived through.

"I asked him if anyone else has been out here since the day your colonel was here. He said they got a big shipment of heavy machinery from Germany. He had to sign for the stuff. Crates of valves and expensive plumbing stuff. And then there was more—heavy wooden crates 'bout two feet square and ten or twelve feet long. That make any sense to you? Boy said the colonel and some others loaded most of it on an old schooner and left here night before last."

"Right after they killed JB. They were right here under our noses and we missed them. That old schooner was sitting right there," Doc said pointing to the pier, "the night we came out here with JB."

"They had just pulled in during that awful storm," Sheri remembered.

"The boy said we should park in there, out of sight, just in case," Josh said and turned the van toward the open doors of the warehouse building. "He said them boxes is over yonder." They pulled into the warehouse and stepped from the van. Stacked beneath a traveling crane were a half dozen empty wooden crates. Doc lifted a lid. Inside, the cut foam liner revealed the outline of a torpedo.

"Seen any of these before?" Doc asked the others.

"Just like the ones in the dockyard," Mike answered and Ian nodded.

"Just like the boy said," Josh said.

"Good lad, now where's the rest?" Ian asked.

"There, the pump house over there," Josh pointed to a second larger bunker. "You go...I'll look after things up here."

It was a bright night. Doc looked out of the warehouse across the yard. The bunker was seventy yards away with little cover between. "We could have parked over there," Doc said and Ian caught the edge in his voice. "Wait here until I'm across."

"Right. Careful now," Ian answered and held up his hands for the others to wait.

Doc eased the Beretta from his belt and stepped into the moonlight. He studied the landscape for ambush points. There were several. The islanders wouldn't set this up, he thought. But Morgan would. He walked easily, slowly, light on his feet and ready to drop and return fire. But he crossed the yard without incident and then crouched in the shadows by the bunker's door.

Just because I'm paranoid doesn't mean they aren't out there, he whispered to himself and raised his arm, signaling the others to follow. Mike and Tom came next. Ian and Sheri followed. The bunker's iron door had a hefty new stainless lock. Doc produced Josh's keys and quickly found the right one. It took two of them to slide the massive door open. When they had all slipped inside and the door was closed again, Tom set down the tool bag and took out the dive lights.

The old concrete bunker was large enough to hold several trucks. It was mostly empty except for four pumps mounted on concrete pads with plumbing that ran to large stainless steel tanks. They reminded Sheri of the condensers on the *Larkington* wreck in Bermuda. The pumps were droning in a deep monotone, but not loud enough to make talking difficult. Eight more torpedo crates, empty food boxes, empty plastic jugs for battery acid, and packing crates for plumbing fittings were strewn about the trash bins at the end of a loading dock beneath the overhead crane.

"For the sub," Doc said and the others agreed.

At the end of the bunker were large stainless steel doors and small windows like those on a meat cooler. They walked the length of the bunker and looked in through the double glass. There was a forklift parked inside and little room for much else.

"Is there a label on forklifts that says 'keep refrigerated?'" Doc asked and Sheri chuckled.

The cooler door was locked. He followed the door's edges with his light and then remarked, "This isn't a refrigerator. It looks like a vault...must have cost a fortune. That must be some forklift."

"What now?" Ian asked.

"We open it," Doc answered. Ian started to speak but Doc cut him off. "Look, I know breaking and entering isn't legal, but neither are those torpedoes or what Morgan did to his..."

"Stow it, Doc. I was only going to ask what you wanted me to do," Ian said and smiled. "I left my badge in Bermuda when I got on a plane to look after your sorry duff. Now let's get to it."

"Get the drill...we need holes here, here and here. Find some way to keep the bit wet so it doesn't lose it's edge."

"Got it."

Doc knelt by the tool bag and removed an assortment of hand tools and an electric screwdriver.

"This is the part where you make black powder out of salt-peter and charcoal to blowup the door, isn't it?" Sheri asked.

"Blowup is just a euphemism, Martha."

"Smart-ass; you think I need that euphemism explained?"

"That's Doctor Smart-ass to you, Martha. Come on, you can help."

Doc had what he needed for the job in the large duffel. As soon as the drilling was done, he loaded and stemmed the holes, and wired the cap circuitry. Next he laid out a firing line and fired the charge with an orange, hand-sized battery operated hell box. There was a muffled blast and a cloud of acid-smelling smoke before the door swung open inviting them in.

"Remind me to tell immigration about your talents before we let you back in," Ian said, staring at the elaborate draw-bolt locking system rendered useless by twenty minutes of work and twenty dollars worth of garden fertilizer and cleaning solvents.

"My recruiter told me the Navy was going to teach me skills I could use in real life," Doc chuckled. His eyes were wet from the burn of the smoke. He wiped them dry and added, "He just forgot to mention that I'd spend the rest of my life in prison if I ever got caught. Now let's see what's so special about this forklift."

He eased the door open a bit farther and stepped in.

"Oh, how clever! It's not a vault after all, boys...it's an elevator. What a surprise!" His sarcasm almost worked.

"You're acting like a nerd, Doc. You knew it was an elevator, didn't you?" Sheri chided.

"I must confess the thought had crossed my mind."

"So where are the buttons? How does it work?"

"No buttons. Keys." He used the electric screw driver to pull the panel off and was looking at the wires. "Let's try the red one and the blue one."

"Doc?" Sheri questioned.

"Oh, you could be right. Let's make it the blue one and the green one."

"Doc, isn't there some scientific way to determine..."

"Sure, like this," he laughed and touched the wires. The elevator lurched a couple inches and stopped. "All aboard, folks. I think we've got it."

Mike was left to guard the rear and they crowded in around the forklift. As soon as he reconnected the wires, they began to drop.

"Can't be too far down. The water table's pretty shallow here...after all we're right on the beach," Ian said. But the elevator kept dropping and the temperature dropped right along with it. "Well, scratch that theory," he said as they continued to drop.

"No, you were right about the water level. We must be in a caisson. See the condensation on the walls? This must have cost a bundle."

The elevator began slowing down, delivering them to a dark cement tunnel. Doc stepped out and scanned the area with his light. There were light fixtures above them. But again the switch required a key, so they went forward with just the dive lights.

"Looks like new construction—none of the iron has rusted," Tom said, pointing to the steel beams overhead and the grate beneath their feet. There was running water beneath the grate. "They must have built this when they built the desalination plant."

In just a few steps, they came to the first vault. Ten by twelve, Doc guessed and the door was a stainless steel frame encasing heavy glass. The locks were internal and electronic. Red flashing LED suggested that they were armed, probably tied into an elaborate security system. Behind the thick glass were racks of flintlock rifles, many still encrusted, but some were beautifully conserved.

"Springfields," Sheri said. "That's Jason's missing gun collection. Those are just like the guns that you and Debbie found," she said to Tom.

"The ones that got us kidnapped," Tom added.

"It could be avacuum chamber," Doc said. "Old Jack went to a lot of expense to build this trophy room. Let's see what else he's got."

There were twelve more locked vaults and room for another ten. The locked ones contained ceramics and porcelain dating back to the Ming dynasty, and Spanish olive jars from the 16th century. And then there were pieces as recent as china from the *Andrea Doria.*

"Most of this stuff is nice," Sheri said. "But it's nothing a good North Carolina or Bermuda wreck diver couldn't have found. I don't understand...some old bathtubs upstairs in the warehouse, like the ones we use at the Maritime Institute, would have worked just as well. Why go to all this trouble if this is all you've got to show?"

"This is all Bermuda stuff," Ian guessed. "I've been looking at stuff like this for years."

"You're right," Doc said. "Morgan didn't build this vault for Jason's Bermuda artifacts. My guess is he built it for the real treasures he thought he was going to get from old Ben Travis. Stuff like Socrates's chalice and statues from Roman, Greek and Egyptian wrecks. And don't forget his golden Madonna and her four hundred-pound solid gold emerald inlaid table. That's what this place was built for."

They kept walking like visitors in a museum, examining

the contents of each compartment with interest but no real excitement until they came to the last vault.

"Treasures like this. Holy cow! Look at all that gold!"

Like the other chambers, this one was ten by twelve feet. But unlike the others, this one was stacked high with crates of gold coins and hundreds of gold bars. Doc's light danced from the coins as if they were diamonds.

"Those are twenty-dollar double eagles, the coins from the *Central America* wreck. That's all the evidence we need to tie Morgan to Behrmann and to the cold blooded murder of *Benthic Explorer*'s captain and crew. Mike deserves to see this, but now, how the devil do we get in there?"

"Remember the first Indiana Jones movie, where Indy's trying to grab the little gold idol but the cave is full of booby traps? That's what this reminds me of," Sheri said.

"I wish you hadn't said that," Doc answered. "I've been thinking the same thing. Let's have another look around before we do anything brash."

He stepped back to the gold vault and swept it again with his light. "I wonder if there's a way in without going through these doors—an air vent or something. Look there in the ceiling...could that be a door?"

"Could be. Hard to tell in this light," Ian said. "Perhaps there's another floor above this one."

"We only tried one pair of wires. We could try the others."

Doc led them back to the elevator. Sheri held the light while he cut and stretched wire from the panel. "Remember which ones got us down here?" he asked. "Blue and red, or was it blue and green?"

"Blue and green," she said.

"Okay, we need the reverse of that so green is out. Let's try red." He arced the wires. Sparks flew, but nothing else happened.

Sheri jumped back against Ian. "Steady, lass, we're all still here," he comforted.

"If not red, then yellow?" Doc said and tried again. This time the elevator responded with a bump. "Bingo! Here we go."

He made contact again and they began a slow rise, stopping twenty feet above the lower chamber. The door was a watertight boat hatch, large but not large enough for the fork-lift. Doc spun the handle which retracted the dogs and Ian helped him pull it open. Doc led with the light. Inside was a large comfortable work space full of work tables and bench racks of sophisticated electronic equipment. Doc walked around looking at the instruments and then at the stacks of components stored in sealed dry storage.

"It's a conservation lab," he said stating the obvious. "Or at least it was."

There were electrolysis tanks, X-ray equipment and plastic casting benches, but the equipment was covered with dust and torpedo parts covered the two large work benches.

Doc examined the torpedo's components and then said, "Looks like these are the old guidance systems. If they replaced the old ones, they must have had something pretty hot they wanted to try. That's something to remember if we get another chance at him."

"Right, mate, but how do we get to the gold? There's nothing here to help us," Ian said.

"We could try the elevator again, or we could do it the good old fashioned way and take out that glass door," Doc answered.

"This place gives me the creeps," Sheri volunteered. "I keep thinking that big stone ball is going to come rolling at us. Just like in the movie."

"I vote for the glass," Tom said. "Let's get what we need and get out of here."

Ian nodded agreement.

"Only take a minute...everything I need is right here," Doc said and opened a box of electronic detonators.

"I just love playing McGyver," he chuckled and picked up a roll of duct tape. "That's it. The only other thing will be a roll of this wire. I left mine upstairs."

They climbed back through the hatch, closed it and Doc reconnected the blue and green wires. The elevator eased them back to the lower chamber. "We need to know how to go all the way up," he said to Tom. "Want to play with it while I rob the piggy bank?"

"Sure."

"I'll come with you, Doc...I guess," Sheri said. "But just remember what happens when Indy grabs the statue."

"Thanks," he said and ruffled her hair. They stepped from the elevator onto the grate and moved down the corridor window shopping until they got to the gold vault.

"How are...?"

"Gently as a baby's cough," he answered. "All we need to do is get this heavy plate glass resonating with two different energy phase waves and when they collide, poof! No more glass."

He worked as he explained. It sounded logical enough. She helped and soon they had the firing wire run back down the corridor and were ready.

"Okay, you go back to the elevator and wait. I'll be along in a minute."

"But I..."

"Remember the movie? Off you go."

She reluctantly complied as he attached the wires to the small orange blasting machine. He yelled "Fire in the hole," held down the arming button and when the red light came on, pushed the toggle switch. There was a sharp rap, like a firecracker in a tin can, followed by the much louder sound of a river roaring down the corridor.

"What the...?" he swore, looking up at a five-foot wave rolling toward him. He dropped to the grate and tried to hang on, but it ripped his grip loose and tumbled him down the corridor. He continued to tumble until he landed at the elevator and Ian pulled him to his feet.

"Did you get the gold, mate?" Ian laughed. They were already waist deep and the water was still pouring in.

"You bet," Doc coughed in disbelief. "Can you get us out of here, Tom?"

Sheri was holding the light while Tom tried various combinations of the wires.

"No power. Listen, even the pumps are dead."

He was right; the chamber had gotten deadly silent. And in the aftermath of the first wave, the water was still rising but more slowly now.

"Dammit, Doc. I knew it. I had a bad feeling about this before we ever got out of the car. I told you..." Sheri sputtered. The water was up to her chest.

"Tell me later," he said while putting his index finger to

her lips.

"Listen," Tom said. "The water is quiet. It's not rising as fast either."

"There should be a hatch in the top of the elevator," Doc said. "See if you can find it. I'm going back for a few of those coins."

He pulled his way out of the elevator and half-walked, half-swam back down the corridor. He saw the glow of the dive light at his feet, dropped under and grabbed it, then moved on. The glass had neatly shattered and had been pushed out by the water pressure. He pulled himself into the gold vault and shoved a handful of gold double eagles into his pocket. Then he began examining the vault. *Where is the water coming from?*

There were no inlets visible. Taking a breath, he dropped to the floor and could feel water moving in through the grate. He grabbed and pulled. The gold was too heavy to move, but he found a section of grate not weighted down and lifted it off to the side. The shaft beneath was four feet deep and went out through the wall. He turned off the light and looked for light, then remembered it was the middle of the night. He surfaced. The salt burned his eyes but boosted his hope. Perhaps the water was coming in from the sea wall by the docks. He took several deep breaths, forcing himself to relax before he dropped down again. This time he pulled forward until he entered a long cement drainage pipe. Twenty feet through it, he saw light. He kicked harder and pulled with wide breast strokes. Then in his light he could see a grate and a lock. There were bolt cutters in the tool bag—new ones in fact. He turned and pulled back for the vault. His brain was screaming for air, but he swallowed hard to quiet it...only a pool length to go. No problem.

He found the entrance and pulled himself through. He pushed up for air, but banged his head on the vault's ceiling—no air pocket.

Now things were getting desperate. He swung the light and got reoriented, then pushed off for the window frame. He swallowed again, but this time it didn't help much. Once in the corridor there was enough space to tread and breathe, which he did with great enthusiasm. However, he didn't rest for more than a moment before swimming hard for the elevator. He didn't get that far.

Ian, Tom and Sheri met him mid-way. There was no hatch in the elevator and there was less than two feet of air space left in the rounded roof of the corridor.

"I knew it!" Sheri started. "Just like the movie, we should have left that damn gold alone and gotten the hell out of here."

"For once, I'd say you were absolutely right. Now take off your jeans."

"Don't you ever think about anything else? Geez, Doc, if this is going to be our last shot, at least you could be a little more romantic about it."

"No party yet. Get them off...I have an idea."

"Yeah, guys usually do." She dropped beneath the surface and worked them off.

"We're going to need the tools. Still in the elevator, Tom?"

"Yeah, back right corner."

"Good. While I get them, the rest of you get out of your pants too and tie knots in the legs. Like the old Navy drill. Try to leave as much air space as you can."

Diving with the light, he swam to the elevator. He found the tools and lightened the bag until he could lift it easily, then rejoined them. He handed Sheri the light, took her pants and used her belt to hang the tool bag from the air bags created by her pants legs. "Come on, there's a way out through the gold vault."

The others floated in their improvised life jackets until they reached the end of the corridor. After Doc explained the rest of his plan and they understood, he dove into the vault, filling the sturdy tool bag with gold until it began to sink. Then he continued bouncing from the air pocket to the pants, blowing air into the knotted legs until the improvised bladders were stretched tight and the tool bag was nearly full of coins. The air pocket was down to a few inches by the time he was done.

"It's a good swim...thirty or forty yards and then we've got the lock to contend with, but there's plenty for both of us. Tom and I will make the first trip and get the lock. I'll come back for you. Tom, remember this air will be compressed. You'll have to exhale when you go for the surface. Got it?"

"No problem, Doc."

"Try to behave yourself while I'm gone," he said to Sheri.

"You know how our neighbors will talk if they see you dressed like that."

"Go to hell, Doc, and hurry," she said squeezing his hand.

He faced Tom. They hyperventilated a half-dozen breaths, gave a thumbs down and dove into the vault for Sheri's pants, now ten feet below them. Doc let Tom get the first breath, waited for an okay and then, dragging their primitive breathing apparatus between them, they worked their way forward to the grate.

It took both of their strength to cut through the steel bars. *This is going to hurt tomorrow,* Doc thought as he felt the strain, *if I'm lucky enough to still be around to feel it.* As soon as the grate was open, Doc sent Tom to the surface and returned to the vault. Ian and Sheri met him just as he entered the chamber. Ian lunged at Sheri's pants and took several desperate breaths. The air pocket was gone. Doc waited while Sheri got a quick breath of air and then pointed toward the grate. Ian nodded but went for more air first. He was panting, unable to get a decent breath. Doc and Sheri dragged him along with them until they were at the entrance. He motioned Sheri up and she darted away. Ian still was trying to get a breath. Doc pulled the blue jeans away and Ian stared at him wide eyed. Doc pointed toward the surface, but Ian reached for the tool bag, spilling the gold and the remainder of the air. He pushed away for the surface. Doc swam up beside him, spun him and grabbed him from the rear in a tight bear hug. The inspector was holding his breath and would embolize if he didn't exhale. Doc clasped his hands and gave a quick inward thrust like the Heimlich maneuver. He felt Ian cough and then fight to get free.

They were still struggling when they hit the surface. Doc released him as he gasped and coughed again. The big Scot looked panicked and ready to fight until he realized where they were. Then he relaxed and nodded. He was in control again.

"Over here," Tom called softly. He and Sheri were crouched on the dive platform of the condo's sportfisherman. Behind them, on the road leading into the plant, police cars were passing, running slowly with their lights out.

"It was a trap," Sheri whispered.

"We've got to get Mike out of there," Doc answered. "Listen, now we've got enough on Morgan and Andrews to turn the tables and clear ourselves. But someone has to tell our story to the right people before it's too late, so here's my idea."

He gave her all but one of the gold coins in his pocket, his cash and credit cards, the Randall and Beretta from his belt. Kissing her goodbye, he wished them all luck and climbed from the boat to the sea wall, and then began a quick trot for the bunker hiding their cars.

Both vehicles were there, but Josh was not. Doc still had the van keys and he eased into the seat and began searching. He found Sheri's 9 mm Smith and Wesson under the seat. He pulled it out and began looking for a place to hide it. No guns on this trip. He settled for a steel I-beam well overhead. Wiping the gun clean, he nested it out of sight. Hopefully, he'd be back for it before it had time to get lonely. He dropped from the window frame he'd climbed to reach the beam, grunted when he landed, slipped back to the van and changed into dry clothes. Now for the fun part.

CHAPTER 19

Doc eased through the bunker door and dropped to his knees. He counted five police cars and guessed that would mean twenty men. But this time the odds were in his favor. He crossed the yard and opened the heavy door to the main warehouse and desalination plant.

Inside, Mike sat on the floor watched by two guards, while other policemen tried to fix the elevator. They looked like real cops; the question now was, were they on the island's payroll, or Morgan's, or both? He saw Josh arguing with the young security guard and two others in plain clothes.

Those are Jack Morgan's boys, he guessed, and the others are cops. Do local murder charges take precedence over whatever charges Morgan might have brought against him? Only one way to find out.

"Evening gents...you fellows ever hear of Harry Houdini?"

Mike looked up in amazement and the burly security guard Doc had met at Morgan's condo slid his hand under his coat. Doc raised his hands, kept smiling and moved forward. Josh was the first to speak.

"Sorry, Doctor Holiday, it was out of my hands."

Doc nodded and kept smiling. "May I ask who's in charge here?"

The man with the hand in his coat stepped forward at the same time as the Caymanian Police Chief. The chief glared at

Morgan's agent and they both said, "I am!"

"Well now, that's a problem. If you're both in charge, which one shall I surrender to?"

"You're coming with me, asshole," the burly condo security agent said, pulling his gun.

"Glad to see you survived. I guess the parking lot wasn't such a bad place to be after all. But it looks as if you may be outnumbered here," Doc laughed. "Unless you're going to blast your way out through a squad of unarmed Caymanian Police. That kind of thinking should certainly impress Jack, don't you agree?"

The Caymanian officers moved forward and Doc held out his wrists to be handcuffed, but Morgan's man hadn't grasped the significance of Doc's logic. "Not so fast, secret service man. I said you are coming with me and that's what I meant."

The Caymanians moved back, but Josh moved forward, standing beside Doc. "What are you doing?" Josh demanded.

"What's it to you, old man? Just shut up and get out of the way."

"You have no jurisdiction here," Josh said and moved closer to Doc. He was standing a little taller now and there wasn't a trace of the dialect which normally dominated his speech.

This is good, Doc thought. *There's more here than meets the eye.*

"I don't have what?" the security agent said, turning his gun toward Josh.

"Jurisdiction. If big words give you trouble, I'll explain. It means this isn't your island and it's not Jack Morgan's yet either, although he obviously thinks so."

The agent was thrown off guard by Josh's directness and an assertiveness he'd not seen before. Josh was speaking with authority and it didn't compute. "Shut up, old man. I haven't got time to play games with the janitor."

The Chief of Police stepped forward. "Joshua, let it be. This isn't our..."

"Not our fight?" Josh turned toward him angrily. "These men are destroying our homes and our island and it's not our fight. When did we give them the right to wave guns in our faces and tell us what to do? No more. It's over. It's our island and we are taking it back—right now." He turned back to the security agent and ordered, "Put down your gun, boy. You're under arrest."

"And who the hell are you, old man? What's your jurisdiction?"

"Chief Inspector, Cayman Islands Customs Service. These two men are my prisoners and you are under arrest for illegal possession of firearms and obstruction of justice. Put your guns down now. It's a small island. Don't be a fool. Morgan is finished here."

"I don't think so," was the response, and he and the rest of Morgan's men began backing toward the door. "Chief Inspector? I think Mr. Morgan's going to want a word with you, janitor man."

"Tell him to call my office. We'll have the indictments ready."

Morgan's men slipped through the door, turned and ran to their car. Doc looked at Josh and smiled. The Chief Inspector nodded.

Once Ian, Tom and Sheri climbed aboard the sportfisherman it didn't take Ian long to hot wire it. They eased away from the slip and made the short journey to Morgan's Landing Marina where they took a cab to the airport. With luck they would be on the first plane back to the States.

Stephanie was already at the airport, checking it out to see if it was safe for them to enter. It didn't take her any longer than walking past the newsstand. The headlines announced that there were warrants out for all of them except Stephanie. She bought a paper and hurried outside to wait for their arrival.

When the cab pulled up, she quickly got in and handed Sheri the newspaper.

"It's no good," she said as they pulled away. "I've never seen so many polyester suits, shoulder holsters and Ray Bans in my life. I guess the shades are their tropical camouflage."

"What now?" Ian asked.

"A boat I guess. Rental cars won't get us very far."

"Funny; ha, ha," Sheri added.

"She's right, of course. We need to find a boat with range

enough to get to the States," Ian said. "I wonder what they've done with *Kratos*?"

Doc's picture was on the front page again, this time with the story of his capture the night before. He looked tired and grubby in the photo. His bedraggled condition and unshaven face made it easy to imagine him as an out-of-luck, desperate criminal. Then Stephanie noticed a smaller photo of *Kratos* under the title 'Terrorist Boat Recovered.'

"Does it say where they took her?" Ian asked.

"No, but the picture looks like the Yacht Club by Morgan's Landing. We must have walked right past her."

"Let's find a fax machine. If I can impound her, she could be our ride home."

"They want to arrest you, remember, Inspector?" Sheri whispered so as not to alarm the driver.

"How bloody inconvenient," he whispered back. "Then I guess we'll have to do it the old fashioned way—steal her. I'm beginning to think that my association with all of you may not be the best thing for my career. As a matter of fact, my pension seems further and further away every moment."

After resting on the beach until dark, they returned to Morgan's Landing. Ian led them down the dock toward *Kratos*. He picked the cabin door lock in less time than most would have taken to open it with the key and once inside, they pulled the salon curtains and set to work.

"How did you get the door open so easily?" Sheri asked.

"Years of experience protecting the innocent and kicking the shit out of the guilty, my dear," Ian answered with a wink. Sheri kept watch while Tom and the inspector used the dive lights with red cellophane over the lens to search the boat.

If Doc had been right about the reason they had not been followed after the hotel was destroyed, they would find a miniature receiver/transmitter and an explosives package somewhere on the boat.

"Well, look at this," Tom said. He'd found a storage locker in the bilge with six, 66 mm LAW rockets. "They missed Mike's stash. At least we won't be empty handed."

While he was in the bilge, Sheri noticed that a new smoke detector had been added in the main cabin's head. She removed the cover and wondered at the intricate wire bundles and numerous black boxes. One look told Tom they'd hit pay dirt. Tracing the wiring led him to two shaped charges in oil filter boxes sitting in a bilge rack. They were easily powerful enough to blow the boat in half.

It was nearly daylight when Stephanie arrived in Josh's van with a load of groceries from the island's only all night convenience store. They had agreed that Stephanie would remain on the island to try and help Doc and Mike. It was a ticklish affair because she needed to avoid contact with Morgan's men who appeared to be everywhere. With the groceries quickly loaded, Stephanie wished them luck and was gone. Ian performed more of his lock-picking magic with the fuel pump and the security chain. When the tanks were full, he eased the boat away from the dock. They had not seen a single soul all night.

"You get the feeling this was too easy?" Sheri said to Tom as the lights of George Town faded behind them.

"You mean like they wanted us to steal her back?"

"Yeah, something like that."

Ian heard her and added, "Doc was right as usual. They could have blown us to pieces anytime. Now at least they'll have to come after us in person, so to speak. Our chances are better, but we'll still need to keep a sharp watch." There was a coldness in his voice, and he spoke without breaking his transfixed stare through the windshield at the hundreds of miles of dark and lonely sea before them. When they cleared the channel, he pushed the throttles to full power.

Doc sat on the edge of the bunk, stretched his aching shoulders and exhaled. The stone walls and floors were cold, the cot uncomfortable, like those he remembered from Navy ships. He moved a bit, but quietly because Mike was still asleep. It was well before dawn and there was nothing to do; no reason to be awake except habit and the need to occupy his mind against the night wanderings of his subconscious.

Thus far the guards had treated them well, especially considering they were suspected of blowing up the condo and killing a dozen men, not to mention John Bentley's murder or the bogus rouse of Jack Morgan's Kuwaitis. All in all, it had been a fairly eventful two weeks. A nice vacation from the tedium of middle-class existence, Doc smiled. Morgan and his crowd would lose whatever game it was they were playing. The truth about *Blackwolf* and Hans Behrmann's submarine would become public, and perhaps his peroxide-powered engines would help save the environment after all.

In the end that would make whatever happened worthwhile. At least this once, the bad guys were not about to retire into fat government pensions with secret service agents to protect them from irate citizens giving them what they most certainly deserved.

Morgan would lose, unless of course, Sheri and Ian were unable to reach Chaplain Stone who could take them directly to the President.

Ian was at *Kratos*'s helm while Tom and Sheri checked the chart and satellite navigation. Their course was northwest, running between the southern coast of Cuba and the northern tip of the Yucatan Peninsula. The twin turbo-charged Detroits purred in balanced harmony as the sleek white hull cut through the dark water. By dawn they were a hundred and fifty miles north. By noon the course line Tom plotted showed they had come three hundred twenty seven miles and the safety of Galveston was another twenty hours north. Tom took the wheel while Ian slept and Sheri sat quietly in the wheelhouse, watching the radar and the horizon for any sign of trouble. Her turn at the wheel was coming, but for now she was content to sit, worry about Doc and Mike and stare out over the empty sea. *Blackwolf* was waiting. She could feel it, and she prayed that her desperate little crew would be up to the challenge.

She opened her hand and looked again at the gold twenty-dollar double eagle, one of the three Doc had given her. The crew of the *Benthic Explorer* would have their revenge, she would see to it. And Doc would be cleared. She rubbed the coin with her thumb as a talisman and then closed her fingers around it again. When *Blackwolf* came, they would be ready.

Hours later, Ian was back at the helm. Tom was watching the radar and Sheri was in her bunk, trying to sleep and still rubbing the gold coin when Ian first saw the lights of

Galveston's Bay Town oil field.

"It looks like a bloody city," he said as they drew closer.

Tom switched the radar from five-mile to twenty-mile scan to get a better look.

"It is a city, thirty miles offshore, working twenty-four hours a day. There must be a couple hundred platforms out there."

"At least, lad," Ian said. "And if that sub knows we're coming, that's where she'll be waiting, hiding like a tabby cat in tall grass...waiting for us to come into range."

"What do you think?" Tom asked. "Do they know where we are?"

"They know," Sheri answered from the hatchway. "Don't ask me how, but believe me, they know."

"It's one of those woman things," Tom said and Ian chuckled.

"Laugh if you want, but I'm right. You'll see," she answered.

"All night long I kept having the same dream," Ian said. "It was of a great sea battle, then I finally realized what it was. It was Lord Nelson against the French at Trafalgar. Do you remember the phrase crossing the 'T'?"

"No."

"Nelson was badly out numbered, but he won because the French had to pass through a bottleneck, single file. And as they came out, he picked them off one at a time, like ducks in a shooting gallery. Crossing the 'T.'"

"And you think..." began Sheri.

"At the entrance to Galveston Pass...it's a narrow channel. We'd be a sitting duck."

"So what can we do?"

"We'd stand a better chance in the middle of those oil platforms," replied Ian. "Maybe draw him to the surface where we'd get a shot with one of those rockets. That's what I've been thinking."

Atlee, the Caymanian guard smiling as usual, opened Doc's cell door and said, "You've got a visitor, Doctor Holiday. Please follow me."

Doc and Mike stood and waited uncertain.

"It's alright, mon. It's a young woman—a pretty one at

that."

At first he didn't recognize her. Stephanie had cut her hair, changed the color and was dressed like a New York teen in oversized ragged jeans, wildly decorated tee shirt and Madonna sun glasses. The transformation was effective. No one would recognize her as the Atlanta accountant and undercover customs agent who had worked for the late John Bentley. She sat nervously in the chair and waited for the guard to leave.

"Josh is gone," she said quietly. "His family hasn't heard from him since the night you were arrested. He took his father's old boat and one of his sons, but he didn't tell anyone where he was going."

Doc nodded and said nothing.

"I've got to get off the island. Morgan's men are looking for me. I just wanted you to know...about Josh, I mean. I'm going tonight...by boat. Some stockbrokers from New Jersey... going to Jamaica. Big boat...hope they've got a decent crew. From the looks of them, I don't think they could paddle a canoe across the boat pond in Central Park. So far all they've done is party. But it's a way off the island and they don't care what my name is, so I think it's safe. Maybe before they dump me, they'll give me enough money to get home."

"When Jack is caught, there will be a trial..." Doc began.

"I know, I've been thinking about it. I'll testify. I owe that to JB. And I wish there was something I could do for you, Doc. But this obviously isn't my week for miracles, and that's what it's going to take to get you out of here."

"I'm working on that. Thanks for coming. There's a call you could make. There's an old friend of mine...he'll wire you some traveling money just in case things don't work out with your brokers, and I'd feel a lot better if he was expecting Sheri. I'd rather not call him from here. Too many ears. Any chance you could do that for me?"

"That should do it," Ian said and put down the open end wrench. "Injector settings are as important to diesels as the right gap is to a gas engine's spark plugs. Open a couple of them up this far and she should smoke like a Bristol factory."

Tom was holding the light as Ian wiped the wrench clean

and put it back in the tool bag.

"Now let's check those LAW rockets again," Ian said when they finished tightening down the engine covers. They had shut down the boat well out of range of the oil platforms. The night sky was just turning pink when they fired up the Detroits again and began limping toward the oil platforms. Now instead of the usual synchronized purr, the starboard engine coughed and hacked out billows of black smoke. Ian was at the wheel, Sheri at the radar and Tom on the tower with the rockets and binoculars. Sheri switched scanning ranges back and forth, first trying to get as much detail as she could, and then searching ten miles ahead of them.

"Anything?" Ian asked, as he had every two or three minutes for the last hour.

"No, just the same four boats. That's all. No, here comes another one. She's really moving too. She's about eight miles out, north northwest, Tom. Can you see her?" she said into the intercom.

"Nothing yet," his voice boomed back. She looked away from the screen and turned down the intercom's volume, then checked the screen again looking for the incoming boat.

Her stomach knotted and for a moment she couldn't speak. When she did, her voice cracked and the most she could get out was a gasp as she pointed at the screen. Ian looked quickly over her shoulder at the round orange display and understood.

"Where was she?"

"There," Sheri pointed to an empty spot.

"Turn up the gain. We still might see her wake."

She switched the scan to seven and a half miles and did as he'd suggested.

"Yes, I see it. They're still coming right at us. About six miles out."

"How sporting of them to stay that close to the surface," he laughed grimly. "Looks like your intuition was working on full power, lass. Makes the game so much more interesting now that we know who the player is. Not to sound morbid, but I never relished the thought of dying in bed," he said.

"Alone, Inspector?"

"Aye, alone is what I meant. However, there are circumstances under which I might retract that statement," he answered with a raised eyebrow and a smirk that reminded her of Doc. He leaned over the intercom to the tower and told Tom they had seen the sub on radar.

"Quick now, lass, take the wheel while I reset those injectors. We're going to need everything this bonnie lass can give us once the fun starts. Sinking a stodgy old freighter is one thing, but hitting us will be quite another. We've got to get them so frustrated they surface and come after us with their deck guns. If they do, our little rockets should do the job."

Sheri held course and speed until the inspector returned from the engine room, then returned to monitoring the radar. They were quiet now. Deadly serious. Tom waited tensely on the tuna tower with one of the LAWs in hand, its muzzle caps removed and the telescoping tube extended. The early morning air was still and quiet with hardly a ripple on the flat calm water. On the radar, she saw the first pair of torpedoes launched. She had the radar on three-mile range and the air from the sub's tubes and the turbulence of the props painted a tiny trail across the orange screen.

"Ten o'clock," she said. "A quarter mile. Looks like two, running on the surface."

"Can you see them, Tom?" the Inspector said to the intercom.

"Not yet...not yet...not...yes! Got 'em...a hundred fifty yards coming fast."

"Now, lads, you get a taste of your own bloody game," he growled and pushed the boat to full power. *Kratos* sprang forward, banked into a sharp turn and ran straight at the oncoming torpedoes.

"Break right!" Tom shouted.

Kratos healed hard to starboard and the torpedoes streamed past within feet of the hull.

"We can outmaneuver them and the sub," Ian said. "And now's the time to prove it."

"I see the sub!" Tom shouted. "Dead ahead. Seventy-five yards." The dark outline of the two-hundred-foot hull caught the light and he could see the periscope at the surface.

"They've fired again," Sheri said, not as calm this time.

"How many?"

"One, I think."

"And one to go. Can you see it, Tom?"

"Got it," he answered and fired the first rocket. They could see the orange trail of the LAW rocket as it converged with the incoming torpedo. The ensuing blast shook the hull and showered the boat with water. Tom grabbed another tube and fired again, this time at the sub which had rapidly closed the distance. The second rocket hit just forward of the periscope and a second blast thundered in the still morning air.

"Got 'em!" Tom shouted and grabbed another rocket.

Sheri looked up at the sub and Ian shouted at her to watch the screen. Good call. *Blackwolf*'s first two torpedoes had circled and were closing on their stern.

"Go left!" she shouted.

Ian swung the wheel to port and hit the starboard throttle. *Kratos* twisted to port and again escaped disaster.

"Their new guidance system is quite an improvement," Ian said.

"Or that's why they're still at the surface—to control them visually. I wonder how long...they're turning...and spreading wider apart...."

"Which way?"

"Right...hard right...."

"They've fired again!" Tom shouted from the tower. "This one's cutting across our bow."

"The stern!" Sheri shouted. "Do something, Tom!"

Tom had been thrown to his knees by the boat's hard turn. He grabbed at the rail, but the rocket case slid across the small deck, dumping the last three tubes which rolled toward the edge. Two had already dropped to the deck below when Tom lunged at the third, nearly falling from the tower himself. He caught it, cleared the end caps, extended the tube, and flipped on the arming switch. He fired, nearly blindly, just aft of the boat's stern.

The explosion shattered the cabin windows. The blast stunned Tom who held on to the tower for his very life. The water blast knocked out the radar, and hurled Sheri and the inspector across the wheelhouse, along with flying glass and a wall of water. Ian lay stunned for a moment and then remembered the other torpedoes. He pulled himself up from the deck and looked out the starboard hatch. The second torpedo passed beyond them and didn't alter course, but the third was headed right at their beam. He leaped at the wheel and slammed both engines to full power. The Detroits growled and again the boat lurched forward. But as he spun the wheel and the torpedo sped past to port, *Blackwolf*'s 25 mm Bushmaster chain gun opened fire. Rounds exploded into their hull and smoke belched from the starboard engine which died with a shattering of steel and jamming of gears.

"Oh shit," Sheri said. "What now?"

"Got your water wings?" quipped Ian.

"It will take angel's wings to get us out of this one."

Tom was flattened on the tower's deck. He looked over the edge and saw the two unused rockets sloshing on the stern below. When he raised his head, the sub opened fire again and he dropped back flat as their rounds cut the air and shredded the aluminum tubing around him. Ian was doing the best he could with one engine, but that wasn't good enough. They'd had it, unless Tom could get to the deck. Above his head was a life ring on a fifty-yard line. He stood quickly, grabbed it and dove into the water from the tower.

He hit hard and it knocked the wind out of him. But somehow he held on to the life ring. And when the line went tight, it jerked him to the surface and towed him behind the boat like a fallen water skier who'd forgotten to let go.

Blackwolf was moving in for the kill. She was twice as fast as *Kratos,* even when both her engines were running. Now it was no longer a contest. She eased forward until she could fire across the sportfisherman's bow and Ian knew he had no choice but to cut the remaining engine.

"Why don't they just finish it?" Ian said.

"Maybe they want us alive? Maybe they want Doc?"

"Let's go on deck and get on with it."

"I'd really like to fix my hair and change. Do you think they'd mind?" she answered in her best southern belle accent.

"You're alright, lass," he said helping her up. "You get my vote in any election."

Tom struggled against the current to pull himself back to the boat. The polypro line burned his hands, but he swam and pulled as hard as he could. As Ian and Sheri walked out onto the deck with their hands raised, Tom pulled himself up on the dive platform. He lay there gasping, trying to ignore the pain of his bleeding hands when he heard the sub's loudspeaker.

He recognized the voice. It was his old friend and boss from Bermuda, Bill Roberts.

"Stay where we can see you, Inspector. We'll come alongside."

Tom crawled through the transom door and kept low as he crawled across the deck. The rockets were laying by the starboard scupper. He prepped the first one and hit the arming switch—nothing. He tried the second. Same result. He heard the whine of the sub's turbines as *Blackwolf* pulled closer. His heart pounded and his mind raced for a solution. *Solution...LPS.* Doc bought it by the case and insisted everything electronic on the boat be bathed in it frequently. Tom crawled low to the tool box in the stern bait station. He lay on his back on the deck and opened the cabinet. There were two of the familiar spray cans. He sprayed the rocket until the first can was empty and then grabbed the second. There was a gentle bump against the hull as the sub pulled alongside. He flipped the first arming switch. He could hear the high pitched loading of the capacitor. The moisture was displaced and the weapon was armed.

He crawled along the stern gunnel back to the dive platform and looked over at the sub. He remembered that the stern was low enough in the water that a swimmer could easily board. He slipped into the water, holding the weapon out of the water and kicked to *Blackwolf*'s stern. He started to rise, but then saw the reflection of the sub's television camera periscope on the water. He dropped back down, tight against the hull and waited. If they saw him, the inspector and Sheri wouldn't have a chance. In the mirrored reflection he watched the camera make another sweep, then it stopped and remained focused on *Kratos.* He held his breath and waited. As he heard the air hiss from the forward hatch, he pulled his knees under him, came to his feet and ran to the top of the sail, just behind the camera as it made another sweep. Sheri and Ian stood stonefaced, watching and praying that whatever Tom was going to try would work, knowing their fate was in his hands.

The hatch opened slowly and Bill Roberts reluctantly appeared. Tom could hear impatient shouting from below as Roberts hesitated on the ladder.

"Jump," Tom said quietly.

Roberts turned and stared wide-eyed into the rocket launcher's muzzle.

"Jump, or so help me, I'll blast you with the rest of them."

Roberts pulled himself clear and lunged over the side. Colonel Andrews was behind him on the ladder and came up waving a short-barreled automatic. Tom didn't hesitate long enough to get the brand and caliber. He hit Andrews in the back of the head, grabbed his weapon and sprayed the companionway until it was out of ammunition. Then he fired the rocket down the hatch, slammed it closed and dove free. Nothing happened. No smoke, no secondary explosions—*Blackwolf* just sat there.

Roberts was swimming toward *Kratos*. Ian went to the helm, started the port engine and eased the boat toward the sub. Tom swam beside Roberts and when they reached *Kratos*'s dive platform, helped him aboard. Roberts looked horrible. He was gaunt and his eyes were sunken as if he'd been living in a cave for years. Tom reached to help him into the cabin, but Roberts pulled away in fright.

"It's over, Bill," Tom said. "Now we've got to make it right. That can't be as bad as what you've been through."

"They've got Petra and my sons. It's not over.... You have no idea how complex this is. If I help you, everything I have left, everyone I care about will be destroyed. You should have left me on the sub."

Ian and Sheri came to the stern.

"We should go aboard, see if there's anything we can do," Ian said.

"She's booby trapped," Roberts said. "If anyone survived, they'll blow her to kingdom come before they let you have her. If I were you, I'd get away from here as fast as..."

A blast of air from the sub and the whine of her turbines stopped Roberts cold. He spun in terror as the bow of the sub dropped and she quickly disappeared beneath the surface.

"You haven't a chance," Roberts said. "They're alive and you haven't got a prayer."

"Then neither do you," Tom answered and grabbed the

frail old man by the arm and shoved him into the cabin. Ian was at the helm with Sheri at his side.

"What now?" she asked.

"The oil rigs, I guess, unless you've got a better idea?"

The boat was hard to handle with just one engine. It was hard to find a balance between the port engine pushing them in an arc to port and the leverage of the rudders trying to hold them on course. The result was a course that looked as if it had been drawn with a cork screw instead of a parallel rule. Tom went to the engine room to see what he could do while Ian handcuffed Roberts to a salon chair in the cabin.

"What do you think?" Sheri asked. "Will they come after us again?"

"The rocket didn't fire because it didn't have enough flight time to arm itself," Ian said. "But the exhaust gas is nasty stuff. It may have gotten them, and at least it should slow them down for a while."

"Don't count on it," Roberts said. "You aren't safe. You will never be safe. They won't stop until all of you are dead."

"And just who are they?" Ian asked.

Roberts snorted and turned away.

Tom emerged from the bilge covered with oil and smelling like diesel. "It's a real mess," he began. "The engine block looks like Swiss cheese—no oil pressure. And we got a cut fuel line from the main fuel tank. I've got it plugged, but we've got a bilge full of fuel. One spark and we're toast. I've got the hatches open and the water hoses on. I hate to dump raw fuel out here, but that bilge is dynamite. How is it up here?"

"The radios and electronics are gone. We can run, but we're a blind mouse now. No more radar," Ian reported.

"Do you think they'll come back?" Sheri asked.

"Bet your life on it," Roberts said contemptuously.

Tom and Ian both turned and glared at him. He got the message and shut up.

"I'll get back up on the tower...let you know if I see anything."

The boat continued to fishtail toward the Bay Town platforms. There was no sign of *Blackwolf* as they entered the cluster of towering steel production platforms. Neither were there other boats or workers on the platforms. That was not unusual.

Crews made regular maintenance rounds, but for the most part the platforms were completely automated. They were still thirty miles from Galveston Pass. Three hours at their present speed. They would all feel better about crossing that last stretch of open water if they could count on the power and maneuverability of both engines. They tied up to a large production platform and Sheri climbed the tower to keep watch while the men set to work in the bilge. Still no sign of *Blackwolf.* Perhaps the missile had done the job as Ian had suggested.

The inspector had decided to pump the diesel fuel and oil into the water tank. It took a while as the pumps were small and they had to transfer more than two hundred gallons. They ate while they worked and kept an uneasy watch on the horizon. Ian commented to Tom that Doc would have a fit if he could see the condition of his usually immaculate boat now.

"I guess I'll be the one getting the grief about bullet holes this time," he laughed.

Tom came up from the bilge to see if he could salvage the radios. Roberts was still handcuffed in the cabin.

Sheri was on her way down from the oil platform to check on the men when she saw the sub surface. She screamed at them to take cover, but *Blackwolf* opened fire before the words were out of her mouth. Tom dropped to the deck, swore and ran back to the cabin. The sub was only a hundred yards away—point blank range—and hammering away at them mercilessly. Debris was flying and Roberts was screaming at him to be set free. Tom rolled across the salon deck just as the cabin windows exploded above him. He crawled through the broken glass to Roberts's chair and unlocked the cuffs.

Flames roared up from the bilge. He was thrown to his knees by the blast, but suddenly Sheri was there helping him. They moved to the rail and Tom shouted, "Jump! We're right behind you." She dove cleanly into the dark water and pulled away from the boat. Tom looked back and saw Roberts lying on the deck. He crawled back and half lifted, half dragged the old man to the railing. He heaved him over the side and jumped in after him.

Sheri screamed when she saw Ian stagger from the bilge and stand, briefly silhouetted against the orange flames just before the boat exploded.

CHAPTER 20

The guard snapped, "Holiday, come on, move it!" Atlee was not on night duty and Doc didn't recognize this guard or the moose in coat and tie with him. He dropped from the top bunk, shook Mike in the lower bunk and grabbed his pants. He fumbled with his socks and shoes, grabbed his only shirt and moved to the cell door. Mike rolled out and stood beside him.

"Not you, Berry. Just Holiday."

"See you, pal," Doc said wondering if he would be coming back in one piece. He didn't like the feel of this at all.

Mike stepped back and the iron door creaked open. Doc was led down the hall to an interrogation room. He stepped inside and stayed on his feet. He began subtle isometrics to wake his defenses up. He knew this room and was certain he was being watched through the two-way mirror. *So what's the game and who are the players?* The door opened again and two men stepped in. The larger, who had been with the guard, stood by the door and Jack Morgan followed him in. Morgan pointed to a chair and said, "Have a seat, Holiday. You and I are overdue for this little chat."

"I must admit this is a surprise. I didn't expect you to have the guts to come back here, not after what you did to your men at the condo."

"Don't you have that just a little backwards? I wasn't even

on the island. That one's going to be a little hard to prove. However, you, I understand, were seen going into the building just shortly before the explosion. The way I see it, that's both motive and opportunity. What a shame they don't have capital punishment here in Paradise, but then I'm sure we'll be able to work something out." He snorted and then changed his tone.

"You're an amazing man," Morgan continued, "and I stand in awe of you. How one man can screw up so phenomenally, it's just...well, it's just unbelievable. Poor old Agent Bentley, my condo, my handpicked security force, my boat, and then my little warehouse. Not to mention my computer net and a few hundred million...no...better make that a billion or two of my very hard earned money. Holiday, if I wasn't such a secure person, my self-esteem could really be damaged here. I just don't understand why you don't like me."

"You're an asshole, Jack. Cut the crap. What do you want?"

"Well, since you put it that way, I want my boat and my money back. I want my condo rebuilt, and I want to watch you rot in hell for all eternity. But like so much of life, we rarely get everything we want. One has to be philosophical, so I suppose I'll have to make choices. For example, I'd be willing to give up watching you rot in exchange for the money, or even most of the money. You can't spend it all, you know. No one could spend it all."

"Got another idea?"

"Oh yes, and it's not nearly as pleasant as what I'm offering this time. Don't be such a hard-ass, Doc. Just focus on you and Sheri on a lush tropic isle, away from the maddening crowds, wealthy beyond your wildest dreams...."

"Or?"

"Doc, have you seen the papers? It's been a terrible week for boating accidents."

"Did you sink another unarmed research vessel?"

"Nothing quite that spectacular. No, just a sailboat full of drunken stockbrokers. I think you knew one of their guests—Stephanie, my little Georgia peach. A terrible fire at the fuel dock. Boat fires can be so grisly, you know?"

Doc remained silent, taking the measure of the dinosaur guarding the door. He shifted his gaze back to Morgan and wondered if he could get to Morgan before T. Rex crossed the room. Spending the rest of his life in prison or in a wheel chair would be a small price to pay for the satisfaction of hearing the bones snap in Morgan's neck. Doc exhaled deeply, forcing himself to relax. *Just give me an opening, Jack, and your ass is mine.*

Morgan reached into his pocket and produced a handful of twenty-dollar gold double eagles. He held them up for Doc to see.

"There was another fire, Doc. This one off the coast of Galveston, just a few hours ago in fact. You'll be glad to know the crew survived. And I was certainly happy to get these back. They're getting so hard to find."

Doc counted the coins. "What's your deal, Jack? Let's hear it."

"I told you, I want the money back. I want the transfer codes you used. That was really quite good. Someday you'll have to tell me how you did it. But for now, the money will do. Well, no...that's not quite true. I want the chalice too, the one you got from old Ben Travis. It was really mine. I footed the bill for the old buzzard's research. He thought it was a government grant of course, and I guess in a way he was right. These things do get complicated after a while. Know what I mean?'

"May I see one of those coins please?"

Morgan hesitated then tossed him a coin. Doc examined it carefully, holding it up to the dim light as if looking for a mark. Then he nodded slowly.

"You didn't get this coin from Sheri. But they were headed to Galveston. That leaves two possibilities: first is you sank *Kratos* before they made port and they are all dead. In that case we have nothing further to discuss...at least for the moment. Second, you knew where they were going, but you missed. And in that case, you came here in desperation to pump me for information. You should have known better, Jack. Unless you can prove you have Sheri, alive and in good health of course, there's nothing to talk about. Oh, no, there might be one little thing—the disks I took from your security files? Want to talk about those, Jack? You see, if you lay a hand on Sheri, those disks go public. Pretty hot stuff on those disks." He looked at the coin again and then tossed it back. Morgan caught it and Doc, having said his piece, now waited.

Morgan glared at Doc and then at the coins in his hand as if they had betrayed him. He thrust them back in his jacket pocket and stood. His face turned ugly. He glared at Doc for a long silent moment. Finally he said, "Don't get too smug, Holiday. Remember what I told you, there's no catch and release in this game. Disks or no disks, you're on my hook and I can reel you in anytime I want."

He leaned forward and jerked his fist up quickly, setting an imaginary gaff deep into Doc's back. Then he laughed, nodded toward T. Rex and they were gone.

Sheri clutched the cold steel of the oil platform's diagonal bracing and tried to keep herself as low in the water as she could. *Blackwolf* was hunting for them. Its searchlights lit the nooks and crannies of the platform and the deck gun tracked with the light. Tom and Bill Roberts were somewhere in the darkness, hiding as she was. Inspector Cord was nowhere to be seen and she feared the worst. *Kratos* was still burning. Surely someone would see the flames and come to the rescue.

She was fifty yards away and she could still feel the terrible fire's heat. The sub's spotlight swept the platform again. A gentle swell passed and Sheri was lifted three feet and then dropped back. The steel was covered with sharp-shelled oysters. She tried to keep clear and yet she needed the protection, just like the little fish below used the massive structure to hide from larger predators.

Blackwolf was moving again, slowly, patiently. Surely the fire on *Kratos* would bring help, but not yet. A boat would take three hours, a helicopter an hour. *What if the sub sent out divers? What if it fired a torpedo at this platform? No more little fish. No more big fish. No more Sheri or Tom.* Another swell...she rose and fell with it, pushing away from the platform leg, trying to stay out of the searchlight. There were some explosions in the fire—probably ammunition—then three flares burst skyward. They arced a hundred feet up, lighting the night sky for a brief moment before fizzling out and falling quietly into the sea. In their light she saw Inspector Cord. He was clinging to a rubber boat bumper, drifting in open water. If the sub had seen him.... She took several deep breaths, exhaled forcefully to lower her carbon dioxide level, dropped beneath the surface and pushed off.

Relax, she kept telling herself. She stretched, streamlining herself as much as she could and imagined herself gliding like an arrow through the dark water. She pulled hard with her arms and followed through with a strong scissor kick. *Relax.* She couldn't tell how deep she was. It was too dark, but when she felt pressure in her ears she arched her back and pulled again. *Relax, glide, swallow to fool your brain. Stroke and kick again.* She surfaced quietly a pool length and a half from the platform. *Blackwolf* was circling, moving toward the far side of the platform again. She side-stroked quietly toward Ian, calling his name softly. There was no answer.

When she reached him, she recoiled at the sight. He'd been badly burned in the blast. His hair and eyebrows were gone and his face blistered. He had tied himself to the white rubber bumper and didn't appear conscious. She reached for his shirt and the charred fabric dissolved in her hand. Gently, she caught him under the arm. He moaned and she shifted her grip and started towing him back to the platform. *Blackwolf* was close enough to breathe fire on them at any moment. They would certainly see the large white bumper. She tugged against the wet line, first breaking her finger nails and finally biting into it to free the inspector's wrists. She nearly lost him as the next swell lifted them apart. At last he was free, but now she had his full weight—nearly twice her own—which forced her under. She shifted him to her hip, grasped him across his burned chest and with her free hand stroked hard, pulling her head up long enough to get a breath. With a strong scissor kick, she continued the swim toward the protection of the towering platform. As the swells lifted them again, she could see the sub passing behind the platform. It was going to be close.

Tom, beside Roberts, was hidden in the cluster of caissons at the center of the platform. He'd managed to climb the bracing high enough to get out of the water and pull Bill Roberts up behind him. They crouched, shivering, hiding from the sub's glaring lights. When Tom saw Sheri struggling to save the inspector, he dove and swam straight to her. The sub was closing on them. The searchlight was swinging right for them. But before it reached them, there was a short burst of gunfire as the light had illuminated another target. Bill Roberts was back in the water, swimming toward the sub, waving his arms and shouting at them not to shoot.

The sub turned and continued to fire. Roberts dove awkwardly, resurfaced waving and screaming again. This time they did not shoot. An amplified voice Tom did not recognize ordered, “Swim to the boat,” and Roberts gratefully complied.

During the shooting, Tom reached Sheri and they were able to tow the inspector into the shadows of the platform’s conductors—large pipe sections, smaller inside of larger, cemented together to protect the well casing. The cluster of conductors provided a forest-like shelter and Sheri felt secure, at least for the moment.

“Now what?” she gasped, still trying to catch her breath.

“Depends on Roberts, I guess.”

Inspector Cord moaned again, the first sign of life since Sheri cut him loose from the bumper. She took his hand and tried to comfort him, but now she was shivering, exhausted from the fear and the cool water. Ian squeezed her hand and groaned, “Thank you,” then he was quiet.

They waited. Roberts was helped below and the sub sat motionless for a while, then the searchlights went dead. The sleek black hull eased away into the darkness. In her wake, *Kratos* slipped abruptly beneath the surface and the night sea became very dark.

“He saved us,” Tom said. “He must have told them we were dead.”

“We’re not out of this yet,” Sheri countered. “We’ve got to do something for Ian and then hitch a ride to the beach.”

“We’ll never be able to lift him up to the platform, but I saw a life raft up there. I’ll get it and we’ll make him as comfortable as we can.”

The next day in the Grand Cayman jail passed slowly, with no more visitors and no word of Sheri or Tom. Doc was quiet most of the time, certain the cell was bugged—certain their every word was being passed on to Jack Morgan, and certain he would kill Morgan if he ever got another chance. He and Mike read, kept to themselves, worried and did push-ups. Several hundred a day. They would push themselves to exhaustion and then collapse in pools of sweat. It was meaningless except that it helped. The endorphins eased the pain and anxiety, and helped them stay focused. There was still a job to do. Whatever Morgan was up to had to be stopped. Sheri and Tom had to be found. Stephanie had to be avenged. But how?

The production platform had legs ten feet in diameter and from the sea floor, was as tall as a twenty-story building. Tom found two rafts near the deck crane. He couldn't get the engine started, but was able to free wheel the cable spool and lower the rafts. The lowest deck was ten feet above the water. Tom jumped back into the cool water, tethered the web-bottom raft to the platform, and helped Sheri roll Ian into one. It was neither dry nor warm, but it would keep him floating until they could think of something better.

The sun had been up for three hours when they heard a boat coming. Sheri was laying on the raft's gunnel, trying to sleep and hold on simultaneously. It was a nebulous effort. But when she heard the boat, it was as if she couldn't quite come awake enough to respond. Her mind wouldn't or couldn't make the leap across the chasm back to reality. *It's the cold,* she thought. *I was shivering all night. I'm hypothermic. Oh God, please let them find us.*

Ian was still beside her, but she couldn't find Tom. Then she heard him. He'd climbed back up on the platform and was shouting and waving frantically at the boat. It passed without seeing them. The sun came higher and it slowly warmed her. Tom found a chipping hammer and they ate a few raw oysters from the platform's legs. She could hardly swallow. Ian drifted in and out of consciousness, but he did not appear to be in great pain. Perhaps the sea water was healing his burns like it healed the road rash from Bermuda motor scooter accidents. Sheri stayed beside him while Tom explored the platform.

There were two small metal buildings. One was full of pressure gauges and valves, the other had a small desk, two chairs and a phone jack, but no phone. He went through the desk drawers and found an old plastic cigarette lighter. It lit at the first flick of his thumb. *There's got to be something that will burn,* he thought, *something we can use as a signal fire.* However, everything around him—the furniture, the building, everything—was metal, as if someone had decided fires and oil platforms were not good company. He was still thinking about it when he heard a helicopter. He hurried from the office and ran to the steel grate stairway. There was a helo pad on the top level, four stories up. He was gasping by the time he got to the top, but the chopper was gone. It had passed miles to the west. He paused to take in the view. He could see twenty other platforms, the closest perhaps three to five miles away, the farthest perhaps thirty. And there were boats. He counted six. Now how the devil to attract them without torching the platform? The platform was spotlessly clean: no trash, no wood, no old tires, no...there were tires. Chained to the platform as boat bumpers on the lowest level. He gripped the lighter tightly and ran back down the metal stairway.

The sea was running out of the southeast, and swells were gently rocking the rafts which were still tied to the crane's cable. The tide was high—the tires were wet and the bands of oysters on the jacket legs were now well submerged. He studied the heavy chains which held the tires. The best plan would be to haul one up to the helo pad. *But they are industrial truck tires and the chains are huge and...and what if* Blackwolf *is still out there, licking her wounds and waiting for nightfall, watching for some sign of life? What if...* He shook it off and sat on the deck, overwhelmed. *Perhaps I should relieve Sheri in the water, let her get dry and warm. It might be a very long night.*

Sheri barely had strength enough to climb the welded ladder up to the deck. She found a place in the sun and was soon fast asleep. Tom was beside her with a half dozen oysters when she awoke. It was the middle of a clear, star-filled night.

"Ian?" she asked, rubbing her eyes.

"Better. He was able to keep a couple of these down," he said, pointing to the oysters.

"Any ideas?" Her throat was dry and her voice cracked.

"I've been watching the wind and the swells. They're pushing northeast, right toward the platforms I saw from the helo pad. It might take a while, but I think our chances would be better there. There were boats—probably working crews. I took the bottoms from the office chairs. We can use them for paddles."

"Alright, I'm game."

She ate more oysters. Getting them down without crackers and cocktail sauce was a battle, and when Tom tried to get her to eat more than two or three, she declined. He helped her up and she shivered as she contemplated another cold night in the water. She hesitated but only for a moment, then dove gracefully into the dark water. Ian was awake when she climbed into the raft.

"I'm better, thank you," he announced. "Ready to eat a bloody horse. And the water's taken the pain out of these burns. Be happy to have my hair back though. Don't want to be taken for one of those skinheads."

"I'll be your character witness," she laughed. "Glad you're feeling better. You gave us quite a scare."

Tom untied the crane cable and pulled himself aboard. The sea was smoother now, and without the cable breaking its natural rhythms, the raft rode easily. They'd been drifting for an hour when a phosphorescent rocket passed beneath them, followed by another, and then a dozen more.

"Dolphins," Sheri said. "They're checking us out." As the pod circled them, they were startled by an air blast an arm's length from the raft. Tom turned to see a large, brown-spotted dolphin giving him the eye. He sat frozen as the huge animal watched and, much to his amazement, came closer. Then for and instant, he felt the soft silky skin pass against his leg.

"She petted me," he said, startled. He jumped and the dolphin vanished. A moment later Sheri had a similar experience, but this time, the dolphin did not surface. It simply rubbed against her leg.

"I want to swim with them," she said and before Tom could answer she was over the side, swimming easily beside the raft. Ian pulled himself up to look over the gunnel. Now there were dorsal fins all around them and the exhaust blasts filled the air with fine sea mist.

Sheri giggled. "Someone's a little curious about clothing...they tugged at my shorts."

"My, these are intelligent creatures," Tom chuckled.

The moon was bright enough that she could see a few feet beneath the surface. She took deep breaths and did a surface dive, kicking easily beneath the boat. Quickly a dolphin, about eight feet long, was beside her, effortlessly keeping pace. She surfaced and dove again. This time her friend moved closer. She raised her arm slowly and at first the creature moved just out of reach, but then moved closer. Sheri gently stroked its side. The creature accepted her touch and came closer still. Sheri reached for its dorsal. She could tell there was hesitation so she moved slowly, and when she could, she gently grasped the dorsal with one hand and stroked the animal's side with her other hand. The dolphin responded with one powerful stroke which pulled them down twenty feet. Sheri was startled, but held on with both hands and felt the water rush past. They were deep and she needed air. She relaxed her grip, ready to break for the surface, when, as if asked, her playmate arched up and in an instant, lifted her into the cool night air.

Exhilarated, she gasped for breath and lay back in the water. Then she realized she was alone. She turned abruptly, looking for the dolphin, but there was nothing around her but stillness. The raft was no longer in sight and she was alone. But as suddenly as a wave of fear broke over her, the water exploded as her friend leapt high in the air and sliced cleanly into the water before her.

She heard Tom calling in an anxious voice and called back that she was alright. "Can you take me home," she said to the dolphin, "back to the boat?" She half expected an answer. Perhaps the magic of the night could overcome the verbal communication barrier as easily as it had her fear. There was only silence and the dark eyes of her friend. She understood. The game was over. The pod had moved on and it was time for them to part. She stroked the soft skin again and with a single thrust of its broad tail, the dolphin was gone.

She called to Tom loudly, and she jumped when he answered in his normal voice from just a few feet behind her. She was back at the raft. The dolphin had understood perfectly and had already brought her near the boat.

They drifted, paddled and occasionally slept through the

rest of the night. At the crest of the swells, they could see bright platform lights far in front of them, and in the troughs only the light of a million stars looked almost within reach. As dawn came, the raft was within five or six miles of the largest cluster of platforms, and by the time the sky had gone from gray to pink to blue, with the sun rising through a cloudless sky, a chopper circled low, and the crew waved. Shortly thereafter, a sleek white shrimp trawler appeared on the horizon.

"Been expecting you," the wiry gray-bearded captain said once they were safe aboard and heading for Galveston Pass. There were three empty thermos bottles on the helm and the old man chattered as if he had not seen another human in months. Sheri was warmly wrapped in a blanket with a cup of hot chocolate, even though the temperature was climbing toward eighty.

"A fellow named Carl Smith's been calling all the boats—choppers too, I guess—asking us to keep an eye out for you. He used to work out here, a diver with the National Marine Fisheries, I think. Married a pretty little local girl and she keeps him on the beach these days. Teaches biology at the high school. My grandson, Mickey, had him last year. That boy's going to be sixteen next month. Lordy, how time does fly. Best teacher in the school, the kid says."

Tom looked at Sheri and nodded. It was the name Doc had given them just before sending them on their way, that last night in Grand Cayman.

"Carl will meet us at the dock, but if there's anything you need, anything at all, you give my wife a shout and she'll see to it. And don't you worry none about your friend...we got the best hospitals in the state. Right here. Yes, sir. The wife's a nurse, patched me up plenty of times. I know. He's going to be good as new. Better even, you'll see." Sheri thanked him and slept, dreaming of dolphins until the old diesels changed their tune as the captain eased the boat into her slip.

Carl Smith had kind eyes and a handle-bar mustache. He was about Doc's age, sturdy, with a bit more of a paunch, and an easy manner that let you feel right at home.

There was an ambulance waiting for Ian, who protested it wasn't necessary until he saw the attractive nurse who would be taking care of him. Tom and Sheri would follow in Carl's car. Carl quickly told Tom of the strange call he had gotten four days before. "She sounded plenty scared, like she couldn't talk for long, you know. Said you were in danger and that Doc wanted me to watch out for you. Told me about your boat and said something about a sub. What's that all about?"

By the time they reached the hospital, the stories had been told and the game plan formulated. Carl would drive them to Houston, provide money and airline tickets, and watch after Ian until they returned. Tom called Debbie who in turn would get word to Doc.

There would be no Coast Guard report and nothing said to the police. Nothing that would delay their arrival in Washington, DC. The banquet for Chaplain Stone was eight hours away and there was not one of those hours to spare. There were dress shops on the way to the airport. Sheri got what she needed without trying anything on, and the clerks were amazed that anyone would buy a three hundred-dollar dress in less than six minutes. So was she. Makeup came from the airport shops and when Sheri emerged from the limo in front of the White House, the transformation was stunning. Tom held the door for her. She took his arm, whispered "Wish me luck," and then disappeared up the stone stairs into the White House.

CHAPTER 21

"I don't have an invitation," she explained to the Secret Service agent "but I left a message for Chaplain Stone. I hope..."

"Miss Benson? Sheri Benson? Captain Stone asked that we take you to him the moment you arrived. Will you come with me please?"

He led her from the vestibule to the formal East Room so quickly that she hardly had time to notice the several parlors they passed on the way. Most of the hundred or so guests were seated at tables below a low platform holding the speaker's table and podium. Chaplain Stone rose with his hand outstretched to welcome her, but she nearly stumbled into him before he caught her and kept her from falling. Jack Morgan was seated at the head table two seats down from the chair reserved for the President. He stood and smiled at her. When she didn't respond, he laughed and snapped his fingers, which got the immediate attention of someone Sheri guessed to be a Secret Service agent. Jack Morgan whispered instructions and the man glanced toward Sheri and nodded. She turned to Chaplain Stone and asked, "Is there somewhere we can go? This doesn't look good at all."

"We'll find a place. Come on." He took her arm and they started across the room. The man Morgan had spoken to started after them. He was moving along the edge of the room, trying not to disturb the guests or draw attention to himself. He reached the door first, but Sheri pushed past him and broke into a run in the hundred-dollar three-inch spike heels as Chaplain Stone followed. The man quickly followed them down the hall. She tried several doors which were locked. As she pulled on the next door, it opened and she found herself face to face with the President. She gasped and turned to leave, but her spike heel caught and twisted in the carpet. She lost her balance and fell at his feet. Chaplain Stone knelt beside her and the President extended his hand to help her up.

"That man," Sheri glared at the man in the doorway, "was chasing me."

"That's my job, Miss. Colonel Morgan wants to speak with you. I was only trying to give you his message."

Sheri looked at him doubtfully and then at the President. He looked younger and taller from the floor. He hesitated with his hand still outstretched. She took it without trying to stand.

"Sir," she began meekly, "I came through great danger to find Chaplain Stone in the hope that he could get me in to see you. I've just come from Grand Cayman and there's a lot of trouble there. Jack Morgan's men killed a customs agent and tried to kill us. He was responsible for the sinking of that research vessel off Charleston and we think we know about the money."

"The money?"

"Yes, sir. Several billion dollars, and there are these...." she said, reaching into a small purse. Morgan's aide dove at her. Chaplain Stone caught him by the coat and threw him clear. Morgan's aide went for his gun as Stone stepped in front of the President and two Secret Service agents leveled weapons at the now bewildered young man. "She was going for a weapon," he stammered. "Colonel Morgan told me she's dangerous and to keep her away from you, sir."

"I don't believe I've seen you here before," the President said, helping Sheri to her feet. "I believe you've got some explaining to do, and why don't we hear what Colonel Morgan has to say while we're at it. I'm sure our guests would enjoy some champagne while we sort this out. Rick, will you?" he nodded and the agent on his left produced a small radio and gave the orders.

The President then turned back to Sheri. "Now, what were you going to give me, Miss...?"

"Benson, sir. Sheri Benson," she smiled and handed him the purse. He opened it and removed three gold twenty-dollar double eagles. He admired them but looked up without comprehending their significance.

"From the wreck of the *Central America*," she said. "The crew of the salvage vessel was killed for those when *Blackwolf*, the submarine that Captain Behrmann built, torpedoed an unarmed salvage vessel. The sub is working for Jack Morgan and these prove it. We found them in a secret vault he's got in Grand Cayman."

"*Blackwolf*? The prototype sub that was destroyed off Bermuda last fall?"

"Yes, sir, that's the boat. But it sure wasn't destroyed. She sank our boat in the Gulf of Mexico two days ago. She was trying to keep me from getting to you."

"Colonel Morgan is gone, sir. Left just a moment ago."

"Find him," the President said calmly. His voice had the edge of a winter blizzard.

"Yes, sir."

The young man on the floor was disarmed and led away as the President led them back to the Oval Office where he offered Sheri a drink.

"I'd really like a beer, but I don't suppose..."

He smiled and picked up the phone. "I'll join you. Anyone else?"

She asked if Tom might be invited in and then the storytelling began in earnest. She told about Doc's dive on the sunken yacht and his suspicions about the torpedo parts. Tom laid out what he could of Morgan's illicit financial empire.

"And how much did you find?" the President asked with amazement.

"About six billion, so far. But that was only what he had ready access to in Grand Cayman. He's been there for years with a network all over the world. We still don't know how much they had hidden or where before Doc put me on to them. But my guess is...well, quite frankly, I don't have a guess. Just pick a number, sir, one with lots of zeros."

He shook his head in bewilderment. "Where could they

have accumulated so much? How can any of this be possible? Your story certainly intrigues me, son. I'm not sure it convinces me, but it sure as hell intrigues me."

"Sir, the guests have been waiting over an hour," his senior aide counseled.

"I want the two of you to wait for us. Rest and eat. We'll talk more later." As they walked down the corridor to the state banquet room, the President asked Chaplain Stone, "What do you make of all this?"

"I believe them. And I believe John Holiday."

"But the implications are mind boggling. Jack Morgan was a trusted advisor to three Presidents—this would be nothing less than treason."

"These people have nothing to gain by lying to you. Does Morgan?" Stone replied.

They were at the doorway. The President paused, straightened his tie then looked to the agent on his left. "Well, where is Colonel Morgan?" The blizzard was back in his voice.

"Nothing yet...sorry, sir."

The President nodded then raised an eyebrow at Stone. They entered the banquet hall to the applause of the guests.

The dinner ended shortly after midnight. Tom and Sheri had been given guest rooms and were asleep when the phone rang just after one. They were escorted to a staff room and met by twenty important looking men drinking coffee and waiting for the President who entered moments later. As the men turned to face the President, Sheri recognized Secretary of the Navy, Andy Anderson. She smiled, but he remained poker faced. Chaplain Stone entered behind the President and took a seat between Sheri and Tom.

"What's happening?" she asked in a whisper.

"He believes you," Stone whispered back. "Now he's trying to find out who the players are."

"I want to know," the President began, "where Jack Morgan got six billion dollars."

There was silence around the table. He made eye contact with each of them before speaking again. Some were nervous, some glared with contempt, others nodded as if approving his boldness.

"Alright, let's begin again. I've just verified that this young man and his friends found six billion dollars from accounts set up by Colonel Jack Morgan. I want to know were Morgan got that much money and what he intended to do with it. And by God, gentlemen, career decisions are going to made here tonight if I don't get some answers."

The silence was heavy as lead until an older man with a southern accent cleared his throat and in a bourbon-smooth voice said, "His daddy was in the oil business...lot of money made in Iran and Iraq. Then there were rumors Morgan has been making some deals."

"What kind of deals are worth that kind of money, Senator? What did he do, sell Camp Pendleton?"

"I don't believe so, sir. But Morgan's a cagey one. The fellow knows how to find money; sniffs it out, like a pack of hounds on a coon."

"I heard he was in on the Savings and Loan scam. Made a real killing," another offered.

"How much did that cost us?" the President asked, turning to his newly appointed director of the budget.

"Roughly five hundred billion, but the first estimates were only one hundred forty to one hundred fifty billion."

"How the hell do you lose five hundred billion dollars? That's not like losing your car keys or forgetting your anniversary. Where did it go?"

There were chuckles around the table, then the budget director tried to answer. "Bad construction loans mostly. Inflated loans and a lot of fraudulent auditing...."

"Perhaps all of it wasn't really lost, Mr. President," Tom said. Sheri turned in her chair, amazed that he would presume to speak.

"Go on, say what's on your mind, Tom. You've certainly earned the right," the President encouraged.

"Well, sir, I think the business about the Savings and Loans is a smoke screen. Morgan's records show some of his money came from arms deals with the Middle East—Iraq as well as Saudi Arabia and Iran. And I'll bet he's been laundering money for years. That's what the customs agent they killed thought too. There was the Bank of Credit and Commerce International, BCCI, twenty billion in assets, a million investors, fraudulent from the very beginning. That's the kind of banker

Jack Morgan is. And if you get me a computer and a little time, I think I can prove it...and get most of that money back."

"Get the money back? Now there's an idea which just might topple Washington. No one here ever gets anything back. Just let me know what you need and Rick will take care of it," the President said and Agent Rick nodded.

"These charges are absurd," General Fulpott snorted. "Jack Morgan has been a trusted member of our team for twenty years."

"Then you're prepared to tell us where Morgan got that much money?" the President responded.

The general looked down at the table and shook his head.

"It has something to do with Kuwait," Sheri said and all of them turned to stare at her. "He had meetings with them, long meetings and they argued a lot."

"About what?" the President asked.

"I wasn't invited, but I know they were real mad at Jack when they left. We were told never to talk about the meetings."

"Could you identify any of them? That would certainly help." The speaker was the Secret Service assistant director.

"I can do better than that. There were pictures in the Cayman newspaper and video tape of the raid. The customs office in Grand Cayman should have all of it."

"Mr. President, do you think some of that money came from a deal Morgan made with the Kuwaitis?" a three-star general asked.

"Good assumption, General. Now figure out what kind of a deal Jack could have made that was worth that kind of money and we're home free," the President said and looked at his watch. It was nearly three.

"Alright, that's it for tonight. Get to work on it. I want to know where Morgan got that money and what kind of deals he's been making and..."

"And Doc needs to get out of jail," Sheri blurted out. "He needs to talk to you."

A smile curled at the edge of the President's lower lip. "Yes, and see what you can do to spring the good Doctor Holiday. I have a feeling we're going to need him. I want a report by nine. Secretary Anderson, please stay. Thank you, gentlemen, and good night."

Anderson sat back heavily in his chair. Chaplain Stone waited until the room emptied, then got up and sat on the table at Anderson's side. "You told Doctor Holiday the President knew about the sub and the attack on the research ship. You lied, Andy. And you were going to let Doctor Holiday and that young lieutenant rot in a Caymanian jail after you recruited them to help you. Are you in this thing with Morgan?"

Anderson hesitated before answering. He glared at Bill Stone as if he were looking at a traitor, then he turned to the President and said. "Never. I was never involved with him. At least not until these past few weeks. Morgan offered to help us get our sub back and I...well, we can't let that sub fall into the wrong hands. That's all." Anderson was staring at his hands, nervously twisting his academy class ring and avoiding the President's eyes.

"I think you'd better start at the beginning, Mr. Secretary. That wouldn't be the three billion-dollar prototype you reported lost off Bermuda eight or nine months ago, would it? Are you now telling me we need to revise that report?" the President said and pulled his tie loose. He turned to look at Sheri and Tom and nodded. She nodded and smiled back. Now they were finally getting somewhere.

CHAPTER 22

It was four in the morning three days later when the President awoke and glared at the phone. It rang again and he picked it up. He recognized the gruff voice from calls the past two nights. "Don't be a fool. You're going to end up deader than Kennedy if you don't quit rocking the boat."

"Who the hell is this?" the President demanded, but the only response was a dial tone. He lay back staring into the darkness unable to sleep. At seven he called Bill Stone and asked the new Chief of Chaplains to join him for breakfast. He was on his third cup of coffee when the chaplain arrived. After briefly exchanging amenities, he offered Stone a chair and pointed to the coffee thermos. When Stone was seated and his cup filled, the President got to the point.

"I had a rather disturbing phone call last night. It's the third one this week. Always the same muffled voice at four in the morning, threatening to kill me if I don't mind my own business."

"That's outrageous," Stone said alarmed. "Can't the Secret Service put a stop to it?"

"Apparently not without diminishing their chances of catching the bastard. So he calls, I answer and they listen, but so far no luck nailing him."

"That must be very unnerving. What do you suppose it's about?"

"Well, it started the night after your party in the East Room. The investigation we started into Jack Morgan's affairs has rattled some cages and the old lions are growling. He has interesting friends."

"Those old loins still have teeth, Mr. President. If I were you, I'd take those threats quite seriously. What has your investigation turned up so far?"

"The file is sparse at best, considering he's supposed to be working for us. Anyway, Morgan was some kind of a financial whiz kid with a background in the Middle East. The agency set him up in Grand Cayman to deal with the Arab states somewhat like Ollie North dealt with the contras during the Reagan administration. Apparently, they sent the fox to watch the hen house, because before anyone realized what he was up to, he'd made millions. He built up one hell of a war chest and to do it, he had to have friends, so he bought some of the very best."

"So now, he's using that wealth against your administration, is that it?"

"Exactly. As the war chest grew, so did his influence and ambition. Now word is out that funds are available for political campaigns—if you're on the right team, of course."

"And did you take advantage of those funds?"

The President raised an eyebrow at the directness of Stone's question. "No. I was the bad guy, at least as far as the military was concerned. I promised to cut federal waste, balance the budget, and pay off the deficit."

"And why did that make you the bad guy?"

"Because it meant stopping the military's financial merry-go-round. And believe me, no one wants that to happen. But..." he paused and shook his head in frustration, "but apparently, I was the only one too naive to know that."

"You and a few million voters."

"Yeah, well, I wonder if anyone's calling them in the middle of the night?"

"I appreciate the history lesson, but isn't there more to this? We could have both used a few more hours sleep," Stone said and smiled gently.

The President nodded. "Everything I've told you is necessary for what I'm going to tell you now. And I must have your word that none of it will ever leave this table."

"Agreed."

"There is a faction of our government, a very large faction in fact, who have their own solution to military downsizing. You will recall that on the eve of our Civil War, it was suggested to President Lincoln by his staff that declaring war on France would be a more viable option than armed conflict on our own soil. It's the same solution being offered to me. Some of the old lions think now's the time for us to use our military strength to stabilize the world's political turmoil."

"Isn't that what Attila the Hun, Julius Caesar and Adolph Hitler all said when they set out to conquer the world?"

"Good point. It sounds too insane to ever be taken seriously, yet..." he paused and ran his fingers through thick wavy hair. Then he looked at Bill Stone with frustration and a look of helplessness. "Yet, the military argue that the world is more at risk than anytime during the cold war. Small nations with big attitudes and bigger bombs—Saddam and Iraq specifically. His most recent raids in the north support the argument that he is a prime candidate for permanent stabilization. Our bombing runs were good public relations, but they were a band aid on a brain tumor. He has weapons and delivery vehicles—long range diesel subs capable of delivering nuclear war heads—courtesy of the Germans and the Russians."

"That's certainly frightening."

"Damn right it is! The Navy thinks one of them killed the Secretary of State...blew that yacht in half with our people on it. The more I listen to them, the more I wonder if they might be right...or if the Pentagon is just trying to fill their rice bowls by giving us a new enemy to fear...a new reason to keep the merry-go-round turning. And I can't get a straight answer to save my ass!" He let his anger cool for a moment before going on. "That's the real scary part. I'm the President, for Christ's sake...oh, sorry. The answers I get have been spun so many times you get dizzy before you get to the first comma...like that damn sub that never existed in the first place. Now what the hell am I supposed to believe about all that?"

"I know the girl and her friends. If you're asking me, I'd say believe what she tells you."

"Thanks. Of course if I decide to believe her and go after Jack Morgan, it will probably get me killed."

"Would you have to get involved? Directly, I mean?"

"It's the only way I'll ever be satisfied I'm getting straight answers. These are frightening times, Bill. Treason isn't a word we hear a lot, but it's the only word I know that describes what might be going on. Morgan may be behind it, but he has a lot of friends. In fact, the whole wood pile may be infested; catching Morgan may not be the end of the problem."

"So what will you do?"

"I want to meet the people Morgan has been dealing with. We've got to find out what he's been up to. If he's double crossed people we trust, it could upset the whole Middle East apple cart. Our allies over there don't have much of a sense of humor. And as we are painfully learning, they have the ways and means to express their anger."

"Terrorism."

"Exactly. Even though I didn't carry New York, I'd hate to see it vaporized by our fundamentalist friends. So I've asked our team to set up a meeting in Grand Cayman. The Kuwaitis obviously know where it is," he chuckled at the irony of his comment. "However, because of that little incident our Doctor Holiday staged, they don't want to meet on the island. That's fine...we'll entertain them at sea. A task force is cruising down there now and I'll fly down next week. It will give us a chance to look into what was really going on down there and I've always wanted to try my hand at marlin fishing. I used to love fishing.

"My grandparents had a cabin on Trout Lake. That's up in the Boundary Waters, between Minnesota and Canada. Not another place around for miles. Fantastic fishing. Another night like last night and I may move the White House up there for keeps."

"If you go after Morgan, I'll be right beside you, and you know, I've got a powerful friend or two myself," Stone answered confidently.

Blackwolf surfaced in darkness off the coast of Key West. Rudy Geist pulled himself up the main ladder with his remaining usable arm. His right one hung useless at his side, crudely bandaged and beginning to putrefy. He knew the stench of gangrene, but he, Roberts and Johnson were the only crew left alive and he was not about to let either of them put a knife to him. Andrews had been hit by the rocket, which without detonating, had ample thrust to splatter his head. The three survivors had been too busy saving the sub to be concerned with the little things, like globs of Colonel Andrews's brains hanging from the overhead.

Roberts was uninjured. Johnson was flash burned and had lost most of his hearing. But because the dark glasses he wore most of the time had protected his eyes, he was still able to see well enough to rebuild or bypass critical operating systems that would have left most engineers stymied for weeks. Within hours he and Roberts had *Blackwolf* functional, if not mostly operational. And after receiving Morgan's message, they sped submerged, averaging better than fifty knots southeast across the Gulf of Mexico to the tip of the Florida Keys.

Jack Morgan met them accompanied by two men. One he introduced as the doctor Rudy Geist had requested. The other looked like what he was, a young army officer named Charlie, with the fresh-scrubbed look of Ft. Bragg.

"Sink it," Morgan snapped and Charlie produced a razor sharp boot knife and slashed the inflatable.

"Get us down as quickly as you can," Morgan ordered as soon as the hatch was closed. He glared at Geist, or what was left of him, and said, "The girl certainly looked healthy for a ghost, Rudy. Especially when she was talking her sweet little ass off to the President. There I am, sitting at the head table, thinking we've got it made and that little bitch comes waltzing down the isle. You assholes told me they were dead. All of them dead! You know how I hate surprises...." He sniffed the air and quickly looked around the compartment. "What the hell is that disgusting smell?"

"Our dearly departed Colonel Andrews," Geist said and lit a cigarette. "Don't worry, you won't notice it after a day or two. Except perhaps when you're trying to eat. Then it gets a little thick."

Morgan stopped and for the first time noticed the extent of the damage: smashed monitors and scorched instrument panels.

"What happened down here?" he asked, his voice losing

its drill sergeant bluster.

"To Andrews? He sort of went to pieces on us. It was a rocket. We surfaced to finish off their boat and....well, it didn't detonate, it just ricocheted around here like a round in a pill box...." His voice trailed off the rest.

"Your arm?"

"Yeah, I hope your doc brought a saw. He's going to need it."

Morgan was silent. The losses of Andrews or even Geist's arm were insignificant compared to the cost of repairing the sub, or his losses on Grand Cayman. He was unable to speak for a moment, suddenly overwhelmed by the abyss into which he had fallen.

"Where to, boss?" Johnson asked from the helm.

"Back to Grand Cayman," Morgan answered. His voice had a hollow, distracted ring. Then he added, "We've got some diving to do and a score to settle." He tried to add a little enthusiasm to give them something to look forward to, but for the moment all he could think of was how much he had lost, not how much might still be saved.

The American Consul and two attorneys were brought to Doc and Mike's cell early the next morning.

"Diplomatic immunity?" Doc laughed. "That's cute. Will the Caymanians buy it?"

"They already have," the Consul answered. "But only because the President himself went out on a limb for you. You have some mighty persuasive friends, Doctor Holiday."

"And Jack Morgan, what kind of friends does he have?"

"He just made the President's most wanted list. Does that answer your question? Got any ideas about where we might find him?"

"A couple," he said and looked at Mike. "You ready, partner?"

"You bet."

"Now wait a minute, the President wants you back in Washington."

"Not much I can do for him there, but if you leave us here and give us a little help, I think we can find Morgan. Try that out on the President and see what he says. In the meantime, we need to see a man about a yellow submarine. Got your MasterCard or Visa? I don't think they take American Express." He stood with his hand out waiting for the Consul to reluctantly hand him a credit card.

"We'll call you this afternoon. If my plan works, I'm going to need your help and a lot more money than the limit on this card. Tell the President we know where part of Morgan's loot is and that will be the key to catching him. Get the money lined up and then stay where I can find you."

The Consul looked worried. Doc smiled a boyish smile and patted him on the back. "Don't worry, Sam. This is going to be fun. You like submarines, don't you?"

Soon they were on Harbour Street, walking past gift and camera shops, south to the Atlantis and Research Submersibles Limited offices. Mike started asking questions.

"You think Morgan will try to salvage his sailboat, don't you?"

"That's affirmative, pilgrim. Josh found millions in European bearer bonds stashed in the master cabin. After what Tom did to his computer piggy bank, Morgan may need to cash a few of those bonds to buy groceries. So we've got our bait. Now all we need is a trap."

They crossed the street in front of the gleaming white fence of the Cayman Museum, continued down Church Street until they saw a yellow Perry submarine on blocks in the parking lot next to the Atlantis office and gift shop. Tourists from cruise ships crowded the sidewalks and filled the shop. Doc moved between them to Research Submersibles Limited's booking desk, introduced himself and asked the young, dark haired, starched and pressed Caymanian attendant if Captain Terry Edmonds was available.

"He's on his way. He got your call and he's expecting you." Her accent was as charming as her smile. Doc nodded and said he'd be happy to look around the gift shop. A map of the Cayman Wall caught his eye and he went over for a closer look. Mike was already there.

"There's the *Kirk Pride,*" Mike pointed to the island freighter wrecked at eight hundred feet. "I remember the National Geographic article about her. Sank in the mid-seventies and no one had a clue where she was until eighty-six, when these guys found her. Pretty much by accident, if I remember the article correctly."

"Your memory serves you well," a tall blond man in his mid-thirties said from behind them. He wore blue military shorts and a white shirt with epaulets and captain's bars. He had a tan surfer look, and the kind of eyes that made you think he'd be good with young kids.

"Doctor Holiday?" he asked, holding out his hand to Mike.

"No, Doc's the crusty, skeptical, old jail-bird type. I'm the dashing, young naval officer. Mike Berry's the name," Mike laughed, shook hands with Captain Terry Edmonds and nodded toward Doc.

"I am not a skeptic," Doc protested. "I'm a devout optimist seasoned with a little realism...that's all. How could you possibly call me a skeptic?" He reached forward and shook Terry's hand firmly while still glaring at Mike with a perturbed look.

"How may I help you?" Terry asked, wondering what the devil he was getting himself into.

"For starters, I'd like to know a little about the topography and geology of the island," Doc said. Mike was taken by surprise. Their visit had little to do with a geology lesson.

"Sure. The islands were once part of a limestone mountain range that ran to the south end of Cuba. Changes in the level of the great abyssal sea carved the face of the wall, like this notch here at three hundred feet," he said, pointing to a smooth half-pipe trough running horizontal around the island. It looked as if it might have been made with an ice cream scoop.

"Interesting," Doc said. "And these big boulders that look like glacial erratics?"

"Glacial erratics? That's good...do you have a background in geology?"

"No, English. I read a lot."

"We call the boulders haystacks. Some are seventy or eighty feet tall. They were pieces of the mountain which broke off and fell. That's what kept the *Kirk Pride* from sliding the rest of the way down the wall. If she hadn't hit the haystacks, she'd have been gone. A couple thousand feet deeper and we'd never have found her."

"Interesting," Doc said. "And do you find these haystacks

in other places around the island? Say off the north end of Seven Mile Beach?" Doc said, pointing to the area where *Bluebird*, Morgan's sailboat, would be waiting.

"Yes, as far as I know."

"How about the depth in this area? Shallow enough to dive there?"

"Assuming the bottom contours are consistent, yes, I think so. Is there something there that interests you?"

"Is there somewhere we can go and talk, and perhaps get a sandwich? I'm starved."

They walked across the street to the Island Taste Restaurant and climbed the stairs to the second floor balcony with its spectacular view of George Town Harbour, the cruise ships and two unique sailing vessels, replicas of old pirate ships. A young Scandinavian tourist with long blond hair caught Mike's eye. He smiled, but she turned away and then glanced back, looking just for a moment before warming into an approving grin then turning back to her companions.

"Oh, yes I would," Mike said under his breath.

"You've been behind bars too long...she's only a child," Doc chided.

"See, skeptical. You're getting old, Doc. They all look too young to you."

Two waitresses by the cash register talked quietly and pointed Doc out to the manager.

"Looks like you're famous," Mike observed.

"Infamous is more like it," Doc answered.

The waitress then approached the table cautiously and whispered to Terry, who she obviously knew. Terry nodded and replied to her quietly then smiled. They ordered beer and burgers and when she had gone, Terry said, "She recognized you from the newspapers. I guess I should have as well. There's so little excitement on Cayman, so little crime..." he hesitated, feeling that he'd made a social blunder and was not certain how to recover.

"It's alright," Doc said then paused. "Well, on the other hand maybe it's not. This is going to take a while to explain, Terry. I hope you've got time for a long lunch."

CHAPTER 23

The day passed so quickly and Sheri was so exhausted that time was a blur, like trying to watch a merry-go-round at full speed. She nodded off frequently in her chair beside Inspector Ian Cord's hospital bed. The President had arranged for the inspector to be transferred from Galveston to the burn unit at Bethesda Naval Hospital. He had been flown in early that same morning and after three hours of surgery, was sleeping off the anesthetic. Tom had been given an office at Fort Belvoir, the center for Army Satellite Intelligence just south of the city, where he was deciphering the transactions initiated by his computer program in the seconds before Morgan's condo was blown to bits beneath them.

Ian was still sleeping and Sheri was dozing off when the telephone rang. She grabbed for the phone, hoping to keep it from waking Ian. Doc had called twice already and she guessed it would be Tom this time. She was surprised to hear the voice of the President.

"I just spoke with the commanding officer at the hospital, Sheri. He told me Inspector Cord's going to be good as new. A little plastic surgery later, perhaps, but the salt water cooled the burns before the deep tissues were destroyed. He was very lucky. If he's awake, I'd like to talk to him...thank him for all he did to help you and Tom."

"No, sir, he's still asleep, but I'll tell him that you called."

"There's something else. I need to talk to Doctor Holiday as quickly as possible. I was hoping you'd know how to reach him. Now that he's a free man again, he's hard to find."

"Yes, sir, I know where he is. They're in a submarine somewhere off the Cayman Wall looking for Jack Morgan's sunken sailboat. Give me your number and I'll ask him to call you tonight."

Late that same afternoon in Grand Cayman when the last of the tourist sub rides were over, one of the two yellow submersibles was docked aboard its mother ship—a strange looking self-propelled barge, built specifically to transport the sub at more reasonable speeds than could be made towing her. Terry, Doc and Mike stood by the helm as the awkward rig plowed across glass flat water toward the island's north end.

The sub, *PC 1203*, a twenty-year-old Perry Cubmarine was, like Doc, a veteran of oil field diving. With much of the deep inspection work now being done by remotely operated vehicles, several of the Perry vehicles had become available. For the first time, tourists had the chance to dive beyond the limits of scuba or of the shallower diving subs like the *Enterprise* in Bermuda or the *Atlantis* in Grand Cayman. This was a unique opportunity because Grand Cayman was the only place in which such vehicles operated. The strange looking barge passed the remains of Jack Morgan's condo. Even a mile from the beach, they could hear the racket of bulldozers clearing out the debris and the honking of frustrated drivers who normally drove the uncongested road as a Le Mans course straight-a-way.

"Beach umbrellas," Terry laughed. "You came down eight stories on beach umbrellas?"

"There were thermals from the explosions in the basement," Doc tried to explain. "All that hot air gave us a lot of extra lift."

"Now, that was definitely worth the price of admission," Mike laughed. "Next time you hear about someone blowing up a building, I might like to try it again."

"Whatever gave you the idea?" Terry asked.

"I'm an optimist," Doc answered and winked at Mike.

"Got any idea how far off the beach you were when Morgan's boat sank?" Terry asked.

"Hard to tell," Doc answered. "It was dark and we were being shot at. All hell was breaking loose, but we could still see the condo...even see Morgan's men launching the inflatables."

"I'd come round the point past the turtle farm when I first saw them," Mike offered. "I remember because I'd been running on a following sea and when I turned the swells really bounced me around in the tower."

Terry had pulled a chart from the helm and was making notes.

"If we're lucky, you were here, still in a couple hundred feet, but if you were out this far," he said pointing to the thousand-foot curve on the chart, "the boat could have hit the bottom and slid right over the edge of the wall."

"Unless she landed in the haystacks and they caught her like they caught the *Kirk Pride,*" Doc said.

"You are an optimist. But perhaps you're lucky too. Our depth limit is a thousand feet...I wouldn't be comfortable going deeper."

"But you could?" Doc asked.

"Not much. If anything happened, the insurance company would go nuts and I'd get crucified."

Doc took the chart and looked from it to the coastline several times. Then he pointed to a spot just at the north end of Seven Mile Beach. "Let's start here and work north and west. There's no way to tell how long *Bluebird* drifted once she started down, but my guess is we were somewhere, about here, when Mike pulled us out. What do you think, Mike?"

"Looks good. Let's do it."

Doc was impressed by how quickly Terry and his two-man crew got the sub ready to dive. It was smaller on the inside than its twenty-two-foot external length and nearly eight-foot diameter appeared. Terry dropped down the hatch, swung the pilot's seat back beneath the hatch to double as a step and then helped them aboard. Once they were seated on cushions in front of the dome port, Terry closed the hatch and secured the dogs. After a brief sequence of radio and systems checks, he turned his attention back to his passengers.

"In the unlikely event that something happens to me, this

red valve will dump a thousand pounds of water ballast. And if that is not enough, there's another thousand pounds we can drop by turning that lever on the deck forward, just between you. We carry a week's worth of oxygen and have lung powered CO_2 scrubbers. About the only thing we don't have is a barby to put the shrimp on if our return is delayed."

"How deep is it down there?" Doc asked.

"Just over a hundred feet. Notice how the dome port makes everything look so much smaller and closer, like looking through a wide-angle lens. I get a more normal perspective through the flat ports up here, but after a while, you get used to the dome. It's very useful for close maneuvering."

"It looks like we could reach out and touch those little coral heads," Mike said.

"Only if your arms are eighty feet long," Terry laughed. "If you're ready, we'll go to work."

Doc turned to watch as Terry added just enough water ballast to start them down. Then with a control box sitting on his lap, he hit toggle switches to activate the three thrusters, main engine and diving planes which controlled the boat.

"It's a lot like flying, isn't it?" Doc asked.

"I was a flight instructor in California, that's why they hired me. Believe me, this is a lot more fun."

There was still enough light to see clearly, but as they passed the shallow top of the wall, the plate corals and sponges looked dark. There were white sand chutes, playground slides to oblivion, and then there was darkness. The wall dropped at a steep slope to over twelve hundred feet. Rather than go straight down, Terry began running grid patterns, frequently confirming his position with the surface support ship who tracked and plotted their position.

At two hundred feet, they saw large grouper and white-spotted eagle rays, then much smaller blackcap basslets and jacks—horse-eye jacks in the shallows and blackjacks as they went deeper. Looking up, they could sometimes see the lonely silhouettes of large barracuda motionless near the surface. But what they did not see was any sign of Jack Morgan's sailboat. An hour passed and then another. Doc wanted to stand up and stretch. Terry's comments were fewer now, and the water, while still clear, was dark, penetrated only by the powerful Burns and Sawyer lights mounted on the pipe frame protecting the acrylic dome port.

Tiny fish swam rapidly to the lights, became confused and quickly swam away again. They briefly saw a shark who darted back under a ledge, and Doc remembered the nurse shark he'd upset in the tunnel beneath the Bermuda Dockyard. A third hour passed.

"I'm afraid that's it for tonight," Terry said and reached for the radio. He reported time and depth to the surface officer and confirmed their location and heading. "We've got a full day tomorrow and the batteries will need all night on the chargers. Sorry we didn't find her. But we haven't gone into deep water yet. If she drifted like you thought, she could be down there in the haystacks. We'll need all the sunlight we can get to be able to see much that deep. We'll start earlier tomorrow. Don't worry, we'll find her."

Doc watched as Terry dumped water ballast, restored trim, and asked for an all clear from the surface officer. When they got it, they started on their way up.

"No, sir, bringing a lot of ships down here is not a good idea. *Blackwolf* could easily avoid them just as she's done for months, or worse, she could blow half of them out of the water and then slip away undetected. Remember, she just took on a full load of very effective torpedoes. And frankly, Mr. President, I'm not sure that if you deploy the entire Sixth Fleet, they could give you better odds of finding her than what I have in mind."

Mike had been sitting quietly for over thirty minutes, listening and watching as Doc paced back and forth in the tiny Research Submersibles Limited office. Doc reached the end of the phone cord and turned to retrace his steps just as the phone was about to be launched from the receptionist's desk. Doc caught it and then was off again, this time pulling it to the opposite corner before again stopping just in time to save it from crashing to the unswept white tile floor. Mike had seen Doc get hyper before, but never like this. Of course, he'd never seen Doc argue with the President of the United States before either.

"Yes, sir, I think I understand, sir. But please realize that your situation in Washington does not mitigate our situation here in Grand Cayman one bit, sir. We still don't have a clue where that asshole is...excuse me. I meant Morgan. And finding his sailboat is the best shot we've got to find him. Sooner or later, he's going to come after that money. I'm betting it's sooner."

There was a long pause during which Doc chewed vigorously on the left half of his lower lip. Then shaking his head negatively and closing his eyes, he said, "Yes, sir, we'll give it our best shot. Good luck to you too, sir."

Doc put the phone down and then sat beside it on the desk, staring through the window at the gutted yellow Perry lockout submersible on the slab in front of the white stucco Atlantis building. Its diving days over, it now served as a landmark and museum piece. It was in better shape than the numerous rusting cannon in front of restaurants, liquor stores and the treasure museum, but still old and unused. *That's what I am,* Doc thought, *a useless, rusty old cannon...or a sub in dry dock, sitting there for birds to crap on and boot camp sailors to paint. What am I doing? Getting us all killed, that's what.* He looked at Mike and scowled. Mike waited.

"Now I know why I didn't vote for him," Doc began. "He's nuts."

"What's up?" Mike asked.

"He's announced a meeting with the Kuwaitis. Wants to know what kind of a deal they made with Morgan. He's going to hold it here on an aircraft carrier."

"That's crazy," Mike said. "He's setting himself up as a target. He'll get his butt blown out of the water and what will that prove? That someone with a lot of torpedoes doesn't like him? He shouldn't take that kind of risk...that's what we get paid for."

"No, that's what you get paid for. I'm an unemployed volunteer, remember?" Doc chuckled and shook his head.

"Do you think Morgan would actually be dumb enough to attack the President?" Mike asked.

Doc thought about that for a while and then he raised an eyebrow and turned to Mike. "What would be the point? Morgan wouldn't risk something that dumb unless there was a really big payoff.... You don't suppose...well, I'll be damned! Thank you, Lieutenant. I think I finally understand what this is about."

"Well?"

"If your country had been overrun, your family wiped out and your source of income destroyed, what would be on your mind?"

"Revenge, with the big R."

"Right, and where would you go to get help?"

"To the last superpower on the planet?"

"Right again. So, Morgan sees an opportunity and makes a deal. He gets a big deposit, and then sells his pals in Washington on the plan."

"So the plan was to get revenge. What do you think, a contract on Saddam?"

"Makes sense to me. We were probably already trying to hit him, so Morgan might have collected without having to do a thing. But it didn't happen, and when a year or two passes and we don't deliver, the Kuwaitis get hot under the collar and show up here."

"Only to fall victim to the infamous Doc Holiday Condo Raid, for which they blame Washington and probably Morgan," Mike said.

"So now they are really pissed, and Morgan has skipped town. Men like Faud are not likely to write this off as a bad idea—not until they've collected a pound or two of flesh—so I'd say we've got a really big problem to deal with. What do you think?" Doc asked.

"'Problem' may be the understatement of the year. So have you got a plan yet...another of the famous Doc Holiday stratagems?"

"It's fomenting at this very moment."

"Sounds dangerous. What's the first step?"

"Terry keeps on looking for *Bluebird,* but this time from the surface with the best side-scan sonar we can find. We can't risk his dropping in on *Blackwolf* and that robot spider thing unannounced. You are going to get that old lock-out sub back in the water," he said, pointing out the window. "And I'm going shopping."

"Looking for anything special?"

"You don't want to know."

Atlantis and Research Submersibles Limited used a metal warehouse near the airport as a maintenance center for the subs. It was a perfect place for what Doc had planned. He could work in private, and nearly everything he would need was immediately at hand. The lock-out sub arrived at the warehouse by flatbed and a second truck delivered four steel drums with orange oxidant labels. The delivery men were quite careful unloading them and when Mike read the labels, he understood why. Doc had found high grade nitro-methane used for making cleaning solvents and as a fuel additive for race cars. Next came a load of hydraulic hoses and scrap aircraft landing gear from the airport. When Doc returned at sundown, he was carrying enough electronics to open a Radio Shack.

"But what are the telephone answering machines for?" Mike asked as he helped unpack. Behind them the RSL maintenance crew were busy checking hoses, valves and cables on the old yellow sub. There was a sudden blast of air as a rotting low pressure air line burst.

Mike jumped and nearly dropped the answering machine he was holding.

"If I can get the servos, which activate the recorders to respond to commands from the portable phone, and get the portable phone to respond to calls on the very low frequency radio, we can turn that old sub into a radio controlled drone."

"But doesn't VLF have a fairly limited range?"

"Yep."

"And just how big a bang are you intending to make with two hundred and twenty gallons of that rocket fuel?"

"As big as I can."

"And just where are we going to be when you set this thing off?"

Doc laughed. "Getting jumpy?" And without answering the question, he turned back to the workbench.

"Oh shit," Mike said softly and continued emptying the box.

They worked until well after midnight. They ordered chow from a local bar and the owner dropped it off after closing at two AM.

They sat out on the flatbed trailer, leaning back against

the sub to eat. It was a beautiful clear night and they watched a falling star blaze across the star-filled cloudless sky.

"Doc," Mike began after washing down the last of the shrimp sandwich with a lukewarm half-pint of Bass beer. "Why are we doing this?"

"Why?"

"Yeah, why aren't we having real ordinance flown in from one of the bases in Florida or Texas? Or better yet, why aren't we just waiting until the Navy ships arrive? Why aren't we letting the big kids handle this?"

"Because I'm a hardheaded old fart, is that what you mean? Well, if it is, you're right, but it's also because of what the President said. Who can we really trust—our friend Andy Anderson?"

"I don't think so."

"That's what the President thinks too. That's why."

Mike sat quietly looking out over the water and then took another pull at the beer before expounding. "The President may be nuts, but then it's all relative. Compared to this plan, his is probably relatively sane."

By the next morning, they were ready to test the Perry sub they had converted to a drone. The large red crane lowered it from the flatbed into the water. Doc sat at the makeshift control panel on the pier and Mike stood at his shoulder. The salvaged aircraft hydraulic units operated the steering and diving planes. Solenoids opened and closed high pressure air valves and the drone responded reasonably well, on the surface at least, to Doc's commands.

"What about range?" Mike asked.

"No way to know until we're both submerged," was all the reassurance Doc would offer.

"When then?"

"Soon as possible. Morgan has to know the longer he waits, the more vulnerable he'll be."

"Doc, I've been thinking. I should be the one to take the sub down.... Now hear me out on this...there are two parts to our mission: take out *Blackwolf* and protect the President. That means we've got to be in two places at once. Now I understand how to push the firing button and solve our first problem, but I haven't got a clue what to do about the second. You would be a lot better on that one than I would." He was looking out across the water, avoiding Doc's eyes.

"I haven't forgotten how you tried to get yourself blown to kingdom come the last time *Blackwolf* came out to play. Do you think I've gotten so old and senile that I'm going to let you try it again?" He put a hand on Mike's shoulder and continued, "I'm not planning this as a one way ride, partner. Remember, I didn't vote for this guy; and I sure as hell am not going to forgo the remainder of my conjugal visits with Sheri just to get my name misspelled in some obscure historical footnote.

"Now as to plan B of our mission, you're right. We will have to be in two places at once and I, as usual, do have a plan. Unfortunately, it has just as much potential for you to become immortalized for monumental stupidity as plan A. Because being as astutely cognizant of your basic psychointellectual developmental deficiencies as I am, I knew that if I made this plan too safe, it wouldn't keep your cartoon-length attention span focused long enough to bring it to fruition. And further, because I do so hate to see a good plan fail, I..."

"You're full of shit, Doc."

"Impossible...that only comes with tenure. Now, pay attention. See if you can grasp the unparalleled sagacity of this strategy within the confines of, let us say, no more than three presentations."

CHAPTER 24

The tow boats that would take the two subs to the reef arrived at eleven and by one AM, the drone was sitting in a sand patch at a hundred feet and Doc was aboard the smaller Perry submersible on the surface, running his fourteenth systems check. After getting them on location, Terry had joined the side scan sonar crew which had flown down from Texas A & M. Operating on a rented dive boat, the crew was having problems calibrating the unit but were confident the problem would and could be solved shortly.

Doc had the VHF marine radio on and picked up the mike when he heard Mike call the tow boat from the fishing docks in Great Bay. Doc acknowledged the call, gave the new channel, then switched and waited. "It's a go, Doc. It might work even better than we thought."

"That's affirmative. Everything here's ready also. We'll standby on sixteen. Good hunting, partner. Out."

The sun came up and climbed higher in the sky until it was directly overhead. The sub became too hot for comfort even with the hatch open, so Doc dove in and swam to the tow boat. He grabbed a cold drink, made a sandwich and joined the young Captain Dan watching television in the wheelhouse.

"Anything about the President?"

"Yeah, he announced a big meeting down here. His ship and its escorts are on the way. Arabs are flying in, but I didn't catch when."

"Sitting ducks," Doc said to himself.

"What?"

"I said they'll be sitting ducks."

"Yeah? For what?" the young man answered skeptically.

"For him," Doc answered. A mile away, a periscope cut cleanly through the water.

"What is it?"

"About seven hundred million, give or take a nickel."

"I mean whose is it. Is it what you are looking for?"

"Ours I think." He dropped down to the deck to get as low as he could to the water.

Captain Dan dropped beside him. "What are we doing?" he whispered.

"Trying to see how much water she pushes. See the bulge? That's what satellites look for. She's one big boat and running just beneath the surface, she makes the water bulge. Probably a Los Angeles class, three hundred and sixty feet, nearly seven thousand-ton displacement. She's what I'd send if I were hunting for another sub. She's the best there is."

"Wow."

"Right."

The radio crackled and Doc got up to answer it.

"You guys see that?" Terry asked from the sonar boat.

"Yes," Doc answered.

"It blew our sonar unit off the charts when it went by. It's looking too. That must be some hot sonar."

Doc rubbed his chin for a minute and then shook his head before speaking again. "Terry, how many times have you covered the area I showed you on the chart?"

"This is the fourth time, Doc. Still nothing."

"How far are you from the *Kirk Pride* wreck, the one on the edge of the wall at eight hundred feet?"

"I know where it is, Doc. We dive her everyday, remember?"

"Sorry. Listen, make a pass over her and tell me what you see."

"Sure, call you back in about an hour."

"Thanks. We'll be standing by on sixteen." Then he turned to Captain Dan and asked, "You got mask and fins on board? I sure could use a swim."

The mask leaked a little and the fins were too tight, but it was a small price to pay for the release of getting back in the water. He swam over the drone a hundred feet below and took in a half dozen deep breaths exhaling forcefully. On the first free dive, he dropped down to thirty or forty feet, hung suspended, neutral, studying the reef and the drone until the sensation behind his eyes told him it was time to go up. Then he stretched his arms upward and surfaced in a relaxed series of full-body dolphin kicks.

Stay loose, he told himself. *Enjoy the reef, stretch and breathe, relax and glide. Be part of it.* He made a second dive and then a third, pushing further down with each, remembering the days when he could have easily reached the bottom, taken a fish with a pole spear and glided back up, stringing the fish on the way. Not so today. He doubted that his best dive reached sixty feet and his brain was screaming for revenge when he finally reached the surface. He caught his breath, cleared the leaking mask and turned toward the shouting coming from the tow boat. Captain Dan was waving at him to come back. He rolled on his back, kicked to the dive platform with easy strokes and pulled himself up.

"I was watching you free dive. You must have been really good, once, I mean."

Doc was sure the boy had meant it as a compliment, but it was awfully hard to thank him. He tossed the mask and fins on the bench seat and grabbed a towel.

"What's up?"

"Terry says he's right on the Loran C numbers and the sonar won't show the wreck. The machine must be broken. He wants to know if you want to have a look at it?"

"No, tell him to get back in the center of the area we charted. Tell him *Blackwolf* is down there and she's been jamming us. It's time to go diving."

"But aren't you supposed to wait for Terry? You can't dive our boat alone, man. That wasn't part of the deal."

Doc looked at him patiently. "Is Terry your friend?"

"Yeah, sure."

"Then you don't want him on this dive."

"What are you talking about, man? What's down there?"

Without answering, Doc pulled on the fins and mask and did a forward roll over the side. The mask flooded. Doc did a three-sixty and caught a breath, cleared the mask and kicked easily to the sub. When he surfaced and climbed aboard, the young boat captain was yelling frantically, first into the radio telling his office their sub was being stolen by a madman, and then at Doc threatening and then begging him not to do it. Doc waved before unhooking the bow line, then climbed aboard and bolted the hatch. The sub's radio was blaring with the angry voice of the Atlantis operations manager. Doc politely turned it off, swung the pilot's seat into position and picked up the control box. There were four toggles on the eight-inch-square metal box, one for the main motor and one each for the three thrusters. He checked the Fathometers and barometer and wrote down the barometric pressure. Drops in pressure would tell him when to add oxygen. He added just a little water ballast and hit the bow horizontal thruster. The bow dropped fifteen degrees and the sub started down. He leveled her and watched the Fathometer's needle continue to rise. During his dive with Terry, the descent rate had been about sixty feet per minute. Doc hit the ballast pump just long enough to slow his descent, which was better.

Beneath him was the drone. He nested the four-toggle control box in its rack by his right knee and picked up the bulkier control box for the drone. The memory bank from the answering machine dialed the number to the portable phone in the drone. The connection was made and they were in business. Bring the drone up, slow the descent of the mother ship. Lead out with the drone. Have mother follow as far back as possible. It was ungainly at first. Like any new helmsman, his tendency was to over-control and then follow by over-compensating. But it didn't take long to get the feel of it; and it wasn't as hard as he'd imagined to get both subs trimmed to neutral buoyancy. Once that was done, he soon had his yellow ducks in a row, marching north along the face of the wall.

Doc had Terry's chart in the sub. He would need Terry's help to keep him in position and hopefully to convince *Blackwolf* that there was only one yellow duck conducting the search. Doc checked his watch and then the LED which was easier to read. He'd give Terry a few more minutes before turning the radio back on. He held tight to the wall. Sunlight softly filtered down even at two hundred feet. The view was spectacular. Plate corals stacked like shingles gave the buttresses at the edge of sand chutes the look of castle watchtowers. At some points the corals at the lower levels joined, roofing over the chutes, creating large tunnels and caves. Large red and orange basket sponges, purple sea fans and precious black corals decorated the wall, and schools of brilliantly colored fish were everywhere. It was hard to keep focused on the drone and not be overwhelmed by the beauty of the wall.

He leaned back to the radio on his right and switched it on again. "*PC 1203* to surface control, our depth is two hundred and ten feet. I make our position in the northeast quadrant of sector sixteen. Can you confirm, please?"

"Negative, *1203*. None of our sonar or depth sounding equipment is functioning. Over."

"Roger, surface control. Can you give me your position? Over."

"Standby one."

"Roger." Doc nudged the drone a little further from the wall. He estimated it was two hundred feet ahead and a hundred feet beneath him.

"Looks like sector eighteen, quadrant four. Everything under control down there, *1203*?"

"So far so good, Terry, thanks."

"Wish I could say the same for my home office, *1203*."

"Sorry...I'll take the heat. I think you understand."

"That's affirmative. Let's just get this job done and sort out the rest over beer. Take good care of my boat, Doc. Without her, they sure as hell don't need me."

"No problem. Now let's activate our counter measures. I could use a little music. How about you?"

Terry laughed and turned on the CD player Doc had wired through the steel-coned waterproof speakers. The 1812 Overture thundered down over the wall. It wouldn't completely knock out *Blackwolf*'s sonar, but his guess was it would render the operator a whole lot less interested in trying to determine if the motor sounds he was hearing were coming from one sub or two.

Doc held to the wall until he had entered the eighteenth

sector. After they had studied the charts, factored in what they knew about the currents, eliminated what had already been covered, and tried to outguess the downward drift of the sinking sailboat, the good and bad news was sector eighteen. Good because it was the logical place for the boat to be; bad because most of it was deeper than a thousand feet, the rated working depth for the *1203*.

Doc glanced down at the Fathometer and back at his dead reckoning plot line and then at his watch.

"Surface, this is *1203*. Our depth is five hundred feet and we are approaching sector seventeen, quadrant four. We should be entering sector eighteen in about six minutes, over."

"Roger, *1203*. We are getting some kind of feedback in the transponders at eighteen, quadrant three. I can't ID the sound...it's just different. Could be hitting a thermocline or something. It's deeper and colder there...might be worth having a look."

"Affirmative, thanks, surface."

Doc made a note on his chart and then looked back through the dome port for the drone. For a moment panic seized him as it was nowhere in sight, lost in the darkening gloom. He hit a button on the side of its control panel and beneath him he could see its lights. He would need to stay closer.

The steepest drop in the wall, nearly vertical, began at a hundred and fifty feet and continued nearly straight down to four hundred feet. Then the wall began a gentle curve. It was barren now except for gorgonians, sea fans, and then stony corals atop occasional outcroppings. A beer can here and a deck chair there made Doc tighten his jaws. *What kind of assholes...*the thought wasn't worth finishing. He knew the answer.

He was amazed at how much light penetrated to six hundred feet. He could still see the bottom clearly—not that there was much to see. Here it reminded him of the lunar photographs: stark and dark. He saw a flatter bottom coming up to meet him and a boulder here and there. At seven hundred feet, he found the haystacks. Beneath him, the drone hovered. He used the thrusters to keep it off the bottom while correcting its buoyancy. He was still dropping silently, showing no lights. He hit both the noisy vehicle ballast pumps simultaneously. It was tricky trimming them both at the same time. *There, close enough. Honey, I'm home; who's for dinner?*

The landscape changed again at eight hundred feet and it was cooler—sixty-two degrees—and much darker. He could still see, but the haystacks, some sixty or eighty feet in diameter, cast dark shadows and *Bluebird*, Morgan's sailboat, or for that matter *Bluebird* and *Blackwolf*, could be hidden behind any of them.

He put on the sonar headset and gently turned up the volume. Terry had switched CDs from Beethoven to Barefoot Man. Doc listened to the reggae rhythm as he lifted the drone over the largest haystack and used its lights to explore the shadows. He could barely hear the whine of the thrusters and main engine. The drone was less than a hundred yards away. He checked the chart, holding it close to the shielded red LED of the clock. Sector eighteen, quadrant three. He guessed he was close.

"See the thing in the reef, with the big shiny teeth...It's a moray... Put your hand in the crack and you won't get it back...from a moray." Doc was humming along to Barefoot Man's clever lyrics. He lifted the *1203* and moved closer to the drone. This was going to take time. He was looking out through the flat ports now, not the dome. He felt better being able to look over his shoulder from time to time and the perspective was better. It was easier to guess the distance to the drone and her distance from the haystacks. He didn't want to bang her into the hard limestone; not with the cargo she was carrying and not at this range. In the lights of the drone, he could see delicate white sea lilies, fan corals and brittle stars. It was amazing that anything could live down here. He wondered if he was the first person to see this part of the reef. Terry had said they had not dived here yet.

He hovered the *1203* a hundred feet or more above the drone and worked through a trail between the haystacks. Nine hundred feet. The drone was at a thousand and according to the depths on the chart, he was entering the third quadrant.

"Big John, big John, six foot six with flippers on, the biggest, baddest diver in the sea." He remembered watching Barefoot Man crooning to his audience at the Holiday Inn and watching the

girls go wild. *Too bad I never learned to sing.*

On his left further down the wall, there was a dim glimmer of light. He looked back at the drone and then back at the glimmer to make certain he hadn't confused them. He wanted to tell Terry, but this was not the time. Nine hundred and fifty feet. The drone was over a thousand. *How low can you go?*

He had converted the drone to a bomb. It was like a high tech version of the fire ship Francis Drake and his captains used to destroy the Spanish Armada. Beneath the drone's hull were two fifteen-foot sealed eight-inch diameter pipes carrying nearly two thousand pounds of his home-brewed liquid explosive. A third tube had replaced the drop weight beneath the *1203*. The time for negotiation was over. The game had gotten too dangerous and the stakes too costly. This mission had one objective: kill *Blackwolf*. Doc had become a sniper looking for a kill shot. *Blackwolf* could only go after one of the agile little work subs at a time. One of them would get close enough. One of them had to.

He turned off the drone's lights and moved it closer. Eleven hundred feet and the drone at twelve fifty or thirteen hundred. The lights were brighter. His chances of being seen in the *1203* were much greater in open water, but he could hide between the haystacks. Let them see the drone and then, like an angler fish distracting its prey with the false bait on its forehead, strike with the *1203*, perhaps....

Twelve hundred feet. Terry wouldn't like this. Twelve fifty. Thirteen hundred. He inched forward, moving past the haystack's cover out into open water. There, before him with her rigging still standing, gleaming white in the *Blackwolf's* work lights, was Jack Morgan's magnificent sailboat. *Bluebird* was definitely on the other side of the rainbow now.

They had been working on her. There was a large hole cut in her side and another through her deck. He moved the drone toward the sailboat. *Faster now. Get their attention, but hit them before they have time to move. Full power to the 1203. Climb and then release the bombs. Hit her with all three.*

He was now fully clear of the haystacks, closing in on *Blackwolf*, when suddenly there was the crash and clatter of metal hitting metal and the *1203* went crashing to the bottom. He couldn't tell what had happened, but then he saw the black metal claw of the ROV *Black Widow* grasp the crash bar in front of the acrylic sphere. Somehow, the spider-like robot was riding the *1203*. He heard the screech of metal and saw the dogs on the main hatch twisting open. The spider was trying to open the hatch. He lunged upward to grab the handle. Too late. The bolt snapped and the handle clattered to the deck. They crashed into the side of the haystack and Doc was thrown forward from the pilot's seat. The sub was diving straight to the bottom under the weight of the ROV. Terry's heavy red steel toolbox came sliding down the deck toward the sphere. Doc blocked it with his leg and instantly felt the pain.

The sub was rolling now, pulled over by the weight of the ROV on the deck. Doc was thrown hard against the radios and the tool box followed, smashing the VLF and the Fathometer. The spider held the sub in its deadly grasp and even as they fell, it began cutting the power cables. Sparks flew as the metal claw cut into the main power cable and everything went black as they hit bottom at the base of the eighty-foot-high haystack. The *1203* crushed the ROV into the mud and rolled just enough to lodge, upside down, against the towering limestone boulder's base.

The pain in Doc's leg reminded him of the last time he'd been shot during his one man commando raid on a drug runner off Bermuda. The damn toolbox had hit almost in the same spot and he was bleeding. Not that he could see the wound. The sub was so dark he wasn't even sure his eyes were open.

He pulled off his shirt and tied it around his leg. Finding a towel he remembered hanging from the plumbing on his left, he struggled to tear it in strips and wished he had his Randall, which he'd asked Sheri to hide along with the video disks and log books from the condo. Then there was light. *Blackwolf* had come for the kill. He crawled to the dome port and used the light to check his leg. It needed stitches, but it didn't look broken. The black hull moved closer. Now the lights were blinding. Doc turned away, looking quickly around the cabin and trying to memorize the location of the valves.

"Remember what I told you, Holiday?" It was Jack Morgan's voice booming out over underwater speakers. "There's no catch and release in this game. Goodbye, Doctor. You cost me a fortune, but in the end I win again. Don't worry about a thing,

Holiday. I'll take good care of Sheri for you. Die slowly, Doctor, and remember I told you this would happen if you crossed me."

The lights went out leaving Doc in total darkness.

Mike's words came back to him. *"How big a boom...?" The drone. Where the hell is the drone?*

He scrambled to find its control box knowing that without power, all but one of the operational systems was useless. There was only one circuit that might still be functional—one circuit that he had given its own separate power source to make certain none of the other circuitry could bleed over and activate it. He raised the safety cover from the dual firing switches and pushed both toggles forward.

Sheri choked back her sobs as she put the phone back on the hospital night stand. She was trying not to wake Inspector Cord, but now, that didn't really matter. The inspector rolled toward her. His face was covered with dressings from the surgery and he'd remained sedated for most of his time in the hospital.

"What's happened?" he asked. His voice still graveled from the smoke he'd inhaled.

"It's Doc," she sobbed, trying to catch her breath. "He went after *Blackwolf* alone in one of those little subs." She dropped into the chair beside his bed and clutched his hand.

"Bloody cowboy," Ian growled and then coughed. He pulled himself up on his elbows.

"There was an explosion. They think Doc is..."

"Now wait just a minute, girl. If they said they think, that means they don't know. But we know that old scoundrel too well to be counting him out before the final bell."

She shook her head and the tears kept coming. "The blast was too much," her voice was soft now, full of pain and loss. "They said no one could have survived it."

He squeezed her hands tightly enough that the pain made her wince. "Stop it, girl. Now let's start at the beginning. Who the bloody hell are 'they' and how soon can you get on a flight?"

The President got the message aboard Air Force One enroute to Houston, the first leg of his journey to meet the Kuwaitis.

"What about Morgan and that prototype sub?" he asked.

"I'll try to find out, sir. There was no mention..." The President raised his hand, stopping the conversation mid-sentence. His aide de camp was young and eager. He just needed to listen more and talk less.

"Just ask what we're doing to find Doctor Holiday, Allen. I want to know for certain what's happened to him. Got it?"

"Yes, Mr. President. We're on it."

At the RSL office, Mike Berry, Terry and three other company officers were working over a chart table with Charlie Bradshaw, captain of the USS *Atlanta, SSN-712,* one of three Los Angeles class subs brought to the Cayman Islands to provide security for the President.

"He should have been here, in sector eighteen, quadrant three," Terry repeated for the benefit of Captain Bradshaw. "Thirteen hundred feet, right in the middle of this cluster of big haystacks."

"Tell me again what happened just before the explosion," asked Bradshaw who was a lean, mean six-foot three with short hair and an Annapolis class ring. He was very confident but soft spoken.

"We heard a voice, clear as a bell. He said something like 'There's no catch and release in this game,' and 'Don't worry about a thing, Holiday. I'll take care of Sheri for you.' That's Doc's girl friend, and then there was laughter. Real ugly laughter," Terry said.

"And then the explosion?"

"Yes, sir. It rattled every window on Seven Mile Beach. Some are now claiming they felt it in town."

"Just one explosion, no secondaries?" Mike asked.

"Just one...why? What were you thinking?" Terry answered.

"*Blackwolf*'s torpedoes. If Doc got her, there might have been secondaries."

Terry shook his head. "Sorry, no such luck."

"Then what?" Bradshaw asked, trying to bring them back on task.

"There was a surface eruption, lots of gas, dirty water and spray."

"Debris?"

"None, but I doubt anything would come up from that deep."

"Life support in your sub?" Bradshaw asked again, firing questions like bullets. "Cut the crap...give me the bottom line."

"Oxygen for seven or eight days. No food, one or two liters of water."

"CO_2 scrubbers? Hydrogen burners?"

"The scrubbers are lung powered. Could last as long as the oxygen. All the batteries are carried in pods outside the hull so we don't need the burners, but do you really think there's any chance he could have survived that blast?"

"I get my orders from the CO of our fleet, who gets his orders from the CNO, who gets his orders from the Secretary of the Navy whose only question is 'How big a pile?' when the President says 'Shit.' The President intends to be off this coast in..." he said as he checked his watch and without counting on his fingers, continued, "three and a half hours. He wants to know what happened to Doctor John Holiday, and the entire U.S. Navy has orders to find and destroy *Blackwolf* or whatever the name of that other sub is. What I think may or may not have happened has nothing to do with my part of getting this job done. Now, is there anything else...anything at all that will help us find Doctor Holiday or that other sub?"

Mike held back the smile he felt creeping across his mug. Doc would have liked this guy's attitude.

"One more thing," Terry offered. "Right after the explosion, our side scan cleared up. There wasn't anything to see, but..."

"Doc got *Blackwolf*, or at least knocked out her jammers," Mike said with excitement.

"Let him finish, Lieutenant Berry," Bradshaw snapped.

"Yes, sir...sorry, sir," Mike answered, suddenly realizing he was back in the Navy.

"Is that what you're saying? Do you think Holiday could have actually destroyed that sub?"

"I don't know. All I know is, our sonar problems resolved themselves the instant we felt that shock wave and if the unit is still working when this meeting is over, my crew and I are going out to find our boats, or what's left of them."

"I appreciate your offer, Captain. But, until the rest of our battle group arrives, I'd appreciate your standing down, at least for now. I assure you we'll do everything in our power to find your boats. That renegade could still be operational and your presence down there might complicate things if my boys find her first. I'd hate to see you and your crew added to the list of casualties. I'm sure you understand."

Terry poised himself to protest, but Bradshaw held up his hand as if to say, as far as he was concerned, the conversation was over. Terry looked to his operations manager who nodded in obvious agreement with Bradshaw.

"Lieutenant Berry, I'm told you've actually been on board this phantom sub, *Blackwolf.* I'd appreciate your filling me and my staff in. Care to join us aboard the *Atlanta* while we have a look down there?"

"My pleasure, sir."

"Good hunting, Captain. Please let us know if there's anything..." Terry said, offering his hand.

"Thanks, son, we'll be in touch," Bradshaw answered, taking Terry's hand and giving him a pat on the back.

Terry had a sinking feeling as he watched them climb aboard the inflatable launch and clear the harbour. It was as if he were watching any hope of finding Doc or the company's boats sail off into the sunset.

It was Mike's first time to board a Los Angeles class sub. As the launch approached it, he was amazed by how much larger it appeared up close than at the dock at the base in Bermuda. Three hundred and sixty feet long, thirty-three feet in diameter with thirty tons of IBM sonar and weapons control systems more sophisticated than anything else in the water. The launch came alongside and in the finest naval tradition, Captain Bradshaw was the first out. A speaker on deck blared, "Atlanta arriving," and Mike started to salute the flag and then the Officer of the Deck before remembering he wasn't in uniform. The outer hull was covered in thick rubber tiles. Mike remembered Doc telling him from his reading that the tiles were to defeat an enemy's active sonar. It was another German development used on the last of the U-boats. They went down through the stores hatch, aft of the sail, which Mike quickly learned was now called a "fairwater" in Navy parlance. The hatch opened into the forward escape trunk, a larger version of the one they had used on *Blackwolf*, and dropped them into the enlisted mess where a young chief was conducting a class on damage control. Just forward of the mess deck was the officer's wardroom. It was small—everything was small. The second thing he noticed was how soft-spoken all the sailors were and how quiet the boat was. Captain Bradshaw offered him a seat and coffee. Mike accepted both while the captain passed the word that he wanted the core of his officers to join them.

Soon the space, which was by no means spacious with only the two of them, was filled by the addition of nine other men.

The captain related the story of the renegade prototype, which seemed to have the nine lives of a cat, then turned to Mike. "What can you give us, Lieutenant, that will help us find this piece of plastic sewer pipe and send that old Nazi to hell with the rest of his shipmates?"

"The first thing is, don't underestimate him, sir. Everyone who has is permanently in the Davy Jones locker. And until someone actually stops him, Behrmann and the crew of his plastic sewer pipe come and go as they please, strike whenever they want and leave behind nothing but what I think you guys call flaming datums."

There was silence around the table and several of the younger officers looked at the deck. One did not usually call out the captain and expect to survive.

"Your observation is noted. Please go on."

"That's the most important thing, sir. The boat is about ninety feet long, roughly twenty feet in diameter and goes like a bat out of hell. Probably faster than fifty knots. She has four tubes forward and two aft, and carries fourteen torpedoes with two hundred-pound warheads. They are not as fast as your fish, but so far *Blackwolf* has only fired at point blank range so their speed hasn't been a factor. Only one hit the research vessel salvaging that gold off Charleston, but it blew that hundred and eighty-foot boat to pieces. She has a remotely operated deck gun and an array of topside and underwater television cameras. She has more acoustical recording gear than you do, although I'm not sure what it was for, and she has sonar. But again, I can't tell you what model or how effective. I remember some other screens and a plotting board. My guess is, whatever she's got is state of the art. And in clear water at close quarters, she'll be able to see you before you see her, outshoot and outrun you."

Captain Bradshaw's right eyebrow went up slightly, a facial expression his executive officer had rarely seen. The captain leaned forward on one elbow and looked around the table.

"I see," he said softly. "Your description is somewhat different than the briefing I received. I was told she was hardly more than a research boat, put together to try out that new turbine they were working on."

"She was a lot more than that, at least based on the scuttlebutt I got from one of the engineers at New London," the engineering officer said.

"Go on, Scotty," the captain encouraged.

"She was a prototype all right, sir. And that new engine they were building was supposed to be for *Seawolf*. But the word was they couldn't get the bugs out of her and the CNO decided to stay with conventional nuclear power. Anyway, the plan was that she would be a hunter/killer designed to compete with the new Russian Kilo class diesel electric boats, or the German Type 205's and the like—the ones our friendly little neighbors are buying up as fast as they get built. And then we know the rest: New London woke up one foggy morning and the barn was empty."

"*Seawolf*?" Mike asked.

"*SSN-21*. The future," Bradshaw replied. "Two billion dollars a copy, most advanced ever; should send the first one down the ways in a year or two."

"Or three, or four..." the exec laughed and got a dirty look from Bradshaw.

"So now we have *Seawolf* and *Blackwolf* being laid out and built at the same time. *Seawolf* very high profile, every captain's dream," the exec said and pointed his thumb at the captain. "And then in the other end of the barn, poor little *Blackwolf*, old Hans Behrmann's dream. Kept so secret she got no PR, no hoopla, no funding. It's almost like she wasn't there. It was a good name, *Blackwolf*: the little sub that wasn't there. Or perhaps," he paused, "perhaps she was the little sub that none of us were to think was ever there."

"What do you mean?" Bradshaw asked.

"I was thinking about the satellite business. You know, we hear all about the new scientific satellite that's going up and how it will let us look at all the stars, all the new galaxies. And then after it's up there, we find out it was as black as the ace of spades. Black like covert operations. Black like what it really does is count the hairs on Omar's camel."

"There are two more things for you to consider, Captain," Mike said. "First, it's possible that Doctor John Holiday, who got as close to taking out *Blackwolf* as anyone has so far, is still alive down there somewhere and needs us to find him. And second, it's very likely that at this minute you're sitting in the cross hairs of *Blackwolf's* sights. And having heard the screams of dying sailors and felt the heat of burning oil from my last encounter with him, it makes me uncomfortable enough that, with your permission, I'd like to go back ashore now and continue working on a little scheme Doc and I cooked up, just before.... Anyway, I'd sure appreciate anything you can do to find him. Good luck to you and good hunting."

Captain Bradshaw nodded and a junior officer got up and led Mike back through the mess deck. "Wait a minute...is that what I think it is?" Mike said, pointing to a tall stainless steel ice cream machine.

"Probably French vanilla, the captain's favorite," the ensign replied.

"May I?" Mike asked.

"Of course."

"What's going to happen now?" Mike asked, filling a cone with six inches of pure decadence.

"It's a tough one. My guess is the captain will call for some destroyers and a chopper or two. Try to set a sound net with sonobuoys...get an active sonar search going...try to flush that sub out."

"Can't you do that active sonar stuff with this boat? I thought you guys carried tons of sonar gear."

"We do. Problem is, if we go active, it gives us away a long time before we would see the target. And if we stay passive, well, like you said, no one's been able to find that puppy yet. I doubt that we will either."

"But you will look?"

"We have been, every minute since we got here."

"And you would need your sonar in active mode to find the little sub Doc is in, especially if he's not making much noise, or the blast covered him in a mud slide?"

"I'm afraid so."

"Damn, what are we going to do now?" His hand felt cold and when he looked down, it was covered with melted ice cream.

CHAPTER 25

Sheri and Tom waved from the pier as the Navy inflatable approached.

Mike grabbed the handrail to pull himself up then turned and thanked the coxswain. Sheri gave Mike a hug and Tom shook his hand. "We came the minute..." Tom started, but Sheri cut him off with, "What are they doing to find Doc?"

Mike shook his head. "They're so worried about protecting the President..."

"Finding Doc is the best way to protect the President; maybe it's the only way," she countered.

Mike nodded. It was no use trying to explain.

"Then it's up to us," she said with determination and then added, "Again."

She turned to Tom who nodded and patted his oversized briefcase. "Let's do it," he said. "Mike, I need a satellite dish, a phone and a place to set up my computer and our new color printer. Got someplace we can work without drawing a crowd?"

The girl on the bass boat was naked. And to make things worse, she was catching all the fish. How the hell's a guy supposed to concentrate on bass with a body like that on the front of the boat? Sheri turned toward him in the swivel seat and said with a laugh, "Don't blame me, asshole. You're the one who wanted this dream to be about fishing, so you fish the way you want, and I'll fish the way I want. Loser cleans and cooks; that's the bet. Toss me the lotion, will you? I want the fish to be the ones to get cooked, not me."

He watched as she rubbed oil on her legs, then on her flat hard stomach, and finally on those world class, beautiful breasts. She smiled as if to remind him again of what the dream could have been about. Her rod, with his lucky red ambassador reel, lay at her feet and while she rubbed and teased, the rod tip twitched. And then twitched again.

"You've got a bite," he said begrudgingly. What the hell kind of fishing dream was this anyway?

Huge oaks, overhung with Spanish moss, lined the canal banks while beyond stretched saw grass marshes with cattails and palm trees. The dark-stained water was shallow and clear like strong tea. Her rod tip twitched again, or rather his favorite rod that she, by some ugly twist of fate was using, and then the line started moving.

"Set the hook," he said.

"You sure?"

"Just set the hook."

She picked up the rod and hammered it back. The line began screaming from the reel and the rod, of course, bent double. The boat began to move and waves crashed over the bow.

"What the hell?"

"Don't ask me, it's your dream. What do you want it to be?"

A blue marlin rose magnificently from the two-foot-deep water, twisting and turning, flashing in the sunlight.

"Hey, that's my marlin! Give me back my rod."

"No way, you caught him the last time."

He moved from the stern pedestal seat toward the bow. But now the huge marlin was towing the bass boat through four-foot blue-green waves. He lost his footing, reached out to Sheri and they fell together into the water. They were sinking and she was slipping away, then she was gone and he was alone. He looked for her all about him, but she was gone and then there was the fish. The rod was in his hands and the marlin was pulling him deeper and deeper. He could see its huge eye and feel the power of its angry strokes. Light was fading. He was getting cold.

He awoke with a shudder. It was dark and cold, and he was lonely and hungry. *How will I know,* he wondered, *when I'm dead? Will the pain be gone? Will I be able to explore outside the sub without opening the hatch?* It was darker than any darkness he had ever experienced. Darker than sleep. Perhaps even darker than death.

He remembered reading that when the body approaches death, the systems shut down one at a time. Food and drink are no longer required. Peristalsis stops and in place of the hunger pains, the body produces its own narcotics—endorphins. The endorphins help the soul get through the pain—the pain of release from the old and now useless shell. *Is that what's happening now? Is my subconscious trying to make this easier? Are endorphins the reason my leg has stopped hurting and that I'm not as cold? How many days have I been down here? How many more can I last?*

He was drifting back into sleep. *Sheri where are you? To hell with the fishing—let's hit the sack!* He rolled on the cold hard deck and in doing so, rolled over the hammer.

"Oh, yeah," he said aloud and was startled at the sound. He swung the hammer against the hull, tap, tap, tap, blam, blam, blam, tap, tap, tap. He repeated the SOS twice more until his head was ringing and his arm was tired.

I'm here, he heard Sheri whisper from just beyond the border of his subconscious. *Come on, let's play.*

Terry and the Atlantis crew watched in amazement as the satellite images of the wall appeared on the television screen and Tom's computer simultaneously. The graphics were layered in colors and as Tom created masks—small selected portions of the screen—and zoomed in on them, they were able to identify the cruise ships at their moorings and even the small launches shuttling tourists back and forth to the docks.

"Will it work deeper?" Terry asked.

"Thermoclines and scattering layers will hurt us, but it's a steel hull and we'll find him," Tom answered.

"And what about the other sub?"

"I wish. The satellite doesn't like things made out of plastic. It refuses to image them for us. Wait...what's this?"

Terry bent in for a closer look. "Should be the *Kirk Pride,* but it's not very clear." All that appeared was a red blotch west of George Town Harbour nearly beneath the cruise ships. Tom put it in memory, made a note of the time and position, and went on.

They moved north along the wall, over condos and dive boats. Tom noted several other hot spots, saved them to the disk and continued on.

"Now we're getting there," Terry said. "Come further west. There, look there," he pointed.

Tom zoomed in. At first there was nothing.

"Thermocline. Must be carrying a lot of sediment."

"From the blast."

"Makes sense. Let's see if we can cut through it."

Tom used a series of filtering and enhancing sequences, and the screen changed as if the camera had been lowered through a cloud layer and could now clearly see the bottom.

"Haystacks," Terry said. "That's the place."

Sheri had been sitting quietly beside Tom, biting her lip. "Come on, Doc," she said softly. "Here's your chance to moon the camera. Come on, dammit. Help us find you."

Tom turned quickly and nodded.

"There!" Terry shouted, pointing to a cluster of red dots. Tom zoomed in more then closed his eyes. The screen showed fragments of metal scattered on the bottom. Sheri looked away with tears coming.

"No. Keep looking. That's probably the drone, remember? Keep looking."

Tom put the section in memory and continued sweeping the bottom. There were more fragments but nothing large enough to be the *PC 1203.*

"We're losing it," he said. "We'll have to try again on the next pass."

"When?" Sheri asked.

"Six hours."

"What if the *1203* were buried or our view was blocked by a haystack? Could we still see it?" Terry asked.

"Probably not. Not if there was very much cover."

"Can you do what you did with the thermocline? Could

you wipe out a haystack like that?"

"Possibly. I'll play back the tape and give it a try."

"He's alive," Sheri said. "If he were gone, I'd know it. I'd feel it and so would Debbie. He's alive and we've got to keep on looking."

Bradshaw and *Atlanta*'s senior staff officers had moved to the control room to the first of its two plotting boards and were laying out the lanes they would follow using the powerful sonar of the destroyers.

"Captain Bradshaw, excuse me, sir. Sonar is on the blower and they sound real excited."

The captain picked up the phone, identified himself and then listened. "You're sure?" was all he asked before replacing the receiver.

"They heard an SOS," Bradshaw said to the exec. "Sounded like it was coming from inside a rain barrel."

"Could they get a fix on it?"

"Yeah, somewhere down there," Bradshaw answered, pointing between his feet.

"Any ideas?" the exec continued.

"Yes. As soon as the destroyers get here, we're going to do what we get paid to do: find that damn sub and blow it the hell out of the water."

The exec knew the destroyers would not arrive on station for at least three more hours. "Until then?" he asked.

"We sit tight, we listen, and if that was Holiday, we hope he hangs on for a few more hours and that he'll signal again. But until we've got the destroyers, we sit tight."

Tom pushed back from the monitor, rubbing his eyes. He'd been enlarging and rearranging pixels for four straight hours. The picture he had so far wasn't any better than the one he'd had four hours ago. There were small pieces of iron, shards from the explosion of the drone scattered across a large stretch of rugged terrain. He had found what he suspected was the sailboat, but if his imaging was accurate, there wasn't enough left of it to hide a toothpick, much less a twenty-two-foot sub.

Sheri pulled back the warehouse door, picked up her packages and crossed to the workbench where she nearly dropped the cardboard coffee tray. As Tom flinched, she made a sad goofy face and went back to close the heavy door.

"Mike been here?" she asked.

"No, he hasn't been back."

"How's it going?"

"Slow, real slow. Hope we do better on the next pass."

"You're amazing," she said and pulled a stool up to the bench. She began opening the bags and laying out their meal. "How did you put all this stuff together, anyway?"

"They left me alone at Fort Belvoir a little too long, that's how. I just hope we find Doc. If we don't, and when they figure this out back at the Fort, I bet I'll be kissing my security clearances good-bye."

"Finding Doc is worth the risk."

"Yes, yes of course, it is."

He picked up the fish sandwich, ate with one hand and continued typing with the other.

At first the blip looked just like all the others, but as he cut away the haystack, the blip grew and grew some more.

"What the...?" He set down the sandwich, wiped his hands and moved closer to the monitor. As the image kept changing, he started to breathe faster. Sheri realized what was happening and moved behind him.

"That's him, isn't it? That's the sub and it's still in one piece? Oh my God, Tom, you found him!"

"That's the sub alright, but there's no way to tell if he's alive, Sheri. And who knows how we're ever going to get him out of there. It's fourteen hundred feet deep. That nuclear sub can only go to a thousand."

"We'll get him out if I have to do it in scuba. He'd do it for us. You know he would. Now let's find Mike and Terry."

Aboard Air Force One, the President's nerves were showing.

"Allen, you told me you were taking care of this. What the hell am I supposed to expect when someone says something like that? It means something is being done. That's what it's supposed to mean. Now, find out what the devil is going on, or we're going to turn this plane around and go back to Houston. Do you understand?"

"Yes, sir, I'm sorry, sir. There just isn't anything to report yet."

"What time does their plane land?"

"Twenty-three hundred; ah...eleven P.M., sir."

"I know what time twenty-three hundred is, Allen. Thank you."

Mike, Tom, Sheri and Terry pulled alongside the *Atlanta* in their inflatable. Terry asked permission to come aboard in proper Navy fashion and was asked to wait until permission was granted by the captain. The duty officer returned with the ensign who had been Mike's escort earlier. "Back for more ice cream, Lieutenant?" he asked with a warm smile.

"Something like that," Mike answered. "We need to see the captain, on the double."

"He's waiting in the wardroom. Let's go."

They dropped through the hatch and several enlisted men came to their feet as Sheri stepped out onto the mess deck. She smiled politely as they were escorted quickly to the wardroom.

"Sir, these folks think they've found Doctor Holiday," Mike began.

"Oh really, Lieutenant," Bradshaw answered skeptically. "And just how did they do that?" His eyes had bypassed Tom and Terry and were busy doing a fitness report on Sheri.

"With KH-35," Tom said.

Bradshaw's attention snapped back to Tom. "With what?"

"Keyhole-35," Tom repeated. "It's a COMIREX imaging reconnaissance satellite."

"It's a top secret reconnaissance satellite," Bradshaw corrected. "And just how did you happen to have access to it?"

Tom passed across his NASA identification and then answered, "No disrespect intended, sir, but that information is on a need to know basis and what you need to know, sir, is that we found the *1203* and we intend to go after her."

"Show me," Bradshaw answered and offered them seats.

Atlanta's exec, the navigation and weapons officers and the chief of the boat entered the wardroom as Tom spread his printouts on the table.

"That's her, the *1203*."

"Get Sonar in here," Bradshaw snapped.

"Aye, aye, sir," the chief answered and left the table.

The navigation officer looked over the printout and started measuring the distance from the beach with a pencil as a rule.

"I've been looking at the charts. It's deep down there, isn't it?"

"Yes, sir, fourteen hundred feet," Terry answered.

"How you going to get there, Captain?" the exec asked.

Terry appreciated the sign of respect which earned the exec a raised eyebrow from Bradshaw.

"We have another sub," Terry said. "She's an older Pisces. But she can make that dive and I'll take her down."

The sonar officer joined them and began examining Tom's prints. "Man, that's beautiful stuff. Where on earth did you get these?"

Tom looked at Bradshaw and remained silent.

"It's classified, Jim. Just tell us what you think...could that be a sub?"

He looked back at the printout and then at the captain and nodded. "I could hedge my bets and say maybe, but I'll go out on the limb a little further than that. If it's not a sub, it's one hell of a big beer can. That just might be our missing doctor, sir."

Bradshaw nodded and looked at his watch. "Gentlemen and Miss," he nodded toward Sheri. "The President will be arriving in less than four hours. Captain," he said looking at Terry and then at the exec who returned the raised eyebrow, "Captain, how long will it take you to make this dive?"

"My crew is setting the boat up now, sir. My guess is three hours, perhaps four."

"And you understand that the other sub, *Blackwolf*, is probably still in the area and just might think it's great fun to use you for target practice?"

"Begging your pardon, sir, but your boat's the target I'd be worried about. And if *Blackwolf* did attack us, it would be the luckiest break you'll get this year and you know it. That's why you're going to let us make this dive. And if you'd like, we'll even have a look under your hull on our way down."

Bradshaw chuckled and looked at the exec who nodded approval. "Captain, if you ever need a job, you come see me. Now, go find your *1203* and bring Doctor Holiday back home. At least that will get the President off my back. And if you've got any ideas about how we can find *Blackwolf* and sink her, I'd sure like to hear them. When a man's on a roll, it's foolish not to ride with him."

They decided that Tom would stay on shore for the next satellite pass; Mike would continue on his project and that left Sheri who insisted on accompanying Terry in the Pisces submarine.

"What's that?" Terry asked as Sheri handed a brown knapsack through the Pisces hatch. The bag felt heavier than the peanut butter sandwiches he'd hoped for.

"It's Doc's diving knife. He gave it to me the last time we were together. It's kind of a good luck thing for him."

She opened the knapsack and showed Terry the oversized Randall in its well worn leather scabbard. Terry felt the weight of it and admired the thick blade. "That's serious iron," he said with respect and handed it back. When she was seated he closed the hatch and ran through his pre-ops check list with the surface.

When the surface officer cleared them to dive Terry said, "Your job is to help me watch. It will be a little crowded, but stand up here beside me. I want you to be the eyes in the back of my head. I don't think *Blackwolf* is interested in us, but there's no use getting caught with our shorts dragging."

This would be no sightseeing trip down the wall. Terry had positioned the V-barge directly over Tom's co-ordinates and they were dropping straight down. The sun was low on the horizon and the water was dark when they passed three hundred feet.

"This boat was originally certified to two thousand feet," Terry said. "But we haven't had her this deep in a long time. Just no need till now."

"How deep are we now?"

He checked the Fathometer. "Five hundred sixty; we're dropping about sixty feet per minute. I'll slow us down when we start getting closer."

All she could see now were shadows and she found that unnerving. It was easy to imagine *Blackwolf* waiting just beyond her limited range of visibility. A chill went up her spine at the thought and she shuddered.

"You okay?"

"Yeah, just a little cold. Do you suppose..."

"Do I believe in things that go bump in the night? You bet your sweet ass. Sorry, no offense intended."

"None taken. It's just that the shadows, I thought..."

"Yeah, I saw it too...only I was hoping it was just my imagination working overtime."

"How deep?"

"Coming up on eight hundred." He picked up the mike and informed the surface officer.

"How will we find him?"

"Unless the current has messed with us, we should be just about on the money. When we get within the range of our lights we'll turn them on, pick a reference point and start a search pattern. I'm reading bottom at thirteen hundred eighty. We should be real close."

"Pisces, this is Surface."

"Go ahead, Surface."

"The destroyers are here and *Atlanta* says he's going to start an active sonar search. He just wanted to warn you."

"Pisces, aye." He put down the mike and said, "Crap!"

"What?"

"Wait a minute, you'll see. The sonar the big subs carry will break glass at five miles. Dolphins and whales hate it...they run like hell when the subs start pinging."

The first ping was more tangible than audible, as though Pisces had been hit with a wrecking ball.

"See what I mean?" Terry shouted.

Sheri was still holding her ears. "They must be right on top of us."

"Now you know how fish feel when dolphins use sonar to stun them."

"Stunned!"

"You got it."

The second was not quite as intense and the third was only

moderately painful.

"They can directionalize the sound and probe like a bullet. They call it 'knife-fighting,' and they use it to get range to targets that the passive sonar won't give them. Then the sonar feeds the data directly to the weapons system and controls the torpedoes. I imagine they'll use it to keep an eye on us while we're looking.

"We should be able to see the bottom now." He turned on the lights and Sheri gasped and buried her fingernails in Terry's shoulder. A huge shadow loomed out of the darkness into their light and passed above them like a great blind blimp: slowly, slowly, tapping the bottom with its acoustical cane. They could see every detail of the hull and its huge single screw turning slowly enough that they could count the blades. They could hear popping and creaking as she passed. Terry checked the Fathometer—nine hundred feet. The gigantic sub was a hundred feet above them. "She's close to her limits. That's why the hull is sounding off."

"Pisces, this is *Atlanta.* Over."

"Pisces, aye," Terry answered on the VLF.

"Pisces, we have a Sierra contact; your bearing two hundred eighty-three degrees; range six hundred yards; depth one thousand four hundred twenty-two feet. Over."

"Is Sierra sonar?" asked Sheri.

"Yeah." Then he grabbed the mike. "Pisces copies. Thank you, *Atlanta.* Pisces standing by."

"*Atlanta.* Out."

"They're really hanging it out, using active sonar and the radio. It's an open invite for *Blackwolf* to go to the free throw line and take a couple."

"Why?"

"Because the minute *Blackwolf* fires, she gives herself away and the destroyers blow her out of the water."

"And us too. Them and Doc and us."

"That's the deal."

"You know," she began with the affected Georgia Peach accent Doc hated, "my poor little tummy is gettin' so hungry. So why don't we'all just hurry up and find ole Doc and then take this pretty little boat and go get poor little ole me a nice little lunch."

"That's a hell of an idea," Terry laughed. He hit the thrusters, changing their attitude to a two hundred eighty-three-degree heading. At thirteen hundred feet they could clearly see the haystacks and the bottom in shadows below.

The haystacks here were huge, over a hundred feet in diameter and close enough together to form dangerous canyons. Terry would have preferred to stay above them, but then it was impossible to see what the shadows below were hiding. He dropped into a canyon to get a better look and then guided them over what appeared to be the largest haystack, and there before them was a valley strewn with the wreckage of huge broken boulders. He circled, looking at Tom's charts and then at the bottom again until he could orient himself to both.

"Over there," he said and maneuvered the Pisces toward the opening of another valley. Sheri saw *Bluebird*'s mast and standing rigging mangled and half buried in the silt. There were shards of the drone embedded in the limestone walls of the towering haystacks and deep fissures where boulders the size of cars had been shattered loose. *How could anything have survived a blast like that?* Terry thought. He guessed Sheri was thinking the same thing because he could feel her breathing quicken and she leaned more against his back. *How was she going to take it if they found him and....*

"There," she said.

He'd seen it too. As they came round the haystack's rim, the *1203*'s stern was sticking through a pile of silt and boulders. She was upside down and eighty percent buried.

"That's why he couldn't get the hell out of here," Terry said. "You have to be right side up to drop the safety weight or blow ballast."

"Do you think...?"

She was close now. He could feel her weight against him and her grip tighten on his shoulder. "Easy now. Don't go jumping to conclusions. We haven't knocked on his door yet."

"But how? What can we do?"

"I think we can get him out. It will take a while, but what the heck...I'm not that hungry yet. Are you?"

"No, not now."

He picked up the mike. "*Atlanta*, Pisces. We've found him. The hull appears intact, but we're going to have to dig him out and that may take a while. Over."

"This is *Atlanta.* Roger, Pisces. We haven't got long. Please keep us advised. Over."

"Pisces. Out."

"This first part's a little tricky—we put hooks on our skid frame. I'm going to hook our stern up to his. He'll be our anchor and then we'll use the main engine to blow away the mud."

"A prop wash, like the treasure hunters use."

"Exactly."

Terry turned to look through the stern ports. Sheri dropped out of his way as he carefully maneuvered the tail hook into position. He hit power enough to jar the *1203* and then waited. There was no response. "I'm going to cut the lights now to save power. We're going to lose the viz anyway."

"Okay."

He eased the rheostat to full power and the sub began to vibrate. He watched a red LED bottom timer and after three minutes, cut power and turned on the lights. They had opened a crater halfway down the port side and everything looked alright. Then a small boulder fell from a crevice in the rock above and then another. He aimed the lights to see where they had come from. "Oh shit!"

"What...what is it?"

"We've got the makings of a first class rock slide. The vibration...here, look."

The limestone haystack's face was fractured into a cobweb of fissures like a shattered windshield. The higher in the pattern they looked, the bigger the pieces were.

"If that goes..." he began.

"It would get us too?"

"Good chance, I'd say. How hungry are you now?"

"I've lost my appetite completely." The words were right, but the crack in her voice betrayed her fear.

"Sure?"

"Yeah, I'm sure."

"Okay, I'll ease off on the power and keep our lights on. You watch those rocks and yell if anything starts falling."

"Okay," she answered meekly.

When he brought the power back to half-thrust, mud and

sediment swirled away. Small rocks tumbled away and above the *1203*, the rock pile shifted minutely, showering down basketball-sized boulders. Terry used the vertical thrusters to change the thrust angle and concentrate on what was beneath the *1203*. The bottom sediment was soft and quickly washed away. Ten minutes passed and then twenty. The port side and most of the battery pod were now exposed, and the rock pile above was holding.

"There's no way to keep that from coming down, but when it starts, there will be a moment in which the *1203* is free. That's when we hit full power." He caught the battery pod leg with the tail hook and brought up the power. Huge cyclonic swirls of mud rose into the darkness while he watched the rock pile and used the secondary thrusters to control the blast's focus. He worked the full length of the hull and then back again. He could see the rim of the sail and its ports, then the lifting eyes were exposed. Small rocks continued to be washed away and then the *1203* shifted for the first time. Terry hit full power and moved her again before a pile of rocks showered down from above.

"It's okay," he reassured Sheri. "It's working. None of the really big stuff fell. We can move these. Limestone doesn't weigh much down here."

Now he used the Pisces's crash bars to nudge rock away. Sheri was amazed at how nimble the old sub was.

"We're getting close. I think we can roll her on the sail and snatch her free before the wall comes tumbling down. Pretty soon now."

"Could we...could we look in the dome port and see if...?"

"Are you sure?" he asked and reached down to her.

She took his hand and squeezed it. "Yeah, I want to know. I'm ready."

"Okay. Let me finish up here, then we will."

He was moving as much material from beneath the *1203* as he could, hoping that he could snatch her out and up in one quick power burst.

"Pisces, this is *Atlanta*. Request status report. Over."

Terry stopped and took deep breaths before picking up the mike. He was sweating as if he'd been moving rocks by hand.

"We're close, *Atlanta.* I sure could use a D-9 Caterpillar and a CH-54 Sky Crane, but we're close."

"Pisces, you need to be out of the area in twenty minutes. Over."

"Roger the twenty minutes. We should be on our way in less time than that."

"Affirmative. *Atlanta.* Out."

He dropped the mike back to its hook and looked down at Sheri. "Let's just do it. We're not going to leave him down here, no matter what. So let's just do it."

She understood what he was trying to tell her. There were tears as she nodded agreement.

In order to roll the sub out clockwise toward the haystack, Terry needed to get leverage as low beneath the boat as possible. To accomplish this, he set about blowing a crater large enough to back Pisces into in the hope that he could snag *1203*'s short lifting cable with his tail hook. The minutes ticked away. He tried. The crater was still too small. He cleared out more material and tried again. Success. Catching the cable would be easy. But once hooked in, he had no way to release it until they were on the surface. He looked down at Sheri. Doc was lucky to have her. Here's hoping his luck had lasted.

Terry walked the Pisces tightly into position and caught the cable on the first try.

"This is it," he said and spun on the seat to look forward. He smiled at Sheri who was back on the deck in front of the dome port. "Let's do lunch."

"It's a date," she smiled back through the tears streaming down her face.

He turned back again to watch the stern, hit full power and braced himself. At first there was nothing, but then in the swirl of mud and the clatter of falling rock, they moved and moved again. *It should have been easier,* he thought. *What the devil was holding them?* He could hear metal grinding against the limestone, and the rumble of the rock slide grew louder.

"Pisces, this is *Atlanta.* Over."

They can hear this, he thought but ignored the radio for the moment. Then they were sliding down the gentle slope toward the opposite wall. "Let go! Lift!" he shouted. Nothing happened. He opened the red emergency ballast valve and compressed air displaced a thousand pounds of the Pisces's water ballast. Still nothing. They continued to slide in the shifting rubble and the larger fragments of the shattered haystack were beginning to fall. "Lift that floor panel and twist the handle!" he shouted at Sheri. "It releases our drop weights."

She scrambled to her knees, twisted the lever frantically and another thousand pounds of ballast was gone.

"We should be up," he shouted over the avalanche. "A thousand pounds of lift should have us both on the way up." He eased off the power. The rock and mud slide carried them to the opposite side of the canyon where the *1203* landed upright against the wall with sediment beginning to rebury her. And now, two thousand pounds positively buoyant and anchored to the *PC 1203*, the Pisces bobbed toward the surface throwing them both off balance. Sheri slid down the short deck onto her knees and held on until they could both stand on the aft bulkhead.

Terry pulled himself upright and twisted to get to the controls. He could barely see the *1203*. Sediment swirled around them blocking his vision, so he turned his main power back on, blasting it away. As the prop-washed crater beneath the *1203* grew larger, he saw a large black mechanical claw clutching the starboard battery pod strut.

"What the hell?" he said in amazement.

Sheri crawled up beside him to look. As they watched the prop wash clear away more of the mud, they could see all of the arm and then another and a third. Finally, a portion of the thorax became visible. The creature was nearly *1203*'s size and now Terry understood why he'd not been able to lift them free.

"What is that thing? It looks like a leftover from a bad Japanese sci-fi flick."

"An ROV—the biggest one I've ever seen," he answered. "I'm going to call *Atlanta* and let them know what's happened."

He began to move, crawling over her in the crowded space, when she grabbed him and gasped, "Wait, it's moving!"

"What?"

He scrambled back up and squeezed in beside her.

Black Widow was struggling to free itself from the soft silt which was holding it like quicksand. It grasped *1203* with its other manipulator claw and pulled itself up, causing *1203* to list and sink the starboard battery pod.

"Look at the size of that thing. It's huge," Sheri said.

As it climbed to the top of *1203*, the research sub sank further into the silt. Once perched on *1203*'s dorsal, it reached for the tether between the two subs and gave a stout pull, violently bouncing Pisces like jerking a balloon on a string.

The spider carefully repositioned itself, clasping *1203* with its hind legs and freeing both its manipulator and claw arm. Then it began pulling on the cable.

"Oh shit!"

"That's affirmative," Terry answered.

"I'm getting really hungry now."

"Me too. Any ideas?"

"I'd settle for McDonald's."

"If we get out of this one, it's the Lobster Pot or Chef Tel's...on me!'

They heard a scraping as the ROV's claw tried to grasp the rudder.

"Maybe," Terry said and climbed down from the sail.

He found the control box and put all horizontal thrusters in full reverse, while at the same time flooding the water ballast tanks. Pisces began to drop and the spider reached higher for a better grasp. Then Terry hit the air valve, dumping the ballast and reversed the thrusters. He was able to snap the cable taut and the ROV lost its grip.

"Did we move *1203*?"

"Yes, I think so."

"Pisces, this is *Atlanta*. Please achnowledge. Over," the radio blared.

Terry grabbed the mike and responded.

"You are out of time, Pisces. Leave the area at once. Over."

"Sorry, *Atlanta*. No can do. We're sort of stuck and we've got company. We're being attacked by some kind of large mechanical spider. It's an ROV, but so far we haven't seen anything of the operator. It has television cameras and isn't tethered, so the operator could be anywhere."

The Pisces was jerked severely again and Terry prepared to jerk back. "Tell me when," he said to Sheri.

There was silence from the nuclear sub and then they returned. "Pisces, this is *Atlanta.* We're going to try jamming low frequency signals. Maybe we can help you out. Pound on your hull if we do anything that works. Over."

"Right now we need all the help can get. Thanks, *Atlanta.*"

"*Atlanta.* Out."

"He's nearly at us again," Sheri said.

"Here goes," Terry answered and reversed the thrusters. Again the spider lost its grip. "We can't keep this up forever," Terry said. "Our batteries won't last. I wonder where that thing gets its juice. Sheri, do you see any cables on that thing—anything we might be able to cut through with our prop?"

"No, nothing. Not even an antenna. Here he comes again."

"There's got to be something," he said with frustration. "What if we just backed into him at full power? Think we could hurt him?"

"It doesn't look good. Better do something...it's just about on our tail."

"We're going for it. Climb down. I need room for the controls."

She dropped beside him apprehensively. "You sure?"

"I'm sure if we don't do something, we're going to lose. If it gets to our bow, it will cut our power cables and we are screwed, just like..."

They heard scraping and Terry pushed his way up into the sail. The spider was trying to tear away the rudder. Terry bounced the Pisces again and then again without dislodging it.

"Okay, mother. I'm the lawn mower and your ass is..." He hit full power again then used the stern's horizontal thruster to twist the boat, changing his attack angle. The prop cut through the ROV's armored shell until their lights went dim and the blade stopped. Terry released the toggles and the ROV changed its grip. Now it had them. "Blow the buoyancy!" Terry shouted and Sheri turned the red-handled Whitey valve. The cable snapped taut again, but now the ROV held them with both claws. It released the *1203* and shifted its weight to the Pisces, which crashed toward the bottom.

"Hang on!" Terry shouted.

But just as they were about to smash into the bottom, they stopped short. Terry was thrown from the pilot's seat. Battered and angry, he crawled back up to see what had happened. The *1203* was rising to the surface, taking them along for the ride. The spider's camera head rotated to look back up the short cable and the image its camera recorded was of Doc, sitting in front of the dome port, giving *Black Widow* and whoever was at its controls, the bird.

Terry started laughing.

"What...what is it?" Sheri asked.

"Doc tried to drop the thousand-pound bomb he was carrying instead of safety weights. It probably just wouldn't release while he was still pinned to the bottom. But when that ugly mother finally got off his back, he broke free."

"He's alive?"

"He looks too pissed off to be dead," Terry laughed.

She laughed too. "And that awful robot?"

"So far it's just sitting there. Maybe the Navy found the right frequency or maybe we've drifted out of range for the operator."

"Let me climb up. I want to see Doc."

"Sure, but he won't be able to see you with our lights on."

"It's okay. I still want to see him."

Once again she wiggled in close to Terry. The water was still dark. With the weight of the ROV they were rising slowly, but they were certainly rising because she could no longer see the dark bottom below. Mud and silt streamed from the *1203* as they rose and she could see the severed power cables and scratches. It was hard to get a good look at Doc who had climbed back up in the pilot's seat. But just knowing that he was alive, that was enough for now.

The water was getting lighter. He tried to contact the surface, but the radio didn't work.

"Hope we don't come up under anybody. Maybe you should climb down and watch from the dome."

"Okay." Before she climbed down, Sheri put her arms around him and gave a squeeze. "Thanks. Doc would have died down there if you hadn't made this dive. Thanks."

When they passed two hundred feet, Terry began taking on more water ballast to slow them down, and they broke the surface as if they were ascending from a normal dive. They were greeted by the *Atlantis* V-barge and two Navy destroyers.

Terry picked up his hand-held VHF and called the destroyers.

"I'd feel a lot better if you could get this thing off my ass before it comes to life again. It's yours for the asking, but I'd sure as hell chain it down. And my friend in the other sub probably needs medical attention."

One destroyer lay abeam to the sea giving the Pisces a flat calm while the other lowered two bowswains mates with chains and cables to lift the ROV. Only after it was off the Pisces did Terry open the hatch.

"Me first," Sheri said and pushed up past him. She climbed up, quickly dove in and swam easy strokes to the *1203*.

CHAPTER 26

At the Grand Cayman Holiday Inn, Doc lay back in the steaming tub with his wounded leg elevated on the tub's rim while Sheri shampooed his hair. He had a second chocolate shake standing by, and had begun his rehabilitation with two cheeseburgers and a large order of onion rings. The leg was infected, his hearing was impaired and he'd lost ten pounds. All in all, not a bad thirty-six hours.

"I think I understand it now," he said and rolled his head while her fingers worked over his scalp.

"Go on, tell me."

"Scrub harder."

"Yes, master."

"Sorry. Harder, please."

"That's better."

"I'm certain *Blackwolf* is still out there like the waiting coyote of death in Tony Hillerman's stories. I can feel it, but I didn't understand it. Then something Mike said helped me get it."

She stopped scrubbing and got comfortable by the edge of the tub, waiting. "Well?"

"Remember what Mike said about the Secretary of State's ship being torpedoed? As the sub that did it was leaving, the Navy got a tape, which they later identified as one of Saddam's Russian-built Kilo class subs. Not only could they nail down which sub it was, they even knew the name of the boat driver."

"Right, so there goes your theory that *Blackwolf* did it."

"Yep, that's what I was thinking too, and then I remembered all that acoustical recording equipment *Blackwolf* had on board. So ask yourself, was it real—or was it Memorex? Behrmann wasn't carrying all that equipment to record horny humpbacks. Think how easy it would have been for them to sneak up on Saddam's sub, make a recording and then, months later, use the recording to create an international incident—one which would provide all the justification Morgan needed to escalate the war against Iraq. And if my guess is right about the deal Morgan cut with Kuwait, that was all the justification he needed to send our teams in to assassinate Saddam."

"Wow, that's pretty hot, and it sure fits with what happened with the Kuwaitis at the condo."

"Yes, and it would have worked perfectly, except..."

"Except, we have a new President and he wouldn't play."

"Smart girl."

"For figuring out that scenario, you get a reward."

"And what might that be?" he asked with a laugh.

She was already undressing. "Before you go anywhere, we need to make sure you're fully, and I do mean fully, recovered."

The phone rang just as they were leaving to meet the President's plane. Sheri told Doc to be brief as she didn't want to be late. He nodded and said hello to Tom.

"Look, you asked me to find out what I could about the University of Mass at Amherst, remember?"

"Yes?"

"Well, there may be a rabbit in that hole. Novel agents are genetically altered forms of naturally occurring poisons or viruses, like rattlesnake venom or anthrax, which can be used in biological weapons...and are designed so that known precautions, like gas masks or normal antidotes, are useless. Your Doctor Lin Kee was one of the best in the business according to a professor of mine. He knew her; she was on full scholarship at M.I.T. and every graduate program in the country wanted her. He described her as absolutely brilliant, ambitious as hell, and cold as ice."

"The dragon lady," Doc said. "What else?"

"That's it so far."

"Great work, Tom, thanks. We're on our way to the airport and I've got another project for you. I'm going to leave a computer disk at the hotel desk. Pick it up as soon as you can and look for the part with Morgan in the conference room. He's pouring drinks and then they toast an op with a Russian or Slavic name. I need to know what that's about. And when you find out, call us on the cell phone on the double. It could be really important."

"Okay. Good luck with the President."

"Doc, we've got to go," Sheri insisted.

"Right," he answered. "Thanks, Tom. Remember, call as soon as you've got something."

Doc grabbed Sheri's cell phone from the dresser. "Put this in your purse. Tom's onto something hot. Let's go."

They met the President's plane at the airport. Chaplain Stone greeted Doc and Sheri warmly while the President took full advantage of the photo opportunity. Secretary of the Navy Andy Anderson looked subdued. Not his usual intrusive self, he stayed in the crowd of staffers, and while Doc knew that Anderson and Chaplain Stone were longtime friends, he noticed they were at opposite edges of the gathering. He also noticed that Anderson avoided making eye contact with either him and Sheri, or the new Chief of Chaplains.

Helicopters were waiting to take them to the aircraft carrier USS *Kennedy*, which would serve as the flagship and host vessel for the meetings. Doc and Sheri climbed aboard the SH-60F Sikorsky Oceanhawk helicopter behind Stone and two Secret Service agents. On the flight to the *Kennedy* a crewman briefed them on Oceanhawk's anti-submarine warfare capabilities. She was specifically designed to protect carriers from enemy subs and carried an impressive arsenal of homing torpedoes and anti-submarine mines.

George Town Harbour now held the carrier and three Spruance class destroyers, while the SSN *Atlanta* cruised slowly just beyond the edge of the wall. The *Kennedy* was turned into the wind for the helos to land and all three approached in tight formation and set down neatly. The crew was waiting in dress whites. Hail to the Chief was played over the bitch box as the President stepped from the chopper and was greeted by the captain and senior officers. The President waved to one and all, and was quickly escorted to the island and to the wardroom. This time Anderson was in the forefront. He took on the role of plantation owner, guiding the President on the palatial tour. He eyed the sailors with raised eyebrows as if scrutinizing them for any breach of naval perfection. As they entered the island structure, he ran his gloved fingers over hatch combing faces checking for dust. Anderson still had not acknowledged Doc although he walked past him, within touching distance, as they wound through the narrow passageways to the escalator which would take them to the wardroom. Doc turned to Sheri and raised an eyebrow. Something was definitely up. They followed, but slowly as he was walking with a noticeable limp at half his normal pace.

"Bring back memories, Doc?" Chaplain Bill Stone asked as they ducked and stepped through watertight hatches.

"I think some of this gray came from slamming my head into one of these," Doc said, slapping a hatch combing. "They just weren't made for anyone my size."

The ship looked much as Doc remembered all the Navy ships he'd been on. It was gray, here and there a little white or blue, but then there was gray, and then there was a lot more gray. The wardroom was a bit brighter, blue walls with the traditional brown imitation leather padded steel chairs. When they entered, the President broke off a conversation with Anderson and made straight for Doc and Sheri.

"Doctor Holiday, it's about time we met. You had this young lady mighty scared. And I'll admit, the rest of us were plenty worried as well." His handshake was solid and his manner sincere. Stone stood back smiling.

"I think this meeting is a bad idea, Mr. President. And I think you should get off this ship as quickly as you can."

"Now that didn't take long, did it?" the President laughed and one or two others followed suit. None of the Secret Service agents, however, believed Doc's remark humorous.

"I don't know what you've been told about *Blackwolf* or Hans Behrmann or Jack Morgan or any of the rest of this, but let me assure you that this is high stakes poker and there are thousands of lives at risk because we are here."

"That's absurd...." a crisp commander Doc had not seen before said a bit too quickly. He looked at Anderson as if suspecting support, but Anderson remained poker faced. What he got instead was a glare from the President which said, *I've got your name and tag number, Commander. Open your mouth again and you'll spend the rest of your career in the bilge.* The commander bit his lip and dropped his gaze to the deck. The wardroom had suddenly become very quiet.

The President's demeanor flashed back with a warm smile.

"Wouldn't be much of a trap without bait now, would it, Doc? Come on, it's time for you and me to have a talk. Gentlemen, if you'll all excuse us, the Doctor and I have some catching up to do. Bill, you, Sheri and Rob, please stay," he said, nodding to the Chaplain, Sheri and his senior aide.

Anderson looked offended and was the first to leave. The wardroom quickly cleared in his wake. The President pulled off his tie and sat on the table. When the door had closed behind the last Secret Service agent, he began. "Doc, none of these guys believe it's Behrmann's sub. They think your *Blackwolf* was destroyed in the explosion in Bermuda."

"Anderson knows better...and how do they explain the fact that I saw her, right here thirty-six hours ago? Or that we saw her attack and sink the *Benthic Explorer*? And what about the coins? What more proof could you want than that?"

"Even the coins don't prove *Blackwolf* sank the research ship. All they prove is that Jack Morgan had them...if you can even tie him to the warehouse."

Doc felt the veins in his neck beginning to bulge. He took slow deep breaths and tried to remain rational. "Then what's their story? What are they telling you?"

"The night the Secretary of State was killed, we had two destroyers and two nuclear subs—SSN's—on patrol as escorts. *Atlanta* was one of them. As the sub that sank the yacht pulled away, *Atlanta* got an acoustical signature on her. We sent out the fleet to find an acoustical match to that signature. It's a dead match to Saddam's second Russian-built Kilo...you know, those small, long range diesel electric boats. We know the boat's name, Doc, and the name of her captain."

"No, sir, I don't think so."

"What?"

"I know what they heard, but it was a recording of Saddam's boat...."

"Doc, that's a bit of a stretch..."

"Please, sir, just hear me out. It's taken a long hard ride to get here, and you may be the only man who can stop this madness."

"Okay, I agree you've paid your dues. Let's hear it."

"Morgan made a deal with the Kuwaitis. My guess is that he promised to take out Saddam. And, I've just found out that he's involved in very sophisticated biological warfare. We have a computer disk of a meeting with..."

"That's absurd. Nixon put a stop to our work with biological agents in '69 and Reagan's Secretary of Defense pulled the plug on the Big Eye chemical bomb and our chemical weapons testing in 1990."

"Begging your pardon, sir," the President's aide began. "But that work was funded again during the Iran and Iraq war when we found out Iraq was using mustard gas. Saddam used gas and other agents against the Kurds. We think fifty thousand casualties or more and then there was the Gulf War..."

"I get your point, Rob. Sorry, Doctor Holiday, please continue."

"Okay, if Morgan made a deal with Kuwait as we believe he did, he hasn't been able to deliver yet. On the disk I saw he was talking about delivery vehicles, and the scientist he was talking to was trying to convince him that thousand-pound bombs were the only safe way, but Morgan didn't like it. Now suppose the scientist was right. Suppose Morgan has to then create a situation which will justify another series of air strikes to deliver whatever kind of weapon he and folks from the university cooked up. An incident here—an attack on your life, no matter how inept, could be all the justification he needs as long as it can be blamed on Iraq."

"Then the killing of the Secretary of State might have been a set up. Is that what you're saying? Interesting...go on."

"Yes, sir, that's what I believe. You see, sir, I found pieces of a torpedo at the wreck site. They were from one of *Blackwolf*'s torpedoes, not a German, a Russian or an Iraqi. I'm sure of it."

"Oh. I never heard that. Who did you report it to?"

"Secretary Anderson, sir. And that wasn't the first time I tried to convince him of *Blackwolf's* involvement. At first I thought he was just skeptical. Now, because of the surveillance disks from Morgan's condo, I believe there's more to it than that."

"You believe he is involved with Jack Morgan?"

"Yes, sir, there's no doubt. When you see the disks, you'll agree."

"This is serious stuff, Doc. How certain are you that you've got it right?"

"It's serious enough that Morgan tried to kill us to keep you from hearing the story, Mr. President," Sheri said. The President nodded and ran his fingers through his wavy hair.

"I've got it right, sir. I'll bet my life on it."

"Yes, well, that's exactly the ante in this game, Doctor," the President answered. "I've had similar suspicions, and my life has been threatened because of them. We need to play this hand very carefully. Will you trust me to do just that, and sit on what you know just a bit longer?"

"Yes, of course, sir," Doc answered.

The President looked at Sheri who nodded her agreement.

"Bill here tells me I can trust you, and I trust him. So you need to hear what we're up against. Our people believe Saddam is very close to having a nuclear weapon. We know he bought fissionable material from the North Koreans; you remember that incident, I'm sure. That makes it all the more important to stop him now. This meeting with the Kuwaitis is a set up, an invitation for him to take a shot at us. But this time if we're attacked, the consequences will be immediate and massive. Actually, we know where he's building those nukes and we're going after the site before he's far enough along with them to launch against us.

"Now you've got the whole picture. I'm sorry we couldn't tell you before. It's a replay of the Cuban missile crisis. It's not acceptable to our national security for that madman to have nuclear weapons and the capability to deliver them. We can't afford another twenty years of cold war, pouring billions we don't have into defensive measures we don't want to take because he's got an attitude. Better just to end it now."

Doc sat thinking for a moment then rubbed his jaw. "If he's building nukes, why should he attack us now and risk certain retaliation before he's ready? We've obviously got the advantage."

"It would make him a hero in all the Arab states, especially if it's a one way trip for his subs. He hates the Kuwaitis. And he knows they would give just about anything to get his head on a pike. So, this is strategically and politically a great opportunity for him."

"How far will we go to retaliate?"

"We have a pretty good chance of getting him this time. Surgical strikes, of course...we're not at war with his civilians. And there is another faction—less radical—waiting in the wings if we're successful."

"So it's a done deal. We're going after him and that's it."

"Now wait a minute, Doc. It's not like Saddam hasn't been asking for it. You know that as well as anyone."

"No argument there, sir. I just hate to think about what happens next. There's no such thing as a surgical strike and we both know it. I just wish there were another way."

"We'll do the best we can. I don't want civilian casualties any more than you do, and that's a promise."

"So then what's the plan?" Doc asked.

"I meet with the Kuwaitis in just a few minutes. I want to find out exactly what kind of deal Morgan made. Then we play our little game and when that's over, we'll deal with Morgan and Anderson. Sound about right?"

"Yes, sir. But then, is there any reason for Sheri and I to remain on board? I'm not much for just taking up space."

"Doctor Holiday, I want you to know that I didn't want any part of this. But in spite of how I feel about it personally, until I can see proof that what you're telling me is honest to God fact, I think I've got to go with the plan. I hope you understand. I know you've been through a lot and as soon as this is over, I'll do everything in my power to get to the bottom of things and find out what Anderson and Morgan have been up to. Now, I'd appreciate it if you stick around until we see how this hand plays out. Is that agreeable?"

"Yes, sir, thank you. Of course, we'll stay. And, sir, good luck. I just hope that when this hand has been played, there will still be time to stop Morgan before he puts you and all of us in a terrible position. I don't think blistering Iraq and killing half their civilians will play well during the next election."

The President looked at him for a moment without speaking, then nodded to his aide and with a look back over his shoulder at Doc as if he were still thinking about what Doc had said, they left the room.

"What do you think?" Doc asked.

"I think Jeremiah was right," Bill Stone answered and then quoted the second verse of chapter fifty-one.

"And I shall send winnowers to Babylon
Who shall winnow her and empty her land.
For in the day of doom they shall be against her all around."

There were six men in the Kuwaiti delegation. They were given a royal welcome aboard when their chopper landed, and from where Doc and Sheri were standing on the second deck of the island structure, Doc recognized two of them. Much to his surprise, one was Faud, the leader of the group at the condo, and the other was the one Bentley had believed was wanted for possible terrorist connections in the States.

There were twelve seats at the wardroom table. After formalities were exchanged, coffee poured and snacks consumed, they gathered at the table with the President centered on one side and Faud across from him on the other.

"Gentlemen," the President began, "the reason we are gathered is to clear away the misunderstandings which may have been created during meetings I understand you had with Mr. Jack Morgan, who at one time represented the White House. In the interest of our continued good working relationship, it's my hope that we can discuss whatever agreements were made and see where we go from there."

Faud leaned over to his right and spoke to an aide who in turn said, "Mr. President, are we given to understand that Mr. Morgan no longer represents you or your administration?"

"Mr. Morgan never represented me or my administration, that is correct."

Faud spoke quietly again, and the aide responded, "And if agreements were made with Mr. Morgan on behalf of your predecessor, are we now given to understand that you have no intention of honoring those commitments?"

"Sir, it is my fear that agreements may have been reached which were never communicated to me or to my administration. That's why I asked you here, to help me do whatever is best to protect the interests of both my country and yours."

"And are you also telling us," Faud said, this time speaking for himself, "that you have no knowledge of certain arrangements of good faith, involving rather substantial assurances paid to Mr. Morgan, as part of these agreements?"

"Unfortunately, that is also true, sir. And again, that is precisely why I asked for this meeting. If you have been wronged in the name of my government, I will do everything in my power to put things right."

Faud stood, his face flushed with anger. "The honor of my country has been trampled by the feet of dogs—your dogs, sir. And now you have the temerity to deny your hand in this outrage? How clever, after the insults of our last visit to these islands, to ask us to return and then take all honor from us with your lies. You may take my life, as you have taken my honor, but I assure you, there will be justice. My people will have an eye for..."

"Now wait just a damn minute," the President said, standing and towering over Faud. "We asked you here in good faith. Talk to me, dammit. Let's try to work this out before we start making threats. Talk to me, please. What did Morgan promise you?"

Faud glared with hatred, like a trapped animal. "Talk? Alright, we'll talk. Clear the room and we will talk, just you and I. And we will see just how good this faith of yours really is."

"Done," the President answered, and waved his arm for his side of the room to be cleared.

When it was only the two of them, Faud began. "My daughter was raped and her children abused. My fourteen-year-old granddaughter took her own life because of her shame. The same is true for every man on my side of this table. My business was destroyed and the land of my family for hundreds of years was desecrated by Saddam's devils. In a thousand years we will not forget the shame he brought to us. Can you imagine living with such shame? We were a wealthy and proud people. He destroyed us. He destroyed our families and our spirit. Can you imagine what that would be like?"

"No. No, I cannot."

"That is an honest answer. No one can."

"You have suffered terribly, and I can't imagine your pain."

"That is why we came to you. Only your country has the might to give us what we so desperately need to begin our healing."

"And what is that?"

"We live in an ancient land, with ancient rules, Mr. President. In our culture, there is only one way to avenge the death of a loved one."

"And that's the deal you made with Morgan? Revenge?"

"Yes, revenge. But my arrangement was not with Jack Morgan...it was with the United States of America. And the price we agreed to pay was..." he hesitated and looked directly into the President's eyes. "The price was worthy of the deed."

"And exactly, what was the price?"

"Your national debt, how much is it?"

"Four trillion, maybe more. But surely..."

"Oil concessions, stock, gold, loans, land, military bases, a trillion in cash. What is a new heart worth to a dying man? Everything. You are the last superpower, and everything, everything we own is tribute at your feet. Our country is nothing without honor. And there will be no honor until we are avenged."

"A trillion dollars in cash?"

"Five billon of that was given as a down payment. Morgan promised us it was going directly to your government. Now you tell me he lied...our money is gone. What am I supposed to say, Mr. President? Are you going to write me a check for five billion dollars? How strong is your good faith now?"

The President slumped into his chair and folded his hands. "And if we carry out the contract? If we kill Saddam? Does that end it?"

"Saddam is a grain of sand in an hourglass. Kill him if you wish, but more will come. This is a holy war. If you've read your Old Testament, you know what that means."

"Total destruction. Oblivion. No survivors."

"To leave the land unfit for habitation for one hundred years. That was the agreement."

"It's impossible. I can't order a nuclear strike against Iraq. We would never have made that kind of a deal."

"A nuclear strike would threaten the entire Middle East... that was never part of our discussions."

"What are you saying?"

"You are a good man, Mr. President. And so am I. But unlike you, I am not so naive. The vengeance we seek is bought and paid for. It begins within the hour and we will witness it. Saddam will attack, and you will keep the bargain your country made with us, or believe me, there will be consequences too horrible for you to imagine. Now please, be reasonable and do what you know you must. It is the only way."

Faud stood, extended his hand to the President who was too much in shock to notice. Unperturbed, Faud turned and left the wardroom. The President sat stunned in his chair and by the time he regained his composure, Faud and his men were in their chopper and were gone.

CHAPTER 27

The hollow pinging of active sonar echoed from the darkness beyond the wall, from beyond the haystacks, from beyond the abyss of the Cayman Trench twenty-four thousand seven hundred twenty feet deep. It was an eerie sound, one that grated and kept men on edge. It was the unexpected knock on the door in the middle of the night, or the creak in the old oak floor just outside the bedroom.

Johnson sat at *Blackwolf*'s sonar station listening to the battle group passing above them. Five or six ships now and at least two big submarines. The men had not spoken in normal voices for days—whispers and hand signals only. Johnson found himself even worrying about the sound of his computer keyboard. It was loud compared to the silence around them. Except, of course, for that infernal pinging.

"Is it coming from the destroyers?" Johnson asked.

"No, Spruance Class destroyers have only passive sonar. It's coming from our subs."

"How the hell do you know what sonar those destroyers have, much less what kind they are?" Johnson smirked.

"Good question. Why don't you tell him, Admiral?" Morgan said, looking at Geist.

"Because he doesn't need to know," Geist snapped, glaring back.

"Now, what kind of team spirit is that?" Morgan said. "If

we're going to get blown out of the water together, there's no use keeping secrets. Captain Geist was a submarine commander and then an instructor in New London, and then a specialist in anti-submarine warfare at the war college in Rhode Island. He was up for admiral with a good shot a making it—academy grad with a good record and all. But then something happened, didn't it, Rudy? Why don't you tell us about that?"

"Yeah, tell us, Admiral," Johnson joined in.

Geist glared back at Morgan and then shrugged off his anger. "What the hell," he said and turned to Johnson. "I backed the wrong team. I wanted to see us develop Behrmann's turbines, but the Navy is committed to nuclear power. I questioned the logic of that; they questioned my willingness to be a team player. I got my nose out of joint and things escalated. Then Colonel Morgan here made me an offer I should have refused."

Morgan laughed again and checked his watch.

"How much longer?"

"As soon as we're sure Saddam's subs are here. It wouldn't be fair to start without them now, would it?"

While the President was in the meeting with the Kuwaitis, Doc and Sheri were offered a tour of the ship and assigned to the care of Chief Billy Wolf, a diver and ordinance disposal specialist with twenty-six years in. Chief Wolf took them through the diving locker and then through the sick bay. Doc was amazed at the changes since his days as a hospital corpsman, although most of his time had been spent "in country," not in the comfort of a floating city and its community hospital. One of the corpsman changed the dressing on Doc's leg and offered pain pills, which Doc declined. He accepted the use of a phone, however, and was able to reach Tom at the RSL warehouse.

"Sorry I haven't called," Tom began, "but things got crazy here. KH-35 just made her last pass and you've got company. Two Russian Deltas are on your backdoor."

"That's no surprise. But what about the other...that Russian name?"

"That took a while. The name was Sverdlovsk and like so

many towns in the Soviet Union, it disappeared when the union dissolved. Now it's got a new name, totally unpronounceable."

"So it was a dead end?"

"Hardly. Listen to this. The Russians had a biological weapons plant there. In 1979 there was an accident and hundreds, maybe thousands, died. The Soviets denied it, of course, at least until '92, after the breakup, when Yeltsin finally admitted there had been a problem. And there's more, Doc. The guy I talked to at the Army's Center for the Study of Infectious Diseases at Ft. Detrick, Maryland said there was a rumor..."

"Don't tell me—there was a rumor the accident was really a black op. Our op."

"You got it. Looks like Morgan has figured out how to get the revenge the Kuwaitis are after. Think we can stop him?"

"I don't know, Tom, but we're sure going to try." Doc hung up the phone, looked at Sheri and shook his head sadly. If the President didn't stop this whole thing now, Iraq was doomed. Doc was more certain of that now than ever.

"So what's that called again, the network transponders off Bermuda?" Doc asked the chief.

"SOSUS, seabed-based sound listening network. And this seamount we're going toward, the choppers are out there now, covering the bottom with enough sonobuoys to hear a starfish grope a mollusk, or whatever the hell they do. If Saddam wants to play games, he's come to the right place. We brought all the toys: Sea Lance anti-sub missiles, the new Mark 50 torpedoes, and some kind of torpedo-firing mine they call CAPTOR."

"So we're actually going to Twelve Mile Bank? That was a lucky guess," Doc said.

"Yes, you know it?"

"It's a fishing ground...the islanders say it's bad news. Lots of things that go bump in the night. So do you really think the Iraqi subs will show? Then things could get pretty interesting. Chief, do you suppose you could show us the bridge, if that's what they still call it? I bet Sheri would love to see all those dashing young officers in their nifty uniforms."

A young ensign met them at the hatch, introduced himself, eyed Sheri appreciatively and then, on behalf of the captain, welcomed them to the bridge. They followed him to an escalator which took them to the flight deck level and the pilot's ready room. Another escalator took them to the bridge.

The captain was cordial. "There was a radio message for you, Doctor. I hope you enjoyed your tour. You were a SEAL, I hear?"

"Yes, sir. Thank you, sir. The message?"

"From a Lieutenant Mike Berry. He said, 'Everything is ready.' That's all. Is there anything I should know about that?"

Doc smiled. On the horizon, he could see the running lights of the three fishing boats Mike had commandeered as part of their plan. "It's an idea we had. Probably won't be needed at all, but...you see that trawler with the reel? He's got five miles of sturdy fishing net. Perhaps sturdy enough to stop a torpedo or..."

"Foul the screw of a small sub and disable her? I like it. But how did you know we would come to the seamount?"

"It's the only shallow water in three hundred miles, why not use it?"

"My thoughts exactly. Show me how you planned to deploy the net," he said, pointing to a plotting table.

Doc drew two lines across the reef. "We create a corridor and use the destroyers to guard the ends and the subs to patrol the edges. You have room to operate in the corridor, but nothing running shallow gets through."

"English teacher, you say? Too bad you didn't study tactics, Doctor...this is very good. Please have your lieutenant deploy those nets immediately."

Three thousand feet below and still between the carrier and the seamount, *Blackwolf* began to silently rise toward the surface. Assured that the Kilo class subs were now in the area, Geist, still scowling but now back at the helm, had guessed they would move into the shallowest water available. Johnson was at the sonar station; Morgan and Roberts were in the bow to reload the torpedo tubes. The turbines were still. The only noise in the boat was the movement of water over the hull as she pushed her way up, and the quiet corrections Geist made to the ballast to slow their ascent. The pinging suddenly stopped. The game had begun. Geist was playing for position now and if he did it correctly, they would be untouchable. If he didn't, they could be dead.

They came up as quickly as they could without creating a doppler effect—water cavitation caused by propellers or water rushing over the hull. They stopped at camera depth, motionless, undetectable, hidden in the night sea by the darkness, the silence and the soft plastic of her outer skin. Hidden, yet within firing range of her quarry. They waited next to the coral wall and just above the narrow, coral-covered canyon in which they had been hiding.

One destroyer led the carrier and the other followed. Oceanhawk helicopters patrolled on each side while two submarines protected the surrounding waters. *Now, how would the battle group commander deploy his most versatile and agile warriors,* Geist pondered. The carrier was making abrupt turns, evasive maneuvers and was closing on the seamount. Geist could see them clearly now through the forward cameras and three dimensional sonar. He smiled and looked at Johnson. This was going to be textbook and it was a book he had written. Geist nodded at Johnson who gave him a thumbs up.

"Attention on deck!" the radar man yelled as the President came through the hatch to the bridge. Secretary Anderson entered behind the President.

"As you were," Anderson snapped.

"Welcome, Mr. President, Mr. Secretary," the captain responded, but by his look it was obvious the intrusion was the last thing he needed at the moment.

"Can't anything be done about those infernal sirens?" the President asked. He looked very tired and was nearly ashen gray.

"Sorry, sir, they're battle alarms," the captain answered. "We have a serious situation, gentlemen. The *Atlanta*'s sonar has just picked up two subs—Russian Kilo class subs."

Doc looked at the President. Tom had known about the subs an hour ago. Surely the *Kennedy* had the same intel, so why the theatrics now? The President looked away and Sheri thought she had never seen a man look more wretched. An hour ago he was confident and poised; now he looked hopeless and panicked. Obviously, something was terribly wrong.

Rudy Geist glanced down at his watch from *Blackwolf*'s four large screen monitors. How considerate of everyone to be on time—how navy. Even the Iraqis had cooperated. Morgan told them that the Navy's newest sub, *Blackwolf*, was going to be on ops with the President's battle group and that Iraq didn't want to miss the chance to observe the new sub before it began ops against them. They had paid Morgan well for the information and the chance to stay a step ahead of the Americans. Now the waiting was over. Just as the *Kennedy* crossed the seamount's wall into the shallows, Geist raised the covers on the four torpedo firing switches. As the huge ship came closer, within a half mile, he fired.

"Sonar reports incoming torpedoes, sir. Range one half mile. We're going to be hit, sir...port side. "

"Captain..." the President began.

"Not now, sir!" the captain snapped.

"Right full rudder. Sound crash alarms. Get us behind those nets. We're dead if we get caught out here. Give me full power on anything we've got. Range on those torpedoes?"

"Eight hundred yards, sir."

"Get the choppers up. Go after his ass. Tell the destroyers we've been fired on. Tell them to find those two subs. What's the range now, Sonar?"

"Five hundred yards, sir. They're correcting course to follow us."

Sheri started to speak, but Doc took her arm and pulled her away from the glass. His eyes never left his watch. He was counting the seconds. He glanced up, only for a second to see Secretary Anderson facing starboard, silently glaring into the night sea. The President was beside him.

Doc jumped to his feet and pulled the President to the deck. "If that glass goes...."

"Of course," the President gasped. "I didn't think."

"How many?" the captain asked.

"Four, sir. Slightly staggered," Sonar answered.

"Time since firing?"

"Two minutes, sir."

Doc nodded agreement and looked up from his Rolex.

There were three anti-climatic muffled explosions, two seconds apart. They waited for the fourth. Nothing.

The captain stood, unruffled and snapped, "Damage report."

"Nothing yet, sir."

"Well, get me something. How many casualties? How many compartments flooding?" Anderson snapped.

"No casualties, no damage, Mr. Secretary. The net caught 'em, sir. Doctor Holiday's plan worked," the captain replied.

"Well, I'll be damned. Good work, Holiday. You may have saved the President and all of us as well!" Anderson said with amazement, but there was no real enthusiasm in it.

"Sonar report, sir. We've got a signature on the sub, sir. Computer says it's a Russian Kilo class, diesel-electric alright. It's the same signature *Atlanta* got after the yacht was sunk, sir. She's haulin' ass it for deep water, sir."

"Roger the 'haulin' ass, Sonar...."

Anderson spun on his heel, looking for the President who was now facing Doc and Sheri. "Mr. President," Anderson began with a cold stare and commanding tone, "firing on this vessel is an act of war. We must retaliate now! We have the bastards right where we want them, sir. Now is your moment. Give the order now, sir!"

"Doc," the President said quietly, turning his back to Anderson. "You were right about everything. They're going to destroy Iraq with some kind of biological weapon. We've got to stop them."

"Wait, Mr. President, don't give the order yet. Listen to me for just a minute, please," Doc said. His voice was resolute and calm, yet loud enough to demand attention.

"Yes? What is it?" came the worried reply.

"Captain, you're telling us we were just fired on by a Russian sub owned by Iraq. Is that right?"

"That's exactly right...not that any of this is your affair."

"And Kilo class subs carry Mk 53 torpedoes, is that correct?"

"Since when did you get to be an expert on Russian submarines, Doctor Holiday?" Secretary Anderson snarled.

"I'm an English professor, remember, Mr. Secretary? I read a lot. Now do Kilo class subs carry Mk 53 torpedoes or not?"

Anderson glanced quickly at the captain who acknowledged with a subtle nod and then answered, "Yes, yes they do. So what?"

"Mark 53 torpedoes have a payload big enough to level a tall building, not make the guppy farts we just heard, and they travel at over sixty knots, just like our Mark 48s. It took those torpedoes over two minutes—two minutes and seven seconds to be exact—to reach us. Now what does that suggest to you, Mr. Secretary?"

"*Atlanta*'s calling, Captain. They are asking permission to fire at the aggressor."

"Permission granted," Anderson said with authority.

"No!" the President snapped with anger. "They are not to fire without my order. Go on, Doctor Holiday, what's the rest of it?"

"It's a set-up, Mr. President. I'm sure of it."

"That's nuts, Holiday," the captain snapped. "You just heard Sonar's report."

"That's Doctor Holiday to you, Captain, and can your Sonar tell the difference between the real thing and a recording of the real thing?"

"What?"

"Think about it. You only got that acoustical signature because *Blackwolf* played it loud enough so you couldn't miss it. Why didn't you hear the sub approaching? Because they didn't want you to, get it? Morgan's playing games with you. He knows the Iraqi subs are out there somewhere; he invited them. But they didn't fire those torpedoes. *Blackwolf* did and she's loaded with sophisticated acoustical recording equipment. It was no problem for them to slip up on one of Saddam's boats and get that recording. With enough planning, anything is possible... even a little charade like this one."

"Arrest him!" Anderson yelled. "He blew up the condo and killed our agents. We have tapes...."

"Forget it, Andy. We know about Operation Sverdlovsk. It's over," Doc said quietly and all eyes turned to the Secretary.

Anderson turned ashen gray and his jaw dropped open.

He stood speechless for a moment and then tried to recover with a feeble "That's a lie...I didn't...you can't..."

"That's enough!" the President ordered. "Just what do you have in mind, Doctor Holiday? Can you prove it wasn't the Iraqis who fired at us?"

"I think so, sir, if we can recover that fourth torpedo. If it's not a Mark 53, and I'm sure it's not, that's the proof. Sonar, can you help me out?"

The young petty officer turned to him and shrugged. "Must've been a dud, sir. We've lost track of it now."

"Can you give me a position and depth on the detonation points of the other three?"

"It will just take a minute, sir."

Doc's eyes were narrow now in that look that Sheri recognized instantly as trouble—big trouble.

"Doc, you're hurt. You're not thinking of..." Sheri began. But the glare she got silenced her immediately. Obviously, that's exactly what he was thinking.

"Got it, sir. Sat nav co-ordinates and depth. It was about two hundred and thirty feet. The trajectory would have been toward a little deeper water, say two twenty to about three hundred."

"Can you plot the trajectory and give us a search grid?"

"Yes, sir, but it would only be our best guess."

"Now wait a minute," the captain snapped. "We haven't got enough divers or the equipment for a job like this. And are you forgetting we've just been attacked? What are you planning to do with the Iraqi subs while you're down there?"

"Call them on the VLF radio. Tell them what's happened and ask them to help find *Blackwolf*, that's what. Give them a chance to prove they didn't fire at us before you blow them out of the water. Mike and I will lead the diving. You've got plenty of equipment; just give me your dive team and one of the subs."

"That's preposterous. We verified the sinking..." Anderson said, recovering some of his poise.

"No, sir. You created the story of *Blackwolf*'s sinking as a cover-up, just like the cover-up of the killing of the salvage boat's crew off Charleston, and probably the killing of the Secretary of State as well. Now I'm tired of being treated like some country boy who fell off the turnip truck. No one wants to see your bases close, Andy, but this isn't the way. Don't take us into another war just to fatten pigs like Jack Morgan."

The President, who had been watching Doc's little show with amazement, moved closer. He stood staring into Doc's eyes, his jaw set and his mouth in a thin, tight line. His eyes were narrow and penetrating. The carrier's bridge, darkened for battle with only soft red lights glowing, was silent with all eyes on the President. Doc met the President's stare and waited.

There were no words spoken at first, only a long and cold silence while the President's eyes met Doc's. The President looked into the crags and scars of that weathered face, praying to find there simple truth and answers to the confusion and lies that still hung heavily in the air. One man in that room had clung desperately to his search for truth. One man had risked everything time and again, refusing to quit, refusing to die, refusing to be silenced. Doc Holiday looked back into the President's eyes and smiled. This was his moment of vindication. Finally the truth would be known.

"Can you find that torpedo, Doc? Can you really prove what you're saying?" the President asked softly.

"Yes, sir," Doc answered. "Stop it now, and we'll give you the proof you need."

The President nodded, smiled and then turned to face Secretary Anderson and the captain.

"Mr. Secretary, I accept your immediate resignation and order you to be placed under arrest. Captain, Mr. Anderson is under arrest. The charge is treason against the United States of America. Please remove him to some secure place until such time as we may deal with him in an appropriate manner."

"You won't..." Anderson began, but then stopped himself short when he caught the captain's glare.

"Take him to my cabin and post guards," the captain ordered.

Anderson's gaze shifted to Doc then abruptly back to the President.

"Sir, if you'll follow the corporal..." a tall sergeant said quietly.

Anderson turned and pushed his way to the hatch where the younger Marine was waiting. He paused at the hatch for a moment as if going for the last word, thought better of it and followed the corporal.

"Mr. President," the captain began when Anderson was removed from the bridge.

"Is there something you want on the record, Captain?" the President responded icily.

"No, sir. I just hope you know what you're doing, sir. That's all."

The President turned again to face Doc and Sheri. "Don't let me down, Doc," he said quietly. "Please don't let me down."

The carrier's diving locker was staffed by a team of six SEALs assigned to explosive ordinance disposal. Their CO, an academy graduate named Carter, was joined by Chief Wolf and his team around a work table. Mike was choppered over from the fishing trawler and joined the meeting just as Doc began the briefing.

"The fishing net is still there. We'll check it first, then lay search lines and divide the area into quadrants. It may take a while so the *Atlanta* will be ready to pick us up on the bottom and we'll do our decompression in her chamber. Now, when we find the torpedo, I'll disarm it before we try to move it. I've seen the detonating systems before; nothing hard, just a little different. When I'm done, we'll load it into one of *Atlanta's* tubes and head for George Town."

"What happens then?" Carter asked.

"We put a bunch of scumbags in the brig, I buy the beer, and we all get shitfaced. With your approval of course, Lieutenant."

A half hour later, at 0200 hours, four divers in Westinghouse Mk-16 closed circuit mixed-gas recirculators began their descent. They dropped down the lines in darkness, planning to save the batteries of the big dive lights until they began the search. They entered the clear, warm water at the net and dropped to the impact point of the three torpedoes which had fired. As Doc had suspected, there was little damage. What he had not counted on were the sharks.

He should have remembered from his oil field diving days that sharks are attracted to explosive blasts like bees to wildflowers. Underwater detonations kill fish, hundreds of them and stun hundreds more, but strangely the sharks survive and feast on the carnage. Their silver bodies glimmered in the moonlight and flashed past in the excitement of the feeding frenzy.

It's hard to be ambivalent about sharks. At a distance they are majestic, graceful, powerful, awe-inspiring. In your face, well.... Salvaging an oil rig three hundred feet deep in black Mississippi River water off the Louisiana coast, the plan had called for explosively cutting up the platform. No problem—until the blasting convened the largest congregation of sharks in the Gulf of Mexico since the last convention of The Association of American Trial Lawyers in New Orleans. Sharks were everywhere, trying to eat everything. When the divers opened the bottom hatch of the diving bell to go to work, sharks stuck their heads in like hungry dogs waiting for the master to fill the bowl....

Doc shook it off with a shiver as he continued to descend. Two months diving in the middle of a thousand feeding sharks and not as much as a scratched finger. Sharks big enough to eat a bus and not a single incident. Still it was hard to be ambivalent about sharks.

He checked his console. They were below the bottom of the net, at two hundred and twenty feet. The bottom rose quickly to meet them. He nodded at Mike and they turned on the search lights. The coral formations below were unbelievable in the bright lights. Oranges, reds and neon blues over a rugged terrain of hard and soft corals. And sharks. Sharks everywhere.

They defined the search in hastily laid out grids and went to work. The viz was over a hundred feet, but even with the lights they would need to work tighter. The torpedo they were after was ten feet long by eighteen inches in diameter and could easily be lost in crevasses and crannies of the rugged coral bottom. As they descended, the shark delegation sent an ambassador to greet them. The eight-foot bull shark eyed them curiously, and when the lights became uncomfortable, did a snap roll and returned to the bottom. Doc looked at Mike who nodded, and they began to search.

Doc missed the scooter that had served him so well in Bermuda. With his injured leg, swimming was painful and frustratingly slow. Mike found himself alone and glanced back to see where Doc had gone. The shock at what he saw caused him to nearly swallow his regulator. SSN *Atlanta* had moved in behind them. Silent, hovering motionless, the massive three hundred sixty-foot-long hull, three stories high, was a stunning sight. Mike pointed and Doc turned. It was comforting there in the darkness, surrounded by questionable companions, to know that big brother had arrived. Now all they had to do was deliver the goods.

The first half hour passed like the quick twitch of a shark's tail. In the second half hour, they covered their quadrants and extended the search area. Even Mike, whom Doc considered to be the best search and recovery diver he'd ever seen, found nothing. Now the dive team would need serious decompression. They had covered the area carefully and were beginning the second attempt when Doc had a frightening thought. Perhaps it wasn't the last of four torpedoes fired. Perhaps the first or the second had stuck in the net and then along came the third or fourth and boom! No evidence! He signaled to Mike to follow him back to the net. As they approached it, Doc suddenly felt visually disoriented, as if he were experiencing vertigo. He closed his eyes and when he reopened them, looked only at his hand and then at the bottom. No problem. Then he brought the light back up toward the net. It was moving. The monofilament wall in front of them was moving and as they rose further from the bottom, they could hear the deck winches banging and clanging away on the boat above them.

They exchanged shrugs. Who had ordered the net be pulled in? What was going on up there? Doc checked his computer. Their decompression ceiling, or the depth of their first stop, was now fifty feet. They planned to do the decompression aboard the *Atlanta*, but it was important that they not rise above their ceiling until then. They were at seventy feet when Mike saw the torpedo precariously dangling from the net above them. He grabbed Doc's arm and pointed up. The torpedo was on its way to the fishing boat's stern. If it slammed into the fishing boat, it would blow the boat to toothpicks and perhaps even assure a nuclear launch against Iraq. Mike bolted for the surface to warn the boat crew and Doc headed for the torpedo. If it dropped from the net the boat might be saved, but the divers below wouldn't have a chance. Doc visualized the torpedo's internal components and wiring; if he could only get the cover off the firing system.... A tool bag hung from his shoulder harness, his long bladed Randall balanced his other side. He grabbed for it, wanting assurance it was still there.

The net was moving quickly. His injured leg ached as he kicked hard toward the torpedo. Finally, he reached the bottom of the net and begin climbing. His breathing was heavy now, coming in gasps. He fought his way against the net and the current until he reached the torpedo. Hanging on with one hand, he pulled a folding tool bag with the other and removed a large screw driver. Six screws held the waterproof plastic cowling. No good. He needed both hands. He stuffed the screwdriver into his weight belt, pulled off his fins and let them drop. Now he could wrap his feet into the net and hang on. He grabbed the screwdriver, stuck the light under his arm and set to work. One good twist loosened the first screw and it was quickly gone. The second came just as easily. He felt himself lurching and looked up. He was within ten feet of the surface and the swells were taking their toll. The torpedo jerked in the net and shifted position. He grabbed it and held on. The sound of the boats' winches were louder. *Where the devil was Mike?*

The net was jerking violently now, but somehow, he got the third screw and started on the fourth. Then the racket stopped. Mike had gotten their attention and probably gotten a good case of the bends as well. However, the boat was still rolling, and hanging on was like riding a greased pig bareback, not that he'd ever tried but the simile worked well, he thought, as he finished the fourth screw and started on the fifth. The net jerked and started moving again—they were letting it back down. *Good idea...thanks, Mike.* A set of large swells hit the boat and Doc was nearly thrown off the torpedo. Scrambling to hang on, he lost the screwdriver and only the wrist lanyard saved the light.

The torpedo swung violently and the first of three strands of monofilament holding the tail fins gave way. It dropped far enough to give Doc a good jolt before the next strand caught and held. Doc looked up and saw the sharp fin edge cutting through the second strand as the torpedo swung with the boat's movement in the building sea. Doc grabbed the Randall and went to work on the last two screws. He got one screw out before the next monofilament strand parted. He held on for dear life and prayed the last strand would hold long enough...no such luck. Suddenly, he and the torpedo were dropping to the bottom two hundred feet below.

He got his legs wrapped around the tube and tightened his grip on the Randall. With his forefinger, he traced the rim of the cowl. He tried to visualize the electrical components and wiring bundles which made up the firing system. Then he raised the Randall and betting all the marbles, he stabbed through the cowling.

The thin plastic was no match for the Randall, but his reward was an electrical shock, which, while it lasted only for a milli-second, was ample enough to take his breath and jolt him from his seat. Doc was left disoriented in deep water, finless and with a flooded mask. A silky gray shape slid past his left side close enough that he could see it through his flooded mask. Doc took a deep breath and cleared the mask. There would not be time enough to escape the torpedo's blast if it detonated. He thought quickly of Sheri and his daughter Debbie, and the grandchild he might never see. Would Jack Morgan win after all? He didn't have to wait long for his answer....

The torpedo struck bottom and lodged upright in a sand patch. It did not detonate. A large bull shark followed it down and nibbled at the tail fins when it landed. Finding the plastic fins unappealing, the shark went off in search of more succulent fare. Doc took several deep slow breaths, exhaled forcefully, recovered the light and started down. A hundred feet beneath him the torpedo was waiting. He would make certain the firing system was deactivated, attach a transponder to it and the recovery team would come from the sub. Then he would join Mike and the other divers for hours of decompression.

Behind him the silent nuclear sub *Atlanta* opened a hatch and two divers with lift bags emerged. It was time to collect the evidence and set the record straight.

Atlanta's weapons officer quickly confirmed that the torpedo was not Russian, German or Iraqi. In fact, it was not like any he'd ever seen or read about. Most of the components were made in the U.S. and purchased at any decent hardware store that sold PVC pipe and trolling motors. It would be a real stretch to build an Iraqi plot based on this evidence. The weapons officer reported to *Atlanta*'s captain who called the carrier.

The President was sitting in the wardroom with Chaplain Stone when the captain brought the news.

"So Holiday was right," was the President's terse reply.

"Look's that way, alright," the captain nodded and then left them.

CHAPTER 28

Stone studied the President's face, saw the sigh of relief last only momentarily and then replaced by nervous agitation.

"I've got to ask a favor," the President asked. "Go with me to talk to Anderson. What we've done saved Iraq, but it could put the U.S. at risk when the Kuwaitis figure out we're not going to be the swift arm of Allah's vengeance. Anderson can help us, and I'll bet he knows were Morgan is."

"Of course. Let's go."

Chaplain Stone followed the President and a Marine escort up the escalators and through narrow gray passageways to officers' country and the captain's cabin where Anderson was confined. There was a tall Marine on duty who saluted smartly and then grinned. The President smiled back, asked his name and where he was from, then nodded and asked the Marine to inform Anderson the President wanted to speak with him. There was no response to the first knock or the second.

The President shook his head and looked at Chaplain Stone who nodded his concern.

"Try the door, son," the President said.

"Yes, sir."

It was locked from the inside.

"Andy, this is Bill. If you can hear me, please open the door. Andy, are you alright? Answer me, please." Stone knocked loudly and called his old friend's name several more times.

"Get some help," the President said and the Marine hurried down the passageway. He returned a moment later.

"Captain's coming, sir. Be here in a minute."

When the captain opened the door, they discovered the Secretary of the Navy, Andrew Stillwell Anderson, hanging from the overhead sprinkler system. On the carpet beneath him was a pool of urine and a pile of feces. His face had turned dark purple and his eyes were bulging grotesquely.

"No wonder they used hoods," the captain said. "That is not a pretty sight. Cut him down, get a flight surgeon to do the paperwork, and get that body off my ship. The son-of-a-bitch ruined my carpet and hung himself with my ties...."

"That will do, Captain. Thank you. That 'son-of-a-bitch' was your superior officer and my friend." Bill Stone had the look of a combat-blooded, pissed-off Marine and his voice was as cold as a December gravestone. The captain wisely retreated. Stone walked to the desk and picked up several handwritten pages. He scanned them quickly and then said to the President, "Here it is. Operation Sverdlovsk. The whole thing. They were going to make it look like a biological accident. Iraq would be destroyed, completely depopulated and we would be blameless. Just think of all those dead children. How could he have even thought of something like this?"

Blackwolf left the seamount immediately after firing on the carrier and broadcasting the recorded acoustical signature of the Russian Kilo class sub. It was the same recording they had played after sinking the yacht and killing the Secretary of State. Once in deep water away from Twelve Mile Bank, they ran undetected, straight for their secret island base. Johnson and Geist were sleeping. The sub was rapidly approaching the cave's entrance and Bill Roberts sat uneasily at her helm while Jack Morgan paced the deck behind him, swearing frequently as he re-played the game like the losing coach at a national championship.

"We should have finished it ourselves," Morgan fumed. "We should have delivered the packages another way. I knew Anderson didn't have balls enough the see it through. He was supposed to have taken care of the President if there were going to be problems authorizing the air strikes."

"We'd have given ourselves away," Roberts said.

"Do you think for one minute they didn't think it was us?" Morgan scowled. "Of course they knew. Come on, Bill, think! We had it all in the palm of our hands and we blew it. All Anderson had to do was order the launch and send his subs after the diesel boats. In twenty minutes it would have been over. Iraq is hot sand and we're the richest double-dealing bastards in history. The perfect deal. Eat your heart out, Uncle Henry."

Roberts was silent, trying to come up with a plan to protect himself and his family from Morgan. He was still in shock that Morgan had actually fired on the carrier. Now even if Morgan escaped, *Blackwolf*'s fate was sealed.

"I handed them the perfect solution, years of planning, millions spent setting it up, and they don't have balls enough to pull it off. And now what happens? Do I go home a hero? Does our flaccid flunky of a President send a few fat contracts our way? You can bet your ass that's not going to happen. I'll be lucky to get out of this with a few hundred million and a shack in the middle of the booger woods—if the Kuwaitis don't find me first."

"The question now is..." Roberts started, but his voice failed.

"What? What did you say?" Morgan snapped.

"I said the question is..."

"Oh, that question," Morgan interrupted with a half-laugh, half-sneer. "The problem with you is you worry too much, Bill. Don't worry about things you can't control. You'll live a lot longer...then again, perhaps you won't," he finished with a taunting chuckle.

"What about me and my family? My sons? You said..." Bill Roberts's desperation showed through.

"Look, Bill, we had plans, but they didn't work out. In case you haven't noticed, I've got challenges and opportunities of my own here. Once we get my cargo unloaded, what happens to your family and the infamous Herr Behrmann is no longer my concern."

Roberts didn't believe him. Not for a six fathom second. They were within an hour of the cave and Roberts's brain raced for a way out. He had grasped at enough straws during the past weeks to fill a scarecrow and still couldn't come up with a plan. As the sub drew closer to the tunnel, he felt his stomach knot and had to tighten his grip on the controls to keep his hands from shaking. Like the pirates Morgan admired, Morgan wouldn't leave a witness alive or a trail uncovered and that was that. What could be done to stop him? Once *Blackwolf* surfaced in the cave, it was over. Petra and his sons wouldn't have a chance. Roberts was faced with one desperate alternative. He glanced at Morgan who was watching the monitors, and then focused on the torpedo firing switches a foot from his quivering right hand. They had reloaded the tubes immediately after firing on the aircraft carrier. Perhaps....

The time passed quickly and soon Jack Morgan was counting down the seconds until they would pick up the laser which guided them into the cave. Roberts bit his lip and tried to pull himself together. This was his last chance to save his family.

"Depth is good...start your turn in nine seconds," Morgan said.

"Got it."

Roberts brought the bow into the turn and reversed the port turbine, increasing the starboard power slightly.

"We've acquired the laser. Come to starboard just a bit."

Roberts could see the guidance system as clearly as Morgan and the coaching was completely unnecessary, if not in fact, a distraction. However, as long as Morgan's attention was occupied, there was a chance. Roberts eased the sub forward through the narrow fissure and began bringing up the bow.

"Steady, steady," Morgan said as if teaching a thirteen-year-old to drive.

Roberts clenched his jaws and slid his hand toward the red switch covers.

"What the hell are you doing, Roberts?" Rudy Geist snapped from the hatch behind him. Roberts had not heard Geist and Johnson enter the control room. Morgan looked down and saw Roberts's hand on the firing switches. He lunged for Roberts's arm as Roberts pulled the joystick back to the peg, pulling the nose up with full power. Morgan was thrown from his feet and Geist dropped to his knees, pinning Johnson against the aft bulkhead.

"You fool! You'll kill us all!" Morgan shouted.

Geist went for his 9 mm Glock with his free hand and raised it to fire.

Captain Hans Behrmann sat in the shade of tall palms at the lagoon's edge, drinking a cool lemonade and watching Martin and Randy row the skiff back to the schooner. They had few personal effects worth taking to their new home. The boys had described the beauty of the Colombian coastline, the opulence of the chateau and the life of security and comfort which awaited them. His daughter, Petra, came to his side to refill his glass. The weeks of rest and solitude had been good for Behrmann. Petra felt confident that once in their new home, safe from stress and conflict, he would be manageable, perhaps even tolerable as old wounds healed and painful memories faded.

Jason came from the cavern carrying another crate to the beach. Karen, now early into her ninth month, was napping in the cool cavern air. Jason set the crate down and looked uneasily at the schooner. In spite of reassurances by the Roberts boys, Jason had grave doubts about the safety they had been promised. Still, they were completely cut off from modern medical support and what if Karen's delivery did not go well? He felt trapped as if his world were tumbling down around him. He had taken precautions, crude at best. But he was afraid. Afraid for all of them, but especially so for the simple and kind golden-haired girl he had come to love.

He was absorbed in his work and his concerns, so that at first he didn't recognize the sounds coming from the cavern as pistol shots. Karen came running from the waterfall. She screamed to Jason as she stumbled and fell, got to her feet and by then Jason was at her side. "It's the sub," she cried, pulling him toward the bungalow. "It surfaced and there was shooting. I saw someone fall into the water."

Jason lifted her and ran to the bungalow. Petra and Behrmann ran to help him. When they got her up the steps, he eased her into a chair. Petra knelt beside her, offering comfort and attempting to determine if she was injured. Her ankle was twisted and her knee scraped. Karen called to Jason, wanting him at her side, but Jason had business to attend to. Randy and Martin stepped from the inflatable and ran to join them on the bungalow's deck.

"It's Morgan," Behrmann growled. He was fully attentive now.

"What, Papa?" Petra looked up from Karen's bloody knee and through the clearing, saw two ragged men dragging each other and a large duffel bag from the cavern entrance.

"It's Morgan," Behrmann repeated. "Stay with her, boys. Take her inside and keep out of sight until we find out what's happened."

Randy looked at his mother who nodded her agreement. Randy helped Karen up and they went inside.

Petra took her father's arm and they hurried back through the trees to the clearing. The stump of Rudy Geist's right arm was bleeding profusely as was Morgan's scalp wound.

"Where is Bill?" Petra asked.

"Your husband..." Geist began with disdain. He'd pulled off his shirt and was using it as a pressure dressing on his arm. He was obviously in great pain.

"There was an accident," Morgan corrected. "An explosion and fire in the control room. We barely made it to the surface. I think the sub is still on fire. Johnson was killed. I'm sorry, but I think the fire got your husband as well."

"Oh, Bill," she said in a sadly maternal sigh. "Oh, Bill, this is all my fault. I'm so sorry...."

"We need your help, Mrs. Roberts. Our wounds need attention. Do you still have medical supplies?" Morgan said impatient with her lack of attention to his needs.

"Yes." She wiped the tears from her eyes and tried to focus. "Almost everything has been loaded aboard the..." She paused, realizing she had given Morgan more information than she'd intended.

"So the schooner is here. Good, let's get underway immediately. The boys can get us out of here while you patch us up."

"What about *Blackwolf*? What about Roberts?" Behrmann demanded.

"It's too dangerous to go back on board, Captain. The fire destroyed the control room. There was an explosion. It's still burning and if the torpedoes go...we need to get out of here.

It's over, Captain. It's time for us to go."

The old man shook his head. "My torpedoes will not fire by accident," he said flatly. "And there is an automatic fire control system. Now, you tell me what really happened. Where are the others?"

"We don't have time for this now, old man," Morgan answered. "I'll write you a report in triplicate once we're off this island. Now get your grandsons up here. We haven't got all day." He started to push past Behrmann, but suddenly found himself held in the old man's bear paw grip.

"I built that sub...she was mine. If you had kept your word—delivered what you promised—there would have been no accidents. None of this would have happened."

"Let go of me, you crazy old fool, or there's going to be another accident right now!" Morgan twisted to get away, then reached for his gun only to discover it was not in his belt. He felt his arm being crushed by an old man twice his age.

"Rudy, get this maniac off me!" Morgan growled.

Rudy Geist had to let go of the dressing before reaching for the 9 mm Glock shoved into his belt, and before he could make the move, Jason stepped into the clearing holding a crudely made bow with a metal tipped arrow. The bow was drawn and Jason had target lock on Geist.

"Well, if it isn't my old double-crossing partner, Jason," Morgan said. "They tell me you don't have much to say these days, Jason. How convenient."

Behrmann shook Morgan and spun him around so that both were facing Jason.

"What did you say, 'partner'? Tell me what you meant by that," Behrmann demanded.

"Oh, didn't your grandson tell you? He made a deal to sell me the plans to your submarine, old man. And if he'd delivered, we'd have been rid of you ages ago. Isn't that right, partner?" Morgan laughed, but Jason shook his head angrily and pointed the bow threateningly at him.

Behrmann eased his grip and Morgan pulled away.

"I knew that," the old man said sadly, his strength gone now. "I knew that, but I had forgotten. But it doesn't matter now. Do you think I would have been so childish to put the secrets of my engines on paper, where you or any of your fools could find it? You laughed at my ideas. But now it's my turn. You could have had wealth beyond your dreams, but you won't get a dime now. My secrets are safe, safe up here," he said, pointing to his thick round head and nodding with a confident grin. "And there's nothing you can do, do you hear me? Nothing that will convince me to trust you again....never!"

Petra moved forward and took her father's hand. She could feel him trembling although his countenance was rock solid.

Randy stepped into the clearing behind Jason. He stopped short when he saw Morgan and Geist held at bay by Jason and the bow. Morgan ordered the boy to disarm Jason, but Behrmann shouted, "Don't do it, boy. They mean to kill us all. Let them have the schooner and go. Admiral Donitz won't forget us. He'll send someone to rescue us. He's a close friend of the Führer, you know."

"I'm sure you're right, Captain," Morgan said. He studied the old man for a moment then shouldered the duffel's strap, strained under the weight and with Geist following, pushed his way past them toward the lagoon. Jason followed, keeping the bow drawn and with Randy at his side.

"Come on, Papa. We have to find Bill," Petra said and nudged him toward the cavern.

"Ya, ya," he answered. "I must see what they have done to my *Blackwolf*."

In the dim light *Blackwolf* was barely visible. The cavern smelled of smoke, but from gunfire, not an electrical fire.

Behrmann moved slowly, clumsily. Petra realized the old man had taken off his glasses. She helped him clean them and put them back on.

"What has happened here?" he asked her several times.

His attention was failing again and each time she answered patiently: "There was an explosion, Papa. We have to find Bill."

"Ya, ya," he would answer, "but what happened here?"

When they reached the water the floating dock was gone, crushed by the sub when she blew to the surface out of control. Petra sat her father down with instructions not to go exploring, then dropped her sandals and long cotton skirt, and slipped into the dark water. She waded out, ready to take the first of the few strokes to the sub, but in chest-deep water she suddenly jumped back with a scream. She had stumbled into a submerged body. She closed her eyes and dropped beneath the surface. With a trembling hand, she groped until she found the body again. She sobbed as her fingers locked into a tangle of thick long hair. It was not her husband. She raised the body to the surface and opened her eyes. It was Johnson, the robotics and electronics genius. She rolled him over to see his face and choked back another scream. He'd been shot twice in the chest and his blood swirled around her in the dark water.

She let Johnson slip away, back into the dark water, and swam to the sub. The climb up the stern left her panting for breath, and the fallen rock and dust which covered the boat caked her wet body in mud. She stood, slipped to her knees, got up again and in a crouch, moved forward. A faint glow of red, like the red eyes of a scallop gleaming from beneath its shell, led her to the partially open hatch. It opened more easily than she'd expected and she cautiously, reluctantly peered over the rim. Her eyes adjusted to the light and then she saw her husband. He was slouched in the helm seat, his head on the control panel and he was not moving.

"Bill?" she said tentatively. No answer. She dropped cautiously down the ladder and went to his side. He was still breathing. She could hear the rattling of his torn lung tissue and air wheezing through his sucking chest wound even before she touched him. She grabbed a battery-powered battle lantern and hurried down the passageway to the tiny sick bay, found a shock-trauma kit and hurried back to her husband in the control room.

The control room lights were on when she returned. Jason was kneeling beside Bill's chair, holding his shirt over the wound while Randy examined the control panel, activated the computer and began a damage assessment. Petra opened the medical kit and began cleaning her husband's wounds. With Jason's and Randy's help, she moved him to a mattress, carefully positioning him on his wounded side.

"How bad is it, Mom?" Randy asked.

She was taking his blood pressure now and when she finished, she shook her head sadly. "We need a real hospital."

Jason went back to the helm and turned on the three dimensional Fathometer. As the screen cleared, he adjusted the unit until he could see that the bottom of the cave, three hundred feet below the entrance, was still open. He slapped his palm on the console to get their attention and pointed to the screen. Randy got up from his father's side to look at the screen.

"Think we'd have a chance?" he asked.

Jason answered by opening his hands and shaking his head.

"You're right. What chance have we got if we stay here? Stay with Mom and Dad. I'll get the others."

Petra started an IV and listened carefully to her husband's chest. The uninjured lung was still functioning, but she knew that internal bleeding could fill the chest cavity and collapse that lung as well. She was wondering how she could try to rig a suction apparatus when she felt the sub vibrate and the lights flicker as Jason started the engines and shifted the electric load from batteries to the gen-set. Roberts felt it too. Dazed, he suddenly tried to sit up. His eyes were wild and afraid. Petra grabbed him and tried to calm him. Jason moved quickly from the helm to her side to help.

Roberts looked at her, struggling, thinking that he was still fighting with Morgan and Geist. She spoke more loudly and held him until he recognized her and then fell back into her arms. He clutched her hand tightly and spoke in a painful, gasping whisper, "Can't take the boat out...stay here...Navy...too dangerous."

His breathing was labored and he coughed up bright frothy blood. Petra put a gentle finger on his lips and told him not to talk, while Jason helped him lay back on the mattress.

"We have to leave the island," she said softly. "It will be alright. We have to get you to the hospital."

He shook his head. "Morgan tried to kill..." he gasped painfully before finally getting the rest out. "Morgan tried to kill the President. The Navy.... If they find us..." He squeezed her hand and looked up with sad eyes. "It's over...call them...save yourselves."

Petra looked at Jason. "Can you do it? Can you let them know where we are?"

Jason nodded and stood up. He went forward to the diving locker, searched the compartment for a moment until he found the recirculator he was looking for. He opened the MK-XVII's shell and removed a piece of plastic pipe with rubber stoppers in both ends. A quick hammer blow shattered the pipe and there were the notes he'd gotten from Debbie Holiday—the price he had demanded for helping her "escape" from his grandfather. The notes were the key, the access code to Roberts's secret control of the Navy Keyhole Satellite. A radio message might never be received or could be easily misinterpreted. It might even be intercepted by Morgan, but the right kind of satellite message was guaranteed to get the response they needed.

Jason grinned as he thought of the reaction his message would create at Ft. Belvoir in Virginia or at the NASA computer center on Bermuda. As he moved back down the passageway to the control room, he heard the sound of angry voices. Petra Roberts was shouting at her father.

"They tried to kill the President! Don't you understand? It's over, Papa. It's time to go home."

"Never!" he shouted back in German. "How dare you talk back to me. Shut up! I will never surrender my boat! Never!"

Karen was cowered in the corner beside Roberts who was unconscious again. Randy and Martin stood by their mother uncertain what to do. Jason felt the sub vibrate as the engines came up to power and then eased off again. Behrmann was doing a pre-dive systems check. Then the bow started to drop. The old man was diving the boat. Jason shoved Debbie's notebook inside his shirt, gathered his strength in preparation for battle and entered the control room.

"Where are we going?" Karen asked as Jason touched her hand and then glared at his grandfather. He stepped past Petra and the boys, pointed at Behrmann and motioned for him to stop. Behrmann laughed and increased the dive angle. On the monitors they could see the steep cavern walls blurring past the cameras. Jason lost his footing and fell forward. He rolled back to his knees and tried to stand, but the dive angle was too steep. Roberts's mattress slid forward and Petra lunged after it in a futile attempt to save him from crashing into the bulkhead.

"Stop him, Jason," Behrmann mimicked Karen's plea in an ugly falsetto. "You spineless whining traitor! I should have finished you in Bermuda. This is all your fault. If you had the balls of a piss-ant, we would be billionaires by now."

Behrmann slammed the boat into full reverse, stopping the dive and causing the sub to hover just a few feet from the rock hard cavern bottom. On the monitors they could see rocks partially blocking the entrance. Behrmann swore and looked threateningly at Jason.

"We'll blast our way out just like we did in Bermuda. One torpedo and we'll follow it out before the cavern has a chance to fall on us."

Jason shook his head emphatically.

"Papa, don't!" Petra screamed and rushed toward him.

"I am still captain!" he shouted at her and with his left hand fired the torpedo.

The explosion was deafening and the hydraulic pressure wave it created pushed out the lower cavern walls, but it brought down tons of rock from above them. The sub was trapped within an instant of Behrmann's launching the torpedo. Alarms blared, the engines shut down, they lost power, and the sub was battered violently. Behrmann was thrown from the helm seat. Jason pulled himself to his feet and in a vengeful rage, lunged at the captain.

Randy and Martin heard the fighting in the darkness and tried to help. During the struggle to pull the two men apart, Behrmann suddenly pulled Jack Morgan's pistol, tried to fire at Jason, but could not release the slide safety and in frustration, struck a glancing blow with the pistol butt to Jason's head.

The red emergency lights came on. Behrmann lurched free from Randy and towered over Jason's limp body. He slowly raised the pistol and took aim. Karen screamed and lunged at the captain, taking him down with a tackle. The old man went down hard and the gun went sliding across the deck. Karen screamed in pain as she twisted to free herself from Behrmann's weight.

"It's the baby," Karen sobbed. "He hurt the baby."

Petra looked down. Karen's water had broken and she cried loudly, pulling herself into a fetal position and wrapping her arms around her knees to protect her abdomen.

"You bastard!" Petra shrieked at her father who was still on his knees. "I'll kill you myself."

The old man turned, wanting someone to help him up, but in the ghoulish red light, all that he saw was the vengeful anger of his clan. Still on his knees before them, he backed into a corner to avoid them. Martin tracked Behrmann's movement with Morgan's automatic. The determination in the boy's eyes left little doubt that the gun would be used.

"Aaahh," Jason moaned and tried to rise to his elbow. "Karen?" he called anxiously. It was the first word he had spoken since the submarine crash which had caused his injury nine months before.

"Jason," she cried in astonishment, crawled to him and pulled him into her arms, sobbing.

"Karen, I love you," he said. "Oh, God, how I love you."

He held for a moment, kissed her and then rose, pulling away from her tight grasp. "We have to get help," he said, moving to the computer console. Jason set to work entering the secret codes Bill Roberts had created to control the Keyhole satellite and its communication links.

Karen's cry broke the silence which had thankfully come like the calm at the eye of a hurricane. "It's the baby," she gasped, still recovering from the surprise and pain of the contraction. Petra and Jason were instantly at her side—Petra telling her to take deep breaths and exhale slowly, while Jason held her hands and whispered how much he loved her.

"Who has a watch?" Petra asked and Randy offered his. "We'll keep track of the time," she said. "Don't worry. That baby's going to be just fine. Now you let Jason figure out how to get us out of here. Go on child, let him go. You and the baby are going to be just fine."

Jason kissed her and went back to the computer. A few minutes later he pushed back from the keyboard and said, "That's it. I've programmed the computer to keep sending the message until we get an answer. We just have to hope our signal is strong enough to reach the satellite."

"How long?" Randy asked.

"If it worked, they could be formulating an answer right now."

They waited. Karen had another contraction and Petra reported that an hour and twenty-six minutes had passed since the first.

"Do you think they got it?" Randy asked quietly enough for Karen and Petra not to hear.

"I doubt it," Jason answered. "Our signal must not be strong enough. We should deploy the antenna array. Perhaps we could let the current carry the towed array out from under this rock pile. We could get a look at how badly we're pinned at the same time."

"We wouldn't stand a chance diving against the current along the wall," Randy said.

"If you were tethered, and one was working, the other tending a safety line, that would work."

"And do what?"

"Clear the antenna's hatch and let it play out into the current. If that doesn't work, you climb the mountain and start sending smoke signals. Karen and Bill need real doctors. We've got to do something now."

CHAPTER 29

It took nearly an hour to prepare for the dive. Randy was the first into the diving lock. It was a confining, cramped space and even though he had come and gone from it before, he had to fight the claustrophobic discomfort that began when water came rushing in. He cleared his ears repeatedly and when the pressure inside the lock became equal with the outside, he opened the outer hatch. His first impression was that it was twilight. The water beyond the bow was deep blue and empty. He might have been standing on a mountain pinnacle looking up into the heavens. He checked his watch and depth gauge—five PM and two hundred sixty feet. He turned to look aft. *Blackwolf*'s bow was protruding from the cavern entrance. If they'd made it just another sixty feet, the sub would have dropped clear, and they would have been home free. But that was no surprise to Randy, who now believed the boat had a spirit of it's own—a very pissed off and bad tempered spirit. He remembered reading Clive Cussler's account of his search for the confederate sub, CSA *Hunley*. The *Hunley* took twenty lives in three different sinkings, trying to convince her creator, Horace L. Hunley, also one of her victims, that she didn't want to play. *Blackwolf* had been telling Randy the same thing since the first ballast control valve failure. Now, here he was again, risking his life to match wits and will with the sub's malevolent spirit.

Blackwolf's stern disappeared in a wall of darkness, buried under tons of fallen rock. He could not tell how much stone they would have to move to get to the antenna reel's compartment, but it was obvious that *Blackwolf* would not be going anywhere anytime soon. And he could feel a very strong current coming from the cavern. The rock pile in the cave's entrance had formed a venturi, greatly increasing the water's velocity. Moving against that current was going to be tough. Martin was banging on the lower hatch. Randy bent down to close the hatch valve so that Martin could come out, but he inadvertently bumped the dry suit inflator button on his chest on the hatch combing. Before he realized what had happened, the air rushing into his suit filled his boots, and unable to get upright quickly enough to dump the unwanted buoyancy, he was lifted into the full force of the current. It snapped him out of the lock, snagged his foot on the rim of the hatch combing, and flattened him hard against the hull, dislodging his mask. He caught it, quickly cleared it and reached frantically for something to tether himself to on the smooth, streamlined hull. He felt his boot slipping over the hatch rim and realized that if he didn't find something to hang on to in the next moment, he'd be drifting with the sargassum weed for the remainder of a very short life.

He turned, looking desperately for a hand hold, but could reach nothing. There were mooring rings on the forward deck, but he would have to let go to reach them and if he missed, he was a goner. His foot slipped further and then the situation was no longer academic. He was flying across the deck in the current, struggling toward the mooring ring which was not directly on his flight path. He kicked frantically and pulled with a strong breast stroke. It would be close. Another quick stroke, but not enough. He let go of the nylon tether and tried a full body roll to gain the lateral distance he needed. He ended up on his back looking into the lonely blue extending nearly three hundred feet above. He rolled again and to his horror, realized he was no longer over the sub. The nylon tether trailed behind him, and as he screamed through his mouthpiece in terror, its snap-hook caught between the hatch covers on the bow storage locker. The line pulled taut, jerking him like a paratrooper landing in trees. The jolt cost him his breath, but he wasn't complaining.

He was gasping now, hoping that Martin would emerge to help him, when reality struck; The outer lock hatch was still open and there was no way Martin could get out. Unless Randy could get back on deck and close that hatch, he was bait on a...no sooner had the thought blazed across his brain than he saw the first shark. It was just a dark shadow above, perhaps only a figment of his imagination, but it sent a major chill up his spine and left him talking to himself rather unkindly.

Come on, asshole, get a grip, he thought, focusing now on the tether and trying to ignore the shark. He grabbed the tether and pulled. The hook slipped a bit giving him a good scare, but then lodged securely. The next time he tried it, it held. He began fighting his way forward, grunting and groaning like a weight lifter. An inch at a time, he worked his way back to the sub. The current was strong enough to break the seal on his mask and when it began to flood, there was nothing he could do. He needed both hands on the nylon strap. The saltwater burned his eyes and he closed them. *At least now I won't have to worry about looking for that damned shark,* he grunted to himself with a grim laugh.

He gasped, moaned and groaned his way forward. His mask was now useless—completely flooded. He tried to stay focused on his breathing, and keeping the mouthpiece securely in his mouth. If he lost it, he wouldn't be able to hang on with one hand and he'd be back at the end of the tether again. After what felt like an eternity, he brushed something with his shoulder and thinking it was the sub, he opened his eyes. Even through the flooded mask he knew it wasn't the sub. He was nose to nose with a ten-foot hammerhead.

He shouted into the double-hosed mouthpiece and nearly lost his grip on the line. The shark, less than a body length away, eyed him with quiet deliberation and in no hurry, turned and descended. Randy was exhausted. He wrapped his legs around the tether and rested. He had never worked as hard before, and for the life of him, it looked like that malevolent spirit was going to win after all.

Rest helped. However, he was surprised to discover that while he wasn't at the end of his rope as he had feared, he was in fact at the end of his tether. Now he was stuck at the bow storage locker, with no way to move the ten feet forward to the diving lock. He rested again and then got another idea. Perhaps there was something he could use in the storage locker. He tied the tether securely to the locker handle, opened it and twisted it to the side, pushing the lid open. Both boats were gone, but there in the bottom of the locker was what he needed—a telescoping boat hook.

He crawled out of the current into the hatch and thankfully rested his aching arms and cleared his flooded mask. As the last of the water was cleared, he looked above into the blue. He could see silhouettes of sharks and a big manta swimming along the wall high above. The sharks had no doubt come because of the explosions and their insatiable curiosity. Perhaps the gentle mantas were curious as well. The aluminum boat hook was badly oxidized. He worked at turning the sections until he could extend them and when he was finally successful, he peered over the hatch rim toward the diving lock hatch. He braced himself against the current and stretched forward with the boat hook. Almost.

After letting out slack on the tether, he inched his way up over the boat locker's edge and hooking his boot tips in the rim, pushed his way forward along the deck. He kept his breathing shallow and wished he were wearing a lot more weight. By staying flat against the deck, he was able to hide from some of the current. Now when he stretched the boat hook forward he was able to catch the diving lock hatch rim and pull himself forward. With a victory shout that was more of a satisfied grunt, he shoved the hatch down and spun the hand wheel until it was tight. He heard the rush of air as the diving lock was blown dry and then the slamming of the inner hatch. The inlet valve opened and water rushed in to bring the lock to bottom pressure.

While he waited for Martin, Randy checked the MK-XVII's wrist display once again. Green lights. But what felt like only a hiccup in time had in reality taken over an hour in which he'd used three hours of oxygen. Without the engines to power the compressor, they had no way to refill the recirculator's tanks and they were using the last of the helium and oxygen bottles.

The hand wheel on the dive lock hatch twisted and as the hatch raised, Martin's head emerged. He looked angry and wanted an explanation. For once, Randy was glad the diving rigs did not have communication.

Randy helped his brother avoid his own traumatic experience by attaching his tether to the hatch cover handle. Then Martin inched his way forward on the deck and when he was braced with his feet against the hatch, he signaled for his brother to use him as a ladder until they could reach the hand railing on the sub's sail and from there, work their way to the antenna's hatch. Both were breathing heavily by the time they crawled their way to the rock pile. Limestone boulders, some half the size of cars, covered the sub's stern and created a solid wall blocking the tunnel. Martin looked up at the rock pile and imagined an hourglass with an obstruction at the neck holding back the thousands of grains of sand above. If they moved the right boulder at the wrong moment, they would be crushed in another avalanche. The locker which held the reel of antenna cable was just behind the sail, but it was buried under tons of stone. It was hopeless, Martin thought. They would just have to find another way to send that message. Perhaps if they.... He struggled to come up with an option—one that he could use to convince Jason that moving these rocks was not the way to go. It was time to go back to the barn and come up with a better plan.

Randy approached the rock wall without looking up. They would have to clear six or eight feet of the rock to reach the antenna hatch. From his engineering studies, he remembered that limestone has roughly the same density as cement, twice the weight of the water, but therefore weighs only half as much in the water. Even though the boulders looked large, given the right leverage, the job wouldn't be half bad. Perhaps they would beat *Blackwolf*'s evil spirit one more time. He looked back over his shoulder. Martin was several feet in back of him, staring off into space. Perhaps it was narcosis. They had lost enough time already. Randy laid hold of the first boulder and gave it a healthy tug. It moved as he'd expected it would. He congratulated himself on correctly analyzing the situation and really laid his back into his next effort.

Martin felt the wall move before he saw the avalanche begin. He tried to warn his brother, but with no communications, there was nothing to do but grab Randy's tether and jerk it violently. He tried to pull his brother clear, but he was too late. Boulders were dropping from the top of the pile thirty or forty feet above them. Martin jerked frantically on Randy's line, but his brother was ignoring him, frozen with panic. And then the rocks started landing. They careened off the slope setting others in motion and the domino effect took over. The hourglass was unplugged.

Martin lost sight of Randy and was transfixed by the wall of stone coming at him. Boulders hammered the boat. Martin fought off his own panic and in a moment of uncanny lucidity, hit the dry suit inflator valve and released the death grip on his brother's nylon tether. The current blew him backward while his increased buoyancy lifted him out of the avalanche's path. Suspended now, like an astronaut from a space capsule, he watched the mountain disgorge itself. When the thunder was over, the sub had survived but was still buried. In fact, now Martin would have to dig his way back to the diving locker hatch.

He hit the deflator valve on his left arm and made a controlled descent to the deck. The silt was still settling over the rock pile and deck level viz was non-existent. At least that's what he told himself to quiet the nagging little voice inside which told him he should go look for his older brother. He muscled his way down the tether to the rock pile covering the hatch lock. Already exhausted, he began digging his way back to the hatch. As he worked, he tried to imagine what he was going to tell his mother. Finally he could open it. He did so and lowered himself into the lock.

Petra Roberts was not waiting anxiously in the diving locker as Martin had expected. Her concern about her sons had been displaced with an overwhelming sense of impending disaster. In the midst of her fear, she remembered Doc Holiday, wounded and covered with blood, standing over her husband's limp body on the stretcher. Hidden beneath Bill's blankets, Doc had brought two EPIRBs, emergency transmitters which would instantly tell the Navy exactly where the sub was. Afraid that her father might have been eavesdropping she had smashed one, but had quickly hidden the other. Perhaps even then she had known their adventure would come to a desperate end. Now, in her terrified mental state, she frantically searched the tiny sick bay. She dumped storage cabinet drawers and ripped through storage boxes. She was certain she had lost both her sons in the deafening avalanche above and knew her husband was near death on his mattress in the control room. Then there was poor Karen whose contractions were coming every hour, and a submarine trapped three hundred feet beneath the surface was not the place for her to have that baby. Petra did not hear Jason the first time he called to her from the passageway. Even when he repeated himself, the message barely registered.

"Come on, Martin is in the diving lock. He may need your help."

"Oh," she looked at the wreckage she'd created in frustration and confusion. "Doctor Holiday gave me a little transmitter and I hid it in here. It's got to be here somewhere. I'm sure I put it right here. If only I could just.... You go. I'll be there in a minute."

Jason nodded. The stress has finally gotten her, he thought. Why would Holiday have given her a transmitter? Wouldn't he have just hidden it on board himself? He hurried back down the passageway to the diving locker.

In his stateroom, Captain Hans Behrmann struggled against the belts binding his wrists to the desk chair. He was in a rage and stronger than a bull. His forearms were bleeding, but he was indifferent to the pain. The chair was an elegant old leather-bound mahogany relic and when he finally snapped the oak trenails fastening it together, he was free. He opened his desk, dropped a six- by two-inch electronic device in his pocket, and kicked through his stateroom door—no problem, because it had not been repaired after his last escape.

He'd seen Martin put Morgan's gun in the chart table drawer. He went straight for it, chambered a round and was on his way to a family reunion. He heard glass break in the sick bay and from the door, he saw his daughter on her knees, searching through the debris.

"So it was you," the old man said with a scowl. "I thought you were the only one I could trust and even you betrayed me."

"What do you mean?" she asked, but as he raised his right hand, she knew her lie was futile. He was holding Doc Holiday's little EPIRB.

"You would give them my boat, my life's work? You would hand over everything just to save your miserable life? Just like your mother, you're nothing but a cheap whore who would sell anything to save her worthless..."

She stepped back against the stainless steel cabinet and eased open the surgical instrument drawer just enough.

"Shut up, Papa. Shut up about mama and give that to me. Shut up or I swear on mama's grave, I'll kill you myself."

Behrmann's eyes narrowed to deadly slits. He raised his left hand, the hand she had not seen, and in it was Jack Morgan's lost 9 mm Glock.

"You threaten me? I was right, you and your mama. Now you can join her in hell."

She pulled a scalpel from the drawer and lunged at him. He stepped back and fired twice. She dropped to her knees, the scalpel fell from her hand and her hatred melted into disbelief.

"You killed mama?" she said as she fell face forward into the debris.

Jason heard the shots, grabbed a pneumatic speargun and pushed open the dive locker hatch. Behrmann fired first and the round hit Jason in the right knee. He dropped to the deck and fired the speargun on the way down. The stainless steel shaft caromed off the deck before striking Behrmann squarely through the chest. The old man emptied the gun at Jason who was hit again, this time in the left shoulder. Behrmann, still standing, kept squeezing the trigger and tried to take a step forward but fell. Now face down in a pool of his own blood, he raised himself on an elbow and tried to speak. No sound came as he tried to give one final order. He raised his hand and pointed a crooked index finger accusingly at Jason and then collapsed.

Karen screamed for Jason. He pulled off his belt and shirt and made a pressure dressing for his knee. Pulling himself up with his good arm, he staggered along the bulkhead until he got close to Hans Behrmann's still body. He hesitated before coming within the old man's grasp. He remembered the power of those short thick arms and vise-like hands. He eased closer and tried to slide by the corpse unnoticed. He was trembling as he dragged his wounded leg over Behrmann and held on to the bulkhead with all his strength to keep from kicking his grandfather.

As he passed over the body, Behrmann's corpse gasped its last gasp. Jason jumped with fright and then fell, landing on the dead man's back. Terrified, he pulled himself clear, crawling to escape before Behrmann could return to life and grab him. Jason was still scrambling like a crab, halfway into the control room, looking back at the passageway when he crawled into Karen and she grabbed him. He jumped so hard he thought his heart stopped and when he realized he was safe, he collapsed into her arms. She held him and kissed him and they cried together until he felt her arch with the pain of her next contraction. When it passed she asked, "Ever deliver a baby?"

"No but I think there's a book in the sick bay."

"This might be a good time to read it," she said, trying to force a laugh.

"Don't worry. By the time you're ready, I'll have it memorized."

"What happened to Marty and Randy?"

"Marty's in the chamber. He needs a couple more hours decompression. Randy didn't make it back. Dear old granddaddy shot Petra too."

"I heard. How could he do that? How could he have done any of this?"

"He was sick—very, very sick."

"What now?"

"There was a signaling device, an EPIRB. Doctor Holiday gave it to Petra. That's what she was looking for when..." He stopped at the horror of what had happened.

"I know, go on. What about it?"

"I'll send it up through a torpedo tube. It will tell a Navy satellite where we are. Don't worry, someone will find us."

CHAPTER 30

The EPIRB's signal was received by satellite, instantly relayed to Ft. Belvoir, Virginia and then passed again to Tom's hastily assembled Grand Cayman field station.

"Trouble in paradise," Tom whistled when he got the transmission. He called the *Kennedy* who in turn called the *Atlanta* and a radioman ran with the high priority message to find the captain, Doc and Mike.

An hour later, after Mike and Doc had finished their decompression, they were circling the island in a twin-rotor CH-46 helicopter looking for a place to land. The island was a rugged mountain range thrust up out of the sea. Roughly fifteen miles long, it was divided by steep rock walls with magnificent waterfalls. There was a small fishing village on the southeast end, but the only sign of life was a ragged old island schooner at anchor in a small bay. Following the co-ordinates Tom had given them, they flew to the north end over a deep volcanic lagoon surrounded by mountains and hidden from the view of passing ships. Doc remembered Josh describing such a lagoon. Certainly this was the same place. They found their LZ on the lagoon's narrow sand beach and landed.

Doc opened the chopper door and dropped to the sand. He was wearing a borrowed set of camos and carrying an M16. The Randall once again hung from his belt. Mike dropped beside him and as they quickly moved away from the chopper;

six Marines and a Navy hospital corpsman followed. The narrow strip of jungle went deathly still when the pilot cut his engine. Doc pulled the maps Tom had printed for them from his pocket and checked a compass.

"Up there," he said pointing to the bungalow and Mike nodded. "Let's spread out and go slow, just in case there's still a reception party."

They worked their way forward cautiously to the bungalow, quickly searched it and then sat on the deck looking at the map and Tom's co-ordinates.

"Can't be right," Mike said. "According to this, that sub is dead center under that mountain. It just can't be."

"Josh told me about this place," Doc answered. "His father knew about it, but Josh said the old timers wouldn't come here. They believed the caves were haunted and they wouldn't even fish here."

"Caves big enough to hide a sub, like in Bermuda?"

"Don't know. But I guess a look at that mountain would be a good place to start."

They moved out, up the trail to the waterfall. It didn't take long to find the cave behind it and Doc entered cautiously, keeping the M16 ready for business, taking advantage of all the cover he could find. But there was no sign of life or the sub. He paused to give his eyes a chance to adjust to the dim light before easing toward the water. A glimmer of brass caught his eye and there, at his feet, were three shiny 9 mm shell cases. He picked them up and held them to his nose. The cordite smell was still strong. Around them were the remnants of a camp crushed beneath fallen rock. Doc called out for Petra and Karen. No answers. He stood and called the others in.

"Have a good look," he said and handed the shells to the Marine captain. "See if you can find the shooter or the shootee."

The water was clear enough that the Marines found the remains of *Blackwolf*'s pier and Dennis Johnson's bullet-riddled body in the shallows.

Doc and Mike climbed through the rubble looking at the remains of the base camp. They found a cable coming down from a small fissure in the ceiling which led them to Bill Roberts's demolished computer station.

"Not exactly the Southampton Princess, is it?" Doc said.

"Not even Motel 6. How long have they been hiding here? Six months?"

"Who knows, six or eight? A week would be enough for me. But at least they were alive. I wonder what started the avalanche...an earthquake? Not likely here. And where's the sub?"

"Doctor Holiday," the Marine captain called. "Sir, you'd better see this."

Bobbing on the surface at the far side of the cavern's lagoon was a small plastic yellow object.

"Remember that?" Doc asked.

"Bingo. It's the EPIRB you gave Roberts's wife."

"Wonder what's under it. Want to go for a swim?" He was unbuttoning the camo shirt.

"Looks deep," Mike said when they'd swum to the EPIRB.

"Yeah, one up, one down. I'll go first, okay?"

"Roger that. Be careful."

Doc took several deep breaths and exhaled forcefully. Then he filled his lungs, did a forward roll, and with a strong dolphin kick, plunged down the line. It was deep, deeper than he'd expected. He tried to guess at the depths as he descended—thirty feet, forty, then deeper. Without a mask all he saw was a blurred darkness, but he could feel the temperature change. He continued the rhythm of the full body kick that began in his shoulders and ended at his feet. The dive felt good, his best in years. Sixty feet? Seventy? Impossible to tell, but it was deep and as he pushed beyond the limits of most free divers, he smiled with inner satisfaction. If you can't run with the big dogs, stay the hell on the porch. He kicked harder, driving himself deeper into the silent tingling coolness of the darkness below.

There was light below, but how far below he couldn't tell. A little deeper, just a little more, there was still time. He pushed harder. He could feel it now, the pressure on his chest and his brain starting to scream. His carbon dioxide was building up telling his brain it was time to breathe. It was important not to exhale too much at this depth, not yet. He didn't want to lose the buoyancy. Not until he was back near the surface. He swallowed a little water and kicked deeper.

The light beneath him was brighter now. And in its arc was a dark shadow, long and slim, dark and deadly. That was what he had come to see. *Blackwolf* was there, waiting. He looked up into the darkness above him and began his ascent. His head was pounding and he realized he had pushed himself too far. He kicked hard and for the first time, matched the kick with powerful arm strokes. The darkness was disorienting because he couldn't see the surface. He kicked again and swore at himself for having gone too far, for having grown older. He blew out a small stream of bubbles and pulled up again. He had lost the tether and the rhythm of the powerful dolphin kick. His effort was now jerky and uncoordinated. He reverted to a feeble scissor kick and a half-hearted arm stroke. He heard something in the water, something tapping. He tried to focus, but the darkness was closing in. He closed his eyes and saw stars. *The damn darkness. Where the hell is the surface? What is making that infernal racket? Where is...* His head was spinning; he was out of control and then Mike had him.

"Doc, what are you doing? You were down for over four minutes. Man, you scared the hell out of me."

The dank cavern air was the best he'd ever tasted. It was a full three minutes before he could speak without gasping.

"It's down there. The sub is there, but she's deep, real deep. I heard something."

"I heard it too...they're tapping an SOS and broadcasting it over the PA system. Must be some powerful speakers. I wonder what happened here?"

"We need to let them know we're here and find out what kind of shape they're in, Captain," he said loudly enough for his voice to boom across the lagoon and echo throughout the cavern.

"Over here, Doc."

"Got any Dupont fishing lures handy? We want to let the sub know we're here.

"Mark 60's should do the trick. Got a six-pack right here."

"Perfect. We'll swim in."

At the water's edge, Doc pulled the pins and threw three grenades, counting to keep them five seconds apart. They detonated far above the sub, but the blast achieved the desired result and the message from the sub's speakers immediately changed. "W-O-U-N-D-E-D—H-A-V-I-N-G—B-A-B-Y—N-E-E-D—H-E-L-P—N-O-W."

"Well?" Doc asked. His Morse code was forgotten years ago.

"They need help now," Mike answered. But before he could finish, he was interrupted by a shower of gravel and rock which fell from the cave's ceiling. It was quiet for a moment and then a boulder the size of a truck came crashing down and sent large waves across the lagoon.

"Get the others out...only one guy on the bank who can relay messages to someone outside. Now tell me the rest."

Mike gave the orders and the Marine captain elected to stay. Doc watched the rest of the team scramble to safety then nodded at Mike to continue.

"They have wounded and someone's having a baby."

"A baby? Well, it isn't Behrmann. Karen maybe? How the devil are we going to get a baby out of that sub?"

"How the devil are we going to get down there?"

"Find something to bang out some code on. Ask if their diving lock is clear. If I make it down there, can they get me in?"

"Doc, how are you going to pull that off with no equipment?"

"Oh, I can get down there. The question is, can you get me back up if this doesn't work?"

"I get it. We're experiencing another electrical storm in the left hemisphere of the notorious Doc Holiday's unlimited cranial capacity. Which means that we are going to again venture where even angels and cosmic comic book heroes fear to tread. Right?"

"What a joy you are to have as a student. Keep up the good work and you'll be riding the long school bus before you know it."

"So what's the plan?"

"Find out if they can get me in the hatch. I'm still working on the rest."

"Sometimes you scare me, and I'm fearless," Mike answered, shaking his head and then looking up at the ceiling. More gravel fell and the mountain groaned as huge plates of rock shifted, grinding against each other. They tensed in anticipation, but this time there was no grand finale...only an anti-climatic shower of gravel.

Doc surveyed the rock and rubble pile for anything that might help with his plan. He spotted the leg of a folding camp chair sticking up out of the debris, dug it out and examined it. It was a standard camp stool with a canvas seat and zippered storage pouch. He turned it in his hands and nodded. Just what the doctor ordered. Now all he needed was a way to attach it to the EPIRB's tether. *Fill the pouch with rocks and use it as a dive sled. Save my air and energy for finding the hatch and getting it open. If anything goes wrong or the sub is just too deep, simply drop the chair and let them pull me up. Piece of cake.*

It took twenty precious minutes to set everything up. Mike swam out with him, helping tow the camp stool full of rocks, now suspended beneath a hastily constructed raft. A stout fishing rig with heavy monofilament recovered from the bungalow would be the safety reel. Mike and the Marine sergeant would wait at the raft—Mike was the safety diver, the Marine, the line tender. It was a good plan. Only one problem. Doc knew that he would only have the strength for one attempt. His first dive had shown him how deep it was, and how easily he could become disoriented in the darkness. He estimated a minute and a half to the bottom, and that left only a minute or so to get into the hatch. After that, he would lose focus and things would get serious, real serious.

He floated on his back with his eyes closed, breathing deeply, exhaling slowly and forcing himself to relax, almost to the point of sleep. He remembered stories of Jacque Mayole, the famous record-setting French free diver who used yoga meditation to relax.

Inhale...exhale—blow out carbon dioxide. Slow metabolism to nearly nothing. Feel your pulse drop twenty beats. Relax, let the water support you, become one with its eternally slow rhythm. Inhale... exhale—clear your mind. See only the blue-green light around the sub. See the hatch. You're there. He took the knotted end of the line holding the improvised sled to the raft and after inhaling deeply, filling his lungs with all they could hold, he pulled the slip knot and launched himself toward the bottom.

The sled jerked him down so quickly that there was not time to clear his ears. He swallowed rapidly several times, moving his jaw forward and back, trying to stay ahead of the pressure. *So far, so good.* But if he can't clear fast enough, it would cost him an eardrum—a price he was already reconciled to. He was dropping at well over a hundred feet a minute and had guessed the depth at one fifty to one seventy feet. He tried to stay focused and relaxed, but it was difficult because the water was coming at him too fast to see through, and all he could do was hang on while the improvised sled plunged deeper and deeper.

The tingling started at a minute, ten seconds. He swallowed hard, pulled in a little water and held it in his mouth. He wanted to be there, but could just now see a little of the light surrounding the sub.

At the surface, Mike glanced up from his watch at the line flying from the fishing reel.

"A minute, twenty-six seconds," he said. "Must be deeper than he thought."

"How long till we haul him up and get the hell out of here?" More gravel and small boulders had fallen just as Doc started the dive.

"He did four minutes on the first dive, but he was nearly out when I found him. Three minutes and not a second longer."

"Got it. Just give me the word," the Marine replied.

The water temperature had cooled at least ten degrees and Doc could see the cool blue light around the sub again. He was beyond the point of having to clear as often and knew that he was deep.

The sled hit bottom before Doc saw it coming and he crashed painfully into the jagged rock pile. Even though they had tried to pull all the scope out of the line before he started the dive, the line had not been taut and straight, but still had enough of the gentle curve of an anchor line to leave him well away from the sub. But now at least he could see it. Or at best a blurry image of it. He pulled on the EPIRB's line. It felt secure and he began pulling himself down the rock slope toward the sub. His head was still clear and with something to focus on, it was easier to force his brain to ignore the pain.

He was nearly at the stern of the sub when he began to sense the power of the current. It was pulling at him now, trying to lift him from the rock and sweep him out under the ledge. As long as the line held, he might be able to use it. He lifted up and launched himself toward the sub. The ride was more than he had bargained for. He was tumbled across the bottom like a leaf in the breeze, but held on to the small diameter EPIRB line even when it burned into his hands. He hit the sub's deck, bounced off the streamlined sail and tumbled across the bow until he came to the end of the line and stopped with a painful jerk. The current had pulled him twenty feet past the hatch and he would have to fight his way back to it. *Why can't it ever be easy? Why is it always so damned complicated?"*

He began the fight for the hatch but realized he was being held back by more than the current. The heavy monofilament fishing line, which was his safety line, had tangled on a deck fitting and was holding him back. He tugged it hard enough to determine it was not about to release him and after a brief moment of grim hesitation, cut it with the Randall.

"How long?" the Marine captain shouted from the bank.

"Two minutes, forty-five seconds," Mike answered. "We haul him up in fifteen seconds."

"Oh shit," the sergeant holding the rod and reel said emphatically. "We've lost him. The line just went slack and he didn't give the signal before he released it."

Doc put his head down trying to streamline himself as best he could and worked his way forward on the quarter-inch buoy line. His head was reeling now and he knew he could not hang on to the line or consciousness much longer. He fought the current, ignored the pain of the small line cutting into his hands, and inched his way to the hatch. When he reached it, he was exhausted and nearly gone. Thank God, it opened easily, and he pulled himself in out of the current's drag and collapsed. He closed his eyes and felt nauseated as his head filled with shooting stars. He was startled back from his stupor by loud banging on the bottom hatch. Shaking off his mental fog, he realized the hatch above him was still open. He stretched up for it and got it closed, then spun the hand wheel which dogged it down. The roar of life-restoring air filled the diving lock as the water rumbled out through the exhaust. He was too far gone to realize that he was breathing again. He simply remained on his knees, stuporous and exhausted, until the side hatch opened and a battered and wounded Jason Richardson helped him out of the lock and offered him an oxygen mask.

CHAPTER 31

As Doc's head began to clear he could hear Jason telling him: "We've had a little excitement since the last time you were onboard."

"Behrmann?" Doc asked.

"Dead. Killed my Aunt Petra and nearly got me. Bill Roberts is badly wounded, Martin just got out of the decompression chamber, and Karen is just a few minutes away from having the baby. The rest are either dead or gone."

"Jack Morgan?"

"Gone. Killed Johnson. That rocket in Galveston got Colonel Andrews. Morgan and Admiral Geist are the only ones left. They took the sailboat."

"No radios?"

"The VLF still works, but we couldn't raise anyone on the surface. The mountain must be causing too much resistance. So it's the pipe wrench telegraph and the boat's PA system. We tried to deploy the towed antenna array. Managed to get Marty bent and his brother killed. Not such a good idea against this current."

Doc nodded and pulled another deep breath from the oxygen mask, then set it aside before he pulled himself to his feet.

"Take me to Karen. Then send a message to the surface and let them know I made it and that we're going to need some help. Tell them about Morgan. He can't have gotten far. Then tell them to get out of the cave. We'll signal them again in thirty minutes."

"How bad is it up there?"

"Pretty unstable. We don't need to waste any time getting out of here."

"Thanks for coming, Doc. You certainly didn't owe us any favors."

"Save it, Jason. You and I still have unfinished business. But I'll patch you up and get you back to the surface before we reopen that file. Now, where is Karen?"

As Doc helped Jason down the passageway over Behrmann's corpse, the boat shook violently with the impact of more rock hitting the hull.

"Feels like the whole damn mountain's coming down on us," Doc said. "I hope we can convince Karen to wait awhile to have that baby."

The cave was filled with dust from the last good shake. Mike and the sergeant clung to the raft, still hopeful the sub would return their inquiry about Doc. They had been signaling constantly since the fishing line went slack. Finally their answer came.

"He made it!" yelled Mike. "Now let's get the hell out of here!" They swam hard for the bank while gravel fell constantly. The cave gave an angry growl as tons of stone shifted and new cracks opened in the walls and ceiling.

"Man, this is one angry mountain," Mike said as they hit the bank and scrambled for the entrance. Behind them more rock fell and the cave belched them out with a low rumble followed by an enormous crash.

The falling rock thundered down on the sub below which, for the first time since hitting bottom, shifted and slid forward. Again Jason and Doc were pitched to the deck. The boat momentarily lost power and they were surrounded by the silence of the inoperative ventilation system and bathed in the red glow of emergency-battle lanterns. When they entered the control room, Karen was sitting next to Bill Roberts, holding his head and talking to him softly.

"It's going to be alright. I had a wonderful dream and the Lady in the pool told me everything is going to be alright."

Roberts lay motionless in her arms. When Doc reached her, she didn't acknowledge him at first, but kept talking to Roberts in her gentle maternal voice. The boat shook again and Jason dropped to her side. She recognized him immediately and took his hands.

"I had a dream about the old mission," she began. "The gentle Lady in the pool..."

"How long since your last contraction, Karen?" Doc asked.

"The Lady in the pool came to me and touched me. She said not to worry, that our baby was going to be just fine. She was so beautiful."

"How long...?" Doc asked again. He checked Roberts's carotid pulse. He was dead. NASA and the Navy were going to be very disappointed. Jason looked at Doc who shook his head. Jason nodded sadly.

Karen's lower lip started to tremble and she grabbed her abdomen in pain. Jason took her hand and eased her back while Doc quickly checked her dilation.

"There's still time," he said. "We've got to get off this boat before the diving lock gets buried or we slide over the edge. It's three thousand feet deep down there."

"Our hull could take that, no problem," Jason answered.

"Yes, but it's too deep for the Navy to get to us. Your kid might be old enough for college by the time we see sunlight again."

"What are you suggesting? Karen's in no condition to make an ascent and neither am I."

"You'd better rethink that unless you plan to spend the rest of your lives on your granddaddy's boat. She can make it and so can you."

"But there's no equipment..."

"We'll improvise."

"But..."

"Jason, if you stay here, you're dead. That's the choice. Now you decide. I'm going to the dive locker and I'll check on Martin. You stay here with Karen. Keep her as relaxed as possible...we don't want her to have that baby yet."

"But what if she has the baby while we're in the water?" he

pleaded.

"Dolphins and whales do it all the time. So what's the problem?"

"But..."

But Doc was gone. Jason looked hopelessly at Karen who smiled back with a peaceful, serene smile. "It's alright," she said, comforting him. "Our baby is going to be just fine. The Lady told me."

Martin was hiding in the corner of the dive locker with his arms wrapped around his tightly drawn up knees. Doc heard him weeping in the darkness and turned on the emergency lighting. Martin covered his eyes and tried to make himself smaller. He looked up over his knees and asked between sobs, "Did you...did you kill my grandfather and my mom?"

"No, son, I didn't." Doc began rummaging through the diving gear. There were two mixed-gas recirculators. He checked the tanks. One set was empty and the other nearly so.

"Are there any more bottles for these?"

"No, my brother and I used the last ones. He didn't make it back."

Doc nodded. "How about scuba tanks?"

"No, we use the recirculators for everything. You planning on going somewhere?"

"Yeah, I thought it might be nice to get us back to the surface while we still can."

"The current is a killer. We'd never make it back into the cave against the current."

"I wasn't planning to try. We'll go out and up with it."

"Then you'll surface in open sea and there's nowhere to climb the ironshore. You might be adrift for days before the sharks get you."

"Think your chances are better down here?" Doc answered. He continued to open lockers and was building a pile of masks and fins. The sub shifted again.

"Look, son, I'm sorry about your family. But if this boat goes over the wall, we won't have a chance. I think my friends will be waiting for us when we hit the surface and if not, at least they will be looking. Now, Jason and Karen will need our help. And there's not a thing more you can do for anyone down here. So if you can get it together enough to help, you just might save your own life and theirs as well. If not, I'll just turn off these lights and save the batteries."

"There is some scuba gear. No tanks but everything else. Morgan's men brought it. They were using it with hookah rigs from the sub when we fixed the rudders. Come on, I'll show you." Martin pulled himself to his feet and led Doc to the torpedo room. He pulled open a large green gear bag and produced three black horse-collar style buoyancy compensators."

"Good work. These are our ticket out of here. Let's go share the good news."

They hurried from the diving locker to the control room and as they moved aft, Doc realized that they were climbing the passageway. He could hear instruments in the small sick bay shifting in the mess Petra Roberts had made in her search for the EPIRB. The bow had dropped significantly as *Blackwolf* inched her way toward the long drop into the abyss.

Doc wasted no time. He scooped Karen up against Jason's protests and ran with her back to the diving lock. Martin followed with Jason and it was only as Doc finished strapping on the recirculator and checked Karen's mask and buoyancy compensator for the third time that he stopped to explain.

"Fill the vest with the oral inflator. But when you come out of the diving lock, the pressure will collapse it again. I'll be there to refill it from the recirculator. Then all you have to do is breathe normally from the oral inflator until we're on the surface." The sub shifted violently. Karen threw her arms around his neck and held on.

"That's it. Here we go."

"But..." Jason protested.

"No buts! Here we go!"

It was a tight squeeze to get Karen in the lock beside him. When the hatch was closed he checked her mask again and reminded her to keep the vest's oral inflator in her mouth like a regulator.

"It's going to be alright, Doc. I had a dream and I know a secret. I'll tell you now if you want."

"Tell me when we reach the surface, honey. I'm going to let the water in now. Remember, just breathe normally all the way up. You ready?"

"Okay."

He spun open the valve's wheel and cool water rushed in. Even louder than the rush of the water, however, was the scraping of the hull against the bottom. When Doc forced the hatch open and climbed out onto the bow, he could quickly see the rock pile which had trapped the sub. It had become so heavy that the narrow ledge could no longer support it. The sleigh ride into the abyss had started and Doc had no desire to go down with this ship. He pulled Karen from the hatch and closed it behind her. He took a lungful of gas from the recirculator and exhaled into her oral inflator. He could feel her start to rise and had her grab the hatch fairing. The sub was sliding quickly now followed by a falling wall of stone. *What the devil was keeping Martin and Jason?*

Martin appeared first. Doc inflated his vest and pushed him off toward the surface. Jason didn't have the strength to pull himself out of the hatch. Doc grabbed him, pulled the inflator from his mouth and filled the vest. Then he pushed Jason away. The only way to go was up. Doc took Karen's hands, nodded and with a powerful kick lifted them both from the sub. Karen had lost touch with reality, but at this point that was a blessing. Hopefully, wherever her mind had gone, her pain had followed. *Perhaps there really are guardian angels for children and fools. And if so, this would be a great opportunity for one of them to log a little overtime.*

He looked down at *Blackwolf.* The sub looked like a small harmless toy as it slid over the edge, followed by tons of crushing stone. Behrmann had gotten his last wish. He had taken his creation to the grave with him. Doc could almost hear the old man's evil laugh in the roar of the sub-sea avalanche.

Karen's hands tightened on his and he looked quickly back to her mask. Her eyes closed for a moment and he knew she was having another contraction. It quickly passed and when she opened them again, she was smiling as if there had been no pain at all. He gave her a diver's OK signal and she nodded her response. That angel was certainly on the job.

He looked up and could see Martin and Jason fifty or sixty feet above them. He guessed their depth at just over a hundred feet. Now they could take their time and when they reach the surface, rest in the warmth of the sea until they were picked up. Karen smiled at him again. Her face was radiant now as the first sunlight from the surface filtered down to caress her. Her long hair flowed gracefully behind and her eyes sparkled in the light. Her breathing was easy and slow. There were fish to see now and she pointed at a dolphin who came close enough to smile back at her just before they broke the surface.

"The dolphin knows I'm going to have the baby...she's come to help," Karen said when they surfaced. The swells were gently rocking them and the water was warm and soothing.

"Of course," Doc answered. He was scanning the surface for Martin and Jason, and for a rescue ship.

"The boat won't come, not yet...not until the baby comes," she told him with authority. He nodded and kept looking.

"Doc," she tensed and breathed deeply. "Doc, it's time. That baby wants to be born right now!"

"Now's as good a time as any, honey. Just give a good push and let's see what happens."

He moved into position and hardly were the words out of his mouth when he found himself holding a tiny baby girl. He lifted her high out of the water and she took her first breath, filling her lungs in preparation for the first cry with which all babies announce their entry into the world. It was a gentle cry and a happy sound and then Karen took her and held her gently. Doc pulled the plastic tie wraps from beneath his watch band, put there just for this occasion, tied off the cord and cut it between the ties.

"Look, Doc, we have company."

The dolphin, now accompanied by her own young, came close enough to touch and raised her graceful head from the water to see the baby.

Doc heard the roar of the CH-46 helicopter as it cleared the rim of mountains and approched them thirty feet off the water. It hovered directly overhead and a wet-suited medic jumped into the water and helped rig Karen into the winch seat. Within minutes they were all onboard and searching for Jason and Martin. As the chopper followed the blue-green ocean's drift, they spotted the men waving frantically at them. Again the pickup went smoothly.

Although in great pain, Jason reached towards his newborn daughter and smiled weakly. However, in preparation for working on his wounds, the medics injected him with pain medicine and he collapsed into a deep and much needed sleep. On the way to Grand Cayman, Doc sat beside Karen who held her now sleeping baby and began telling her story.

"There's a golden Lady with a baby and a treasure, Doc—a huge treasure on that mountain. I saw it in my dream. The Lady wants us to use it to care for children everywhere. Promise me that as soon as we can, you'll help me find it."

"I've always been a sucker for golden ladies, especially rich ones. You've got a date."

Mike was waiting for him when the chopper landed on the hospital's lawn.

"Did the crew tell you about the President?" Mike began.

"Tell me what?"

"Air Force One blew up right after take off. They killed him, Doc. They killed the President and most of his staff. I just can't believe it."

"What about Bill Stone?"

"No. He waited for you to come back. He's here."

CHAPTER 32

No bombs—chemical, biological or conventional—were dropped on Iraq. That was the good news. During the next week, Doc underwent a debriefing by the Navy during which he was asked at least a thousand times if he was certain *Blackwolf* had either been destroyed or was at last permanently out of commission.

"Yes, the oil cartels are safe," he caustically responded. "*Blackwolf* and the genius who created her are asleep in the deep, finally and forever."

Doc was angry about the President's death and unsatisfied with the official statements about Morgan's disappearance. The battered old schooner had been found adrift half-way to Cuba with no trace of her crew. At least that's what the Navy said. Doc got a very familiar uneasy feeling in the pit of his stomach as he read the report. "Presumed lost at sea." That was the official conclusion.

"Experienced sailors, lost on a flat calm day, with a duffel bag full of European bearer bonds worth millions. Bullshit!" was Doc's official conclusion.

With Ian's help, Doc was confident they could lay a trap which would bring Jack Morgan out of hiding. Doc's leg healed quickly and he hit the exercise room hard everyday. By the end of the week, he was ready.

On Friday night, Doc, Mike and Sheri waited at the Holiday Inn lounge listening to the Big Kahuna batter the tourists with rowdy lounge humor until it was time to meet Ian's plane. Sheri sat between them, nursing a beer and wondering who was going to say it first. Finally, in frustration she gave them an opening. "Well, do you really think this will work?"

Doc pushed up the bill of the Atlanta Braves ball cap and said over the top of his thoughtfully folded hands, "Well, there are still a few interesting loose ends."

"Like what?" she prompted.

"Like where we're going to get the extra men we need to pull this off. And then there's the question of who helped Morgan and Geist escape. And what's being done to round up the rest of Morgan's men, the ones you met on his sailboat? Once that's solved, we might go after whoever put the bomb on Air Force One."

"There were a couple of Morgan's boys I wouldn't mind seeing again," Sheri said and winked at Mike. "Hot stuff, if you get my drift."

Doc gave her a vile look and then she laughed. "Lighten up, grandpa. I'm not ready to trade you for two twenty-year-olds quite yet."

Doc scowled and she laughed again.

"Let me sally forth a query to this august body in the hope of stemming the abuse of this loquacious wench," he countered.

"Now I'm a loquacious wench? Just because I tried to bring a little life to this wake? Oh, brother. Alright sagacious one—that means old, very old, like older than dirt. I've been saving that one," she quipped to Mike.

"It means wise, not necessarily that old," Doc corrected.

"What'd you say about Sally's body?" Mike asked, looking through the bottom of an empty green beer bottle.

"Back to the short school bus for both of you," Doc retorted and waived three fingers at their short-skirted waitress who nodded and gave the order to the bartender.

"Consider something for me. Do you agree that Morgan is still on the prowl?"

"I agree. They hitched a ride with the loot and he'll turn up again when he wants to," Sheri said.

"I'll go along with that," Mike affirmed.

"Right. Now, what's the one thing that might bring him back? And I'll give you a hint. It's not money or stock certificates or computer files or even another roll with the dragon lady. It's ..." he paused, waiting for them to fill in the blank.

"The golden Madonna," Sheri said. "He was nuts about the Madonna, but how does that help us?"

"On the chopper Karen told me that she had a dream, but it sounds more like a vision in which her Lady showed her a treasure of gold coins which Karen believed were Spanish, like the one Jason gave her in Bermuda. The Lady told her the treasure was hers...if she would promise to use the money to help kids. When I asked her about it today at the hospital, she told me she has seen the Lady several more times in her dreams. Now here's the spooky part. She and Jason found an old mission up there on the mountain, and it's identical to the one in her dream. Also in her dream were a bunch of children. Very unhappy, silent children."

Sheri's eyes were wide. "It can't be. Doc, that fits right into the story Jack Morgan told us about the golden Madonna and the kids who were tortured by Henry Morgan's men. That stands the hair up on the back of my neck. It's too bizarre to be believable and yet it's so close...."

"To be coincidence? That's what I thought. And..." he paused and pulled the Braves hat low over his eyes. "And that's exactly what Morgan would think if he were to read it in the papers."

"Interesting," Mike said. "I'll stick around for that."

"It's also pretty ambitious for someone with no money, no weapons and no boat. Just how had you planned to get back to that island, anyway?" Sheri asked.

Doc looked up and smiled. "Women have such a limited perspective for adventure. Finish your beer. It's time to go to the airport. Help is on the way."

They got a pleasant surprise when Chaplain Stone came out of the luggage area along with Inspector Ian Cord. Bill Stone had conducted the funeral over the President's empty casket and had moved the nation to tears with his compassionate eulogy. Now he helped Ian down the plane's stairway and waved at Doc and Sheri. Inspector Cord was walking with a cane and wearing an inverted sailor's hat to cover the missing patches of hair he had lost in the boat fire.

"What's the word on the Hill about the President's death?" Doc asked Bill Stone as soon as they were in the rented van heading back to the hotel.

"They'd love to blame Saddam," Stone answered. "But because of that torpedo you found, and the report of *Atlanta*'s captain, Congress is afraid the public won't buy it. It's so paradoxical that we're protecting a country that's gone so far out of its way to incur our anger, but even what Saddam has done doesn't justify genocide. His people don't deserve that. And there's going to be a big congressional investigation into the whole *Blackwolf* affair. The media loves it of course, and resignations are hitting the Pentagon like hail in a summer storm. Anderson's last letter had a list of names. Most are being given the chance to retire, but some will face serious charges. It's the closest thing to a military coup since the Civil War."

"And Morgan?"

"No one believes he was lost at sea. So far, there's no trace of him, but the bad news is, he and the Vice President were pretty chummy around election time. Morgan's companies made big contributions. So Morgan may not have to resurface to get what he wants."

"I remember him saying he didn't have to be president," Sheri said, "as long as he could buy one."

"How long until we know which way that wind is blowing?" Doc asked.

"Hard to say. Every committee in Washington wants a piece of Morgan right now, but if I were you, I'd watch myself," Stone answered. "If Morgan is still pulling strings, you can bet he's going to try to pull one of them around your neck."

"At least we kept him from obliterating Iraq. I hope Saddam knows how close he came to being the flattest of all camel patties."

"I think so, or we'd have heard a lot more noise about our capturing his subs."

"How did his crews explain being in the area anyway?" Mike asked.

"They were ordered to spy on our newest mini-sub, *Blackwolf* and to record it for their ASW boys. Ironic, isn't it? Morgan told them if they liked what they saw, he might be able to sell them a few."

"That's our boy, the knight of the double cross," Doc laughed. "I can't believe they fell for that."

"Well, they did and it cost them two subs. Perhaps they'll be smarter next time."

"I have a plan to get Morgan," Doc said. "But I'm going to need help from all of you. And I want to be up front about this...I'm a lot more interested in stopping him than convicting him. Like old Captain Behrmann, he's too dangerous and too clever to come out of hiding if we play by the rules, so we're going to bend them a bit."

They all looked at Bill Stone and waited. The Chief of Chaplains thought for a moment and then answered, "*Onward Christian Soldiers* was always one of my favorite hymns. Let's just pray that what we're doing is right and then let's make sure we do it right the first time."

Karen gave her amazing story about the baby's birth, the dolphins and her vision of the treasure to the local press with the agreement that it would not go to press for twenty-four hours. From the satellite station on Bermuda, Tom was able to monitor the island which still remained geologically unstable. And with the satellite watching over them, they could be relatively certain there were no other visitors on the island. At least not yet.... It had taken three days to outfit the creaky old boat for their return to the island. No one paid much notice when the old schooner slipped away from the dock just after midnight, with its ragamuffin crew of old men and cripples, and a woman with a newborn baby.

They beat the old schooner northeast against the wind arriving at dusk the next day. Jason, wearing his fiberglass leg cast, sat by the helm and guided the boat into the hidden cove. When the anchor was down, they used a new inflatable to move the five men ashore. After an adequate reconnaissance, they returned to the boat to spend the night and plan the next morning's climb.

That evening Doc made notes on the satellite photos Tom had faxed from Bermuda, while Mike and Ian made a final check of the weapons Bill Stone had helped them borrow from the Navy. When the work was done and the packs loaded, Doc climbed the ladder topside to join Sheri on her watch. The sky was clear and the only sounds were small waves against the hull and the island night birds. The bright three-quarter moon had just passed the mountain's rim, lighting the lagoon elegantly.

"Are the others sleeping?" Sheri asked.

"Most, I think. Karen was feeding the baby again. That's the hungriest kid I ever saw. And the most content. I don't think I've ever heard her cry."

"The boat is like one big rocking chair. She just loves it."

"You ever think about having kids?"

"Someday, perhaps. I came from a big family and my mom had a pretty rough time. Guess I wanted to explore the other possibilities. Besides, there hasn't been much conversation about marriage here lately. Have you noticed that?"

He put his arm around her and stared into the moon's reflection. "Is that a proposal?" he asked and kissed her neck.

"No, it's more like a prod. Just to get you thinking, that's all. I'm not sure you're mature enough for me yet. Saving the world is nice and all, but just look at the life you lead...you don't even have a job. So how could we afford kids? I'm afraid if you did ask, I might have to think about it for a while."

"Oh, I see," he laughed.

"Probably not, but you're getting better. But I know what I do want. I want us to have a home, a real house and a dog."

"Water?"

"Of course on the water, with a big boat in the backyard."

"I've got just the place. My grandfather built it before I was born."

"Really?"

"Yep, all we need is the boat and the dog."

"Good. I'm ready. How about a swim?"

"While you're on watch? I'm not sure that's authorized."

"Okay, I'll swim. You watch...and make sure to keep your eyes on those trees over there. If someone were going to attack, they would probably do it from those trees and I'd hate to have them sneak up on us while you were watching something else."

"What else could possibly get my attention?" he laughed.

"I was kinda thinking this might," she teased and slipped out of her clothes. Before he could reach her, she was over the side with a graceful and quiet dive. The moonlight bathed her in white as she swam easily through the clear water. Doc shook his head, quickly scanned the beach again as he undressed and followed her over the rail.

"And just what do you think you're doing?" she asked as he surfaced beside her. "Aren't you supposed to be on watch or something?"

"I came to rescue you," he laughed and reached for her.

"With what?" she smiled and slipped into his arms.

At dawn the boat smelled of strong coffee, eggs, bacon and fried potatoes. Doc used the grill on deck to cook a massive breakfast. After eating, the men loaded into the inflatable and motored to the beach. They pulled the inflatable up on the sandy shore and cautiously moved forward to the waterfall and the cave behind it.

Inspector Cord moved slowly and it was obvious he was in pain. However, he was as adamant as Jason had been that he was not going to be left out of an opportunity to even the score with the man who had put him in the hospital and caused him so much pain...and he had no intention of letting Jason out of his sight.

Chaplain Stone had not forgotten his days as a combat decorated Marine, and an able-bodied seasoned warrior was a welcome addition to Doc's tiny and battered invasion force.

On board the old schooner, Sheri leaned back on the cabin's roof against a salon cushion she'd hauled up from below. A hand-held radio lay close at hand and a 9 mm automatic was right beside it. Karen, who was nursing the baby, rested nearby in the shade of a tarp they'd rigged over the boom. It was hard for Sheri to believe that Karen was the same person she had known as the calculating Georgia State co-ed, or as Jason's playmate in Bermuda. Now, in the comfortable privacy of the lush lagoon, Karen began to tell the story of her months aboard *Blackwolf* and their eventual arrival at this beautiful but desolate island.

With Doc at the point, the men began the steep climb up the rugged trail to the mission. Cracks and crevasses had opened in the mountain face and twice they had to rig rope bridges. What was left of the trail was covered with loose gravel and footing was precarious. Trees on the mountain face had fallen, pulling the vines of the upper canopy with them, blocking the trail and making the climb much more difficult. Halfway up, they entered a clearing with a spectacular view of the sea and stopped to rest.

"It's hard to believe it has changed so much," Jason said. "Karen and I would climb this in an hour even when she was eight months pregnant. We've not even gotten to the hard part and we've been at it twice as long."

"Do you really think Morgan will come after us?" Mike asked.

"After us and after the golden Madonna," Jason answered. "He was obsessed with it, like an addiction. I understand that kind of obsession. He'll come. He can't help himself."

"How did you meet Morgan?" Doc asked. He had a pair of binoculars and was scanning the horizon.

"He came to Bermuda because he wanted to see the old sub base under the dockyard," Jason answered. "He was the one who showed me the hidden entrances. Once he was sure the base was operable, he convinced my grandfather to liberate *Blackwolf.* I don't think he had any idea how difficult grandpa could be. When he found out later, he tried to make a deal with me."

Doc lowered the glasses and turned to look at Jason. "You got any idea who he was really working for?"

Jason laughed. "That is the sixty-four thousand-dollar question, isn't it? He had some horsepower with the Navy, that's for sure."

"Yes," Chaplain Bill Stone added. "And Andy Anderson paid for that mistake with his life. Other good men destroyed their careers. Men who weren't traitors. Men I've known for years who would have sacrificed themselves for the country without hesitation. I don't understand it at all."

"You expecting company this soon?" Mike asked. Doc was using the binoculars again.

"Morgan had quite a network on Grand Cayman. I wouldn't be surprised if he got an early phone call about Karen's story."

"Give me the bloody bastards phone number and I'll give him a call," Ian growled. "I've got a bit of a score to settle with that one, I do."

"That's why we're here," Doc smiled. "And now, if we're through with this little tea party, the mountain is waiting to show us that treasure."

The climb took until noon. Doc was the first to reach the plateau where the waterfall thundered into the small, deep pool. The clearing around it allowed the sun to break through the heavy canopy of trees and vines high above. The jungle looked impenetrable and dark, and shrouded the ancient mission walls from view.

"I was afraid the place might have been destroyed," Jason said. They were resting and eating now. The plateau was seven hundred feet above the lagoon and offered another spectacular view. Doc again scanned the horizon with field glasses and then put them away.

"We should keep someone on watch up here," Mike offered.

"I'll do it," Ian replied. "That climb about did these old bones in. Give me those glasses and a radio. This spot is lovely, it is, and I'll be perfectly fine just right here."

They finished lunch quickly. Leaning on Mike and Chaplain Stone, Jason led them to the vine-covered mission wall. Mike went up first. Ground birds squawked and scattered when they saw him. Startled, he leveled his M16 toward the brush where they retreated. "Holy Mother," he said under his breath as he got his first look at the mission. Twenty yards directly in front of him, the ancient buttressed stone walls were dark with moss and, in the dim light beneath the forest canopy, looked as foreboding as a medieval castle. The air was heavy and still and suddenly, so was the forest. Sweat dripped into his right eye and burned. He blinked to flush it and tried to remain motionless. On his right, across the courtyard, a bird fluttered in the underbrush, seeking better cover. He ducked low and swung the M16 ready to return fire. Nothing. A squawk brought him back left toward the remains of the out buildings. Soon the normal chatter of the jungle birds resumed. Mike exhaled, laid the M16 on the top of the wall and turned to give Jason a hand.

"There must be an entrance, an easier way," he said as he eased Jason to the ground.

"Over there," Jason pointed west beyond the chapel. "But

it's overgrown and I wasn't about to clear it with a machete. This place needs to stay hidden. You'll see what I mean in the chapel."

"Spooky old place. Gives me a strange feeling," Mike answered.

"It's death," Chaplain Stone said. He'd just dropped to the ground beside them and Doc landed just behind him. "It's death, the same way I've felt it on the great battlefields of Europe. What in the name of our merciful Father could have happened in this place?"

As if in answer, the ground shook violently beneath them. Stones fell from the mission walls and birds screamed in terror. The quake was over as suddenly as it had began, leaving them kneeling, fearful of the falling debris.

"What the...?" Mike said.

"An aftershock," Doc answered. "Tom said the satellite and the seismic reports show there have been several. The mountain is still settling, recovering from her wounds and trying to stabilize."

"Because of the explosions in the cave?"

"Exactly."

"The grave where we found the rosary is over there," Jason pointed to his left, "as well as what I imagine were the work sheds. The wall there is where the musket balls are. That's where the killing took place, at least some of it. Come on, I'll show you the chapel and the courtyard behind it."

"If Karen was right about that treasure being up here, where do you suppose they would have put it?" Doc asked Jason.

"Perhaps buried under the church itself. The metal detector should help. We could start sweeping with it now. No use waiting."

Doc nodded and swung the pack from his back. He knelt and began assembling the new Garrett metal detector he'd borrowed from Grand Cayman treasure hunters at the museum.

"Now, how'd you get them to loan you that?" Mike asked with a laugh.

"Ah so, is excellent lesson in power of unspoken word, grasshopper. Very wise honorable old teacher told them we might have to look for mines. Did not say 'gold' mines. Now show me how to work this thing, Jason. Let's get this show on the road."

Ian mopped the sweat from his brow and pulled at the buttons on his shirt. It was unusually hot even for a spring day in tropical latitudes. He shifted his weight from one foot to the other, stretched and felt the twinge of new skin pull on his back and neck. He silently cursed Morgan for the ten thousandth time and mopped his brow again.

In the lagoon far below, the old schooner rested comfortably at anchor and he could see both girls on deck. He focused the glasses to determine just how much of them he could see. Karen was even more beautiful than he'd remembered when he'd carried her months ago in Bermuda, wounded, to the sick bay aboard *Blackwolf.* He smiled as he thought of her clinging to his neck like a wee frightened child. He shook his head with sadness. What would become of her and the baby with Jason in the Dockyard prison? He'd given it a lot of thought. Jason would have to face charges, of course, and he would no doubt be convicted. Too bad...such a brilliant mind, such a....

"Dear Mother of God," he said aloud and fumbled for the portable radio Doc had given him. In the clear quiet lagoon below, a sleek black shape was rising from the bottom. Twice the length of the old schooner, it surfaced close enough beside her to lay over a boarding plank. He saw the girls rise from the bow and run for the cabin. The hatch opened and two men emerged, leveling guns at the schooner. After a moment the girls were back on deck, Karen with the baby in her arms.

Ian looked down at the radio, turned it on and hit the push to talk switch. "Doc, Doc come in. It's a bloody submarine. We've got..."

"Company," a voice he didn't recognize cut him off. "I have the girls and it should be obvious that they'll have to balance the ledger for any checks you write, so let's not do anything stupid, gentlemen."

"Morgan, is that you?" Doc cut in.

"Ah, yes, the intrepid and amazing Doctor Holiday. I was quite surprised to see you on television, Doctor. By the way, it's good to see Sheri again. She and I have a little unfinished business."

"Don't touch her, Morgan. Do you hear me? You lay a hand on her and I'll rip out your heart."

"You're a little late for heroics, Doctor. As usual, I'm holding all the cards. Now, why don't you and your friends join us and perhaps we can discuss this like civilized men? Now come on down. As they say on the West Coast, we'll do lunch."

Mike was standing beside him in the church. They had been sweeping the church floor with the metal detector.

"What do we do now?" Mike asked.

"Punt, I guess. Where's Stone?"

"Jason was showing him the courtyard."

Doc's mind was racing. He looked around them, thinking of possible booby traps if he could just lure Morgan to the mountain top.

"Let's find them," he said. They left the church, carefully picked their footing on the moss-covered stone steps and rounded the corner to the courtyard. Bill Stone was kneeling by the fallen marble Madonna at the wall beyond the deep, clear reflecting pool and Jason was standing behind him awe struck. But they were not looking down at the demolished statue at their feet. There, smiling down through a newly opened fissure in the seventy-five-foot-high stone wall behind the statue's pedestal, was the radiant face of the golden Madonna.

"Karen was right," Mike said. "Her vision was real."

"It would certainly seem so," Doc answered. "But unfortunately, it brings to mind an old native American proverb, 'When dreams come true, trouble can't be far behind.'"

CHAPTER 33

Jason sat at the reflecting pool's edge, looking up at the serene face of the Madonna smiling down from the alcove cut for her in the mountainside. "Down there we haven't much of a chance, but up here...well, our odds might be better if we made them come to us."

"What are you saying?" Doc answered. "Give him the statue? It doesn't seem right after the price the ghosts of this place paid to keep her hidden."

"He's here now and he'll find it, regardless," Jason countered. "But with a little time, we might be able to turn this around."

"I agree with Jason," Mike said. "Morgan came for that statue and he will find it. Our best shot might be to try a little horse trading to buy ourselves some time."

Chaplain Stone nodded agreement and Doc lifted the small radio and keyed the mike. "Morgan, listen for a minute. We've found something up here. Something that interests you a lot. Don't hurt the girls and we can make a deal."

"You actually found the Madonna? Is that what you're telling me?"

"Yes, she's here, hidden in the mountain. We'll have to dig her out. All that's exposed at the moment is her face."

"Don't touch anything. That statue is priceless and she's mine, of course. Alright, Holiday, you've got your deal. We're coming up and the girls are coming with us. Any of your infamous tricks and you know what the result will be."

"I understand," Doc answered and lowered the radio.

"Hail, Caesar, we who are about to die salute you," Jason said forcing a laugh.

"You've got it," Doc nodded. "Let the games begin. Mike, you've got point. Get over the wall and see if you can get a body count while they're still on the beach. Then scout the area. I'll bet they aren't alone. I'd have landed a team before surfacing in the lagoon. So watch your back."

"Got it." He hesitated for a moment then asked, "Doc, who are these guys? And where did they get that sub?"

Doc turned to Jason, "You want to tell him?"

Jason shook his head, "Doc, I wasn't part of that...not then, not now. I only did what I had to do to stay alive, and that's the truth."

"But you did know."

"Some of it at least. They talked. It was hard not to put the pieces together."

"Now wait just a damn minute," Mike growled and grabbed Jason's shirt. "If you know something, I want to hear it. Like, do we end up in Leavenworth when this is over?"

"That depends on just one thing," Jason answered calmly.

"Oh yeah? And what the hell is that?"

"Who wins."

Mike relaxed his grip on Jason and looked at Doc and Bill Stone. Their slow nods, affirming what Jason had just said, confirmed Mike's fears. "So it was true...it's been right in front of us from the beginning, but I just couldn't believe it. A handful of right-wingers off the deep end, that I can believe, but not fleet officers, not a full blown military coup. Not in this country. It was all true."

"Was it?" Doc said. "Can you prove it? Can you prove any of it? There's only one person I know who can answer those questions."

"And he's on his way up the mountain," Mike nodded.

"No, Lieutenant, he's on his way up YOUR mountain. Now get your ass out there and make sure it stays your mountain."

"Roger that," Mike answered. "Doc, this would certainly be a good time for one of your left brainers. It's going to take something really off the wall to save our butts this time."

Doc smiled and nodded. "Don't worry. We'll come up with something. Now go find out what we're up against while Jason and I get ready to show them a little southern hospitality."

Mike nodded and was off to the wall. Doc opened his backpack and took inventory. It was slim picking. There was twine and wire for booby traps but little more. He looked around the garden and shook his head. It looked grim. Still they took the folding shovels and began setting a snare. One good distraction might be enough...enough to give them a momentary edge, or get them all killed. They were covering the wire with leaves when they heard Inspector Cord calling. Doc looked up at Jason and Bill. He signaled Bill to stay and he and Jason quickly climbed the vine-covered mission wall. Two men in camouflaged jungle fatigues were holding the inspector at gunpoint. Two others shoved Mike into the clearing with his hands on his head. At first count, Doc could see another ten shooters peering out from the thick jungle foliage which ringed the clearing by the waterfall pool.

"Guess it's not our mountain after all," Doc said and raised his hands.

"Tell the other shithead to get out here too. Now, asshole!" ordered a cocky twenty-year-old while raising his H & K, MP5 toward Doc.

"That other shithead," Doc began, "is the Navy's Chief of..."

"We know who you are. Shut your face, asshole, or you won't last till the others get up here."

On the trail below, Karen stumbled with her baby and Sheri quickly caught her, helping her back on her feet.

"I'll carry her if you'd like. I'm not as tired," Sheri offered.

Karen hesitated then agreed as one of their guards snarled at her for slowing them down. Then to Sheri's surprise, Karen smiled and said softly, "Don't worry. Remember what I told you. She's got everything under control."

"Shut up, bitch," the soldier snarled again and shoved her. Karen looked at him with a look that made Sheri wonder if the shock of everything which had happened to her had finally overloaded Karen's circuits. The soldier saw it too and shoved her again. As she fell, the mountain shook violently for fifteen seconds and the soldier was thrown off balance. He recovered quickly and looked fearfully at the rock outcrops above them. Karen said nothing. She simply smiled a sweetly vindictive smile and began humming to herself as she started to climb.

"We're going to a party," she giggled to Sheri. "And that one's not going to have a very good time."

Doc and his men were stripped of their weapons, including Doc's beloved Randall, which was thrown into the waterfall pool along with the rest of the weapons. Then they were bound wrist and ankles with plastic tie wraps and thrown to their knees.

Doc sat quietly studying their captors. All were white, young and dressed in special ops gear. They moved with the arrogant confidence of youth untempered by the reality of combat pain. "Who are these guys?" he asked.

Mike leaned forward and whispered, "You have any ideas, Doc?"

"Now would be a great time for the cavalry to attack."

"I'd say they missed their cue. Just thought I'd mention it, in case you hadn't noticed."

Doc chuckled, "I noticed. Thanks."

"Shut up, asshole," the cocky twenty-year-old snapped and booted Mike in the ribs. Mike fell with a groan.

Doc looked into the pool where their weapons had been thrown and remembered the story of Andre Galerne, the French frogman who was captured by German sailors while placing limpet mines on the hull of their ship. Galerne's hands and feet were put in irons and he and his friend were hauled to the ship's fantail for execution. As the Germans raised their rifles, Andre shoved his friend over the rail and jumped. Both men were wounded, but even with his wounds and with his hands and feet still in irons, Galerne was able to tow his friend over a mile to safety. Doc had met the quiet, gentle Frenchman who went on to start International Underwater Contractors in New York, and remembered the look of those ice-blue eyes. He looked back at the cocky young rooster strutting before them in his jungle boots and headband. As Doc was constructing nine ways to kill the arrogant little rooster, Jack Morgan emerged from the jungle at the head of a column of four more young men, Karen, Sheri and the baby. Karen's blouse was torn and her knees were bloody. When she saw Jason crumbled in the grass, she broke from the column and ran to him in spite of the threats of the rear guard.

"Let her go," Morgan snapped at the guard. "Unless you're afraid she's going to hurt you?"

"Doctor Holiday, my, it is a pleasure to see you with the proper attitude," Morgan laughed sarcastically. "No catch and release, remember? This time, I'll finish you myself."

"That's what you said the last time, Jack. We're not off the mountain yet."

"Yes, but some of us will be taking a slightly faster way down than they came up," Morgan retorted, looking at the cliffs on the far side of the waterfall pool. "Hitler refused easy deaths for those who betrayed him, and he was right."

"Now, there's a lovely comparison," Inspector Cord offered. "You and Hitler, I mean."

"Thank you for that, Inspector. Open your mouth again and we'll let you be the first to go."

"Now, Doctor, what was it you said on the radio? You had something to show me?"

"Let the girls go, that was the trade."

Morgan lowered his chin, looking at Doc as if he were an imbecile then shook his head and pointed toward Sheri. "Here's the trade. You behave and I'll consider keeping the girls alive. Not in this hemisphere of course, but we might find a benevolent prince who would prefer them to his favorite camel. Who knows?"

The thought of being sold into slavery sent a chill up Sheri's spine. Still, the look she got from Doc told her to keep quiet and she did. She carried the baby to Karen and Jason, and knelt by Doc's side. Karen whispered something to Jason and then she laughed. Jason smiled and she kissed him.

Morgan watched them and wondered what she could be laughing about, but he said nothing, for beyond them in the darkness of the jungle he saw the mission wall. Snapping his fingers, two soldiers were at his side like obedient dogs. He looked at Doc and curled his lip in a vicious smile. "You really found something, didn't you? I thought you were just up to your old tricks, but you really found it, didn't you."

"Bring him," he snapped, "and kill all of them if he so much as raises a hair on the back of his neck."

They pulled Doc roughly to his feet and cut away the plastic restraints at his ankles. Doc counted quickly as they pushed him toward the vine-covered wall—sixteen men. Perhaps another two in the brush, just in case. Geist was still nowhere in sight. He stretched to get his circulation flowing again and looked back at Chaplain Stone and Inspector Cord. Had he invited all of his old friends to die with him? It was a gruesome thought. No, none of this was acceptable, but it certainly looked as if the outcome was going to be out of Doc's hands.

They climbed over the wall and dropped to the ground in front of the dark walled church. Morgan was amazed. "It's just like the old priest described it. Right down to the musket ball holes in the wall."

"It must be a proud moment," Doc said, "to realize that this is the spot on which your ancestors murdered innocent priests and children."

"Let's see how innocent they were," Morgan countered. "Where is it?"

"In back of the church," Doc answered and Morgan shoved him out of the way walking briskly toward it.

"Get up," his escort prodded and kicked him in the back.

Doc rolled with the kick and came to his feet ready to fight. Then, looking down the MP5's short deadly barrel and remembering the others, he slowly exhaled deeply.

"You some kind of bad ass, old man? Hell, you look old enough to be my grandfather. Be careful, grandpa, or I'll have to hurt you good."

"I'll look forward to that," Doc answered forcing a smile. He turned and followed Morgan and the other two soldiers. In the courtyard Morgan was trying to scramble up the soft rock face to the crevasse. He clawed and kicked and slid until he nearly reached the fissure's edge then his footing gave way and he tumbled roughly to the ground, twisting his knee as he landed. He tried to stand, fell and crawled back to the rock and began clawing his way up again. The result was the same: He got partway up and then fell again, this time tearing his shirt and covering himself with scrapes and cuts.

Undaunted, he shouted at his men, "I found it, by God, I finally found it. It's everything the legend said—solid gold.

It's the treasure of a lifetime." His eyes were wild as he shouted, "Get the men. Get the equipment. We're going to dig her out right now."

"I wouldn't," Doc said.

"Yes, I know you wouldn't, but you are a fool and a dead one at that," Morgan snapped and his men laughed.

"This is an important archaeological site. Just think of what will be lost..."

"Let's see, boys," Morgan cut him off. "Doctor Holiday thinks we should leave this treasure, worth several hundred million dollars, here for some archaeologist to fuss over for the next fifteen years. Now I think we should give that idea serious consideration. I know, let's vote. All in favor?" There was only the call of treetop birds and the waterfall's gentle roar to support Doc's side of the argument.

"Too bad, Holiday. Looks like I win again. But just to show you I'm not a bad sport, I'll let you help. Cut him loose and get him a shovel. Bring the others. Then get a crew clearing that area for an LZ." He pointed toward the clearing beside the church. "We haven't got all day. Let's get moving."

At his order the men scattered, leaving only two with Morgan.

Doc picked up the shovel and began cutting in toeholds. Working carefully, he climbed the twenty feet to the crevasse and then, precariously perched, began widening the opening. The alcove appeared quite large. Sunlight through the crevasse glittered on piles of gold coins and jewels stacked around the statue. Doc clenched his jaws. The thought that Morgan would have the statue was sickening. Then almost within his reach, he saw a heavy sword, gold hilted and with a silver blade in a jeweled scabbard. Perhaps...

One of the soldiers helped Morgan to the edge of the reflecting pool where he perched on a rock, braced his feet on the remains of the marble statue and watched Doc carefully, waving his Glock and shouting constant instructions.

"What do you see," Morgan demanded impatiently.

"It's Spanish treasure, alright, lots of it. Probably enough to pay back at least...maybe two percent of what you stole."

"Don't be a sore loser, Holiday. Putting away a few dollars for a rainy day is as American as mom's apple pie. Especially if one is able to get it from the life savings of some poor less fortunate fool. That's the real American dream—win the lottery, live on the interest."

"Tell me about the sub," Doc asked. "From Iraq or Kuwait?"

"Oh, Iraq. Faud's a bit upset with me, thanks to your interference in our little game. Can't say that I blame him. But that's politics. One week you're up, the next there's a price on your head. Too bad about old Captain Behrmann. Too bad he'll never know that his greatest contribution was to help me avenge my father and bring the Middle East to its knees."

"Illusions of grandeur perhaps?"

"Grandeur, yes. Illusions, not a chance. We lost the first inning, but damn, here I am, and the game ain't over yet, man. You never did figure it out, did you? Well, because you helped me find the Madonna, I'll give you a little political history lesson. Did you ever wonder why Iraq? Why poor old Saddam got baited into becoming public idiot number one?"

"No, and I'm dying to hear your version of it."

"Well said. Price of oil is about two thirds what it was ten years ago. Competition got downright ugly. OPEC set quotas, trying to stabilize the market, but there were a couple of mavericks that wouldn't play. Kept cutting the price, producing more than the quotas. Continuing to drive the price down. Care to guess who?"

"Kuwait, I suppose."

"Oh yes, I forgot. You're an English teacher and you read a lot. Alright I'm impressed, not that it will do you any good. For a while their two key players, Kuwait and Iraq, were in the penalty box. Kuwait was putting out fires and rebuilding refineries, and we had sanctions against Iraq. Now the fires are out and the sanctions are coming to an end. Price stability and our market share are threatened again. Now do you get the picture?"

"What about Project Sverdlovsk and your deal with Kuwait?"

"Cutting edge technology. De-populate the country in twenty four hours and leave the land so hot no one will go near it for a hundred years. Not bad, especially when Saddam set himself up for it so beautifully by using biologicals on the Kurds and against us. So if one of his secret factories was accidentally hit, so what? He was supposed to have closed them all years ago. That was the deal and we can't be blamed. It was a good plan, damn you. We could have made a bundle and neutralized a madman and his oil production with one little air strike."

"And the casualties? What about the civilians...the kids?"

"There are no civilians, Doc. In that country they will all grow up just like Saddam. You were in Vietnam...it's in the blood. They're warriors. They haven't changed since the place was called Babylon and they were fighting the Assyrians and hauled the Israelites off into captivity. Same place, same people, same war. We can't change that."

"Unless of course you kill them all."

"We could, but it would be bad marketing."

Doc swung the shovel angrily into the wall, pulling out large chunks of soft limestone conglomerate and letting them fall. Then he stopped and twisted his upper body to look down at Morgan. The crevasse was now wide enough to twist his upper body in toward the sword. He hooked the sword hilt with the shovel and pulled it closer.

"What are you doing?" Morgan shouted. "What did you find?"

"More gold," Doc answered. "I can just about reach it."

"Show me!" Morgan said and held out his hand, demanding to see some of the gold. Doc obliged and hurled a handful of Spanish coins at Morgan's feet. Morgan lunged to catch them and fell. He looked up from his knees, waving the gun and then scooped up some of the coins.

Morgan's fall gave Doc a moment to scan the area. He was high enough up to see over the wall, and on the outside shadow warriors emerged from the jungle, and like real pros were taking down Morgan's men, one at a time. Not a shot had been fired, but the tables were turning. The cavalry had arrived.

"So you killed the President, and you want to eradicate Iraq over a buck or two a barrel. Jack, did you ever ask yourself if you might be just a little right of center? Most folks we think of as healthy wouldn't be plotting the deaths of an entire nation just to put a little away for a rainy day. There are clinical descriptions for people who behave the way you do."

"A few bucks a barrel? Listen, Holiday, we're talking seventy million barrels a day. So, as even a liberal arts major should be able to comprehend, a drop in the price of a dollar a barrel is seventy million dollars a day. Two dollars a barrel is one hundred forty million a day and three dollars a barrel is, well, it's just unthinkable. And the players on my team don't especially want that to happen. That's why they pay me, you see, to make sure that it doesn't. That's why Behrmann's damn engines were such a threat. Think about it. There's just too much on the table for it to go down any other way. Congress will come around. Iraq gets neutralized and if the Arab's have an attitude about it, so much the better. We'll blast them too. A few less kids at the party means we get a bigger piece of the cake."

Morgan looked up at him with a malevolent grin and held up the fistful of coins. "This, onion-peeler...this is all that matters. This is the power and the glory and everything else is bullshit. Too bad you never figured that out."

Then, as if Morgan's words were the last straw, the mountain began to shake with a terrible vengeance. Boulders crashed down around Morgan. He screamed for his men, and looked back for Doc who had disappeared into the Madonna's alcove. When the quake subsided, Morgan, barely conscious, was dragged to his feet not by his arrogant soldiers but by none other than old Josh.

Josh and his men were in black jungle fatigues and well outfitted, courtesy of the U.S. Navy, thanks to a good word from Chaplain Bill Stone. "Welcome to judgment day," Josh said and raised a big ugly knife.

Doc intervened just in time to stay the hand of vengeance. "Easy now," he said to Josh. "It's over and we want him alive. He's got a lot of explaining to do."

"No, sir, he's going to pay. If we take him back, you know he'll buy his way out. But that dirty money's no good here. There's not even a bank or a single computer here. And here is where it ends."

"Not if you kill him, Josh. If you kill him, he takes it all with him. Don't kill him. Strip him clean and let's take it all back. If you want to keep him here, that's fine, but don't kill him, not yet. Let's have him entertain us awhile first."

"Now wait a minute," Morgan gasped. "Holiday, I want to make a deal. You set it up. I'll tell them what they want to know."

"Yeah, well, who you going to call, Jack? Washington? I think your stock is facing a bear market there. Iraq? Not when they find out the plans you had to 'neutralize' the whole population. Or, how about we call Kuwait? There's a plan. I bet Faud would be delighted to make your bail. But poetic justice has always appealed to me. I can't imagine a better end for you than with you entertaining Josh and his men around the campfire with stories of where you hid the money. And if you do a really good job of entertaining them, I bet they'll even rotate you on the spit every half hour or so. It's over Jack. No catch and release, remember?

"Now, Josh, what are we going to do with all this gold? As I recall, the Lady said she wanted it used to help kids. You know any kids who could use a little help?"

CHAPTER 34

The old schooner cut cleanly through the gentle sea for the third day of their sail, north toward the Florida coast. Doc was at the helm and Sheri lounged in a deck chair beside him.

"I have a question," Sheri asked, "now that you're in a talking mood."

"I am?"

"Unless you want to do the rest of this watch by yourself, you are."

"Okay, fire away."

"Did you know Josh and his men were going to be on the island to help us?"

"Bill Stone helped organize that. Josh left the island to gather his men and Bill got them equipped and transported. It was Josh's chance to take back that dignity he always talked about."

"And you didn't tell me?"

"It was better to stay focused on what we could do for ourselves. Just in case I was wrong about Josh."

"You should have told me."

"Okay."

"I mean, I was sharing the risk...I deserved to know what was cooking."

"Okay."

"So what's Josh going to do with Morgan?"

"Okay."

"Damn it, I want to know."

"Okay."

"That's it! You can sit up here all night by yourself. I've had it."

"Would you be willing to die before giving up the answer, if I told you?"

"Umm? What do you want for dinner? Potatoes and pot roast or pot roast and potatoes?"

"Sounds good. What can I do?"

"Not a damn thing. As far as I'm concerned, you're completely worthless in the kitchen. Excuse me, worthless in the galley. Unless of course you'd be willing to use your talents as a world class sleuth and onion-peeler on a few simple Idaho potatoes."

"You're bad."

"That's why you love me."

The commuter flight from Minneapolis took almost an hour to reach Hibbing, Minnesota. After renting a car and asking a few questions, Chaplain Bill Stone was on his way to Tower and the millions of acres of the Superior National Forest which contains the Boundary Waters Canoe Area, or BWCA as it's known to the Canadians and Americans who live along its borders. The body count on Air Force One was one short. Bill Stone would have bet his retirement that he knew which body was missing. Another hour found Stone on the south shore of majestic Lake Vermilion at Archibald's Lodge, renting a boat and asking Arch, a tall gray-bearded Canuck with twinkling blue eyes and a contagious laugh, about portage into Trout Lake.

"Tree huggers raised hell about the truck, you know, and for a while it looked like folks were going to have to tote the load themselves. Then a young couple who live on the point had an idea. They race dog sleds, yeah, and a small boat, she don't weigh much more than a loaded sled. Worked out for everybody I guess. Anyway, they'll get you into Trout alright. Now, what you going to need for bait and tackle? We got big shiners and plenty of leeches. You know, big walleye like those leeches. Now just yesterday, had some folks in from Wisconsin. They asked me where to go and I told 'em try out by the island. Pettis family from down by St. Peter, stay with us every year, you know. Why, they fish out there a lot and always do real well. And wouldn't you know, those Wisconsin folks, Mowchans I think the name was. Anyhow, they were back here in a couple hours with a boatload of the biggest walleye I've seen in...damn, I can't remember. Told me their oldest daughter, Emily—dark haired pretty thing she was—she hooked into one so big it was pulling the boat. And they must have had.... Hey, friend, don't you want your change?" Arch looked up from the register, scratched his beard and watched the aluminum fishing boat ease away from the dock. With other fish to fry, Stone checked his pocket compass, twisted the throttle of the 25 horse Johnson and headed north to the Trout Lake portage.

It was nearly dusk and the lake was flat as glass. The sun was sinking behind the giant pines on rocky shores. When he cut the motor, he could hear the haunting call of loons across the water and see sunfish and bass feeding on yellow mayflies. He was in the right place. What place on earth could possibly be better for a wounded soul to find peace and strength? He tied the boat and started the climb to the only cabin remaining on the lake.

A lone figure sat in darkness on the screened log cabin porch, a shotgun across his lap. Stone took a deep breath of the cool night air and approached cautiously.

"That you, Bill?" the voice in the darkness asked.

"Yes, Mr. President. It's me."

"Bring a fishing pole?"

"No sir, I'm afraid not."

"Too bad. If you didn't come to fish, then you came a long way for nothing."

A loon called again, mournfully long and low and was answered by another across the lake. A screech owl made it a trio, and when the frogs joined in, it was a full blown moonlight symphony.

"May I come in?"

"Suit yourself. I presume you came alone?"

"I did and I took precautions not to be followed." Stone

took a seat in a roughly hewn cedar rocker and unbuttoned his jacket.

"Oh, if you found me, they certainly will."

"Then come back and put a stop to it. Congress still wants to bomb Iraq. They need to know who really blew up your plane. There will be war in the Middle East when they pull Israel into it. Doctor Holiday is..."

"What about Jack Morgan?"

"Behind bars on the island where the sub was hidden and that's where he's going to stay. There's no chance he'll escape. Holiday saw to that. That's what I came to tell you. With Morgan out of the way, I think we can stop this thing."

"Seth Davidson was my best friend, I ever tell you that? We grew up together. Spent hours fishing together on this lake. Best man I ever could have chosen as a running mate. Once I asked him what his first official act would be if anything ever happened to me..." His voice trailed off as a bass landed on the water with a thundering splash.

Stone waited.

"Said he would make fishing tax deductible!"

"I understand," Stone chuckled.

The President ran his fingers through his hair and then wiped a tear from his eye. Then the tears flowed freely. "Morgan bought him, Bill. And Morgan blew up the plane because I wouldn't play ball. I wanted to fish, just a day or two to myself. So I sent the plane back..."

"Davidson is on the wrong team, Mr. President. Doc and his friends won't be safe until you put a stop to this. Tell the truth about what happened and you'll have the support you need. I'm sure of it. You can stop Davidson. You can still turn this thing around." With that Chaplain Stone set down his briefcase and removed a small video camera.

The video stunned the nation. The newly sworn-in President, Seth Davidson, quickly stepped down and shortly thereafter, retired from public life. Accusations and denials filled the news for days, and just as it looked as if the mud-slinging might go on endlessly, a young archaeologist from Bermuda, Doctor Jason Richardson stepped forward with the bizarre story of a submarine built by his grandfather and operated from a hidden island base for Colonel Jack Morgan. His testimony was supported by enough documentation to be beyond question. The icing on the cake was a collection of video discs and a logbook provided by Doctor John Holiday. Confronted by such overwhelming evidence, the Justice Department handed out indictments like parking tickets. Jack Morgan's associates were put out of business for keeps with one notable exception, however. Doctor Lin Kee, the beautiful and mysterious dragon lady, had apparently vanished from the face of the earth.

To show his approval for what Jason had done, Doc gave Jason and Karen a very unique wedding present—an ancient and ornate goblet, rumored to have held the poison Socrates used to take his life and believed to somehow hold the key to numerous archaeological treasures.

For the first time in many months, Doc felt peacefully at ease. He smiled contentedly as he sat at the schooner's helm watching the night fall on the Florida Intercoastal Waterway. A new life was beginning. Next to the schooner's dock was his comfortable old, tin-roofed house on the water, surrounded by giant oaks dressed in Spanish moss. An old black Bronco with a smiling red seal in the rear window was parked by the garage, and a flop-eared black puppy chewed a tennis ball on the wooden floor beneath the back porch swing. Sheri sat on the schooner's rail and watched the moonlight begin dancing on the dark water.

"It's beautiful here," she said softly. "It feels like home."

But Doc didn't hear her. He had gone into the house where he pulled a large green trunk with a false bottom from beneath the antique sleigh bed. It was time to put the long-bladed Randall to rest once again.

Also by Jon Coon

Thief of the Deep

Ex-Navy SEAL Doc Holiday's daughter and her boyfriend have disappeared while investigating the sophisticated plunder of Bermuda's historic shipwrecks. After reestablishing his old CIA contacts, Doc begins the hunt helped by Sheri, the shapely leader of a college underwater archaeology expedition.

Using his expertise in underwater explosives and high-tech diving, Doc dives deep into the center of a mystery that involves a museum executive, drug smugglers, a revenge-driven police inspector, a desperate old Nazi U-boat captain, and one deadly player that takes Doc by surprise.

Other books from Aqua Quest

Aqua Quest Dive Guide Series: each $18.95

Diving Bahamas
Diving Baja California
Diving Bay Islands
Diving Belize
Diving Bermuda
Diving Bonaire
Diving British Virgin Islands
Diving Cayman Islands
Diving Club Med
Diving Cozumel
Diving Hawaii
Diving Micronesia
Diving Offshore California
Diving Off The Beaten Track

Jim Church Titles:

Essential Guide to Underwater Video $19.95
Essential Guide to Nikonos Systems $22.95
Essential Guide to Composition $19.95
Nikonos Cue Cards $12.95

Other Titles:

Thief of the Deep $11.95
Lost Voyages: Two Centuries of Shipwrecks in the Approaches to New York $29.95
Guide to Marine Life: Caribbean, Bahamas, Florida $34.95
The Cave Divers $19.95
The Fireside Diver $14.95
Dennis Graver's 100 Best Scuba Quizzes $14.95
Essentials of Deeper Sport Diving $21.95
Will A Clownfish Make You Giggle? $14.95

The above titles are available from your local dive center, bookstore or the publisher, Aqua Quest Publications, Inc., P.O. Box 700, Locust Valley, NY 11560; (516) 759-0476: 1-800-933-8989; aquaquest@aol.com.

Aqua Quest Publications is a publisher of books on dive travel destinations, underwater photography and videography, wreck diving, dive-related fiction, marine life, technical diving and safety. If these books are not available at your local stores, call or write us directly for a catalog of our publications.

AQUA QUEST PUBLICATIONS, INC.
POST OFFICE BOX 700
LOCUST VALLEY, NY 11560-0700

(800) 933-8989 (516) 759-0476
Fax: (516) 759-4519 e-mail: aquaquest@aol.com